The Author

EARLE BIRNEY was born in Calgary, Alberta, in 1904. He took his B.A. (1926) in English literature from the University of British Columbia and his M.A. (1927) and Ph.D. (1936) from the University of Toronto. He has always complemented his distinguished teaching career with his poetry, fiction, criticism, and editorial work.

During the Second World War Birney served in the Canadian army as a personnel selection officer in Britain and in Holland, and his wartime experiences furnished him with material for his first novel, *Turvey*, which won the Stephen Leacock Award for Humour.

Birney's reputation as a poet was established with his first two volumes, *David and Other Poems* and *Now is Time*, both of them winning Governor General's Awards. As a chronicler and interpreter of Canadian life, Birney has responded openly and carefully to the many developments in poetry during his life.

From 1946 until 1965 Birney was Professor of English at the University of British Columbia, where he founded Canada's first department of creative writing.

Earle Birney resides in Toronto, Ontario.

EARLE BIRNEY

Turvey

A Military Picaresque

With an Afterword by Al Purdy

Copyright Canada © 1949, 1951 by McClelland and Stewart Limited
Afterword copyright © 1989 by Al Purdy

This revised edition was first published in 1976 by permission of the
author.

Reprinted 1989

Canadian Cataloguing in Publication Data

Birney, Earle, 1904–
Turvey
(New Canadian library)
Bibliography: p.
ISBN 0-7710-9953-3

I. Title. II. Series.

PS8503.17T87 1989   C813'.54   C89-094604-3
PR9199.3.B58T87 1989

All incidents and characters in this novel are entirely fictitous, and no
reference is intended to any actual person, whether living or dead.

Typesetting by S & G Graphics Inc.
Printed and bound in Canada by Webcom Limited

McClelland & Stewart Inc.
The Canadian Publishers
481 University Avenue
Toronto, Ontario
M5G 2E9

Contents

PRIVATE TURVEY
reporting,

and would the gentlemen
kindly remember he's just
a Body, and so are all the
other joes, and they never
really lived, and they got
phony names and outfits.
And he's sorry about some of
their language but the real
guys talked a lot worse,
and he hopes there aint
any sailors present.

ONE

Turvey Is Enlisted

NUMBER Eight was a drawing of an envelope addressed to Mr. John Brown, 114 West 78th., New York, N.Y. It had a New York postmark but no stamp. The squeaky sergeant had told them to draw in the missing part of each picture. Turvey licked his pencil point and tried to recall whether King George had a beard.

He had finished the stamp, except for one edge of perforation, when he remembered the American postmark. It ought to be George Washington. There was no eraser on the pencil he had been given. Turvey was in the midst of a leisurely probe of his trouser pockets when his head, coming up, was transfixed by the sergeant's amber stare. It was a stare of suspicion; it leapt in a straight beam from the sergeant's highstool, over the hunched and shirted backs of the other recruits, unmistakably and directly to him. Turvey blushed, made a show of scratching his behind, and returned to picture Eight.

Implanting a careful X over the implausible head of George, and an arrow to the margin, he began a profile which in spite of himself grew into the head of the sergeant. He shouldnt have put in the Adam's apple. Turvey was laying pencil to tongue again, wondering if the remaining eight pictures in Test One would be as tough, when, like the sudden shriek of chalk on a blackboard, the sergeant's voice scratched the heavy air:

"Lay down your pencils. Turn over the page and fold

under. You are about to begin Test Number Two."

Turvey tried to go more quickly but the camel held him up. It was two-humped and had a guy riding it backwards. The sergeant had, with a precise maidenly firmness, made it very clear to them that in each set of four pictures, one and one only was wrong, and to be crossed out. Since in the other three a man rode an animal frontwards, the camel picture must be wrong. Still, should you ride an elephant with your feet tucked under its ears? Or a horse with no knee-joints in its forelegs? The broad-beamed youth at the next barrackroom table broke wind suddenly and the roomful of silent sweating men stirred in sympathy, squirmed on the pitted benches, sighed as in dreams of anguish. But Turvey continued to regard the little parade of riders; the more he examined them the more he was convinced they were all wrong. All except the camel, maybe. If you rode a camel backwards you could see better. And you had the rear hump to hang on to; it was more pointed; you could get a grip on it. Turvey was neatly crucifying the mahout and his elephant when the gopher voice of the sergeant piped again, and they were in Test Number Three. When it came to the arithmetic questions, Turvey remembered what Mac had said and was careful not to go too fast. Besides, he had caught a far glimpse, through the dusty window beside him, of a girl in the backyard of a store – no, it couldnt be – yes, and unbelievably, in a bathing suit, like a butterfly from the garbage can.

Once the O-testing was over, Turvey began to think his second day in the army much more enjoyable, though he hadnt found any Kootenay Highlanders yet. Yesterday he had stood in long dispirited line-ups before attestation clerks and then naked before staccato doctors. Now, though they had been filed out of the testing room into a big hall where he couldnt discover a window with a view of the girl, there was a lull. He got friendly with two Icelanders and had won a dollar-twenty from them shooting craps in a corner of the lavatory before he heard the bawling of his name and it was his turn to sit down before the Personnel Corporal in a dark corner of the bare hall.

He was a bulky balding chap whose questions came out tonelessly between sucks on a rooty pipe. Turvey was surprised at the number of large stiff papers the corporal had with TURVEY, THOMAS LEADBEATER already typed at the top. And now he was starting to fill out a new one in a big sloping hand, pronouncing each word as he traced it, much as if his arm were phonographic.

"Born thirteenth May nineteen-twenty-two Skookum Falls B.C. . . . white single nextofkin Mr. Leopold Turvey Skookum Falls brother. No glasses righthanded. Ussssp?"

Turvey would not have ventured to halt the flow of the voice and bulbous pen if he had not decided that the last suck of the corporal's pipe was meant to be a question mark.

"Lefthanded, sir . . . except for hockey."

The corporal's pen wavered and his pipe hissed mildly. "Wut about a rifle?"

Turvey smiled ingratiatingly. "Anyway you like, sir."

The corporal pouted his lips at the tip of his pipe and put a curvaceous R in the corner of the big sheet. "Dont call a corporal 'sir', callum 'corporal'." The voice was almost expressionless but Turvey detected a purr and decided he had said the right thing.

"Completed grade nine Kuskanee High at sixteen wotcha chief occupation civil life?"

Turvey thought carefully. "Well, I was chokerman in the Kootenays once. Just a two-bit camp." The corporal looked blank. "Then I was a bucker in Calgary."

"You mean you was a bronco-buster?" The edge in the corporal's voice betrayed a hint of unprofessional surprise.

"No, s –, no, corporal, on a bridge. You know – holdin a bat under the girder for the riveter. I was a sticker too." The corporal kept his eyes on the form, nodding as if he had known all along, but his bald head pinkened slightly and his pen halted. "That's fine. How long you, uh, stick?"

"At stickin? Not very long. I got to missin rivets with my bucket and a hot one set a big Swede on fire and he complained to the strawboss. Then I rode the rods east and sorta bummed. Then I was scurfer in a coke plant. And I was a pouncer once, for a while."

The corporal twisted his ear as if he were having trouble hearing. His face had become a mask of distrust. Turvey felt sorry he had mentioned pouncing and he added apologetically:

"In a hat factory, Guelph. You know – sandpaperin up the fuzz on fedoras. Then I come to Toronto to join the Air Force, cause the war had started, but they wouldnt have me cause I hadnt matric and couldnt see enough green at night or somethin. So my pal Mac and I hit the freights to Vancouver to get in the Kootenay Highlanders but they was filled up. Then in Victoria we worked house-to-house gettin moths out of pianos. Then –"

But the corporal had taken the pipe out of his mouth and was holding it at a monitory angle, and his voice was a growl:

"Dont try no smart stuff here. I ast you wut cher *chief* occupation was. Wut did you do longest?"

Turvey thought rapidly. There was the time he was a popsicle-coater, and then assistant flavour-mixer, in that candy factory. But he quit after, what was it, four months? Got tired of the vanilla smell always on his clothes. Wanted to get east anyway and try the army again. The corporal was staring sullenly at his forms. What happened then? O yes, the army turned him down because he had a mess of hives and his front teeth were out and his feet kind of flat. So after a while he landed that tannery job. How long was he there? Gee, almost a whole winter!

"Wet-splittin."

The corporal's eyes rose, speckled and malevolent, but they saw only a round face beaming with the pleasures of recall and the tremulous smile of the young man anxious to please.

"I ran a machine scrapin fat off hides. Eastern Tannery, Montreal."

The corporal laid his pipe down (it had gone out), wrote "Machine Operator", and asked hurriedly:

"Any previous military experience?"

"Well, we started cadets in Kuskanee High but we never got rifles. But I was in the Boy Sc –"

"That's all. Wait on a bench atta back till the officer calls you, next man!" The corporal looked past him, mopped his veined head with a khaki handkerchief, and whanged his pipe spitefully against the table leg.

Lieutenant Smith burped bleakly. Though it was past four, the June mugginess seemed to be thickening, and there was still another recruit to interview. If he opened the window again all the dreadful honking and crashing of the downtown traffic would leap into the room. And there was always the risk that a draft might blow papers from his desk down to join the yellowing litter in the dark alley below. It had never happened, but it might; you couldnt take risks with a soldier's personal documents. Yet the air was definitely fouling again, that eternal reek of mouldy potatoes – tons of them somewhere under his feet – seeping up through the floorboards from the warehouse in the second storey.

He slid the window up a careful inch, dusting his fingers distastefully afterwards on a rag he drew from a bottom drawer of the desk. He thought with resentment that he, the Personnel Officer in charge of the whole third floor (except Captain Crashaw's corner office), had to keep messing around with a dirty window, while that fat Crashaw had a fan – wangled through Medical Stores. Everybody kowtowing to the psychiatrist. He opened his door and beckoned the last recruit in silently.

A low-score referral from Hodgson, the ass. If Hodgson hadnt been a Confirmed Corporal when he was sent to him he would have had his stripes off by now. All his 169s read the same. Yes, here it was: "Young man of good appearance, average education and stability." He always began that way, whoever he interviewed. Mind like a paint-brush, slicking everybody up to look the same. That's how he could boast he interviewed more men in a day than any other NCO. "Neat appearance, cheerful. Machine Operator type" – what kind of a type was that?

The lieutenant for the first time looked at Turvey, Thomas Leadbeater, saw nothing in that bland waiting countenance to help him, and returned to Corporal Hodgson's Preliminary Interview Report, abstractedly biting his nail. "Seems to have had a lot of rather odd jobs." Now what does the idiot mean by that? That most of his jobs were casual, or, or . . . ? "Perhaps a bit of a smart-alec." Dear, dear, this wasnt the sort of language acceptable in a psychological report. He would have to issue another staff memo – *MFM* 169, *Phraseology of.* Not that Hodgson would ever remember it.

Dear Heavens, what was this final paragraph? "Intelligence below average. Recommend for Engineers"! If the RCE redtab at headquarters ever saw that, what a to-do there would be. Hodgson, of course, was thinking of the Work Company the Engineers had for the strong-backed and weak-headed; but why didnt the fool say so? Anyway, Hodgson must have balled up the whole interview; nobody could score as low as that on an O-test and be literate, have average intelligence, and a grade nine education. He turned once more to the pink expectant face of Turvey. Perhaps a straight approach would be the most fruitful – simple words, and a soothing tone:

"Did you want to be an engineer?"

"No, sir," the fellow looked alarmed – "I got my call-

up so I come here to go Active and be a Kootenay Highlander, please sir.''

"Well, now," the lieutenant remembered to be patient, "that's a unit, a regiment, not an arm, you see. We
can assign you here only to certain general arms, such as
Engineers or Infantry. And that's a B.C. regiment, isnt
it? You couldnt join it down here in Ontario. As for Infantry –'' Lieutenant Smith paused. Here was a chance
to plug another hole in that insatiable Infantry quota; it
was only sixty percent filled today; but with an O-score
of 89 out of 214 there wasnt much you could do except
stick him in a Work Company. Old Fusspot had been
phoning just this morning; the Infantry raising the devil
at getting so many morons last month. This chap *looked*
bright and cheerful, though.

"Did you like doing the O-test, Turvey?"

"Me? O, sure, it was fine, sir. Only there wasnt
enough time. And of course I didnt want to do too well.''
The man said this with a peculiar smile – was it con-
spiratorial? He seemed to feel the lieutenant was a pal.

Lieutenant Smith, however, was shocked. "But you
were supposed to try just as hard as ever you could.
Didnt the sergeant explain that when he tested all of
you?"

"O, yes, sir, but Mac – that's my sidekick – he said
not to make too high a score, specially in the rithmetic, or
I'd get stuck in the Ingineers and have to do a lot of fig-
gerin and maybe not even get overseas a tall. Mac's in the
Kootenay Highlanders,'' Turvey added comfortably as if
it explained everything.

Lieutenant Smith felt his temples throbbing with a baffled undirected anger. Then he remembered – here was a
wonderful chance to try out the new secret instructions
(To Personnel Selection *Officers only*): INTELLI-
GENCE, CLINICAL ASSESSMENT OF: ORAL
TESTING. Crashaw had sniffed and said it was just a
steal from the Binet. Just jealous because it hadnt come

down from *Medical* H.Q. He unlocked his one lockable
drawer and fished out the sheet for "Borderline Intelligence". He was about to begin when he noticed the
top off the ink bottle. That sloppy clerk again. He
screwed it on carefully and shifted back to Turvey. He
warned him carefully – the chap's attention seemed to
have wandered out the window – that he must try his
best if he wanted to make the Infantry.

Turvey sat up in his chair like a cocker spaniel and
repeated six digits after him faithfully, and the little
sentence about Walter and his grandmother. There was
that enigmatic grin still, though, and wider than ever.
The fellow had such a wide face anyway.

"Now," said Lieutenant Smith, in the voice he used
for small children and large dogs, "listen carefully and
see if you can finish this sentence for me: A man who was
walking in the woods near the city stopped suddenly, very
much frightened, and then ran to the nearest policeman,
saying that he had just seen hanging from a tree a –
what?"

"Parachute!" Turvey shouted. His blue eyes shone
with honest excitement. "A Jerry parachute. He was a
spy come down and got caught in a tree."

The lieutenant sighed. The answers in the sheet were all
in a more ghoulish vein, "corpse . . . body . . .", and
yet – excellent morale, at any rate, but had that anything
to do with intelligence? He would try the section dealing
with the subject's COMPREHENSION.

"We should judge a person more by his actions than
his words. True or False?"

Turvey's grin widened to show, the lieutenant was
startled to see, a false upper plate. Had Hodgson got the
age wrong too? And he began to wonder about the man's
hearing, for he had evidently taken the last item as a
statement of opinion.

"That's what I like to hear, sir. All these words, and,
and tests and questions. It's what we can do that counts,
like you just said. That's why I want the Kootenay

Highlanders, sir, so I can get, uh, actions, action."
Doubt flickered in Turvey's eyes but the grin stayed as if
it belonged to another face. Was it a sly grin? Or even
supercilious? Perhaps this man was trying an elaborate
hoax. The lieutenant was aware once more of the room's
heat, the root-house smell from below, the reverberation
of boots from the main hall where his staff were trooping
out for the day. His temper rose.

"Now you take that grin off your face. This is a
serious test. It will decide your whole army, er, career."
"Career" didnt seem the right word and the lieutenant
instantly reproached himself. For the chap's eyes grew
round as a calf's and the grin, instead of disappearing,
lengthened, twisting piteously at the corners.

"Please, sir, I cant help it. I always grin when I'm nervous. I dont even know I'm doin it. My old man used to
wham me for it when I was knee-high to a grasshopper
because he thought I was bein flip, even when I was just a
little kid, but it never did no good. And I'm really tryin,
sir, this time."

For a moment the lieutenant thought Turvey was going
to cry. Nervous! Of course! Here was a psychiatric referral right under his nose and he had almost missed it.
Lieutenant Smith drew out form SP 235 from a cardboard file, lit himself a cigarette, and instantly became
paternal.

"That's all right, my boy. Just relax. We're all trying
to help you here. Now, tell me, how is your health in
general?"

"O, I dont complain, sir." The lieutenant could not
suppress a frown of disappointment. Was it because he
noticed it that Turvey added, ingratiatingly, "Of course,
I do have colds."

The lieutenant spoke with a velvety encouraging softness:

"Ah, yes, and how many colds do you have in, say, a
year?"

Turvey shut an eye and considered. "One, I guess."

Then he added, as if by way of conciliation, "But I wasnt very healthy at birth."

Trying to keep eagerness out of his voice, the lieutenant leaned back in his chair with elaborate casualness. "What was wrong with you at birth?"

Turvey puckered his lips and stared out the window, a man stumbling in the caverns of his memory: "I was thin and cried a lot." He added quickly (too quickly?): "My sister Sally was like that too; she takes treatments; she has a, a weakness in her back."

Lieutenant Smith began to write rapidly, his arm fencing the paper from Turvey's gaze.

By the time the interview was over, the psychiatrist, and everyone else on the third floor, had gone for the day. Turvey just managed to catch the last station-wagon to the barracks for supper, still clutching a slip which told him to report to a Captain Crashaw at nine the next morning. Lieutenant Smith, however, stayed till seven, writing the SP 235.

Under REASON FOR REFERRAL he typed "Possible Neurosis." Then he remembered sadly there had been a DPS directive just last week forbidding the use of psychiatric terms by Personnel Officers in ANY (repeat ANY) written reports. As if the dictionary werent free to everybody, especially to a former University Instructor in English. The Ottawa Medicos were certainly throwing their weight around. He X-ed out the forbidden phrase and substituted "Nervous Condition."

At FAMILY HISTORY he paused, cleaned his glasses, and tried to organize the welter of notes he had pencilled down from Turvey's bewildering conversation. "This man claims to be the second of three siblings and to have had twelve or thirteen older half-siblings of whom ten are alive. His father, a fruit-rancher, married for the second time at the age of seventy and sired two boys and a girl, the latter (according to the soldier) at the age of 79.

Father died at 84. Questioned as to cause of death, a/m soldier replied: 'The doctor said his insides were just wore out!'

"Soldier's mother died at 60 of pneumonia. Family farm now run by soldier's sister and older brother. Whereabouts of half-siblings, also circumstances and health, unknown to a/m. Thinks some of his seven half-brothers might be in the army. 'You never can tell.' Says full brother in good health, inventor in spare time (mechanical toothpaste squeezer; now working on mechanical window-washer)."

Lieutenant Smith sighed. Perhaps the parenthesis was a mite irrelevant. He typed it out neatly and lit another cigarette. "Father a drinker, not religiously inclined, severe with children. 'He used to beat the be-jeezus out of us if we got into any hellery.' " The language these country boys used! But Fusspot was always at him to put down the interviewee's exact words. "No significant factors were elicited in regard to mother's health or disposition. No evidence of dysharmony in conjugal state." DPS directives always spelled it with a "y", and it certainly looked more clinical that way. "Attitude toward father probably poor; to mother and siblings, good; to half-siblings, indifferent. Denies history of familial mental disorders or fits but describes sister as possibly nervous."

He was about to add the sister's complaints but he was growing tired and there was much yet to be covered. Let that fat slob Crashaw find out something for himself.

EARLY CHILDHOOD was next. He must admit he hadnt got much here, but he could certainly work in the time Turvey wet his bed in the Boy Scout camp, and his history of measles, nightmares and, ummm, lefthandedness, and ah yes, accidents. "Accident Prone", he wrote, and underlined it. Then remembering the remotely skeptical way in which Crashaw was inclined to go over his reports with him, he inserted above the line: "Appears to be". Well, my goodness, there was enough evidence.

"When asked about various distinguishing scars noted in medical examination report, soldier said in part: 'The callouses on my behind I got from sitting in a pot of boiling water when I was three. That scar on my big toe is from cleaning a rifle when I was about eleven, I guess.' He admits also to breaking rib in fall from tree, age 14, and being hospitalized at 18 for concussion after contact with iron bed-knob. (Soldier intimated he was on mixed drinking party). Has false upper front plate; says he lost teeth in fight in Vancouver beer parlour, same year." Lieutenant Smith was typing rapidly now, feeling more and more assured:

"SCHOOL HISTORY. Claims Grade 9 completed at 16 but O-score only 89. See under INTELLIGENCE. Active in sports. Admits three truancies."

OCCUPATIONAL HISTORY was next. Lieutenant Smith's back began aching in the usual vague way and he felt a headache coming on. He would just have to summarize here. Besides, no amount of questioning had produced a coherent account from Turvey. Did the fellow make these jobs up? That grin of his. But no, that was the neurosis, that was what this report was all about, drat it.

Well, let's see; first he picked cucumbers but quit because of the fuzz under his fingers; then there were those improbable mill jobs, whistle –, what was it? whistle-punk, and chokerman. Then riding the freights east and being a bucker and sticker . . . scurfer . . . ? Popsicle – well, *really* . . . Oiler on a mosquito-control gang in Banff – *was* there such a job? Why did he quit that? O, yes, seasonal employment, of course. Lieutenant Smith attempted to summarize: "Work history extremely varied, semi-skilled, with periods of unemployment. In 4 years seems to have had about 20 jobs and left, or been discharged, for as many reasons." That would make Crashaw sit up – but was it a neurotic pattern? He crossed out "varied" and wrote "unstable". Yes, that made more sense now.

"RELAXATIONS. Evidently fond of company, dances." He squinted at his notes. Spit-in-the-Ocean? Some kind of poker was it? "Plays cards. Consumption of alcohol: moderate?" He didnt *look* like a drinker, but there was that concussion story. At eighteen too. The lives some people lived! And he was such a nice pink-cheeked boy to look at. "Reads detectives and westerns. Sports: hockey, softball, horse-shoe pitching. Plays to-nette." Some kind of a whistle, wasnt it? Ah, here was a clue: "Cannot swim. Questioned if he had a fear of water, soldier hesitated and replied: 'I'm not really scared of it so long as I know it aint deeper than I am. But I'd just as soon not go in the navy.' CRIMINAL RECORD; None admitted, but see under SCHOOL HISTORY (truancy).

"SEX HISTORY". Lieutenant Smith paused and reached for the aspirin box he kept in his tobacco-tin cache on the window-ledge, along with his bismuth pills. Two would be enough, he hoped, and a bismuth after. He'd better say very little here. Crashaw was so touchy about anyone else asking sex questions. Sat on his great fanny expecting the Personnel Officer to spot all the neurotics for him without letting him ask the real posers. "Single. Says he was 'kind of engaged' to a girl in his home town but lost contact when he left because 'I dont go for writing letters.' Marked interest in women in general but no admitted history of V.D." Lieutenant Smith thought deeply, then added: "Not questioned regarding masturbation." Let Crashaw make what he wanted to out of that. And now for the SUMMING UP:

"This man comes from a broken and not altogether happy family (father previously married, drank); his schooling is incomplete, his health and work history odd." No, "odd" wouldnt do; that was Hodgson's word creeping in. The lieutenant traded it for "chequered", pulled his trouser leg loose from his sticky skin, and lit another cigarette. Was the aspirin going to work?

"His habits are irregular and his answers to questions

are sometimes . . .'' Sometimes what? Odd? Drat the word. Unexpected? But that gave him too much intelligence. Eccentric? That would do. "Eccentric and inchoate''. No doubt Crashaw would purse up his puffy lips at "inchoate", a professor's word. Well, let him hunt up his own cant phrase out of the medical book he kept on his desk all the time. No originality, no imagination; all doctors were the same; certainly none of them had ever been able to do *him* any good.

"Eccentric and inchoate. He blushes easily and there are several other symptoms of nervousness, such as his almost perpetual grin, which he explains as a nervous habit (tic?). See also childhood health history. He seemed very tense at times, particularly when the suggestion was made that he might be placed with an Engineering Works Company. Is set on Infantry but low O-score apparently precludes. Intelligence, however, difficult to judge. Oral Intelligence Test results show memory gaps, attention only fair, eccentric answers but normal score. Conversation seems at times juvenile and rambling, though manner is engaging and cooperative.''

Should he comment on the incredible age of the father at the time of Turvey's birth? He couldnt remember if it was biologically possible and, if so, whether the offspring was any more likely to be neurotic. He'd better play it safe: "Unusual family history, attitude to father, health history, accident proneness, confessed nervousness, doubtful intelligence, tic, all point to nervous disorder sufficiently serious to raise question of suitability for army in any capacity.

W.W.C. Smith, i/c
Personnel Selection Office,
Active Recruit Depot,
50 George St., Toronto, Can.''

The aspirin hadnt really worked. And now he was getting that fluttering in the stomach. Well, he'd shot the works on this one anyway. Crashaw would have to admit this was a really professional job. Perhaps someone in Headquarters would read the copy he'd send them, and duplicate it, and circulate it as a model for all PSOs. Then Old Fusspot would just have to give him that over-due third pip.

Lieutenant Smith fitted the typewriter cover carefully. He would have to sneak into his old civvy doctor's some-time and see about his stomach. That little squirt of an M.O. at the Depot had wanted to send *him* to the psychiatrist for his "nerves" when he had complained about the flutterings and the pain in the back. He would die first.

What a Court of Enquiry that would make! Lieutenant Smith adjusted his wedge at the regulation angle and placed his shiny swagger stick under his left armpit. UNIVERSITY MAN DIES ON SERVICE. Probe death of Lt. Wilbur Smith. M.O. Dismissed for Failure to Diagnose Cancer.

He loped wearily down the stairs and out of the empty building. He would ask his wife to coddle him an egg for supper.

Turvey liked the captain's office better than the lieuten-ant's. It wasnt as stuffy and there was a better view of the backyard he saw yesterday. The lush babe who had been sunning herself in the green bathing suit wasnt there today – too early in the morning perhaps – but a couple of fellows were leaning against a big ashcan by the back-door; one of them seemed to be talking and waving his hands. The other was drinking out of a bottle.

He liked the captain better than the lieutenant, too. A fat man with big moist eyes, peaceful eyes, like a cow's a bit, Turvey thought, and a deep sleepy voice. Not intense and fidgety like the lieutenant. In fact the captain seemed to consider the interview a rather amusing chore. He glanced haphazardly at Turvey's palms and finger-nails, and wheezed out a few queer questions about his health. Did he ever have dizzy spells or faint or see double? But he apparently expected "no" and didnt wait for answers. Turvey tried to look as solemn as possible; if it werent for his grin, maybe he'd be on his way to the Kootenay Highlanders now instead of being quizzed by a Nut Doctor.

But the captain seemed scarcely to look at Turvey. He sat sideways in a big swivelchair; the corners of a gray cushion squeezed out around his fat back, a bit like rising dough; he stared out the window and sometimes there would be long pauses between questions.

Turvey decided the captain must be just staring at the clouds because from his angle he couldnt see what Turvey was watching. The talkative bozo by the ashcan was tight, though it wasnt yet ten in the morning. He would wind up as if to sock the other guy, the one with the bottle, but he would lose his balance and topple back against the ashcan. The other fellow would take a few steps, bottle in hand, walking remarkably like a duck. Then he would return and the argument seemed to start again. Turvey decided this must be a bootlegger's; it was the right district; he tried to fix the spot in his mind so that he could find it from the front street in case of need. Maybe a cathouse too, maybe a floozy in that bathing suit.

But now the captain apparently remembered Turvey was still with him, shuffled the file of papers with a soft thumb, and asked Turvey about his sister's back and his father's chronology. Turvey explained that Maud, the old mare, had kicked Sally, and that his Old Man's age was always a mystery; he probably was younger than he said; he liked to make a story good.

"Do you ever get nervous, Turvey?" The captain's questions had been jumping around a lot but here was the sixty-four-dollar one. He felt his grin widen in spite of him. He fixed his eyes on the sooty porcelain skull the captain used for an ashtray. It grinned back at him.

"Well, sir, like when people ask me a lot of questions I do. Not," he thought he had better add, "not like now, of course, sir, but with the lieutenant yesterday. Course I kinda think he was nervous too, the way he kept bitin his nails. I guess we all do somethin. Now me, it's my grin, sir. People who dont know me, they think I'm happy sometimes when I'm most tied up in knots. Like when I got a girl in the family way once and thought I'd have to marry her; and everybody in Skookum Falls was sure I was real pleased about it, cause I musta gone around grinnin just like somebody else would be, you know, frownin. They knew how I felt, I bet, when I jumped a freight and never come back."

Turvey couldnt tell if the captain was listening any more; he was doodling on a scratch pad; but he said with sudden interest, "Tell me about the time you worked getting orders for piano repairs."

"Well, sir, Mac, that's my old sidekick, he and me worked together on that, for a music firm. We'd go knockin on houses, see, until we found one with a piano. Then Mac would talk the woman into lettin us lift her piano cover, even if she said it'd just been fixed. Shot her a line about moths and all that. Most times we could find some spot that looked as if moths had been eatin the felt, but if not, I always carried a few dead ones in my pocket. Mac would get her attention, like, and I'd reach my hand down pretendin to feel the felts too, and I'd rough up some of it with my finger-nail and plant a moth or two and then show the woman. We didn't do bad at that but I scattered a flock of moths on the floor, grabbin a handkerchief out to sneeze once, and the lady caught on and give us the gate. So we went back to Vancouver to see if the Kootenays would have us, but they was filled up yet."

The captain drew out a form and began a slow scrawl. The two drunks had made it up and gone back into the store. The babe hadnt appeared. Turvey turned his attention to the gap under the partition that separated the psychiatrist's office from what, by the steady rattle of typewriters, must be the civil stenographers'. By shifting his chair a little, he arranged a rather pleasant view of a long nyloned leg, a trifle thin but well turned. Just as this view began really to improve, the captain put his meditations in an envelope, licked the seal, and looked up.

"Do you want to be in the Infantry, Turvey?"

"Yes, sir; Kootenay Highlanders, please, sir."

"O.K. Take this to Lieutenant Smith."

Lieutenant Smith had slept even less than usual and it was another hot and hectic morning, but so far he had been carried along in a quiet, secret elation and anticipation. For, thinking over Turvey's case in bed last night, he had become convinced that he had written a report that would make Personnel Selection history. He expected Crashaw to poke his head in any moment; those buggy eyes would be shining with respect and admiration this time. There was a knock at the door and Lieutenant Smith looked up to gaze into the wide anxious smile of Turvey, Thomas Leadbeater.

Twice he read the insultingly small note he had fished out of the long brown envelope: "Functional enquiry – negative; no indigestion, insomnia, or true facial tics. Smile not unusual as a nervous reaction under stress, and probably less sinister in pattern than, say, nailbiting. May have mild schizoid tendencies; tends to gaze out the window and let his attention wander and should have further psychiatric check-up in six months (by a qualified Medical Officer). No neurosis. Intelligence higher than that of some officers I have met. Recommend he be assigned to Infantry without further delay.

7 June 1942   K.F. Crashaw,
                          Capt. RCAMC, Psych. Consult."

Lieutenant Smith resisted a treacherous impulse to cry.

He would ask for a transfer. He would stand for no more insult from that fat Buddha. But it would never do to let anyone see how he felt. With an effort he assumed his paternal voice. There was even a hint of the godlike in its benevolence:

"Well, Turvey, I've decided to take a chance on you in the Infantry. I always try to put a man where he wants to be, if it's humanly possible. That way he'll give his very best service to the war effort. And that's what you want to do, isnt it, Turvey?"

"Yes, sir. Kootenay Highlanders, sir."

Lieutenant Smith placed his thumb-nail between his teeth but withdrew it instantly as if it might poison him.

"You go to the *Infantry*, Turvey," he shouted with the emphasis one uses in talking to the deaf. "After your *Basic* Training, *if* you pass it, you will get *Advanced* Training. *If* you pass that, you *may* be posted to a regiment; and it *may* be the Kootenay Highlanders." From the sour pucker of the lieutenant's mouth, Turvey gathered that he hadnt a snowball's chance of getting anywhere.

His last memory of Lieutenant Smith was of a gaunt face, and a bony arm reaching out for a round tin on the ledge of the shut window.

TWO

Turvey Marks Time

THE NEXT two weeks Turvey dwelt with several thousand other males in a District Depot. As a talkative platoon mate, Calvin Busby, pointed out, their new home was a little like a fish hatchery. Shiny fingerlings in zinc tanks, the prentice soldiers moved up and down a square world, learning to flip right-angled corners with increasing speed and nimbleness, putting on weight with regular feeding, until they were gamey enough to be dipped out and transferred to larger and larger tanks through which the water ran progressively swifter and deeper. Then one day, said Busby, they would be taken a long journey and dumped in the Lake itself, where anglers waited. Fishers of men, said Busby, Mark One, Seventeen.

But Turvey was not the sort of man to let such a comparison worry him. During the day he was a Body, stabbed with poisoned needles and drilling interminably in a hot sun under the bullet voices of extremely unlikable sergeants and the catcalls of swooping gulls; but after the early mass supper and before the ten o'clock mass bedding-down, he was Thomas (Tops for Topsy) Turvey, learning the multiform escapes of soldiers. He and Busby, and the two Icelanders with whom he had shot craps on O-testing day, would play a little nickle stud or blackjack, an eye out for the Orderly Sergeant, and then walk down, griping happily about the NCOs and the bugs, to the corner of the old Exhibition Grounds to see what girls were sauntering tonight.

The Icelanders were leary of women. They were shy to begin with and now that they walked branded with the Depot's chili-bowl haircut they were struck dumb in female presence. They would stand listening almost fearfully while Turvey went through the preliminary ceremonies of a pick-up. Then they would excuse themselves with great but strictly pantomimic politeness and board a streetcar to a movie, or perhaps just down to Yonge Street and back for the ride. The girls were always disappointed, for Emil, at least, was outwardly a Nordic god. Eric, small and spectacled, was actually the more sporting of the two but was taken up with his protective role toward Emil. The latter, all six handsome feet of him, was timid, homesick, plagued by imaginary ailments, and already cheesed off with the army, which he felt would be the death of him. It had already given him sunburn.

But it was lank Calvin Busby whose attitude to women really puzzled Turvey. He had little good to say about them, yet he had little to say about anything else. He loved to fix a woman with his wild yellowish eyes and deliver a kind of sermon, elaborate and insulting, in a bastard Biblical style. As he told Turvey, he had once had a religious spell and won a Bible marathon in the Heavenly Institute of Badger Coulee, so he could always produce something from the Lord to clinch his arguments.

The third night they were allowed out of barracks was hot, languorous with the scent of catalpa blossoms, a complete waste of a night, thought Turvey, without a woman. Busby apparently thought so too; dropping the mournful Icelanders, they linked up with two young waitresses from a Queen Street restaurant off for the evening. The girls were set on a movie, and Turvey, who was two dollars flush from the poker games, was willing. But Busby spoke first, suggesting a walk in High Park.

"Ja hear that Lavonne?" asked the older one, in a querulous chant; her scarlet little claws and matching lipstick seemed out of kilter with her eyes, which were pale as driftwood. "Aint you guys been on yuh feet enough today? You should work like us from eighta-clawk in the mornin on yuh dogs alla time we wanna sit down."

"Listen, Jezebel," said Calvin, running his fingers with a preparatory flourish through his tarblack hair, "the grass is really swell in High Park – sweet and warm as the hills of Gideon. Come, we will perfume it with aloes, and take our fill of love until morning."

"Jeez watta line he's got. You musta been readin a book. And my name's Gilda, I tole yuh . . . Anyways, les go have a beer wile we decide."

Turvey, who had got his arm around plump Lavonne without need of conversation, was about to agree, but Busby was implacable.

"Beer afterwards. First let us to the hills of frankin-cense. Song of Solomon, Four." His tawny eyes flashed and he seized her arm imperiously.

Gilda wriggled away indignantly and hiked the strap of her shiny plastic bag higher on her shoulder. "Come on, Lavonne. This guy's goofy. Les get outa here." She was genuinely alarmed and pulled her girl-friend off with her.

Turvey eyed the weaving of Lavonne's trim little bottom with such obvious regret that Busby made what he no doubt considered an adequate gesture of peace. Toss-ing a long lick of hair from his eye, he shouted:

"Return, O ye daughters of Jerusalem, for I am black but comely," and he beat his khaki bosom in mock despair. But though Lavonne looked back with a furtive smile, Gilda speeded their pace, shouting over her platinum-dipped curls: "He's bats, Lavonne. Now he's callin us kikes."

Turvey was never one to be dashed when a partridge gets away. Making a mental note of the name of the restaurant where Lavonne said they worked, for future reference, he suggested to Busby that they follow up another pair of girls who, while they had been negotiating with the waitresses, had passed them in the opposite direction, chattering ostentatiously. But Busby had worked himself up into one of his woman-hating moods.

"Tops," he declaimed, "keep thee from the strange woman, from the stranger that flattereth with her words. To the tavern, come. Let's get squiffed . . . Waitresses! Pahh! Painted sisters of Gomorrah."

At Busby's insistence they thumbed a ride downtown and shoved their way into a crowded beverage room on Adelaide Street.

There were other evenings, however, in which Turvey managed to study women at closer hand, so that the night before he was sent off to Basic Training Centre Lavonne actually had sniffles and Turvey had to promise to write her.

Busby and the Icelanders were in the same draft, and they and twenty other recuits jolted out on each other's feet in the same fifteen-hundredweight one Saturday morning. Turvey felt excited. This was the way men rode up to the Front, wasnt it, and who knows how far they might be going even now? Perhaps, without saying anything, the army had quietly planned to take him direct to the Kootenay Highlanders!

The convoy of trucks thumped along for about thirty miles and through a small town, then drew up in a maze of hutments by a treeless marshland on the outskirts. Passing through Main Street those who were at the rear of the truck and could see out began whistling at the cuties. But most of them must have been used to soldiers and walked as if they were deaf. Busby had the loudest whistle of all; it had a shrill toothy sound that made even these snooty women jump. Turvey tried to learn how Busby did it but he felt his top plate loosening and had to give up.

THREE

Turvey Is Basically Trained

TURVEY found that the week-end was a concentrated repetition of his days at the Depot. With the other truckloads of fresh battledress, he was fallen out, warned that he was confined to camp until after supper Monday, fallen in for lunch parade, lined up to wash implements, fallen in for a sergeant-major's parade to hear eight pages of Camp Standing Orders, fallen out to wait an hour under the hot sun for a missing nominal roll, fallen in when it arrived, marched north to a blanket parade, which came to nothing, marched east with his pack and haversack into a board hut furnished so compactly with double-tiered bunks it looked more like a warehouse than a place to live, marched back again on the double because it was some other squad's, marched west to an even more crowded one where he left his kit, brought back to a line-up, given blankets at last, sent to the hut to make his bed but whisked away south immediately into a longer line-up for supper, and another to wash his mug and billytin, and another at the latrine, and another for sunburn oil at the Sally Ann. Then he was ordered back to his hut for the night.

Sunday morning their hut was shaken out at seven and set to tidying quarters. After a sketchy breakfast Turvey spent three hours standing or sitting in wait for three minutes of medical inspection, and four hours in the afternoon for a four-minute Personnel Selection interview. The M.O. contented himself with poking a flashlight at Turvey's pubic hairs. Turvey gathered that the PSO meant to be equally brief and informal but his once-over-lightly system was thrown out of gear by the discovery that Turvey was recorded in his pay book as a Seventh Day Adventist. It took a little time for the officer to understand that Turvey had confessed to this faith, when sworn in, on the written advice of his pal Mac of the Kootenay Highlanders, who had found such a declaration to be of some help in getting out of church parades. Since Turvey was not sure what religion he did follow, the officer automatically changed the pay book to read Church of England. He was about to hand Turvey back the precious little brown document when he noticed the O-score and had to hold the line-up behind Turvey another minute to ask him who was Prime Minister of Canada and which side the Hungarians were fighting on. He didnt seem any too happy about Turvey's answers.

That night the incoming draft was divided into training groups by yapping corporals and issued with rifles and bayonets, and Turvey felt as happy as the first time his father let him take the old .44 deer-shooting.

Monday morning he was shaving by 0550 hrs, in water so cold he was surprised it could run. After rollcall at 0610, and breakfast, he doused his tools in a barrel of greasy water (he was about 180th in the queue), and learned a new way to line-up beds and kits with the aid of a long string and two lance-corporals. Then Turvey and his hutmates, with rifles and full marching kit, joined the general draft on the parade square.

About an hour later the Camp Commandant, an elderly colonel with a sun helmet crowning an impressively big head, addressed them in a loud high voice. He told them how important training was and how they were the glorious soldiers of democracy but soldiering meant discipline too and fitness, because they had to be ready to wipe the Huns off the face of the earth. At first the colo-

nel stood at attention and spoke as if he had it all
memorized but when he began to talk about the Germans
his voice grew dramatic and he hissed. "You men have
got to ssstart *hating*," he shouted, and his fat face red-
dened. He went on excitedly about the crimes of the German Nation in this war and the last. Turvey, who had
grown very hot in his battledress and pack, and was envy-
ing the colonel's sleeveless shirt and khaki shorts,
reproached himself for not paying attention. He tried to
start hating, but his feet ached and his steel helmet kept
slipping over one ear. "Rrruthlessss," the colonel was
shouting, "abssolutely rruthlesss, if need be." His round
knees quivered as he stamped his feet. "I tell you, men,
frankly, I would be proud, yess *proud*, if at the end of
this war I was one of those ordered to sshoot down every
ssurviving German, man, woman and – *and* child." He
stopped suddenly. "All right, carry on, captain."

The adjutant saluted, called the parade to attention
and turned it over to the sergeant-major. The sergeant-
major saluted and, while the officers clumped off without
another look, divided the intake into training platoons.

Turvey was a little dashed when he found that he was in a
different platoon from Busby and the Icelanders, a group
which the tall youth on his right described as the Goon
Squad. They were standing easy, in a corner of the
square, waiting for their first drill.

"It's for morons, brother; you gotta low O-score, I
bet. Watcha make, you know?"

"Eighty-nine."

"Mine's seventy-six," said the tall one, who had
responded at roll-call to the name of Roach. There was a
hint of superiority in his voice. "They dont take em much
lower." He cocked his jaw confidentially. "It's all horse-
feathers though. Aint none a these crystal-ball bastards
can drill a gopher at a hunerd yards with a twenty-two
like I can, I bet yah. Trouble is though, they gointa make

us do extra drill. Ten weeks we gointa be in this dump, brother; mosta them oney goin to be here eight. And they got the collitch boys and brainstorms seprated off and I heard they gointa let them out in six. It's the joes like us gointa do the fightin though, you watch. Can yah wrassle?''

The platoon was "shunned" before Turvey could reply, harried around the parade square for a while and then led off by a stumpy morose sergeant over a windy field and halted near a row of dwarf gibbets from each of which hung stuffed gunnysacks. Another group of trainees was already in action here, bayonets fixed, making involved twisting rushes at the bloated brown torsos and inflicting bright straw wounds as they passed. The sergeant in charge of the stabbing operations broke off and went into a huddle with their own sergeant. Roach, who seemed to have everything taped beforehand, whispered delightedly:

"They's a ballup somers; rookies dont have no baynit drill for a month yet, I heard; we gotta letcher on the parts of a rifle cordin to what our corp said; by geez they oughta have some a these officers right here in the Goon Squad."

A young lieutenant appeared, bony-kneed in undersized shorts. He joined the sergeants fretfully; there was a great fluttering of training schedules among them. The lieutenant's treble, indistinct in the fitful wind, rose higher with impatience.

"Do anything you like with them, sergeant, until the next period but get them out of here. Take them over to the assault course and – ah – show them around."

Turvey's sergeant looked more depressed than ever, and surprised as well. He stood at attention for a moment; the natural sag of his thin lips deepened, his eyebrows rose over round eyes. Then evidently he made a decision. He clamped his long jaw firmly and said, "Very good, sir," with that curious combination of astonishment, submission, and contempt which practised sergeants use in addressing foolish subalterns. Then he saluted with slightly exaggerated precision and led his charges over to a series of earthworks and entanglements at the far end of the camp.

He stood them easy on the top of a high earth bank and warned them to pay attention, but for a long time he just stared at the slouching group. His round bulbous eyes regarded them in a way that reminded Turvey of his father when he was about to climb into the pigpen at Skookum Falls and stab a favourite hog. His father always got attached to his pigs. There was certainly pity in the sergeant's eyes, but when his voice came it was carefully tough; in fact it was like gristle.

"All right, men. This here's the assault course. It starts with this here ramp. When I give the word of command, the three leadin men will walk up the ramp, jump down onto the platform, then crawl *under* the barb wire, *acrost* the water hazard, *over* that there wall, and back *through* them sewer pipes. Now I'll repeat that and remember you gunna do this fast as you can and no holdin up."

Thirty uneasy men stood and regarded the ramp. From the edge of the earth bank in front of them, three parallel planks, spaced about two feet apart, sloped steeply up to a cross beam. The beam was supported by log pillars whose bases, together with the platform to which the sergeant had referred, were hidden by the crest of the bank. Beyond the ramp the terrain dropped; they could see a confusion of trampled mud crossed with spiny coils of wire and spotted with hollow concrete pipe. Beyond these again was a reedy swamp and, on its far side, a kind of billboard at least ten feet high and apparently naked of ledge or handhold.

The sergeant had repeated his instructions exactly, except that his voice had sunk lower and lower until at the end, when he asked for questions, Turvey was almost sure he had said, "Any last requests?"

"How high's the ramp, sarge?" It was Ball, a pot-bellied chap with a little sunburned face. His steel helmet, issued that morning, seemed about to come down like a snuffer and extinguish the orange glow of his nose.

The sergeant gazed at him grimly. "This here ramp is regalation height." There was silence.

"We keep our helmets on?" It was Ball again.

The sergeant moved his thin lips soundlessly like a man at prayer. The surprised arch of his eyebrows seemed to have become permanently fixed and his pop eyes rolled up and down the front row.

"This here is an assault course, see. You supposed to be attackin over broken ground. Theys enemy in the woods beyond that there swamp. So, you gunna keep your helmets on your heads and carry your rifles atta *trail* and" – he surveyed the lot of them desperately – "any bastard gets his barrel muddy –" He left the threat unfinished as if he already despaired of its effectiveness. There were no more questions.

They were brought to attention, right-turned, and steered in column of three upon the ramp. Turvey was in the second triad of shufflers to tackle the swaying planks; in front of him was Roach; they were on the outside right. Halfway up his plank, Turvey heard the first yell. It came from McGuigan, the broad-beamed Irishman who had been the first to poise at the top of the middle plank and been precipitated out into space as much by the prancing board as by the watchful bark of the sergeant standing on the bank behind them. The yell, which had a pained animal quality about it, was followed at split-second intervals by remarkably similar cries from the lead man on the left and from Roach.

Pressing to the crosslog Turvey could see, a dizzying distance below him, the three who had jumped. Roach was already barging on towards the barbed wire, cursing ornately in rhythm with his agonised limp. The lefthand leader was belly down and gasping in the mud like a stranded fish, his helmet several yards off. The Irishman, after his first howl, was now quietly staring at the sky, one arm draped over a corner of the landing platform. As

Turvey gazed, the voice of the sergeant, devoid now of anything but blind relentless command, came pelting up at him from the rear:

"Keep movin, keep movin. Next three over. Get the lead outa your ass. This aint no sight-seein tour."

Turvey tried to balance himself on the rim until he could find the likeliest spot to aim his heavy feet. At least fifteen – was it twenty? – feet below him there lay in wait a rectangle of heel-gouged, sunbaked clay, rimmed with knotty logs and raised about two feet above the surrounding bog. The whole little contrivance seemed scarcely roomy enough for one man to land on accurately, let alone three, abreast, helmeted, and carrying rifles. At least they hadnt been asked to fix bayonets beforehand. He was trying to decide whether he would be more likely to survive if he aimed at the end of the raised sacrificial altar or if he tried to overleap it and hit the mud (there was a risk of crashing on the prone Irishman, either way), when the rifle of the man behind, lurching up the ramp under the impetus of the sergeant's insults, connected neatly with the centre of Turvey's rump. Turvey leapt without further calculation.

His left foot landed exactly in one of the ramp's fossilized footprints; after the rest of his body pitched forward, Turvey's army boot was retained in the clay's grip and Turvey's solid one hundred and sixty pounds pivoted on his ankle before dragging it clear. Still clutching his rifle in one hand and reaching for his ankle with the other, he executed a complicated forward somersault and came to rest sitting in the mud.

Between shoots of pain and while groping for his false teeth, which had shot out, he heard the sergeant urging the third trio over the top, and the fourth, and the fifth. He found his mudcased plate and filed it in his battle-blouse for cleaning later. Then he hopped over and sank beside the Irishman, who had revived sufficiently to drag himself clear of the growing human waterfall. They regarded the fate of this stream which the sergeant was too busy initiating above to observe in its full spate below.

Roach somehow had cleared the first hurdle of wire and had even remembered to hold his rifle clear of the mud, but preoccupied with this soldierly trick, and still limping, he had tried to go over instead of under the second row of concertina. Caught in its intricate fangs he was engaged at the moment mainly in weaving together most of the rather ingenious obscenities at his command.

The bog-fish whom Turvey had glimpsed from the ramp's top had recovered his breath and, sitting up, was now totally absorbed in the job of getting mud out of the interstices of his face.

More victims were flung down to them as they watched. Ball, the sunburned soldier who had starred at question time, came flapping down like a shot grouse, shedding his rifle in mid-air; he ricocheted from the platform and landed on his head by Turvey's feet. Turvey was able to pry Ball's oversized helmet up to his forehead before it could smother him, and boosted him to his feet, whereupon the newest victim, who seemed to have lost his sense of direction, if indeed he had yet got his eyes open, ran straight back into one of the ramp posts, banging his helmet over his ears once more. He slumped gently under the striped shadow of the ramp and took no further interest in the action.

By this time about thirty had cascaded over the little cliff. Of these a dozen, by some mystery of hardihood, had picked themselves up and reached the barbed wire. Five were in fitful rest among its briary coils; the remainder were bogged down at various levels in the water hazard. Except Roach. That hero of the hour had recovered from his limp, and the wire, struggled through the swamp and, still clutching a muddy object that had been his rifle, was leaping galvanically at the billboard in a futile attempt to clutch its top with his free hand. Suddenly a new voice shrieked above the sergeant's:

"Halt!" it cried hysterically. "Call your men back,

sergeant." The spindly legs of the young lieutenant they had seen at the bayonet ground were dancing on the bank. "My God, what's going on here? Who told you to put these men over this course?"

The sergeant advanced stiffly until he was the regulation two paces from the lieutenant, saluted beautifully and froze to attention. "Beggin your pardon, sir, you did. Your orders was for me to take this here platoon over the assault course."

"You imbecile!" screeched the officer, forgetting to return the salute, "I said take them over TO the assault course, *TO* the assault course! I just wanted them out of the road until we found out what the hell we're supposed to do with them. Dont you know the Engineers condemned this ramp yesterday?"

"Yes, sir, but your orders wa –"

"Didnt you read the sign over there?" The lieutenant's voice went into a squeak with rage and he thrust a wavering swagger stick at a notice tacked on one of the ramp's posts, OUT OF BOUNDS TO ALL TROOPS. "Didnt you read your Part One Orders this morning? Where's your bloody hea –" But the lieutenant at last remembered that his audience was too large and unselect for the occasion. He gazed at the little Dantean circle below him, the still faintly writhing field of battle, and made a soldierly effort to sound nonchalant.

"As you were, lads. No, ah, serious casualties, I take it?"

When the various grunting figures had been unhooked from the wire, pried from the mud, and assisted to the bank it was found that twelve of the thirty were indeed intact. Of the remainder all but one were, like Turvey, suffering from nothing worse than a sprained or broken ankle; the exceptions were Joey Deerfoot, the Huron, who had broken a heel and bitten a tooth off on his own knee, and McGuigan, whose back had unaccountably splintered.

FOUR

Turvey Is Hospitalized

HEDY LAMARR snuggled tighter into Turvey's arms. The other dancers cleared the floor to watch, entranced with their grace. Her fingers slid down and caressed his wrist. Lifting her luminous eyes she murmured:

"Come on, lug. Open up your trap 'n lift that tongue."

Turvey awoke in time to gag before the little icicle of a thermometer could slide down his throat. The orderly, who had been holding Turvey's wrist with a thumb and forefinger as if it were a piece of bad meat, dropped it. The time was 0600 hrs. Turvey began his thirteenth day in Ward Two of Number Umpteen Basic Training Centre Hospital.

It began very much like the other twelve. He struggled to the floor with the impossible hope in his heart that the chip-fracture in his ankle might have mended overnight, but two trial steps – and the familiar nest of needles stabbed up through the floor into his foot. He fished his one crutch from under the bed (with eight fracture cases from the assault course alone, the hospital had run out of pairs) and hopped quickly, in his parti-coloured pajamas, to the washroom before that little establishment could be fully occupied. After a while he realized he should have drunk the glass of liquid dynamite the orderly had left with him the night before, instead of swashing it through the window screen after lights out. He reflected that at least he could shave and, taking up a stork-like stance, he proceeded to scrape the cold razor over his cheeks.

Bedmaking and breakfast over, the ward settled down to renewed flippings of the old *Readers' Digests* and other paperbacks available, waiting for the M.O.'s morning visitation. Turvey, though he would have preferred to be out learning to be a Kootenay Highlander, was rather enjoying the camp hospital. From the outside it had looked like any other brindle-green army dump, three barrack huts glaumed together, but inside it was whitewashed clean as a cafeteria. The two wards were small, of course, and theirs, the non-infectious one, was overcrowded even though the sprain cases had all been taped up the day of the accident and sent to their huts for 72 hours light duties. All the beds were occupied and huddled together in pairs to make room for two mattresses on the floor. Turvey, who rated a bed, found it a good deal softer than the wisp of straw on this bunk in the hut. He was disappointed, certainly, to discover that the hospital provided none of the Nursing Sisters, beautiful or otherwise, whom he had read about in the newspapers. The nurses consisted of two definitely male orderlies who divided the night and the day. Turvey had already become pally with Clarence, however, the Night Orderly, and so was able to scrounge the occasional forbidden sandwich or cup of coffee after 2200 hrs, when lights went out and most of the ward lay snoring competitively. The regular food, of course, was as anonymous as in the rest of the camp – Turvey wondered if he had signed something on Attestation Day which suspended his rights to fresh fruits and vegetables for the Duration – but at least the dry beef, old potatoes, saccharine beets and glucose pudding were not all slopped into the same billytin.

And there were always distractions. On the second day the ward had blossomed out in shiny plastercasts. Turvey had a boot that reached almost to his knee, with a hole in front to let his toes wriggle. McGuigan, the unfortunate Irishman, who had surprised the M.O.s by surviving and even, as soon as he was propped up with pillows, resuming an enormous appetite, now lay encased in white armour from waist to neck. The up-patients had gone about autographing all the casts with indelible pencils, and Zapasocky, a needleworker who had always wanted to be a commercial illustrator, decorated the larger surfaces with bosomy nymphs and exotic purple lilies. Zapasocky was an oldtimer from the previous intake who might have graduated from camp by now if he had not been accidentally skewered in the rear by the bayonet of another recruit. By kneeling – Zapasocky couldnt yet bend – and working rapidly, he was able to cover nearly the whole of McGuigan's false back with a lush Petty nude before the Orderly Officer made his rounds. McGuigan was a little miffed at first, because he had asked for a ship in full sail, but he was reconciled by the unfailing public attention he received.

During the first week, too, the Assault Heroes had been the stars of the ward. The brief saga of their action was told and re-told, each warrior adding his chapter. Even Turvey's contained a novel twist. The sergeant had decided his leg was "just wrenched a little" and made him carry three helmets and four rifles, abandoned on the battlefield, back to the hut before he could get his ankle taped. It was only after he had sat down in the middle of the square while acting as marker for the afternoon parade that the M.O. was intrigued into X-raying his ankle.

To such tales the oldtimers appended the previous histories of the sergeant and the lieutenant involved, and visitors from the outside brought fresh rumours of what was to be their fate. Opinion was somewhat divided as to whether the lieutenant would be given another platoon or promoted to a Company Commander; the camp veterans held for the latter, on the theory that all officers who got into trouble were kicked upstairs. The sergeant, it was generally felt, would be court-martialled and reduced to the ranks, but the arguments for this were inclined to be tinged with wish-fulfilment. One notion was as good as another, of course, for the Court of Enquiry which had promptly been set up hadnt yet reached a decision.

Apparently the court consisted of most of the officers of the camp, for each day had brought different ones into the ward by twos and threes, flanked by clerks bearing little pyramids of notepaper and forms. Every assault victim was systematically interviewed in turn, and then interviewed all over again by the next group, on a different form containing the same questions. Turvey had to render up his educational and occupational history once more, and the Personnel Officer came in and gave them all a special twenty-minute Classification Appraisal for reasons that he never explained and were never divulged. It had questions like "Write the letter before the seventh letter from the beginning of the alphabet", with the alphabet carefully printed alongside for aid. Turvey thought it a little odd that he was asked very few questions about the accident itself or how his leg felt. On the contrary, each Enquirer warned him he mustnt discuss the Nature or Cause of his injuries in letters or conversations. But he was always glad of an interview since it broke the monotony and added a fillip to the illegal bedside poker. There were so many officers clumping into the ward that you had to keep an ear always cocked for boots in the corridor and have a hand ready to flip a top blanket over the telltale matches and cards before an officer got his eye around the doorframe.

Then there were the standard distractions. At 0830 hrs Captain S. Hart, the overworked M.O., made his usual lightning visit. There was a belief that his initial stood for Stone, but he was popular despite – or because of – his apparent toughness. His technique was to assume each day that every man had got completely well over night, appear to pay no attention to even the most dramatic of complaints, and hum cheerfully to himself while he examined the evidence of malaise or injury bared to him. Consequently he stirred up a mass fear of expulsion from what, compared to the Basic Training routine, was paradise enow. Today, as on previous occasions, when the captain had loped out whistling, everyone felt lucky he was still a casualty for at least another twenty-four hours.

After the Orderly Officer (0900 hrs) came a dull interlude, and then the mail. Turvey was surprised to receive a letter postmarked Ottawa; he could think of no one he knew there. It turned out to be an application blank for his civilian sugar ration. He was hoping to hear from Mac, now somewhere in Nova Scotia with the Kootenays. He had written Mac as soon as he had landed in hospital, asking him to keep a place for him in the regiment. Bored, he went back to last January's *Macleans* to see if Veronica, the banker's gleaming daughter, would marry the Forest Ranger or the Pilot Officer from her home town.

A century later the noon dinner arrived. It contained no surprises. After he had downed the last of what was known in the ward as "coftea" – they could never be sure which, especially with the added saltpetre – Turvey lay and practised "He's got spurs that jingle, jangle, jingle" on his tonette till the ward made him stop. He thought how much he would like a beer to wash down the last gob of gluey rice. He counted the flies on the ceiling; ten more than ever before. Through the window he could see some of his healthier if unluckier comrades, followed by a barking corporal, going on the double for a Saturday afternoon punishment parade in the bright sunshine. At this distance the corporal's voice sounded deceptively kind drifting in from away across the North Parade Ground, drifting in . . . drifting . . . .

Captain Turvey, V.C., paused in his tour of inspection and turned to his attendant officers. A cool breeze ruffled his kilts. "You know, of course, that we condemned all these ramps overseas. We find dances make the best tests, dances and" – he smiled indulgently at Sgt. Busby standing by, eyes humble with hero-worship – "Bible Marathons." He turned to take a great tankard of beer

from a girl who had just appeared. She looked a little like
Lavonne, with a dash of Dorothy Lamour. But just then
there was a shout behind him. "It's a WOMAN!" He
wheeled. It was the Personnel Lieutenant of the Recruiting Depot. The lieutenant bit his nails hurriedly and then
pointed a warning finger, not at Lavonne, who had
disappeared, but at Turvey himself, at his kilts. "A
WOMAN!" "I'm not a woman," Turvey cried, "I'm a
Koot –"

"A WOMAN!!" The shout was taken up by other
voices and Turvey was wide awake and limping out of
bed to join the rubber-necking patients at the windows.
Slowly he became aware that this was 1500 hrs Saturday
afternoon, that Visitors' Hour had begun, and that
Zapasocky had sounded the amazing news of a female's
approach to the hospital. "Oy, she's got legs!"
Zapasocky was saying. "Two of dem. Wit curves in em.
And, O no, dont tahl me, a box of chocolates she's got
under that denty arm." Whatever it was, Ward Two had
none of it, for the lady, the first they had seen within the
boundaries of Number Umpteen Basic Training Centre,
disappeared through the main entrance and evidently
wasted her sweetness on the infectious air at the guarded
door to Ward One.

"Don't we *never* get visitors?" Ball asked plaintively.

"Visitors, shmisitors," said Zapasocky crawling back
into bed, "two kinds already we got and both from the
sex I never ordered. First come our hearty warriors, wit
suntan – what am I sayin? – last they should come, five
minutes before time is up yet. And what beautiful gifties
they bring me! Any chocolate bars I got, they bring me a
hunger. Any cigarettes around, they should smoke
dem." Turvey thought regretfully that Calvin Busby, for
all his weird oratory, fitted into this type. "Next,"
Zapasocky went on, "they give bedtime stories; sure, all
about the beautiful crittures they been slipping wit, or
they want you should think it –"

"Or they wanna know we got phone numbers of any bims they *could* lay," Leacock interrupted.

"Sure, sure," Zapasocky agreed, "always the big ball they got coming up. Then they slap me where it's sore yet and zowie they're off!"

"Yeah," Leacock chipped in, "they tell yuh they gotta crock and all you get is the smell off their puss."

"That's Mark One," Zapasocky continued. "Mark Two comes in he wants I should sympathize. The sergeant was rude to him, poor fellah, he should cry on my shoulder."

"Or like the guy was in here yesterday seein McGuigan," said Ball, "was still green from the rotgut he got down to the village."

"Gosh, I dont know, there's Roach now," said Turvey, "he aint like those."

"Turvey's got somethin there," Ball agreed. "They dont make many like him. He comes early and he stays till the corp throws him out. And every time he smuggles in cokes."

"And he gives us all the dope on what's goin on in camp," said Turvey.

"Yeah and he *listens*," Leacock added. "I feel like I'm in jail here. What I want is somebody *I* can beef to."

"Hah!" said Zapasocky, "so now we're nut good enough for him."

The two Icelanders, who were Turvey's visitors this Saturday, however, were Zapasocky's Mark Two, Turvey thought, except that they never drank and therefore never had hangovers, and Eric's beefs were not usually for himself but for six-foot Emil. The latter was now lounging over the upper two-thirds of Turvey's bed, looking at leg shots in an old *Life*. Eric took up the rest of the bed and Turvey contented himself with the visitor's camp-chair.

"He oughtnt to be doing all this hard marching and drilling," said Eric solemnly. "He's really kind of delicate, you know. You got something wrong with your back, havent you, Emil?"

"Yeah," said Emil sadly, behind the masking pages of *Life*. "It's my kidneys, I bet. My father had it too. And mom has to take medicine all the time for her liver."

"All his family's delicate, you know," Eric explained confidentially, as if Emil werent there. "His sister's very high-strung too."

"Why dont he go sick?" Turvey asked, shifting his cast from under one of Emil's spreading limbs.

"He does," said Eric with indignation, "he's been on three sick parades. But the M.O. dont do a thing. Just says he cant find anything wrong, and gives him a Number Nine, doesnt he, Emil?"

Emil flipped another page. "The army dont give a hoot," he said gloomily. "Unless," he conceded as an afterthought, "you got somethin simple like a broken leg they can see. That butcher he dont really examine me. Not like my doctor at home. I got a pumpin in my heart too, somethin horrible at times. I told em about it when I was drafted too." He pressed his chest vaguely with one large paw. "You got another cig, Tops?"

"He shouldnt have been called-up, should you, Emil?"

"I dont like hearin guns go off," said Emil, coming out from behind the magazine again. "And they better not put *me* over that ramp. I get dizzy on high places. You got a light, Tops?"

Turvey supplied them both with Players and matches.

"He gets dizzy sometimes just looking out a window," Eric added with fond pride.

"What you goin to do when you get to where the fightin is?" Turvey asked.

"They better not send me over. I aint well enough," Emil said aggressively, throwing *Life* on the floor. "All this doublin and night marchin and wearing shorts even when it's rainin. I tell yuh it taint good for a man. They better watch who they're pushin."

"You see, he only turned Active to stay with me," Eric explained. "My folks went back to Iceland just before the war, so I went Active soon as I got my call-up because they said only overseas units got sent to Iceland, and I'd have first chance to go after I finished Advanced Training. But now, wouldnt you know it, the papers are saying they took the last Canadians out of there a year ago and they wont send any more."

"Mmyeah." Emil registered scornful agreement. "The double-cross is what we got."

"You see Emil knew that even if he stayed on Home Service they would probably send him to some other part of Canada miles away from home and I couldnt keep an eye on him."

"Yeah, so I figgered I'd string along with Eric and Iceland, where I aint never been cause I was born in Canada. But by crikey they better not send me to that Second Front they're all yappin about now. I aint cut out for it."

By the time Eric and Emil had unravelled their tangled web to Turvey it was 1600 hrs and the orderly was shouting, "All visitors out." Emil heaved himself out of Turvey's bed with an envious sigh. "You sure got it soft in here," he said.

Visitors gone, the time until supper began to drag a little. The ward discussed plans for the long hospital leave they were rumoured to be getting as soon as they were convalescent. They pooled a few dirty stories previously overlooked. They grumbled at the Commandant for not permitting a radio in the hospital, and not letting the crutch cases walk fifty yards to the Rec Hut where there was one. They quarrelled about politics, and agreed about women. Some lapsed into reading and others into sleep. The rest listened to Leacock, the newest patient, retelling his accident.

"There I was jus sittin, kina relaxin, firs time all day; ten mile that fuckin sergeant took us route-marchin all over Hannah, an after plowin around on a scheme half the night. So I was jus squattin, see, on the edge a my bunk, wit my boots an sox off, coolin my dogs like on the floor, an waitin for the supper gong, it was jus about doo, and Johansen, the big squarehead – d'I tell yuh how *big* that fucker is? Weighs two hunnern ten he tole me, hones! Well Johansen he was stretchin on his bunk above mine, like I said, nappin I guess. But he dint have his boots off, O no, not Johansen! So bong goes the chow bell an Johansen – he's allus a hungry bastard, cant wait never – I oughta *knew* bettern be where I was – well, like I say, before I finish *hearin* the jeezly gong even, the nex thing I know that big bloody Scandihoovian he's sailin tru the air over my head an whambo! He lands wit bot' dose big gravelcrushers a his square on top a my bare toes! *Son* of a bitch! Cleats on em too, he had."

"So. A lot you got to holler," said Zapasocky, after the wise-cracks had trailed into silence – the story had been funnier the first time – "out ahead of us you'll be yet . . . Yoy, what I am going to do, come my forty-eight!"

Turvey, listening to Zapasocky elaborating plans for his hospital leave, felt restless. It was stickily hot and his skin, beneath the plaster, sweated and itched. McGuigan had perspired so much the cast under his armpits had turned to mush and the Petty girl had lost her trimness in a violet haze. For something to do, Turvey tried lying flat on the tallwheeled stretcher-table the night orderly had carelessly left in the ward; he had just caught on to the trick of propelling it down the aisle, using his crutch like a punt-pole, when the Orderly Officer made a second unscheduled visit, trailing the Orderly Sergeant three paces behind him and the Corporal of the Wards three paces behind *him* again. The officer rebuked Turvey and the sergeant took his name, and the Corporal of the Wards called the Ward Orderly and rebuked him, and the Ward Orderly wheeled the stretcher out meekly, and the procession trailed behind it, and Turvey went back to his bed.

There was no further diversion of any note until 1700 hrs when Clarence, the Night Orderly, took over. He made his usual, excited, unsuccessful attempt to read all their temperatures before the oncoming supper. Clarence was the hospital butt, a fat toothy youth crowned with a tough stand of bristly badger-coloured hair; he talked with an adenoidal snuffle. Turvey rather liked him because he was full of beans and was always willing to do things for the boys, even if what he did was seldom right. He had a great knack for tripping over bedposts, slopping the bedpans, dropping thermometers, and mixing up the medicines. But he also had a St. John Ambulance Certificate and any soldier with the slightest paper claim to medical lore was never transferred from hospital duties short of death to himself or his patients.

Clarence was a conscious clown and had even admitted to the ward with stagey shyness that he had once made a living as a clown diver. "I specialized id fallig off the highboard," he said giggling. Then, climbing on Turvey's bed, he had immediately demonstrated his art by leaping into the air, legs and arms grotesquely tangled, and crashing on the floor. He seemed to be able to fall with any part down and bounce up undamaged, grinning more toothily than ever.

Tonight Clarence had a star turn for the ward. To begin with, this was the first they had seen of him since he had rushed off five days ago on leave not to his home town but to the big and wicked city of Toronto. His reappearance therefore brought out a burst of bawdy questioning from all the ward humourists. Clarence was not the type women came sidling towards and, with the comedian's ready frankness, he always agreed that it bothered him. The ward now registered concern, as one individual, as to whether or not he had found satisfaction for his manly needs. Clarence, the shrewd trouper, waited in grinning silence until the wits had delivered themselves, and then ruffling his cockscomb hair, he announced simply: "I god barried."

There was an awed hush, broken by Zapasocky.

"Jeez, what she look like, Clarence? She got two heads?"

Clarence fished a bedpan out from under a cot and set it on the floor. Then with a sudden show of hauteur he drew a snapshot from his wallet and presented it with open theatrical palm to the nearest bed-patient, Leacock. "The weddig pictures aid developed yet. This here was taket at Diagara Falls."

Leaning by an iron rail against a soiled background that might have been spray from the mighty Niagara was a shortskirted female, somewhat fetching in a hard way, and looking at least ten years older than Clarence, who was twenty-five.

"By Christ she aint bad, Clarry!" said Leacock, surprised. "But who's the zoot-suiter she got with her? You wanna watch that type."

"That, geddlemed," said Clarence with dignity as the photograph passed around, "is her brother. He's a swell guy." He picked up the bedpan, dropping the lid with a crash.

Turvey thought the brother looked like one of the gangster-sheiks in Li'l Abner. He even had a wide snap-brim hat and clammy black sideburns.

"He's doig special work for the govibed," Clarence went on proudly. "They wode let him edlist. After the war he an me is goig into partnership. He can box too. He was featherweight chabbiod of Widsor once. He's goig to teach me."

"You gotta house for the blushing bride yet, Clarry? Wotcha gonna do for a love-nest?" asked Ball, the tireless questioner.

"She lives with her brother. They got a flat od Jarvis Street. She'll stay there till I get her a house dowd here."

"Where you have your honeymoon, Clarence? You take the brudder along?" It was Zapasocky.

Clarence explained with hammy bashfulness that it had taken three days to get the license and they couldnt find a preacher until just before he had to catch a train back to camp.

"I'll get a forty-eight dext weeked," he added, winking grotesquely, and he bore the bedpan dripping out to the washroom.

It was two weeks before Clarence could wangle another pass, however; he had been half an hour late getting back from the last one and the Staff-Sergeant was not his friend. Meantime life in the ward ticked away much as usual. Patients waxed healthy and left, newcomers took their place, but the fractures remained, serving out their minimum six-week sentence. On appointed mornings, in their fourth week, they were taken out for an official hour of sunbathing on a small square of discouraged grass and aspiring weeds under the ward window. Here they were allowed to remove their pink pajama uppers, though on no account the pale-blue lowers. The latter restriction led to a rumour among the group, which soon spread through the whole camp, that somewhere there was a woman in it. The most popular theory was that the venerable Commandant, who had a separate double hut behind the trees in a far corner of the camp, was concealing a mistress. But no one ever saw her.

In addition to its shreds of brown grass and rich green docks, the "Hospital Lawn", as it was officially designated, contained a really prodigious colony of . ants, several light years of them, as Zapasocky remarked. They belonged to a species more inquisitive than intelligent, and never grew tired of racing into the toe-hole in Turvey's cast. They would then proceed in a more leisurely crawl heelwards until Turvey wriggled in an agony of tickling. Whereupon they would bite, in somewhat understandable retaliation for being squeezed to death. Though very few ants ever emerged it did not seem to deter their relatives, so that Turvey and the other legcasts soon began to anticipate the sunbaths much as they would a Chinese water-torture. But so long as the sun shone the Corporal of the Wards firmly refused to let them abandon the field; the outdoor exposure was on the M.O.'s orders and the scene of heliolatry had been agreed to in conference with the adjutant and the RSM and published in Part One Orders.

Among the new patients one day was Emil. It was the morning the first news came about Dieppe. He had fainted while waiting in line for an inoculation and, on being revived, had complained so vigorously about a stomach ache that the M.O. had decided to place him under observation. Emil lasted only the minimum twenty-four hours, however; his interior agonies vanished shortly after the morning visit of the M.O. Captain Hart had seen to it that Emil had a generous assignment of black strap on the evening of his admission and had, the next morning, kneaded Emil's large white belly with systematic vigour. Then he announced cheerfully that if the pains did not clear up by noon he would go to work with the stomach pump. Emil, deprived of his guardian Eric, and sensing perhaps a certain lack of sympathy in the remarks both of the M.O. and the ward wits, begged permission to dress and be officially discharged as cured by 1600 hours.

Clarence finally got away again on a Saturday morning for a forty-eight. He left in a flurry of ribald goodbyes, looking like a plump Disney rooster in his newly-blancoed gaiters and pressed battledress, a spur of pumpkin-coloured hair sticking out from the side of his wedge-cap. He was not back on duty Monday night. After supper Tuesday he came in with a prayer-meeting face incongruously relieved by a large ornate shiner. He made feeble attempts to respond in kind to the uproar his entry caused, but his heart was not in it and he threatened to pour a bedpan over Ball when the latter asked him if his wife was a boxer too. He passed off his mouse as an accident in a friendly bout with his brother-in-law but it was obvious he was holding a lot back.

Attention was diverted for a while by the hospital Staff-Sergeant, a bald saturnine Scot who unbent one afternoon long enough to let drop that he had heard "unoffeecially" that the Commandant had been told to wash out the Court of Enquiry. "The Ottawa laddies a got the wind up their breeks the story'll maybe get in the Press. It ud no be good for recruitin. An the Tories ud be makin a hullabaloo aboot it in Parliament."

"That's why we aint seen any of the brass in here lately. We thought they'd just run out of bumph," said Ball. "Dont nobody get crimed, staff?"

"Ah weel there's been nothin in orrders. But a sairrtin party was sayin there's a lieutenant yull know who's on overseas draft withoot exactly demandin he be sent."

"What's happnin to our dear old sergeant?" Ball asked.

"Him? The British Empire Medal he should get, the shlemiel," said Zapasocky.

"Ah, you've no had today's Parrt Two Orrders in the ward yet? Your sergeant's awa on a Commando course."

"I hope they break his bloody neck," said Ball amid the cheers.

Turvey looked at the silent McGuigan, who had been warned that morning by the M.O. for transfer to a bigger hospital. If the operation on his spine turned out successful he might be fit, after several months, for duty again – but only in Canada, of course, the M.O. had added. McGuigan was staring at the ceiling.

At last a morning came when Turvey had his cast cut off and was able to view the satisfying heap of dead ants curled under his scarred instep. His ankle was massaged and taped; then, restored to his battledress but not his boots, he was sent off in oversized slippers to report to the Orderly Room for Light Duties. The hospital leaves had turned out to be an unfounded belief peculiar to patients. Turvey was set to peeling potatoes in the Officer's Mess kitchen and soon began to remember his prison with a sigh. For a few more days he was allowed to return to it, but only to sleep.

On the last of such nights, before he was to re-commence training, Turvey, now booted and free of his limp, was given five dollars hospital pay and a pass until 2300 hrs. For the first time he was at liberty to walk out of camp. While working in the kitchen he had been able to slip an occasional piece of officer pie to one of the army drivers who brought rations to the cookhouse and in return he now got himself and Roach an unauthorized lift into the village.

On the way Roach reminded him that it was a dry town, without even a beer parlour, and proposed they buy a jug from the local bootlegger behind the barber shop. Turvey's five dollars proved enough for a fifth of watered gin and two bottles of ginger ale. Later they picked up two girls in the park and strolled down with them for an impromptu party on the tree-screened river-bank.

The evening exceeded Turvey's expectation. Roach had a laconic line which rather captivated one of the ladies, and Turvey was able to amble off unobtrusively with the other and find a quiet nook for his own sort of discussion. Roach and Turvey just managed to make camp by the 2300 hr deadline. They separated in the moonlit parade square and Turvey trudged over for his last night's sleep in the hospital.

He was stumbling down the dark hall when he saw the night light in the First Aid room and remembered that Clarence had warned him he should always check in for a prophylactic after being out with a girl. He walked through the open door and found Clarence brooding on the solitary chair.

It was a cramped cubbyhole of a room which served also as a dispensary and was barnacled with bottles and cartons of every shape and colour, littered on shelves extending up to the low ceiling. The surviving wall space was shagged with typed orders, posters warning against V.D., and an appeal to subscribe to the Second Victory Loan.

Clarence seemed so down in the dumps it made Turvey sad just to look at him. "How's chances for a prolifaxis, Clarry?" he asked cheerfully.

Clarence regarded him sourly. "You mead a prophylaxis. You been exposig yourself already?"

"Kinda, I guess," said Turvey amiably. "What's bitin you, old man. Dint you have a good honeymoon?"

Clarence regarded him with a tragic eye and then got up, stumbling over a corner of the wheeled stretcher which occupied most of the room space and almost upsetting a bottle of purple fluid perched on its top.

He made Turvey sit on the chair. "You godda rest that aggle," he said mournfully. Then he propped his pudgy elbows precariously on the enamelled stretcher table.

"Tops," he said, "no bore barriages for be. You know what?"

"What?"

"I didit get my leave till the last binute, see, so she didit know I was cubbig. Ad I didit telephode whed I got to Torodo. Just wed up to the flat ad walked in. Wadded to surprise her." He paused, heaving his round shoulders with a sigh that rippled down to his knees. Turvey had a feeling Clarence was waiting for the right question.

"Well, wasnt she surprised?"

Clarence lifted his eyebrows with satisfaction. It was the right question. "O sure, sure, she was surprised all right. Ad so was the guy id bed with her."

Turvey had rather anticipated this revelation. "Watcha do, kick him out the window?"

Clarence reached up silently and drew a violet bottle down from a shelf, setting it on the stretcher. Then he raised his right hand slowly and cocked his trigger finger at his black eye. "I told you he was a boxer."

"Your brother-in-law?" asked Turvey, genuinely surprised this time. "Was he there? Didnt he take your side?"

Clarence laughed. It was the laugh of a frustrated villain at the close of a movie western. He dug out a carton from a bottom shelf and pulled some cotton-batten from it. "He was the fucker in bed with her."

Turvey stared. "I dont get it," he said finally.

Clarence poured purple liquid from one of the bottles into a shallow beaker and dropped the cotton pad into it. He wasn't ever her brother. He's her husbud."

"Wait a minute! Isnt this the gal you married three weeks ago, the one in the snap with her brother?"

"Yah, sure, I barried her too, but it aid legal, the padre told be today, ad I could get her for bigaby. She was just tryig to get my assigned pay ad allowedces. Then, when I cub out on Jarvis Street agade, an M.P. albost arrested me for beig in a red light district. Now you stad up and swab this od good." He interrupted his story to give Turvey further material and directions for a self-administered prophylaxis. "You see, you're dot supposed to tell, but I was put on overseas draft a while ago, and I got shootig off my face about it first tibe I met them in that beer parlour . . . Go ahead, you shouldit waste doe tibe. Best stuff in the world. Mild as milk to you and rat poisod to all those gerbs you probably got."

Turvey thought the purple liquid had a powerful odour. "They aint *spies*, are they?" he asked.

"Daw. Rackideers I guess you'd call em. I seed the paybaster today too when I got back. He says they figured I'd be goin overseas in a few days an wouldit fide out she was barried. Baybe she's barried four or five other guys, you dever know. Course the Pay boys in Ottawa they got ways of checkig up after a while, but beadtibe these rackideers they get sub of your pay ad skip towd. You're the spart guy, Tops, never gettig barried. As log as you cub an get a prophylaxis like this, you –"

A mounting howl of anguish from Turvey, who had at last freed his mind sufficiently from Clarence's tragedy to essay the little operation, cut short Clarence's remark. Turvey clutched himself as if he were shot and rolled on the floor.

"Holy jeezis," said Clarence, for the first time looking closely at the two bottles on the stretcher table, "I bust have give you the perbagadate by mistake. O dear, I'b so sorry. Wait! Tops! I got to fide you a addidote –"

It was indeed the purple rather than the violet bottle which had been brought into use and since it was a concentrated solution, used only for bathing athlete's foot after considerable dilution, Turvey became the howling vortex of an alarmed hospital. Fortunately he had not proceeded beyond a few tentative dabs and flourishes, being somewhat warned by his nose, but it was nevertheless another two weeks before he was again ready for discharge from hospital. They had not been as pleasant as the previous ones. In fact there had been days when Turvey had thought he would never want to discuss things with a girl by a riverbank again. But at least he had been the cynosure of medical eyes (and of fascinated up-patients whenever the NCOs or the M.O. were out of sight). And certainly there had been time for his ankle to grow stronger than ever.

FIVE

Turvey Guards Niagara

WHETHER the Goon Squad's new sergeant got tired of ticking him off for grinning at attention, or the Commandant was annoyed because he had appeared in the village one night without his anklets, Turvey never knew; for some reason, three weeks after he finally left hospital, he was rattling once more through Ontario in a truck, posted to another unit.

Watching the dusty September orchards roll by, bright with apples, Turvey reflected it couldnt have been the gaiters, because he paid for that with five days C.B. And he must have been getting along with his Basic because, just before he left, the Orderly Room Clerk had stamped his Pay Book "Completed Tests of Elementary Training", and the adjutant had hurriedly signed it. Though this had been done for the nineteen others from his squad who made up this draft, the rest had managed to avoid hospital and had served their allotted weeks. The more he thought about it the more Turvey felt proud. Despite the fact that on his earliest appearance at the rifle range he had very nearly shot the Butts Officer (he had been anxious to be first to hit the target, and the officer had been slow getting out of the line of fire), Turvey recalled with elation that he had made three bulls and an inner, even if they were on the next man's target. It was quite possible he had broken some kind of record and got himself basically trained in three weeks, and in the Goon

Squad at that! The thought salved his disappointment that, once again, he was not going to England and the Kootenay Highlanders (Mac had sent him a card from some arithmetical address overseas), but to some outfit called Number Two Security Regiment. The truck bumped through a sleepy elm-shaded town and, on the far side, came to the usual bald scabby crisscross of huts, fences and squares – an army camp.

After the ordained blanket line-ups and personnel quickies, the new arrivals were given a short-arm inspection. Although this was already Turvey's fourth since enlistment, it was the first since hospitalization and he waited his turn with some apprehension.

The twenty silent soldiers were paraded by a silent corporal into a small room smelling of lysol. They shuffled in single file past the R.A.P. Sergeant, a husky redfaced man with gleaming green eyes and an enormous restless mouth; when this cavern was not roaring words it was chewing snuff or spouting the brown residue into a tin pail in the corner. He had the verbal gusto of a hockey broadcaster but a voice like a file at work on the teeth of a crosscut. Also, his choice of words was more basic than Turvey had heard over the CBC.

"Allri unbuttonyahtrousehs . . . allawaydown . . . evradadose? . . . lesseeit . . . Okaynexman . . . chokeit . . . HARD . . . cmon, can' hurta lil feller . . . nexman, opnup . . . jeeze, Niagara girls'll be glada thisn . . . Okaynexman . . . any R.C.s here? . . . report ta padre right af'er this prade . . . cmoncmon nexman, get em comin faster corpral . . . allri dont be shamed it plup your shirt . . ." The sergeant had the reputation of being the fastest and merriest short-arm inspector in the Canadian Army. But even his magnificent verbal machine sputtered into momentary silence, and the tough carrotty mask of his face took on a look of wonder and respect, when it was the turn of the blushing Turvey to shuffle up and reveal his most recent battle scars.

Turvey soon forgot such little embarrassments, how-

ever, in the stress of more prolonged discomforts.
Number Two Security Regiment, he discovered, was far
less secure than its name. It seemed made up in roughly
equal divisions of men who couldnt and men who
wouldnt do guard duty. An order had gone out from Ottawa some months before that a unit was to be created
for the protection by night and by day of the Welland
Canal, the Queenston Power Plant, and other expensive
improvements on Niagara Falls, from the rogueries of
Hitler's *saboteurs*. Since the plan involved the freeing of
existing guard units for service abroad, it was decreed
that all officers and men of Number Two Security Regiment must be, for whatever reason, certified as unfit for
overseas duties. In consequence Turvey found his new
companions to be a representation of all the unfatal ills
of mankind. There were rheumatics and bronchials, men
with a short left arm or a long army crime-sheet, myopics
and hyperopics, lads with an over-high arch in the foot or
an over-low score in the head, with two webbed fingers or
one perforated ear-drum, successful leadswingers and
unsuccessful deserters, soldiers too lean or too fat, too
short or too broad, detected neurotics, undetected
psychotics, and some whose only undesirable oddity, in
the eyes of National Defence Headquarters, was that they
were not yet eighteen-and-a-half or that they were more
than forty-four-and-a-half. And there was the inevitable
sprinkling of bewildered ones who were whole in mind
and body and of the right size, shape, age and attitude
for storming Nazi redoubts; they were there merely by
mistake, by some unadmitted but apparently permanent
error in a distant Orderly Room, and they were probably
the unhappiest of all.

From the gangways of troopships in Halifax, from
batteries on Vancouver Island, from camps and depots,
goon squads and work companies across a rather too-far-
flung Dominion, the slightly halt and the somewhat blind
were yielded up by delighted Commanding Officers,
snatched by train and by truck to the damp shores of

Niagara, given rifles and live rounds, and set to pacing, in sun, hail or eerie darkness, the long paths and slithery green banks of the Welland Canal.

The Russians heaved the Germans back from Stalingrad; gaudy autumn blew itself away in Niagara. Montgomery advanced from El Alamein; the cold rains of November made a muddy waste of Turvey's morning parade ground. The Allied landings swept over North Africa; a howling December gale buried No. 2 Sec. Reg. knee-deep in snow. The spirits of Turvey and his ailing fellow-guardsmen swayed and dampened and froze with the climate of Canada. And so apparently did the spirits of their officers.

The latter publicly cursed the camp, the army, the men. (The men returned the sentiments in their own way.) When the officers were not inspecting posts or drilling their scarecrow platoons into some kind of recognizable order for the unpredictable visits of the brigadier, they were pressed into the elaborate routine of defending or prosecuting their own soldiers in courts-martial. What with AWLs, desertions of guard posts, donnybrooks, and conversions of army property, the unit averaged four of these full-dress affairs a week, not to speak of the time consumed in representing soldiers in the toils of civilian law for thefts, burglaries, assaults, rapes and the odd murder. Whenever there was a lull, most of the officers wangled leave and those who couldnt got drunk. There were two notable exceptions: a plum-faced captain who took his leaves to go home and sober up; and the Commanding Officer himself, a sad honest soldier whose only crime was being beyond the age for overseas. He seldom emerged from his cubbyhole at the back of the Orderly Room except for meals or to play an evening game of crib in the Officers' Mess with his rheumatic adjutant. For the latter, as for his C.O., the war was a silent inky battle against forms. Most of the soldiers saw the C.O. only when paraded into his office on some charge of misconduct.

The men themselves, when they were not on duty or
deserting it, and had money, passed their waking hours in
the two beer parlours (the only place in the village where
they were welcome) or gambling openly in their huts.
Those who were broke huddled in bull sessions around
undernourished coal stoves in their clapboard hovels.

One night, a few days before Christmas, Turvey sat on a
bench by the squat heater in conversation with a lean
suck-cheeked private, Ballard, who had just been shifted
to the same post and sleeping quarters. The rest of the
hut had decamped to a beer parlour. Ballard was one of
the regiment's tough boys; he had already served 30 days
in the District Detention Barracks for jumping a lance-
jack in the dark and kicking in two of his ribs. He was a
small nimble fellow with permanent pouches under his
eyes and a walk like a prowling tomcat. He was telling
Turvey that he had always been in trouble; in fact trouble
was his earliest memory; when he was four, he had
watched his father drop his mother with a right hook to
the jaw and walk out for good.

"I'm like me old man," Ballard went on, with a note
of hereditary pride. "My ma hadda handle me with kid
gloves after the old bastard lef. And wen I was fifteen I
went on the lam too. I figgered I was too old fer school,
specially in Grade Six, and I waned ta see the fuckin
world."

"Where'd you go?" Turvey slid his tonette into his
field-dressing pocket.

"Oh, me an a guy from my home town, he was a bit
older, we batted aroun. Ontario, Quebec. Panhandled or
got a job fer a few days, see. Wen the weather'd git cold
we'd come home. Go on a bum again wen it warmed up.
That's till we landed in Romanburg."

"You mean in the *reformatory*?"

"Yeah, sure," said Ballard, spitting a tobacco grain
from his cigarette butt with a worldly air, "my firs time

in stir. I was seventeen then. Nick, that was my sidekick, he'd done a stretch before. He was real, that guy, but crazy as a fart. We had more fuckin fun; we'd lift a car, see, just for the hell of it, pick up some beetles and take em for a joyride, then dump em. Nick, he even wanned to make off with a goddam yella plane one day we saw in a field. Wanned to go to the States in it. There wernt no one in it, we coulda made it all right, see, but I dont think Nick really knew how to run one. So I talked him out of it and we snatched another car instead. We shoulda tried the plane, though," he added reflectively. "That was the shitty crate sent us to Romanburg."

"Pretty tough in there, I guess." Turvey was glad to draw Ballard out, there was nothing else to do. "Worse than bein here, was it?"

Ballard spat knowingly at the red potbelly of the stove, sending up a quick hiss of steam. "You never been in stir?" His tone was that of a college graduate speaking to a child just commencing high school. "Felluh, yuh dont know what a tough place is. O sure, sure, this dump is pretty shitty. Sometimes I think I'm back in Roman, but not really I dont." He explained to Turvey some of the problems of life in a jail, such as the dangers of incurring venereal disease from the enforced attentions of older and stronger cellmates. "You jus gotta pick your gang and bloody well stick with em, I tell yuh, and get your fuckin hide really tough, see."

"Gosh, how long were you in?"

"Ten months an eight fuckin days. I would a been out in six, see, but I los all my good time for climbin the fence twicet. Woulda made it the first break, that was the one Nick pulled, oney a fuckin blizzard come down, see, an we hadda hole up in a barnloft fer the nex two fuckin days witout no grub. We give ourselves up to the hay-seed. Got chicken wen our pegs went numb on us. Anyways we had a bellyful a beatin off the rats in that shitty barn. Nick he froze two a his toes. They hadda hack em off. So nex time you betcha I picked me some good

weather. I wen wit a green punk, he was even younger'n
me. We got over the wall O.K., see, an hopped a midnight and wen to sleep in a empty boxcar. But damn if we
dint go on poundin our ear after they shunted us onto a
sidin in the nex bloody town. The cocksuckin yardbulls
jus hauled us out, see, and back we wen to the fuckin
hoosegow.''

"What you do after you got out?"

"I wen straight, fulluh, believe you me. Anyways I
tried ta. Course I figgered I couldnt git no job in Canada,
see, so I beat it crost the border. Hitchhiked an got the
mug was drivin to tell the Yank brassbuttons I was his
son. I got jobs, all sorts, all over the States. Yeah, I been
aroun. New York, Dee-troit, Frisco, Shy, all over. I was
goin straight too, see, till that crazy galoot Nick caught
up with me agin. He'd been in Roman longer, cause it
was his second rap. I'll say this for Nick, he wanted to
make it straight too, and he dint mean no harm; jus
unlucky, I giss he was. And stir-simple too," he added,
on consideration. "Frinstance, what got us in trouble
agin. I was workin in Savannah, see, deliverin rented
typewriters aroun, ta offices, an so on, an I got Nick on
with me. His firs day we wen together, see, to show him
the ropes. Well, about the secon damn office we come to,
up on a top floor, there was a good-lookin steno all
alone. So I'm just settin down the typewriter, see, when
Nick he picks up a paperknife lyin on the desk and holds
it to her throat, yeah – holds it to her throat and says he
gotta have a kiss and a feel-up. Course he woulda done
fuckall to her, I giss, but the silly bitch gits high-sterical
like and starts yelpin and hollerin fer the cops. Then two
big guys come runnin in and I scrammed out the fire-
scape. Din stop till I was out on a highway. Never seen
old Nick since!''

"Didja go straight after that, after Nick was gone?"

"Watcha mean, I was goin straight all a time, see?
Oney I got some bad luck in Daytona, where I wen nex.
That's in Florida, you know," he added condescend-

ingly. "I was workin in a store, see, jista git a few bucks an move on. Dint cotton much to the job, though. So after two weeks I give notice. But the old bastard run the store, he wunt pay me till my month was up. An I was flat, see. So I hefted a chair, one a them cane-backs it was, and tole him I'd throw it right through his fuckin plate-glass window if he dint pay me right there out a the till. And by God he did. Oney the sonfabitch called the coppers soon as I lef the store, see, an they picked me up on a street an took it back offn me. Those cracker cops are tough babies, I'm tellin yuh." Ballard lit a cigarette from the butt of his last, and suddenly assumed an exaggerated Southern accent.

" 'Wheah *yoh* from?' one a them says to me. 'New York,' I says. 'O.K. Mistah New Yohkeh, yoh got foah hours to get outa owah town.' So I hotfoots it out to the city limits an starts thumbin. Then damn if the same cocksuckin cops dint come out in a cruiser car and put the bracelets on me for bein a vag. I got a month in their lousy clink fer that, hard labour too. I got the hell out a the South after that, you bet; dont figger it's any country fer a white man. They dont even letcha plead Not Guilty, them cracker judges. Not like Scotland, now. Nick tole me up there, ever yuh git squealed on, like, but they aint got you with the goods, they dont rap yuh. Yuh plead Not Proven, see, Not Proven, an they cant do nuttin. But I aint sayin I dont like the States, though. I'd like to live mebbe in California, see."

"Where you goin when the war's over?" asked Turvey, since Ballard seemed to have run out of reminiscences.

"Me! O, bugger round, I giss. I like travel, see. Mebbe I can talk some big company into makin me a sales representative or somethin out in China. That's a place I'd like to see. Fulluh tole me there's a big future there. I could take a course and brush up my schoolin. Or mebbe ship over as a Able Seaman. What you gunna do after?"

"Well," said Turvey, changing the leg he was toasting

by the stove and weighing the question slowly, "I'd kinda
thought of stayin in the army, supposin I got to the
Kootenay Highlanders and became an officer perhaps.
But I'm gettin pretty cheesed off with this place. They
aint enough action, least not the right kind. Why I'd better be a woman, that's what! I got a letter from my sister
and she says Tilly Salmonberry, she was just a brat when
I left Skookum Falls, she's in London now with the
CWACs, right in all the bombin and, and things.
Nobody bombin us. Nobody to shoot at. And all this
snow. Might as well be in the Yukon. And, you know
somethin, that's where I'd like to go. After the war, I
mean. Run a business on this new Alaska Highway
they're talkin about buildin."

"What kinda business up there?"

"Tourists. A hotel, maybe." Turvey was brightening
to his subject. "I'd have a saloon with a big long bar, and
a beer parlour too, and any guy who'd been a private in
the army could come and get plastered free. You wanta
come into partners with me?"

"That's a lotta cock. Aint no bars in a Yukon," said
Ballard the realist. "I knewd a guy in stir was up there,
see. Jus like the rest a Canada. Govment liquor stores, or
rotgut, an prices high's a kite. We'd have to go t'Alaska
fer saloons."

"O.K.," said Turvey, not to be downed, "we'll build
it on the border, and have the saloon on the Alaska
side."

"Les have it in California where it aint so chrisely cold.
Les go to the States anyways. Hell, why wait for the
fuckin war to be over? Some guy was sayin he thought
it'd be ten years yet. Les go now!" Ballard actually slid
out of his chair in a catlike motion, as if he were about to
stroll straight over to New York from the hut.

"What you mean, *now*?"

"Les go over the hill. Cmawn. Jus for a few days.
They wont do more than shoot yuh. I know a cluck in

Buff'lo. Two clucks," he added, seeing Turvey begin to
perk up. "Boy, they're lookers too, I'm tellin yuh. They
got a apartment they could put us up. No b.s.!"

"We couldnt get across the border."

"Nuts! You think I cant get through them brassbuttons any time I take a fancy? Aint never got stopped
yet!" Ballard walked around the stove on his little feline
feet.

Turvey reflected. Perhaps it was the rising whoop of
the wind outside, swishing the dry snow up against the
door of their hut. Perhaps it was the thought that his
would-be guide had not been particularly successful in
keeping out of jail in civilian farings. Turvey regretfully
gave up the picture of a cosy Buffalo apartment,
sleeping-in, two luscious American dames, surcease from
sergeants and from stomping the long dull canal banks.

"Let's wait till it gets warmer," he said. His feet were
sore anyway, and besides he had Christmas leave coming
up, his first leave yet.

The afternoon before Christmas a sudden sun spread
ankle-deep slush over the camp. Turvey, with Ballard
and their corporal, sat cramped in a small unheated
guard post by the canal bank. The other two in their
group were out trudging the gooey snow; soon Turvey
would have to relieve one of them. He was bored. The
sergeant had crossed him up somehow on Christmas
leave; the best he could hope for now was New Year's
Day. Meanwhile he was perfunctorily responding to the
latest rumour being retailed by the corporal, a laconic
Nova Scotian with asthma.

"Sykes – the Stores Corp, you know – was sayin the
quartermaster's goin ta catch it from NDHQ account a
Landis."

"Landis?" asked Ballard, "the silly bugger fell in the
canal we had a miltry funeral fer in the summer?"

"Yeah. They buried him with his boots on," said the corporal.

"So what?"

"So Ottawa wants em. Demand come through from Ordnance, Sykes sayin. Boots, moist leather, issue, black, one pair; laces, one pair. Improper burial. Should a took em off, returned em to Stores."

"The QM have to pay for em, eh?"

"Mebbe. I figger he oughta work on the padre to dig up Landis an get the boots back. They'd still be good enough to turn back in Stores."

Turvey was about to remark that he could do with a new pair himself, when there was a sudden rip . . . ping . . . smack . . . plop; chips flew, and a little jagged hole appeared just above head-level in the door-top.

"Well I'll be damned," said the corporal, only mildly perturbed, "was a bullet." Stepping over the prostrate bodies of Turvey and Ballard – who had made the floor in a dead heat – he examined the hole and, turning about, hunted and found a parallel splotch on the cement of the back wall. He was trying to pick up the hot lead slug from the floor when rip . . . ping . . . smack . . . plp, there was another hole in the door, an inch away and at the same level.

"It's the Jerries!" shouted Turvey. "Paratroops, I bet! Let's charge em!" He was scrambling to his feet, one arm reaching for his rifle stacked in a corner, when Ballard pulled him down. For a tough guy, Turvey thought Ballard looked surprisingly pale and worried. His voice was shaking.

"Stay put, yuh mug. They got us cornered, see, aint they, corp? We gotta surrender."

Just then an unintelligible shout floated across the canal. The corporal, despite blasphemous protests from Ballard, edged to their tiny window and peered gingerly through its barred pane.

"McKelvie," he announced, after a breathless pause.

"Wonder what's up."

"That jerk! He'd do anythin fer a laugh. Dont show or he'll pot yuh. I'll bet he's stinkin."

But the corporal had already pushed open the door. McKelvie could be seen standing outside another guard house identical with theirs, sixty yards down on the other side of the canal. His melton cap was cocked drunkenly on his head and he held his rifle in both hands. His voice carried easily across the steep banks.

"How's that for shootin, corp? Jest wanted to wake you christers up. Wotcha doin anyway?" His tone was sober and cheery, as if he had just rung them on the telephone.

The corporal peered at him biliously. "You mighta hit somebody, you know. Where's your corporal? Aint he there?"

"Nah," shouted McKelvie offhandedly, "he and the rest of them hightailed it downtown for beer. They left me in charge! How about a shootin match? Come on, just fer the hell of it, they aint nothin to do."

"The fucker's gone screwy!" said Ballard anxiously. "You better go arrest him, corp."

"You feelin all right?" shouted the corporal. "Better walk around by the bridge and come over here . . . Leave your rifle," he added.

But McKelvie was not to be persuaded, and hoisted his gun. The corporal decided, wisely, to retire. During the next few minutes McKelvie demonstrated his really admirable and sober marksmanship by drilling an almost straight line of holes across the top of their wooden door. The three besieged lay smelling the mould on the cold cement floor and cursing. Ballard easily led in this form of retaliation both in the speed and variety of his responses. "Rip . . . ping . . . smack," went the bullets; "#$%$*#@," went Ballard, before the pellet had plopped to the floor. "We coulda been in Bufflo now, Turvey," he whined reproachfully, after the fifth bullet struck. "Yuh see what happens wen you stick around the cocksuckin army. I dint join up ta git drilled by some fuckin stir-crazy Scotchman."

"He's only got fifteen rounds," the corporal murmured soothingly. "Somebody'll hear the shootin and stop him."

Rip . . . ping . . . smack-smack.

"Ow, jezus, I'm shot!" yelled Ballard, clutching his left wrist. But it was only a glancing burn from the seventh slug, which had ricocheted.

"*We* heard him but he didnt stop for us, you know," said Turvey mildly. "Maybe we better wing him. He's a nawful good shot."

"Holy shit! Now he's startin a lower set. He'll be pickin us off right here on the friggin floor," cried Ballard, whose face had turned the colour of grey goat-cheese. "I'm gittin out a here." The twelfth and thirteenth bullets had started a new line several inches lower on the doorframe. But since his only exit would have been directly into McKelvie's line of fire Ballard didnt actually move.

After the fifteenth bullet there was a long pause, some confused shouting, and a new voice yelled, "All Clear!" Squinting cautiously through the window Turvey saw McKelvie, still surprisingly nonchalant, being led off by an impressive posse of NCOs and guards, under close arrest. It looked as if the posse also had been waiting for McKelvie to expend his fifteen rounds.

Whether it was the indignity of being shot at, however playfully, by his own side, or whether it was Christmas Eve without a pass, or the frustration of not being allowed to shoot back, or just the milder weather, Turvey wasnt sure; but when, after supper, Ballard again raised the topic of going on the loose Turvey found himself listening with more interest. Ballard this time drew a detailed picture of the charms of his two Buffalo friends, the softness of their beds, the comparative variety and abundance of American food, and the bliss of lying-in till mid-day unattended by corporals, sergeants or their betters. By nine that evening they were both on the Niagara Falls road, their cap-badges gleaming in the auto headlights, their right arms twisted out from them, thumbs wistfully curved.

SIX

Turvey Attends a Court-Martial

THE SUN was a colourless wafer in a steely sky, and the January cold, invisible but bitter, filtered efficiently through the cracks in the little wooden nests of Number Two Security Regiment. In the feeble afternoon sunlight four soldiers stood shivering and stamping their feet on the bare porch of a square hut known somewhat grandiosely as the YMCA Hostel. A casual observer would have been puzzled to know why a sergeant, a corporal, and two privates continued to linger in such a cold spot for no apparent military purpose, and without the benefit of greatcoats. They made an oddly chummy and idle foursome; one of the privates was even smoking, in full view of the mid-day camp and of possible prowling officers.

Turvey would have enjoyed the cigarette more if the sergeant, in permitting it, had not added, "It's the last you'll smoke for a month of Sundays, my boy. Nothing like that where you're going. They got a real brassballs from Ottawa running the courts this week. Colonel Sloggin, Old Fishface, they call him. You wont pull your panties over *his* eyes."

The frost-rimmed door behind them abruptly screeched and opened. A little bald soldier peered out, winked heavily at the sergeant and jerked his thumb inwards. "O.K."

"Chuck cigarettes," the sergeant hissed quickly, then

instantly transformed himself into a stiffbacked loud-speaker. "Escort-n-prisner ten-HOWN," he bellowed and, suddenly *sotto voce* again, "allri, allri, corp'ral in front, prisner, then you, Davis." Then the loudspeaker blared. "RrriiiiTUN, weeeeeek MATCH." The little procession clomped briskly into the blessed warmth of a square room, past stacks of upturned chairs and tables, and a handful of officers and men standing at attention beside benches. Turvey heard the sergeant behind hissing something about "headdress" and somebody neatly whipped his melton skull cap from his head. Clump, clomp, clump, clomp they went toward a ruddy Winnipeg heater and a low platform against the far wall, on which three officers were perched behind a table spread with papers.

" 'Scortnprisner, HALLT! . . . Riii TUN . . . 'Scort two-pacestepback MATCH." Turvey felt his companions vanish from beside him, and began absorbing the stare of the three sets of officer eyes on the dais. The middle ones were especially formidable; they were steel blue and glittering beneath an impressive redbanded officer's hat, and above two red neck-tabs and the brassy shoulder adornments of a Full Colonel.

Turvey reached his hand up to smooth his hair, and stopped, his arm paralyzed by the Full Colonel's eyes. They seemed to be saying that, however solidly the officers of the court might squat on their chairs, he, Turvey, the prisoner, was to stand at attention.

The sergeant was right, Turvey thought; the colonel's eyes, behind thick rimless spectacles, looked remarkably like those of a trout, and Turvey unaccountably remembered what Calvin Busby had said about the army being a fish hatchery. This colonel looked about the room with the calm unwinking orb of the fish that knows itself several sizes bigger than any other in his tank. A big plump Dolly Varden swimming in a pool of documents, Turvey decided, with a Sam Browne belt and a bright row of buttons for belly stripes; the two redtabs were his gills.

The way his cheeks sloped into a tiny chinless mouth was fish-like too.

The Big Trout stared down at a paper one of his two flanking troutlings slid in front of him, stared up at Turvey, opened his puckery mouth as if about to gulp air, and, miraculously, spoke:

"Are you B-08654732 Private Turvey, Thomas Lead-beater?" The voice was cold and clear and utterly colourless.

"B-086547 TWO 2, Private Turvey, sir, yessir," said Turvey brightly.

There was a small stir in the papery pool above him until it was discovered that the mistake was the colonel's, not the document's. The colonel sucked air again: "Take your place beside your Defending Officer, Turvey. The court will now be sworn in."

"I swear by Almighty God," the Great Trout said expressionlessly and paused; all the minnows throughout the stuffy little room opened their mouths in unison and echoed the words and the tonelessness: "swear-bymightygad . . . To tell the truth . . ."

He was glad to feel that he was still within warming distance of the stove. His toes and fingers throbbed slowly into life. Then the Orderly Sergeant sat Turvey on a bench on the left of the court and for the first time he was able to look around. Opposite him sat a solemn private with a long nose like a badger's and a lap full of files; next to him was a captain, a newcomer to the unit, remarkable for a large fierce moustache, RAF pattern, set in the middle of a small baby-face. Behind them he identified his old Hut Corporal and Platoon Sergeant, and the provost who had brought him back from the border. He stole a glance behind him and spotted the R.A.P. Sergeant, the M.O., and the Nut Doctor who had visited him in the guard house this morning.

And, beside him, breathing a most exciting odour of whiskey into his right ear, was Lieutenant Sanderson, the paymaster, a devil-may-care character with a literary turn of mind who had been sent back from England officially as overage; he was popularly rumoured to have been returned because he paid off the same regiment twice in one week in a burst of alcoholic benevolence; he was also said to be the author of some plain-spoken ballads of army life circulating in the camp. It was this gentleman who, Turvey had been surprised to learn yesterday, was defending him.

He had received the news from that old terror of the Short-Arm Inspection, the R.A.P. Sergeant, who had breezed into the Camp Brig, redfaced and wild-eyed as usual, slapped Turvey jovially on the back, asked him if he'd been getting lots, and rasped out with bewildering speed an elaborate set of plans for Turvey's defense. There were so many courts-martial this week, the R.A.P. Sergeant had told him, that there was no use Turvey standing on his rights and choosing his own defending officer. The paymaster was the only one available and even he was still busy in a Court of Enquiry regarding six rifles that a guard post had unitedly dumped in the canal last week, so he wouldnt be able to see Turvey personally before the trial. The sergeant had assured him, however, that Pay had a masterly plan for Turvey's defense. The R.A.P. Sergeant himself was going to be Turvey's chief witness. At the most he would only get C.B. and loss of pay to equal the number of days he had been on the loose. Or they might even get him off.

That was, of course, the sergeant had rattled on, if Turvey himself said as little as possible and they could get the Nut Doctor on their side. O sure as hell, yes, said the sergeant, shifting a wad of snoose to his other cheek, Pay had discovered in Turvey's documents that he was due to see a Nut Doctor again any time now. And the M.O. was getting the Area's Travelling Psychiatrist to come over and see Turvey that very day. The sergeant had slammed Turvey over the kidneys again, expressed a hope that the

Buffalo girls had appreciated his battle scars, spat
brownly on the doorstep, and clattered off in a burst of
tremendous bronchial laughter.

And now the swearing was over and the president had
swivelled his eyes to the opposite side of the room from
Turvey, bringing them to rest on the equally expressionless face of the long-nosed private that Turvey had
noticed sitting with a thick file of papers. "The Clerk of
the Court will now read the charge against the accused."

The clerk rose instantly, released by some secret
spring, holding the wad of papers in front of him like a
choir soloist. He began to recite the charge in a shrill
nasal monotone, running the clichés together.

"The accused, B-08654722, Private-Turvey-Thomas-
Leadbeater, on-a-strength-of Number-Two-Skewerty-Reg-
iment, Cam-Byng-tario, soldier – Canain-Active-Armys-
s-charged-with-w'en'n-Active-Service," here he took his
first breath and his voice rose another notch, gaining
speed, "SENTING-SELF-THOUT-FICIAL-LEAVE in-
that-he . . . did-sent-self-from twenty-two-hunrd-hours
Friday cember-twenyfour-nin'n-hunrd-forytwo . . . un'l
apprehen'd-an-return-barracks steen-hunr-sen-hours
Saday-Janwy-fteen-nin-hun-for-three . . ." The clerk's
voice shifted into an even higher gear and raced dizzily
through a computation of the exact number of hours and
minutes Private Turvey had deprived the Canadian Active Army of his activity, and the precise clauses and pro-
visions of the Army Act which had anticipated such
conduct and laid down the appropriate punishments.

"Do you plead guilty or not guilty?" It was the Big
Trout again, the clerk having subsided as abruptly as he
had arisen.

Turvey suddenly couldnt remember how the R.A.P.
Sergeant had told him to plead. But he could see they had
everything down exactly and no argument, and he was
about to acknowledge his guilt, a little surprised that the
president should think it debatable, when the paymaster
came to life and stood up. His leathery, whiskey-veined

face dimpled in a great mock-hearty smile, rakish with a gold molar. He announced to the colonel, as if it were the most natural thing in the world:

"He pleads not guilty, sir."

The glassy vision of the President of the Court-Martial rested briefly on the paymaster.

"You have been appointed, Lieutenant uh-er-"

"Sanderson," whispered the Righthand Troutling.

"Lieutenant Sanson," the president went on majestically, "to defend the prisoner, not to plead for him. Private Turvey, are you guilty or not guilty of the charge as read?"

Turvey shifted the weight on his feet; he was really stumped. Had the president given a peculiar emphasis to the last two words? Perhaps there was a loophole somewhere. And yet, come to think of it, nothing the president had said really had any emphasis to it at all. The paymaster was now elbowing him in the ribs most energetically, and had screwed his mouth up into an elaborate almost-silent "Not Guilty", shaking his head, and winking all at the same time.

"Whatever you gentlemen like." He paused. There was silence, except for a smothered whisper from the paymaster. The president's face for the first time betrayed impatience and even some anxiety. Turvey groped in his mind for something that might please everybody and suddenly thought of what Ballard had said about a nice compromise in Scottish law. "Not Proven," he said, louder than he intended.

"Write down Not Guilty," said the president crisply. "You have not sufficiently instructed the defendant, Mr.-uh-Sansom," he added; even the president's voice was beginning to betray emphasis; there was a sharkish edge to it which did not bode well either for defendant or his counsel. After some general remarks on court-martial procedure, he held a whispered consultation with his two supporting judges, and announced that in view of the inclemency of the weather, witnesses would remain in the court-room until their testimony had been given. "The prosecution will commence."

Up stood the captain with the moustaches. He had been nervously twirling the ends; now one was curled jauntily up and the other hooked villainously down; but the rest of his face looked as childlike as ever. His voice was a jittery imitation of the president's; that is, it would have sounded impartial if it had not quavered slightly. While Turvey listened with interest, the prosecution proceeded to establish the undisputed fact that Turvey had been absent on the dates set down. Turvey's Hut Corporal gave the greasy Bible a gingerly peck and swore, with the clerk's prodding, "by mighty-Gad-tell-trut-whole-trut-nottin-buta-trut." He testified that Turvey was not in his hut at bed-check 2300 hours Christmas Eve. Then Turvey's Platoon Sergeant plodded through the same ceremony to assert that Turvey had not responded to rollcalls since 1400 hrs December 24th, and produced his roll-books in proof. They were duly accepted as exhibits for the evidence of the court.

As the trial droned on, Turvey got the feeling they were talking about someone else; the facts fitted him, but they had all ceased paying him any attention. All, that is, except the paymaster, who kept up a succession of sighs and soothing murmurs beside Turvey's right ear, a kind of punctuating rebuttal to each damning sentence of evidence. Turvey would have been quite comforted if the lieutenant's aromatic gusts had not blown into him a growing longing for a good stiff drink.

Then came a beefy provost corporal, circumstantial and bored. He testified to having received into his care the body of one Turvey, Thomas Leadbeater (whom he also identified as the prisoner) from the custody of a United States Police Officer at the International Border, Niagara Falls, N.Y. He produced signed documents to prove it, and to prove also that he had delivered the same body later the same day to the corporal in charge of the guard house, Number Two Security Regiment.

A slight hitch developed here when the president's left-hand Troutling discovered that the guard house corporal had signed for Turvey on the wrong line. The president reproved both the corporal and the provost for this carelessness, and offered the paymaster an opportunity to enter an objection. But the latter cheerfully waived his rights, as he had waived all suggestions up to now that he cross-examine or in any other way enter the proceedings except by quiet wheezes and grunts to Turvey. The president thereupon decided that the document could be entered as evidence, together with a special emendatory form which the clerk had been rapidly making out in quadruplicate.

Then the clerk, who continued throughout the proceedings to be by far the busiest man in the room, released the secret spring in his knees and bounced up to intone a long series of reports which had been delivered up to the provost along with Turvey's sinful body. Although, from the point of view of an intimate chronicler, these documents revealed disappointing gaps, they nevertheless proved to be the most interesting of the day.

They informed all who might be concerned that the said person, giving his name as Thomas Leadbeater Turvey and admitting to being a Canadian citizen and a soldier in the Canadian Army, had been taken into custody in the bedroom of number nine Paradise Apartments, Raintree St., in the City of Buffalo, N.Y. The apartment, the report went on to specify, was legally and jointly tenanted by a Miss Ruby O'Reilly and a Miss Helga Bolinski, employees of the Earthquake Aircraft Corporation. The soldier had been apprehended in the course of a routine investigation arising out of a complaint by a tenant in the next apartment – who objected to the noise of night parties emanating from the windows of number nine. The soldier had been unable to produce evidence that he had legally entered the United States or that he was on official leave from his unit, and he had therefore been taken into custody as a potential deserter.

This somewhat tantalizing report was duly passed to the clerk, and then passed to the paymaster at the latter's request. Turvey was somewhat startled to gather from Lieutenant Sanderson's chuckles and admiring wheezes that his Defending Officer had not previously examined this document at any leisure, if indeed at all. The lieutenant's tsst-chah's finally became so audible that the president sent a freezing ray from his eye over Turvey's right shoulder, the chuckles ceased, and the document was returned to the clerk.

The Prosecuting Officer, both horns of his moustache now sagging piratically, indicated that his case had been presented. The paymaster again airily declined to cross-examine, and the president called upon him to begin the defense.

With a great odorous wheeze Lieutenant Sanderson arose beside Turvey and beamed at the president. "Well, Your Honour –"

"The President of a Court-Martial is addressed as 'sir'," said the Great Trout coldly.

Lieutenant Sanderson's cheeks purpled a little more but otherwise he seemed unperturbed. "Sir," he said, "our first witness is Sergeant Sawyer here."

The R.A.P. Sergeant, his face a somewhat rosier reflection of the lieutenant's, stumped noisily from a side bench and was sworn in. Turvey thought his expression looked a little unnatural and then realized that for the first time he was seeing the sergeant when he was not chewing snuff.

"Tell His Hon – tell the court, sarge, about the pitiful condition of the prisoner when he was brought into camp."

"At sixtin-fiftin hours on January fiftint," the sergeant rattled on at once, obviously well-rehearsed. "I 'as called from the regmentl aid post to guard hut t'attend a prisner here, Priv' Turvey, wh'ad jus been brought in. I foun him na highly nervous nweakened condition.

Hands tremblin. Pulse slow. Eyes bloodshot. Very, uh-tired." He paused, his green eyes darting over the impassive faces of the judges as if to measure his effect.

"Was he drunk?" asked the president casually.

"Nassir. Very sober. Well, had a hangover, mebbe. Walked kinda splay-legged, but," the sergeant chuckled bronchially, "I'll bet tha was jus a case a lover's nuts."

"Kahumph," the paymaster intervened with a breezy cough. "Tell us what you did for the prisoner."

"Objection," said the moustachioed captain suddenly. "All this is irrelevent to the charge."

"What are you seeking to prove by this testimony, lieutenant?" asked the president.

"Ah, sir, many things, many things." The paymaster made a large vague gesture with one arm. "This lad here, he's a good lad, sir, but nervous, very nervous. We shall present expert testimony to prove this. Impulsive, you know. And penitent, penitent too. Like the Ancient Mariner, sir. 'This man hath penance done and –' uh. Coleridge, sir. The, uh, the sergeant here is giving you first-hand evidence of this, this really pitiable nervousness."

The president looked skeptically at his watch. "The witness may proceed. But make it short."

The sergeant began rasping away at once. "He ast me fer a drink, a drink a – water." He pronounced the last word with a long twist of his great mouth as if the word itself proved Turvey's strange and heart-rending condition. "When he took the glass, sir, his hand shook so much he spilled it." The sergeant paused for the full effect of this to penetrate his hearers. "Had to give him a bit a brandy to pull him to."

"Is that all your testimony?" asked the president with some bewilderment, as the sergeant stood silent.

The paymaster and the sergeant beamed common assent. The president shifted his glittering eyepieces to the Prosecuting Officer. "Do you wish to cross-examine?"

"One question, sir. Sergeant Sawyer, you handed a glass of brandy to the accused after his ah – poor trembling hands had spilled the water?"

"Yassir."

"Did he spill the brandy, too?"

"Nassir."

"That's all, sir," said the captain, his moustache tips quivering triumphantly. The sergeant stood down.

"My next witness," said the paymaster, seemingly as confident as ever, "is not available. He is Private Horatio Ballard who was reported absent without leave at the same time as the prisoner and who has not yet returned. I hope to show that it was Private Ballard who planned this unfortunate uh-expedition and prevailed upon this poor lad to accompany him. He was the brains, gentlemen, the Mephistopheles, and young Turvey here was the uh – was the victim. I now ask for an adjournment of these proceedings until such time as Private Ballard is available as a witness."

Even the president's equanimity was upset by this barefaced bid to derail his trial. He stared glassily, sucked air, wriggled in his seat almost as if he were flicking a great tail-fin, and denied the lieutenant the support of Private Ballard.

The paymaster looked, for the first time, really put out. He licked his lips abstractedly. Then he nodded to himself, bent over and whispered to Turvey: "It's all right, old boy, we'll finagle a little break." He put on his most winning gold-toothed smile:

"With the court's permission, sir, the prisoner asks for a five-minute recess. He has to attend to the duties of nature."

Turvey was startled, since he had made no such request, but the interruption was welcome.

The president agreeing, none too graciously, Turvey was duly marched out and around to the latrine on the side of the Hostel. While his guards were standing shivering outside its partly open door, Turvey was surprised to see the paymaster brush between them into his privacy. Without a word the lieutenant closed the door, reached over Turvey's dutifully seated figure to a dark recess between the roof braces, and drew forth a half-empty bottle of Haig & Haig.

"After you, my boy. And make it snappy. We've just time to finish it. 'Freedom and whiskey go together.' Robbie Burns. The Immortal Memory. Hope you dont mind drinking out of the crock." Turvey didnt mind at all.

When the court had reassembled, the paymaster called briefly on the M.O. to corroborate Sergeant Sawyer's impression that Turvey was of a nervous temperament. The M.O. seemed to have little of any consequence to say, however, and that little was immediately objected to by opposing counsel. He was stood down, to give place to another officer.

Captain Norton Montague, Temporary-Acting-Neuro-psychiatric-Consultant, was a tall, elegant young man – surprisingly young, Turvey had thought when the captain interviewed him in the camp brig last night. Following a fashion popular among officers in combatant arms he had extracted the wire framework from his peaked cap and wore the shapeless residue at a rakish yachtsman's angle. His buttons shone more brightly even than the president's and he was adorned with the neatest black pencil-line of a moustache Turvey had ever seen. After the clerk had droned the oath Captain Montague took the Bible in a gloved hand and casually kissed the air in front of it.

Under the breezy promptings of the paymaster, who had recovered marvellously his normal magenta hue and his confidence, the captain testified that he had indeed examined the prisoner on the previous evening.

"Just give us your report, doctor." Lieutenant Sanderson beamed expansively around the room as if there could be no doubt what the good young doctor would say.

Captain Montague drew a neat sheaf of papers from a shining briefcase, and flaired horn-rims from a leather pouch in his pocket. He seemed to be in no hurry and he managed to smile in a way that suggested he thought the proceedings, however necessary, a trifle quaint. But the Great Fish wasnt intimidated:

"We havent time for you to read all that, you know," he remarked testily. "This case is taking far too long anyway." He glittered briefly in the paymaster's direction.

The young doctor bowed slightly but charmingly to the president. "I will endeavour to be brief, sir. But I must claim the privileges of what this court calls, I believe, an Expert Witness." He began to read in a most professional voice, skimming his papers. "Umm, yes, Turvey, Thomas Leadbeater. Private. Let me see. No admitted history of venereal disease, mental illness, fits. No present symptoms . . . No apparent addiction to drugs or alcohol." He raised his eyes. "For purposes of this court, addiction may be taken to mean a habit marked enough to interfere with, ah, ordinary duties." He flipped another page. "Memory and concentration normal. No certain mental deficiency. No vertigo, tinnitus, parasthesiae, incontinence, nystagmus, diplopia or rombergism. Normal stereognosis and two-part discrimination. Orientation for time and place probably ah – normal. Examination of glands, joints –"

"For God's sake, captain, was this an autopsy? This man is accused of being absent without leave! What's all this gibberish got to do with it?" The president had, for the first time, quite lost his temper. His little mouth puckered in and out and he bounced up and down on his seat.

The paymaster hastily interposed. "What we most

want to know, doctor, is about this lad's nerves, you know. Now dont you think he's pretty high-strung, eh?"

"Objection!" shrieked the Prosecuting Captain, twirling his moustaches, and dropping a paper.

"Sustained!" boomed the president. "This is your last warning, Lieutenant, uh, Samson. If you ask another leading question, the witness will be stood down."

"No signs of organic nervous or mental disease," Captain Montague went on blandly, as if no interruption had taken place. "I rather think, however," and here he paused professorially, "that the subject's personality *tends* towards that of the, ah, constitutional psychopath."

"Constitutional what?" barked the president.

"Constitutional psychopath, sir. Probably of the inadequate type."

"What's that?" the president asked grudgingly.

"Ah, this is a classification sometimes used in psychiatry" – Captain Montague's manner had gradually become that of a somewhat sophisticated professor speaking to an unusually callow freshman class – "to denote a personality which, though apparently not suffering from any of the psychoses which might respond to treatment, nor classifiable legally as insane, ah, nevertheless presents a settled pattern of marked instability. This type – and of course I am venturing only the most tentative of diagnoses, and suggesting in the case of the prisoner merely an approximation to a type – this type is, for example, likely to be reckless with himself and with others, to come into conflict with the law and the, ah, social mores –"

"Come, come, captain. Cut it short! You mean the fellow's immoral?"

"Let us say," the captain permitted himself a worldly smile and an arch of the eyebrows, "the type (to which he *may* belong) is often in trouble over women, ah, is fond of liquor (without necessarily being an addict) and gambling, the usual things. A large percentage of our civilian jail population is made up of such psychopaths.

Unfortunately there is still considerable disagreement as to whether the pattern is acquired or congenital. In either case," he finished brightly, "they are generally considered incurable." He was about to sit down when the president made a sound as if he were strangling and then found breath:

"What *has* all this to do with it? What *are* you trying to tell us? That this man is crazy? Or, or what?"

"O dear no, sir. It is my opinion that he is and has been, for all legal purposes, civil or military, in his, ah, right mind."

"But – ," the paymaster jumped up. He had been winking agonizingly without effect at Captain Norton Montague and looking very much like a boy whose pet hamster had suddenly taken to gnawing the leg of a valued visitor, "but you wouldnt say, now would you, that –" he stopped and looked apprehensively at the president. "Well, would you say that he was fully aware of the nature of his act when he – when he went on the loose?"

"Perfectly aware," said Captain Montague calmly. Then, as if to assure the paymaster he hadnt entirely deserted him, he added, "though to what extent he has a normal understanding of whether it is right or wrong to do such a thing, I couldnt really say. *Or* to what extent –" here the young doctor cast a professional eye on Turvey who happened at that moment to be wearing his fatal nervous grin – "to what extent he actually experiences such common feelings as guilt, penitence, pity or even, ah, fear."

"Have you *quite* finished, captain?" the president enquired with savage politeness.

"Unless there are any more questions?" The captain looked about him with elegant disinterest. The Prosecuting Captain stood up and opened the little pink mouth under his great moustaches, but before he could speak Captain Montague added: "I understand, of course, that the report of an Expert Witness is not subject to cross-examination." The prosecutor sat down, his mouth still ajar. Captain Montague bowed once more to the president.

"Quite, sir," he said and sat down.

The president sucked his thin lips in until they disappeared.

"And have *you* quite finished?" He flashed his spectacles at the paymaster. But the latter, though punch drunk, was not yet on the canvas.

"I claim the time-honoured right, sir, to introduce this poor boy, the – the prisoner, into the stand in his own defense."

The president glared, gulped air, and seemed to be expanding silently. But there was no explosion. The paymaster had him.

Turvey was alarmed. The R.A.P. Sergeant had been so confident Turvey would get off easily he hadnt coached him for rising to his own defense. But there was no time to brood. The paymaster, with one of his large easy gestures, was already wafting Turvey to the stand. The clerk bobbed up in the same instant.

"Ye-swear-a-might-gad-tell-tru-nothin-but-a-trut?"

"Sure," said Turvey, "yes, sir," taking care to implant an especially firm smack between two grease spots on the black Book.

"Say 'I do'," said the clerk unappeased.

"I do."

"Now, Turvey," said the paymaster affably, "suppose you just tell us your story, the one you told Sergeant Sawyer yesterday, you know. How you lost out on your leave, and then didnt like being shot at by McKelvie; and how Ballard, your, uh, evil genius so to speak, how he talked you into going –"

"Objection," yelped the Prosecuting Captain. "The witness is being led!"

"Objection sustained," said the president effortlessly. "Just tell your story, Private Turvey, without further promptings. And," he looked at his wrist watch again, "you are warned that you must be brief."

Turvey obliged. He gave some account of McKelvie's

shooting prowess, his own disappointment at loss of Christmas leave, his conversations with Ballard, and their faring-forth on Christmas Eve. They had been lucky enough to get a lift with an American trucker on his way back from a Buffalo-Toronto run. The trucker, it appeared, had somewhat anticipated the Christmas festivities and had been in the proper mood to smuggle them, under a pile of sacks and empty crates, across the border. Once over, they found that their uniforms and the season together created a passport to free food and a surprising number of drinks all the way to Buffalo. The trucker had by this time grown so enthusiastic about Canada's role in the war that he brought them to his home for the night and for most of Christmas Day. They had then proceeded to an address known to Ballard, the address at which Turvey was later discovered.

"May we presume you had settled down there for the duration?" the president asked, with acidity.

"O, no, sir," said Turvey, round-eyed and earnest. "We were goin to come back next, uh, that night, but the girls wanted, well, that is, it was Christmas and we got hoistin a few and we thought we might just as well hang around another day."

"Tomorrow and tomorrow and tomorrow, creeps in this petty pace from day to day." It was the paymaster, suddenly, beaming with pride at his own literary wit. "He just put it off, sir, a human –"

"Has the defendant anything more to say?" the president cut in grimly.

"Well, sir, only this, sir," said Turvey, stumbling desperately. "I woulda come back right away except I was, I was waitin for Ballard. The day after Christmas he started off to hitchhike to Cleveland. Said he had a nant there he was going to hit up for a loan and I wasnt to go back till he come. He said it'd be better for me if we come back together on our own steam; then he could explain I was, I just went along with him for the ride."

The president sniffed faintly. "How long did you intend to wait for Ballard?"

"O, of course, I was goin to nip back anyhow before my 28 days was up. Ballard told me we hadda do that, or else we'd be charged with desertion and not just bein AW Loose."

"Do you realize," the president retorted implacably, "that the charge against you may still be altered to one of desertion? No evidence has been presented in this court that you were still in uniform when apprehended. *Were* you in uniform, by the way? Remember you are under oath." There was an ominous smile about the president's lips, a thin, icicled smile.

"No, sir," said Turvey, faltering and hanging his head.

"Hah," said the president shortly, "so you admit to being apprehended in civilian clothes."

There was a pause. Turvey ran his finger under the collar of his battleblouse.

"No, sir," he said bashfully.

"Come, come" – the president was irritated – "you must have been in one or the other, you know, unless –" He paused, struck apparently by an interesting new idea.

"I was in the bed, sir," said Turvey blushing now. "I didnt think to take my pajamas when we went over the line."

There was a snicker, which quickly died under the president's revolving stare. "*The* bed?" the president could not quite conceal a note of salacious curiosity. "Was there only *one* in the apartment?"

"Yes, sir." Turvey's voice had faded to a shy whisper.

"Do you mean to say you were sleeping with both these women?"

"Well, not exactly," said Turvey, as one who didnt wish to boast. "You see, sir, one of them was on day-shift at the airplane plant, and the other was on nights." Turvey paused, and added in a burst of honesty, "They did change shifts the second week I was there. Ruby went on nights and took over shoppin and keepin up the uh – liquor supply – I didnt go out, a course, cause I mighta got picked up by a Namerican M.P. or somebody. I always kept my uniform hung over a chair, though, O, gosh, no, I wouldn't put on any civvies" – Turvey seized on the thought with horror.

This time the president allowed the court-room reaction to go unreproved. For a long space he peered at Turvey, as if seeing him for the first time. Then he trained his little glassy headlamps on the empurpled paymaster.

"Lieutenant," he asked with his most precise and military accents, "do you consider yourself a nervous type?"

"Me, sir?" The paymaster was definitely caught off base. "O, dear no, sir. Average, uh – sta-stability, I should say, sir. Hic! At least average."

"Hah! and do you suppose, lieutenant, that if you had spent the previous fortnight taking alternate shifts with two ladies in the same bed, and indulging in apparently alcoholic parties of sufficient, umm, exuberance to prompt complaints to the police from a neighbouring apartment house – do you suppose, lieutenant, that your hand would not have trembled when you were suddenly transported to one of His Majesty's guard rooms and handed a glass of water?"

It was the president's moment; the paymaster had no reply. The Great Trout, having clearly established his greatness, stilled the little commotion his coup had wrought with a finny flick of his hand, and looked left and right to his silent admiring Troutlings. "Does either of my colleagues wish to question the defendant?" But they shook their heads quickly; any question from them would be an anticlimax, if not actually a piece of insubordination, at this moment. Turvey was stood down, and his somewhat deflated counsel began the hopeless task of summing up for the defense. When that was over, the bristled captain had merely to ask tartly for a conviction on the evidence given, and the court-room was cleared, leaving the three large fish to decide on the fate of Turvey the minnow. Fortunately (it seemed colder than ever outside, and there was no shelter) the judges took almost no time to confer. The court was reassembled and Turvey informed that the findings would be promulgated.

"It means you're guilty," whispered the paymaster cheerfully, behind his ear again, "but don't worry, you wont get much."

Turvey wondered how much was much to the paymaster. The length of the sentence had something to do, he knew, with the state of his "crime-sheet", his M.F.M.6. This the Clerk of the Court now proceeded to chant, much like a minister with a reading from the Scriptures. It wasnt too bad, Turvey thought with relief. "Three days' C.B. for being improperly dressed, in that he did appear without anklets in the streets of . . . . Two days' C.B. and one day's Field Punishment for . . . ." His little catalogue of sins having been read without comment, Turvey was informed that they would be weighed in considering his present sentence. His Majesty's Court-Martial was over.

"ULLLef . . . . ry . . . . lef . . . eye . . ."

Next day Turvey had to disrupt some newly formed friendships in the camp brig and betake himself to the much larger and grimmer District Detention Barracks, there to consider, for the next forty-five days, the wickedness of his life.

SEVEN

Turvey Goes Overseas

ONE DAY during the fifth week of his sentence, a guard called Turvey away from his twenty-seventh scrubbing of the Detention Barracks floor and doubled him back to his cell, where he found a tense stoop-shouldered captain waiting to interview him. Turvey tried to control a grin of apprehension when he realized the captain was another Personnel Selection Officer, cumbered with a bulky brown file: Soldier's Personal Documents, TURVEY, THOMAS LEADBEATER.

At first, the captain was stern-eyed and parental in a fidgety kind of way. He wanted to know why Turvey was a problem soldier, and if he had ever been to jail in civilian life. But after a bit he said Turvey had perhaps been led astray and he liked soldiers who could take their punishment with a smile and now he would give him a little test, an interesting new one that he was sure Turvey hadnt had before. So Turvey plowed through the Canadian Army Classification Appraisal Number Two. It was the same puzzle he had been treated to in hospital but he didnt like to disappoint the captain by saying so. He got quite a little farther in it this time. The captain seemed pleased when he had marked it and asked Turvey if he would like to go overseas right away, and Turvey said, "Oh, yes, sir, the Kootenay Highlanders, please sir."

And so it was that a few days later Turvey, the rest of

his sentence mysteriously remitted, was back in the Horse Palace on the Toronto lake-front where he had first met Calvin Busby and the Icelanders. He spent an energetic week executing the same drills as last year, only this time in an interminable March wind that persisted in blowing his rifle askew on his shoulder whenever the sergeant-major looked at him. But though the drills and the pistol-lunged sergeants and the caterwauling gulls hadnt changed, and Lavonne, after some initial coolness because Turvey hadnt written her, became her plump and tender self, Turvey walked the world with a difference. Locked (by official warning) in his soldierly heart was the knowledge that he was on his way to the Kootenay Highlanders.

And on his way he went, before another week was out, buried in kit on half a hard seat over the wheels of a colonist car full of similar crusaders. They played seven-toed pete along the frozen St. Lawrence, crawled out to exercise in the snow-humped Laurentians, piled in again to sleep through the cold forests of New Brunswick, and woke on the windy coast of Nova Scotia.

Until mid-May Turvey's trainload, merged with many others, drilled and route-marched and sat and groused on a sea-marsh in the Land of Evangeline. Slowly behind them the snow slushed down from the hill farms, the land softened under rains and broke with rivulets. All these fluids, it seemed to Turvey, found their way into Number Seven Temporary Transit Camp, there to swell the natural bog that quivered daily around the steps of their unfinished hovels. Gradually the gelatinous waters reclaimed the drill fields under the very noses of the sergeants, so that the training hours were perforce simplified into route marches over the comparative firmness of the soggy hills. Between the labyrinth of huts, duckboards formed precarious bridges and any who wobbled from their safety plunged to his khaki ears in a cold briny goo. Turvey, as he had told the Personnel Officer when he entered the army, distrusted all water deeper than himself, and he ventured out after duty hours as little as possible.

There was nothing to do, anyway. For purposes of SECURITY, the sailing date was being kept secret even, apparently, from the Camp Commandant himself. In consequence, that harrassed gentleman would not allow the rank and file enough leave even to walk to the somnolent village looking dry and cosy on a green hill down the shore; and the village maidens, either from a modesty superior to that which Turvey had encountered elsewhere in his Dominion, or because of the depth of mud in the intervening two miles, stayed aloof from the camp's gate. For Turvey, therefore, Number Seven Temporary Transit Camp was an unadventurous not to say dismal hiatus in his military career.

At last the order raced through the camp and they were stuffed into another train and shunted into Halifax. There was a long day of standing in an embarkation shed rumbling with trucks and echoing with officers. Then with his overcoat buttoned by command to the neck, and his respirator on his left side and his water bottle full of coca-cola on his right, and his haversack slung on his left, and his rifle on his right, and his pack on his back, and his tin helmet joggling on his head, and ammo pouches full of chocolate bars across his chest, and his dunnage bag in his left hand, and a berth card and a mess card and a tag and an extra roll of issue toilet paper in his right, Turvey boarded the grey transport. Though the thought came to him that the Atlantic was even deeper than the transit camp, he descended into the ship's bowels, smelling already of kippers and boiled cabbage, and struggled to the top of a four-tier bunk, with something like relief.

The Atlantic, it is true, proved even more monotonous than their waterlogged barracks: six days of zigzagging in a putty-coloured waste of waters, six days of life-boat drill and kit inspection and lining up for meals, seven queasy nights of rolling on an emaciated mattress in a man-packed hold. Since they were not in convoy, there was nothing to look at but the salt-chuck, of which Turvey thought there was far too much and all the same. Nor was he comforted by the ship's name, *Andes*. It was such a heavy name, much heavier than water.

But somehow the *Andes* buoyed Turvey's body safely, while his spirits, never easy to douse at any time, were sustained by his fairly consistent winnings at black jack and by the thought that he was approaching every moment nearer a glamorous new world.

Even McQua, a gloomy New Brunswicker who was his chief threat in the poker sessions, could not quite snuff the candle of adventure within Turvey, though at times he considerably reduced its flame.

"Gosh, this sun sure feels good," said Turvey on the fourth afternoon, interrupting his own rendering of "Hairy Heelanman" on the tonette. They had shed their tops, after boat drill, and were sprawled, lifebelts over bare skin, with several hundred others on a warm afterdeck.

McQua stirred slightly and squinted from ruffled black eyebrows. "We aint headed right."

"Whaddya mean?"

"Subs." McQua closed his eyes.

"Subs? What they got to do with it?"

McQua seemed to undergo an inner struggle whether to squander more words. He was from a pulpwood section of New Brunswick where speech is seldom given away. His mouth puckered, straightened, puckered again. "Feller was sayin dey was a wolf pack yistedy. We're headin Africa way to miss em."

"Africa! What fellah said?"

McQua opened one eye. "Hotter, aint it?"

"Holy gosh, it aint that hot! It gets hottern this in Kuskanee."

"Hell, this is just good old limey sunshine, you – Canadians," cut in a lordly voice above them. It belonged to a Tank Sergeant sitting on a pile of life-rafts;

he had already spent a year in England, was returning after a three-months' course, and in their hatch was generally regarded as an authority on the Old Country. He had even learned to suppress some of his r's. "Cant you see," he went on, "we're steering straight away from the sun? Iahland off stahboard day ahfteh tomorrow, you watch. And the day ahfteh that, the best ale in the world."

McQua regarded the Tank Sergeant and then the sun suspiciously from under his right eyelid. This far away from the Maritimes he trusted nothing.

But the next morning, when clouds had muffled the whole sky and the temperature dropped almost to freezing, Turvey got McQua to concede they mightnt be nearing the equator after all.

"Shows we aint headin right, like I said, dough." McQua peered hostilely from an aft rail at the misty seas. "Dat wolf pack, fellah was talkin about. Ar'tic mebbe."

Turvey was about to disagree when the ship, as if to join the argument, suddenly heeled over to the right. The engines shifted into a confused new rhythm and the bow swung with surprising speed. McQua clutched silently at a tier of rocket frames, stolid resignation in the face of death. Turvey, caught in an argumentative stance, tumbled to the deck and rolled up against the railing screen. Before he got himself righted, the *Andes* had written a foaming hairpin in the grey waters and was now heading at top speed in the opposite direction.

"Like I said," McQua resumed with dignity, still keeping a firm clutch on a frame, "aint headed right."

"Holy cats," said Turvey dismally, "they're takin us back to Halifax."

Turvey's opinion was widely shared. Security prevented the disclosure of the trooper's whereabouts, and the sun had lost the battle to a great flannelly waste of clouds and fog. Some swore they felt the *Andes* turn back again in the night; others were sure it made only a half-turn. Submarines were sighted hourly for a while, but each resolved itself into a porpoise, a floating board,

or a rather large wave. The First Mate was rumoured to
have glimpsed an iceberg, and a Radar Corporal who had
been stationed in St.John's saw the coast of Labrador
through a momentary hole in the mist. On the sixth evening the news spread that Hitler had been assassinated, the
war was over, and the captain now steering for Quebec
City.

And then with the seventh morning came sunlight on a
bright green headland, and Catalinas in the air.

"Africa, like I said," McQua muttered.

"Nerts. I bet it's Greenland. Taint Nova Scotia
anyway," said a Haligonian.

"I see a castle," Turvey shouted. "Maybe it's Spain!"

"Why dont you chaps get wise to yawselves. That's
Iahland dopes," drawled the veteran Tank Sergeant.

Ireland it was, green as a pool table. And, in a few
hours, the rockier coast of Scotland, real wrecks on
English sandbars, destroyers circling a convoy, and the
bombed docks of Liverpool. Turvey had arrived in a land
where, if the tales of the Tank Sergeant and the warnings
of the Security Officers were true, training schemes were
conducted with live mines and honest-to-god shells,
enemy spies listened in every restaurant, you didnt dare
scratch a match except behind blackout curtains, the ale
was terrific, and the girls all blonde and all lonely. Britain, land of air-raids and thatched-roofed beer
parlours – and Mac and the Kootenay Highlanders. A
new land and a new Turvey, his crime-sheet cancelled in
Halifax, and a shiny new pay book in his pocket in which
the adjutant had forgotten to stamp any of his O-scores.
Turvey straightened his helmet and marched down the
gangplank into the European Theatre of War.

Their detachment was herded straightway into a toy train
which suddenly slid away without a toot or jerk and
rushed them through a bewildering landscape of brick
and hedge and dinky green farms into the grimy outskirts
of London. Then it artfully whisked them out again.

Another two hours and they were marching away from a solid little Sussex station along the edge of a highway roaring with motorcycles, trucks and staffcars whizzing importantly, all on the wrong side of the road. Then Turvey and company were deflected into an immense series of barracks, to which they were promptly confined for the next forty-eight hours. Turvey felt vaguely let down.

The next day the anticlimax continued. There were line-ups, there was an inspection, mysterious delays before and after it, bad-tempered officers bawling for lost documents, burnt beans and a dollop of sour applesauce for lunch, and a general snafu that, it began to appear, attended the moving of a Canadian soldier in any section of the globe. Worst of all, Turvey found that he had not arrived at the Kootenay Highlanders after all, nor at any other recognizable regiment. He had been posted to something called a Canadian Infantry Reinforcement Unit, where he was to remain indefinitely and which, so far, reminded him strongly of the old Horse Palace on the shores of Lake Ontario. Turvey was miffed, and he confided his sorrows to McQua.

The latter, though of a temperament even less pervious than Turvey's to the disappointments of martial life, at least offered sympathy through silence. For McQua also carried a kilt in his haversack. His heart was drawn, as much as McQua allowed it to be tugged by anything, toward the Northwest-Shore New Brunswick Canadian Scottish. The only comforting thoughts that occurred to either of them were that tomorrow night, at last, they were to be allowed out of barracks, and there was a pub only a mile away.

"This beer aint bad." It was Private Archibald McQua's first remark since he and Turvey had entered the *Duck and Maiden* that evening and sat down by a real fireplace with coals. It was in fact one of his first observations on the soil of the Old Land.

"Aint bad!" exclaimed Turvey, "it's got all our Canadian monkey-pee licked hollow! Wish I was a sergeant!"

McQua raised one moustache-sized eyebrow from around the rim of his mild-and-bitter in mute question.

"Hut Corporal was tellin us the sergeants here have a wet canteen and bring in whole barrels of beer, and kina drink it at home like. It's a lot cheaper that way, too, and they aint closed between three and six. And nobody cares if they get stinko."

McQua set the tall glass down and pursed his corrugated lips skeptically. "Private's best."

"You mean you wouldnt want to be a sergeant and get more pay?"

McQua remained silent.

"And have your own mess, and beer with meals, and everythin? And maybe lead a platoon into action?" asked Turvey with mounting amazement.

McQua let his expressionless grey eyes float over the staghorn and the V of Ashanti spears above the fireplace, across to the village dartplayers in the corner, and back to Turvey. He shook his head.

"Wouldnt you even want to be a nofficer?"

McQua lengthened his long pawkish face in denial and silently got himself another pint from the busy barmaid. When he sat down again, Turvey renewed the topic.

"What's a matter with bein a nofficer? Even better than a three-striper. You'd have big dough, and a mess with real hard liquor, and, and, think of the girls they get!"

McQua thought for the space of a long pull on his beady glass. "Dey aint happy," he said finally.

"Who? The girls?"

"Officers. Sergeants is happier nor officers. Privates is happiern any a dem." McQua's fifth seemed at last to be loosening him into communicability.

"Why?" asked Turvey flatly.

McQua prodded a little puddle of beer by his glass with a reflective finger. "Privates is happiest," he said finally. "Yu aint worretin alla time what to make privates do.

You jess do it." He poked the puddle into a neat square on the old oak tabletop. "More stripes you git, more worry. More trouble." He shook his thick pow solemnly.

"I heard the officers over here get week-end passes to London all the time," Turvey began again, after securing two more beers.

"Aint nuttin. Just anudder big town. Seed it oncet seed it all. You seed it from de train yistedy."

"But officers can afford to go to night-clubs and all kinds of movies and things."

McQua wagged his head slowly again. "I'd be afeered to be an officer. More brass you git on, more privates you gotta tink about what to do nex wit."

Turvey, under the unusual flow of McQua's logic, was being convinced. He began to feel sorry for all the sergeants and staff-sergeants and sergeant-majors and lieutenants he had met. Come to think of it, few of them ever did seem very happy, except maybe when they were swacked. He tried to remember what the really high officers looked like, but he hadnt seen any of them close up so far.

"What about General McNaughton, then?" he asked. "Cordin to what you say he should be unhappiern anybody cause he's right up on top."

"You niver seed a pitcher a him?" Worritest-lookin man I *ever* see."

Turvey recalled the recruiting placards showing the long furrowed countenance of the General Officer Commanding the Canadian Army. McQua was probably right. Turvey got another round, and changed the subject. But he made a mental reservation about Kootenay Highland officers. It was impossible to think about one of them unhappy in his job.

Turvey, in fact, was finding it more and more difficult to think of anyone being unhappy. He had never tasted liquid that slipped down so easily. He had never been in such a cosy beer parlour in all his alcoholidays. He beamed at a pert thing in an ATS uniform by the crowded little bar, and thought how pleasant it was to sit legally in a tavern with ladies even though he hadnt brought any; when the ATS shifted her enigmatic eyes to her officer companion's, Turvey eased his along to the funny old mirror above the dark panelling on the wall, grinned quizzically at himself and the pawky profile of McQua and then let his gaze roam tranquilly over a hazy tangle of uniforms and laborers' overalls and beer-mugs and gleaming strange bar-taps, and dartplayers, and two quiet ancients doggedly playing checkers beside the thumping mechanical piano.

By ten, when the barmaid called "Time, gentlemen, please," Turvey and McQua, at least, had become living arguments for the possibility of happiness among privates. They had discovered, a little late, that English wartime beer, however inferior it was considered by the natives to the brews of peace, was a good deal stronger as well as tastier than the fluids sold in the aseptic taverns of their homeland. They were the last to paw their way through the blackout sacking in the porch and into the solid night.

"Whoops," said Turvey, "wash a step, Arshie."

"Wash it yrself, yole stumblebum," McQua's voice in the dark behind him held a high recklessness Turvey had never heard in it before.

"Whish way we go?" asked Turvey, after he and McQua had picked themselves up from the inn lawn (there had been two steps to mind). The other customers had already disappeared.

"Way we come, acoorse," said McQua slap-happily. "You go firs."

Since neither of them could remember which way that was, Turvey decided to steer by the unmistakable sounds of army boots ahead. They stumbled into the blankness, two rolling Canadians over the rolling English roads.

What with their somewhat eccentric pace, and the rule against striking even a match in the open during an alert, a prohibition which had been so dinned into them by a succession of Intelligence Officers that even in their present state they could not forget it, Turvey and McQua had not gone very far before the footsteps ahead died away and they were left with only the inefficient light of murky English stars to guide them. They came to a crossroad. "Whish way now?" asked Turvey.

"You're charge." McQua reeled expansively. "You're ossifer."

"You're drunk, y'old coot. Aint no more oss-officer'n you are."

"Whass date a your 'nlismen'?" demanded McQua, sternly.

"Fif' June forty-two."

"Like – uc! – I said." McQua was triumphant. "Mine steent July. Your Senior Solyer dis resh-rezhment. You're charge. No sense friggin roun." He drew himself up to a weaving attention and saluted solemnly. "Whish way we go, shir?"

Turvey was baffled. McQua might be right about this.

"You gotta return my s'lute," said McQua relentlessly, still teetering at attention.

Turvey saluted half-heartedly, deciding to make the best of it. "O.K. Private McQua. We goin left." Gravely they assumed a file order, Turvey leading. They stumbled along a road which quickly degenerated into a twisting uphill lane which neither of them had ever seen. Fortunately a full moon began to rise, red as a tomato; though it suffered a running interference from a sky-full of lean clouds, it shed enough glow for them to make out a hillside on the right, blobbed with sheep, a field sloping down on their left, and, perhaps a mile beyond it, the blurred roofs and chimney-pots of what might be Lesser Hensfold, the nearest town to their barracks. But now their lane began to bend right.

There was a high barbed fence between it and the field, though beyond seemed clear and inviting.

"Les cut across fiel'," suggested Turvey.

"You're ossifer." McQua halted punctiliously behind him.

Turvey was about to tackle the wire when he made out a sign at the top of a tall fence post. "Mil-it-a-ry Prop-er-ty," he read with alcoholic care. "Dan-ger. No En-trance." There was something more in letters too small to be read by moonlight.

"Guess berr shtay on road," said Turvey with disappointment. He was getting a little sleepy. But the beer at the *Duck and Maiden* seemed to have permanently altered McQua. Awhile back he had been singing a salty North Shore version of "Blow the Man Down", with individual discords. Now he flourished his arms in the quiet lane.

"Hell wit it, ain we Mil'ry? Thish *our* proper'y thash what says. Civvies ga go roun. We're Cnayn Army, see. You're Cnayn ossfer goofus. You orr us go ri' tru. Ulless go."

Turvey began a demurrer which McQua cut short by suddenly grabbing Turvey's little wedge-cap from his wide head and hurling it with a falsetto whoop over the fence. Turvey, always one to enter into games, seized McQua's headdress in turn and threw it even farther in the same direction, and the two of them, snorting with simple glee, wriggled under the lowest barbed strand and zigzagged into the field looking for their caps. The game was so amusing they tried it twice more before they lost Turvey's completely. Feeling suddenly empty of breath and fervour, they flopped under a solitary hawthorn in the middle of the field, heavy with dusty brick bloom in the moonlight. There had been an unusual spell of good weather for May, and the grass was reasonably dry.

"S'funny kina a farm – uc," said McQua. "Musha been drivin tractors all overa grass. Wh-uc, whuh ay wanna do at fer?"

It was true that the meadow grass seemed strangely, savagely gouged and scraped all around them. In their romping so far Turvey had noticed even one or two shallow pits like shellholes and wondered if the field had been raided lately. Bombholes, he had thought, were bigger, but he hadnt seen any for sure yet.

"Mebbe way they farm," he said vaguely. "I heard they was kina old-fashioned over here."

"Mebbe." McQua yawned. "Whas time?"

"Dunno, but sure as hec more'n twen'y-three hunner hours. I'm AWL again, jus aferr gettin a clean Six. 'N no wedge-cap neither." Turvey sighed, feeling sleepy and sad.

"Thass aw ri'. You're osser now. Ul tell you what. You orrer us go sleep ri' here. Fine your cap ina morn'."

"Mebbe we berr try make barracks."

"Naw, thish berr. Allus wannit sleep unner tree 'n jolly ole Englan'. Unner tree." His voice rose in a last burst of beery song. "Unner a greenwood treee who ullovesa lie w'me – shkool reader – Shape – Sha – uk – Shakesbeer."

Turvey would have preferred the barracks; the night was cooling and dampening but McQua had curled his arm under his head and entered a world without sergeants. Somewhere an owl seemed to be talking wearily in his sleep. A low-flying Lancaster was pounding home heavily, steadily. Then the clouds multiplied and shut the moon away. Turvey, after fitful catnaps, drifted into dream-clogged slumber.

He seemed to be wakened almost at once by a great cawing and clawking. He opened foggy eyes to exchange annoyed stares with a large crow a few yards away on the turf. It was bright dawn. As Turvey craned his neck, trying to remember where he was, the crow ran sideways briefly, turned by a buttercup and swore at him. The sentiments were immediately taken up by several of the crow's companions in the tree overhead. McQua snored on, blue-stubbled cheek still wistfully couched on his arm, his grass-stained wedge-cap cocked over his eyes. Turvey's head ached, and the cawing made it worse. He took a fist-sized rock that lay in reach and hurled it, without rising, at the crow on the turf. The rock looped about thirty feet and suddenly disappeared in a blast of noise and a black umbrella that fanned and showered them with acrid dirt and bits of gravel. McQua rolled over sputtering, too suddenly awake and alarmed to find words. The crows left the tree in a great squawking panic. The one on the ground had disappeared. "Wha – squwhut– whas happened?" McQua managed, spitting dirt from his mouth, and waggling his great eyebrows, "Air-raid?"

"Darn'f I know," said Turvey breathlessly. "Just chucked a rock at a crow and it blew up."

McQua, whose taciturnity had come back with the morning, at first only grunted. He stared at Turvey. "You hadda dream."

"I didn't dream that hole, anyway." Where the stone had landed there was a ragged crater at least three feet across, its bottom still obscured with lazy grey wreaths of smoke that drifted toward them stinging their nostrils.

"That wern no rock you chunked. You musta got holt of a grenade."

But Turvey knew it was only a shapeless dew-damp stone he had clasped in his hand. Unless it was some kind of secret weapon the Jerries had dropped. He was mystified.

Suddenly McQua, who had been squinting up at the tree above them in an effort to get his eyes free of dirt, shouted: "Hey, lookit!"

Tacked on the trunk above their heads, visible now in daylight, was a notice like the one they had half-read on the fencepost by the lane:

MILITARY PROPERTY
Tank-Test Field B3-RAC
DANGER
This field is mined
NO ENTRANCE
By order, War Department

"Holy jiminy! You suppose that was a mine I threw?"

"You dint trow it, dumbell, you hit it," said McQua gloomily. "And dey's all over dis field."

Turvey now remembered the Tank Sergeant on the *Andes* talking about the use of small mines to test big tanks and the nerves of their drivers, mines big enough to blow the foot off a man walking but not powerful enough to do more than throw the tread off a tank. Troopers in training sometimes had to drive over a field mined with such devices, trying, by the use of a chart of the danger spots, to navigate unscathed.

"How'd we git here anyways?" asked McQua suddenly. He had been gazing about like a newcomer on the moon.

Turvey had to restore McQua's memory of the events following their departure from the pub. When he mentioned the bit about McQua deciding Turvey was his officer, he thought he saw a foxy gleam behind the bleariness in his companion's eyes. They sat silent for a while, considering the situation. The lane whose safety they had left was only a hundred yards away across the tank-scarred turf. But how many concealed mines lay between, and where? And from their island tree the now sinister field rolled in every direction.

"We gotta figure a way out of here."

"Yissir," said McQua.

"Well, what do you sugges – say, whatya mean, 'sir'?" Turvey turned with growing alarm to the blank-faced McQua.

"Yissir. You're still officer-'n-charge. You git us out." McQua fitted his back serenely against the tree trunk, though he was careful not to move out of his general position on the grass.

Turvey stared wildly at him. "I resign."

"Cant. Gotta lead me back firs . . . sir." He closed his eyes.

No amount of cajolery would move McQua from his role of the Permanent Happy Private and, until Turvey remembered to put his plea in the shape of an order, he would not even join in when Turvey started shouting at the first auto that rolled by. Neither it nor the other vehicles that passed as the morning wore on gave any sign of having heard them. An elderly lady in shorts, clicking stately by on a bicycle, did give one quick look, after a particularly piercing whistle of McQua's. She immediately bent to the handlebars in an impressive burst of speed, and did not return. It was another half-hour before the first pedestrian came into sight, a greyheaded civilian in farmer's corduroys. In response to their now somewhat crack-voiced holloos he stopped, stared uncomprehendingly, and slowly approached the barbed wire.

"You be wantin summat?" He spoke in a burry Sussex, with wary politeness.

"We wanta get outa here," shouted Turvey. "Please go tell the tank men or somebody to fetch us out."

"Yent urt?" asked the ancient, puzzled.

"Aint heard what?"

" 'Urt, 'urt. I'll lay you look middlin able to walk. You ent been urted?"

"O, no. Not yet. But this place is full a mines. We'd get blowed up if we tried walkin out."

The greyhead stared at them suspiciously, and then at the sign on the post.

"How be you fellers got in, 'en?" he asked, retreating a little from the fence.

"We walked in," explained Turvey patiently. "It was night. We didnt know it was mined."

" 'Appen you can walk out way you walked in, 'en."

"But we dont know just where the heck we did walk in," said Turvey desperately. McQua continued to recline against the tree, a carefree spectator, slowly chewing a grass blade. The stranger regarded them silently for a long space.

"You fellers Canide-yins?" he asked suddenly.

"Yeah," said Turvey.

"Ah!" The stranger shook his head as if he understood everything. "Tryin to lead me up the gahden."

Without further words he trudged down the lane, paying no heed to Turvey's shouts and entreaties.

Turvey and McQua, neither of whom could make out what a garden had to do with it, passed the next half-hour alternately yelling at passing traffic and brooding upon the ungrateful English, who could so callously leave their rescuing brothers-in-arms from across the sea in peril of their lives.

Then a British army lorry drew up beside the fence, and its driver, after a brief parley, told them to sit tight and wait for a tank.

And so it was that, about noon, two hungry and jittery Canadian infantrymen were ferried safely across a tank-testing field in a mighty weaving Royal Tiger, interviewed and retained in a guard house of a squadron of the Royal Armoured Corps, and eventually signed over and ceremoniously delivered to a corporal's guard and lorry of the Twentieth Canadian Infantry Reinforcement Unit. The latter in turn transported them to the guard house of their proper barracks. There, after an inadequate but welcome meal, they were both formally charged (a) with being fifteen hours, twenty-three minutes Absent Without Leave and (b) with entering a forbidden area. After the assistant adjutant came in and wearily heard their story, Turvey was in addition accused of illegal discharge of a weapon, in that he did cause to be detonated . . . etc., and with the loss or destruction of one cap, field service, and one badge, cap, Canadian Infantry Corps. Turvey was driven to point out that it was McQua who had thrown the headgear away, but McQua maintained, with monosyllabic firmness, that he had placed himself in Turvey's charge from the moment they left the pub, and had therefore simply been carrying out orders. The assistant adjutant made it plain that he considered both their stories to be highly improbable and that the two of them must have been sent by some malevolent deity all the way from Canada to plague him. He did not alter the wording of the charges.

"Like I said," McQua remarked the first time they were alone in the guard house that night, "it dont pay to be an officer."

EIGHT

Turvey Investigates London

ESCAPE from greater to lesser ills was always, for Turvey, one of the pleasures of army life. For this reason he came away rather cheered from meeting his Commanding Officer next morning. True, he was once more disappointed in a secret hope that sometime he would make the acquaintance of a new C.O. in a less formal way than being paraded before him hatless between guards and on a charge. But once Turvey had agreed to take the C.O.'s punishment sight unseen, Colonel Stimkin had exhibited no more than the usual firmness of army authorities in regard to matters of money; he docked Turvey two days' pay for his temporary absence, and the price of the wedge-cap for its permanent disappearance. And he confined him to barracks for the next week. But he made sure McQua would be his evening companion for the same period and he informed Turvey that the British Tank unit had generously agreed not to press any charge against him for leading a foray into their territory and setting off one of their mines. Turvey wrote Mac in care of the Kootenays, the only address he had, and settled down amiably, if under duress, to a steady diet of barrack life for the next seven days.

The week, and the many that succeeded it at No. 20 CIRU, turned out surprisingly dull. His chief defeats were still incurred in drill strafes and respirator blitzes; his only possible victories were over lance-jacks. There was seldom a blast from the camp's air-raid siren, and never a sky-full of zooming dogfights such as Turvey had expected from the English heavens in June 1943. And he heard nothing from Mac.

"The trouble with you, Turvey," said Potts, over supper one night, "is you're too full of aggression." Potts was a serious-minded Ordnance Clerk who had recently been assigned to type psychological reports for the Personnel Officer.

"Gee, I just want some excitement, Pottsy, that's all. Only difference bein a soldier over here is I have to roll down a flock of skewgee old blackout blinds at night and roll em up in the mornin. And since the Old Man cracked down on poker and craps I havent any change to get out to a pub even or take a biddy out. Or see Phyllis Dixie over at the Empire Palace. Let alone get to London." Turvey sighed, abstractedly wedding a fragment of cold potato to a square of spam on the end of his fork. "Why, I -"

"Yaa, London!" Potts interrupted impatiently, "all you new ones is the same. Suckerbait. Spend all your money. Get pie-eyed, pick a scrap with a Yank over some Piccadilly skirt, and bang the provost's got you."

"O, no," said Turvey virtuously, "that aint what I want to get to London for. You see, I aint even been there yet; I aint ever seen a nair-raid, or - or," Turvey groped for a worthy alternative, "or the Bloody Tower."

"There you go," Potts hissed; he was a little man who packed a great deal of fierce energy into his speech. "Always thinking *violently*. Blood and bombs and things. You should realize it's our *duty* as Canadian soldiers to - to *channel* our aggressions, see, *channel* em. We gotta save up our frustrations -" he paused and thrust his little round chin across the table at Turvey - "to smash the Nazis with."

Turvey felt vaguely he hadnt made himself clear. He swallowed the last forkful of spam and looked at his dessert. "Custard again," he sighed.

Potts, who had forgotten to eat, regarded him with bright fanatic eyes. "Custard, sure, custard! *That's* the real adventure right now. Stop being a, a *Canadian*. Powdered egg omelet and custard and spam and hard-tack and – and – basic training over and over again, and putting up with our officers –"

"What about sergeants?"

"*And* sergeants. Dont you see? That's *our* part of the Battle of Britain! We learn now to suffer, to – to channel. We *discipline* our energies."

Turvey abstractedly wiped his cheek from the spray of Potts' intense vocables. "I dont really feel aggressive though, Pottsy; it's just, well, you hear all the oldtimers boastin about the swell forty-eights they had in London. And – and golly, I dont even feel I'm in a war yet. About my only fun is horseshoe pitchin. Everythin's so sort of humdrum – not like in the Canadian papers."

"Ah, *Canadian* papers – pandering to the aggressions of *civilians*. *We* dont need that. You can get the BBC news every night in the NAAFI, if that's what you want. *We're* hardening ourselves to be the shock troops of the *Second Front*." Potts began his custard and then thought of another phrase. "We're storing our conflicts for the Invasion, steeling our, uh-morale under English skies."

"It aint any rainier than Vancouver," said Turvey, somewhat on a tangent. "Besides, you've been to London."

"Yaa, why do I waste my breath! Call yourself a *soldier*, a Canadian volunteer!" Potts had unaccountably become angry. He snatched his now empty billytin and mug and, neck out-thrust, stamped down to wash them in the swill barrel.

Turvey gazed after him puzzled. He tried hard to look at it Potts' way, but still somehow he kept picturing himself boarding a fast train to London.

And one sunny Saturday late in June, he did. His boots were gleaming, his cap badge twinkling with silvo, his anklets and belt crusted with new blanco. In his front

thigh-pocket was his toothpaste and brush, in the right
pocket of his new battledress a pass till Sunday midnight,
and in a wallet over his heart: four crisp pound notes. He
was bound for the great mysterious exciting capital, alone
but bright-eyed. McQua, who had also managed a forty-
eight, had set off for a nearby farm where he had
established himself recently by helping to milk the cows
and shovel manure for the farmer's daughter.

"Like I said," McQua had reiterated when Turvey
made a last attempt to secure his companionship. "Jist
anudder big dump."

"You havent *seen* it yet."

"Seed it from dat troop train comin in."

"You didnt see the waxworks. Come on. We'll take in
a big show too."

McQua had shaken his head. "Millie's frying me a
mess a real duck eggs."

All the compartments in the London train were filled and
he was lucky to squeeze himself with half a hundred
others into the narrow corridor, one of a squashed little
army of allied soldiers speckled with gloomy civilians and
their splaytoothed children. By the time the train had
started Turvey and two other Canadians had been shoved
right to the corridor's end, around the corner, and into
the pocketsize Ladies. This might have been easier going
if the female children in the coach had not proved ex-
traordinarily weak in the bladder. Their parents kept
passing the more urgent cases to a pair of strapping
Royal Sappers outside the lavatory who would tug
Turvey and his two temporary room-mates into the
vestibule, ram the child in and slam the door shut. Then,
to make room for her return journey, one would pull her
out while the other heaved the three Canadians back in.
It wasnt until Redhill that Turvey, by a little tricky foot-
work, managed to slip one of the sappers into his place.

After a few minutes' judicious edging and pressing he

worked himself back into the main corridor and beside a
trim redhaired corporal in the tailored uniform of the
Canadian Women's Army Corps.

"Hi," he said in his most winning tones, "where you
from?"

The redhead looked at him, then at his arm, and tilted
her pear-shaped chin scornfully. "Horsham," she said.
She had loops lipsticked above a rather thin upper lip.

"I mean back home," Turvey persisted. He had noted
that her cool blue eyes showed more interest than her
voice betrayed.

The CWAC looked away, making him wait. "Vancouver," she said as if she shouldnt have.

"Gee, why I'm practically from there too!" Turvey
tried to make it sound like an amazing coincidence. "I'm
from near Kuskanee." He managed to get an elbow
against the corridor wall and pivoted so that she had to
face him.

She regarded him with careful impersonality. "Never
heard of it."

By the time Turvey had located Kuskanee and
Skookum Falls for her, taken over the care of her haversack for the rest of the journey, and explained that he
was making his first attempt to paint London red, he had
discovered that her name was Estelle and that she was a
condescending veteran of many London leaves.

"How about comin with me to Maddem Tussawds this
afternoon?" Turvey turned on his Number One whee-
dling smile.

"Madame Too-soes?" Estelle managed a smile that
was both motherly and sophisticated. "I'm really more
interested in the theatre. Anyway I sort of promised my
lieutenant friend at CMHQ to see Ivor Novello in The
Dancing Years with him." She turned her little pear chin
in profile. Turvey saw a flicker of her eyelash and following the direction of her gaze detected a suave Sergeant of
Signals beginning to shove quietly toward them. He
decided he had better consolidate whatever ground had
been gained.

"Heck, *you* know the sights. Let's do whatever you want. Let's – let's have lunch together anyway and talk about it." Estelle, after a pause during which the Signal Sergeant deflected his course toward a pair of chattering ATS girls, gave Turvey a sporty little smile and assented.

He was glad at first to have Estelle's pilotage through the swirling confusion of Waterloo station, though he sensed some disappointment in her slatey-blue eyes when, enchanted with the sight of the escalators, he insisted they go down them rather than out to the taxi stand. The slick thundering tubes excited him, and the strange whirlpool of Piccadilly Circus. It was full of sloppy Yanks with cascades of medals under big kid faces, and with arms around the necks of little cockney floozies.

His first real misgiving came when he paid the check and ten percent tip at the queer Scandinavian restaurant up a side-street to which Estelle had guided them and where she displayed a hearty western appetite and a fondness for ale with her mid-day meal. It seemed that though the ancient chicken, anemic sprouts, and dessert were included in the five-shilling tariff for each of them, the ale was extra, and so were the sour potato salad (hors d'oeuvres), the chicory coffee, the concealed fiddler (orchestra), and the cloakroom charge. But there was still eleven-and-six change from the second pound, and two pounds to go.

During dessert (it had a Swedish name but turned out to be unmistakably English custard with prunes) he proposed they take in They Got Me Covered, with Bob Hope, a movie he had seen resplendently billed along the way. But Estelle pouted her plum-red lips and explained to Turvey that there was something called the "legitimate theatre" which anybody really hep would prefer to a flick.

"Now, there's Sweet and Low," she said speculatively, blowing a neat ribbon of smoke in the direction of a British captain toying with a shrivelled jam tart. "Of course, I've seen it, but I wouldnt mind seeing it again. Other Ranks can sometimes get free tickets," she went on, perhaps detecting that Turvey was adding something in his head, "down at the Beaver Club. Then there's Quiet Week-End at Wyndham's."

Past Rainbow Corner and Lyons and the tarts and cinema queues she shepherded Turvey again, and hurriedly through Trafalgar Square to the Beaver Club, lighthouse for Canadian privates on leave. Here a very kind lady was very sorry that all free tickets to the Saturday plays were gone; she even went to the trouble, when Estelle suggested they could pay for seats, of ringing several theatres; but everything was sold out.

"O well, it's only half-past one. We can try some of the theatre box-offices just before the two-thirty curtain. They sometimes have quite good seats people turn in at the last moment."

"I hear Flanagan and Allen are pretty good. And there's somethin called The Windmill," said Turvey, trying to soar to her level.

"Well," she said sniffing gently, "if there's nothing left, we can still go to a flick."

"O.K., uh – swell. How'd you like to go have a beer in a pub first?"

Estelle thought for a moment. "A drink would be nice," she said, with a slight emphasis on "drink", "and I know a wonderful place you must see, a real London bar. You'll love it. We've just time, if we take a cab." She seized his arm, smiled gaily at the kind Club Lady, and before he could talk Turvey was riding up the Strand in a funny square car smelling of old leather, holding Estelle's cool hand, and gawking at the overhanging cliffs of double-decker buses that swayed about him. Outside the Savoy Turvey rendered up another three-and-six.

He thought he had never seen anything quite so high-class as the Savoy lobby, unless it was the one in the old Hotel Vancouver. It was full of pillars and soft grey lounges, and elderly redtabs with very young chicks, and pinkcheeked officers in strange foreign uniforms with older and even more lavish ladies. Turvey looked uneasily around, feeling he was in officers' territory, but Estelle seemed quite at home and marched him unhesitatingly over the mossy carpets and down marble stairs to a cave-like bar glowing with subdued neon lights and chromium fittings and high stools full of Poles and RAF types with really gorgeous biddies. Here they had a double whiskey sour each, and Turvey got back ten shillings from his third pound. Estelle drank hers surprisingly fast and became much more chummy.

"My dear, that was just what I wanted. But we mustnt stay long, must we, if we're going to make a last stab for tickets. I think we should have just one for the road." She spoke as if Turvey had been offering to settle down for an afternoon's steady drinking. When he slid the ten-shilling note a little sadly toward the bartender he noticed the latter looking at it sourly.

"Funny darling," Estelle whispered in his ear, "he expects a tip too, you know."

Turvey blushed, grabbed the note back and not knowing how much silver was needed, fished out his last pound.

"Thank you, sir," said the bartender briskly. "*And* madam." Turvey waited for his change but the bartender had stuffed the note in his pocket and was busy serving two lieutenant-commanders from the Royal Navy. Estelle tugged his arm and before he knew it they were back in the Strand. At any rate the second whiskey sour had touched a spot; and he still had some silver in his pocket, not to speak of a return ticket to Lesser Hensfold. But he stopped at the first corner calculating desperately . . .

"Uh, Estelle, dont you think it'd be more fun, all this sun and everythin, to stay out in a park or somewhere this afternoon?"

Estelle looked at him with a kind of martyred indulgence. "I see you really want to see a flick rather than the theatre. O.K. Let's go to your old Bob Hope."

"Well, uh, to be honest with you, Estelle, I havent got

fixed up with a place for the night yet and, well, I *would* like some fresh air and, uh, just walkin around like."

Estelle permitted a short punitive silence, then spoke with a brave brightness: "We'll go and look at the ducks in St. James'. I guess we dont really need a taxi."

When they had gone, none too conversationally, as far as Trafalgar Square again, past leaning piles of stacked bricks and little heaps of glass and plaster by a newly-bombed store, Estelle remembered a message she had to give a friend and parked Turvey by a large stone lion while she disappeared into a building the other side of Canada House. Turvey spent the next twenty minutes exchanging coos with the pigeons that strutted round like little sergeant-majors, and gawking at bespattered Nelson on his monument – and wondering how he was going to finance the rest of his week-end on eighteen bob in this surprisingly high-priced town. Then Estelle reappeared, without comment, and they completed the pilgrimage to St. James' Park. They strolled past a pond-full of fancy ducks and over a large toy-bridge. Beyond these were lawns blotched with slit trenches, and rows of green chairs, but disappointingly few thick clumps of trees, and far too many people about for Turvey's taste in parks.

They sat down on two of the grass-coloured seats for a moment to watch a softball game between Canadian teams. Estelle said they were ack-ack gunners from near-by batteries. A civilian couple, talking busily in clipped accents, came by towing a spectacled little girl; they stopped just short of the screen behind home plate. The next pitch sent a tip-foul smack on the woman's thick ankle. She yelped, jumped, glared indignantly at the players, and turned back to her family with British aplomb. The next foul missed the little girl's head by a sliver, but the trio ignored it.

"Gee whillikens, they're gonna get hurt standin there," Turvey exclaimed. He went over to them. "Excuse me, sir," he said to the man, "if all of you stood just a coupla feet over behind the screen here you wouldnt be in the way a them fouls."

The man stared down a long nose at Turvey as if he were a fly on it. The woman spoke sharply: "Why should we? It's *ah* pahk."

"O sure," Turvey gulped, "sorry, I just thought I'd –" but all three had turned their shoulders on him.

When he got back to Estelle there was an old man by their seats. He had an official-looking cap. "Gosh, I didnt mean any harm," Turvey began. "I was just –"

"My dear, he wants fourpence for the seats," said Estelle. "Just give him sixpence."

Eventually he manoeuvred Estelle into a bushy arrangement of vegetation and even found a leaf-screened seat in the middle of it. Estelle permitted one kiss but immediately dug out her lipstick to restore the *status quo*, and looked at her watch. She got on to the subject of promotions and asked Turvey what his chances were.

"Not very hot right now, Estelle, but soon as I get out to the Kootenay Highlanders I'll be shootin ahead. My pal Mac was a lance-corporal already in Canada with them, and I'm just waitin to hear he's got a spot for me. Course I generally make some steady spendin-money playin poker with the fellahs; but just now the R.S.M.'s kinda death on it; havin a purge on gamblin. Still, we're fixin up a way to beat that."

Estelle did not seem exactly impressed by Turvey's plans to break into the big money but she did consent to sit in his lap and Turvey was even managing a second kiss when the light suddenly dimmed, the bushes parted, and a tall bobbie looked solemnly down on them.

"You cahnt remain heah, sir, you know." The voice was startlingly like the BBC, not cockney as Turvey had expected, very impressive in fact and quite polite.

"Gosh, officer, we werent doing a thing," said Estelle quickly, with maidenly indignation, before Turvey could think of anything appropriate.

"I'm shaw you wehnt, miss," said the constable equably, "but possibly you did not obsehve the little notice?" He led them outside their thicket where there was indeed a sign:

NO ENTRANCE
By Order – War Department

Turvey thought with alarm of the tank-testing field. "Is it mined?" he gasped.

The officer blinked but went on evenly: "Mined? I couldnt say, sih. My ohdehs ah to see that no one proceeds beyond this notice without oe-thrization. A tempry wahtime inconvenience, sih, you undehstend." He smiled benevolently. "Now theah's a rawtheh pleasant nook if you follow this pawth to the otheh side of the fihst weeping willow. You cahnt miss it. *Good* day, miss. *Good* day, sih."

But just as he was about to take his stately leave a burly Canadian soldier, walking briskly toward them, blocked his way. He was even taller than the bobbie, who seemed a foot higher than Turvey. The ominous precision of the newcomer's movements alone, apart from the claypipe whiteness of his anklets, whistle cord and webbing, the venomous gleam of his buttons and the ornate badge on his flat officer-like hat, betrayed the natural enemy of the private – the professional army policeman. A provost. And three stripes. A provost sergeant!

"Ur these soldiers givin yuh trouble?" There was the dramatic baying of the bloodhound in his voice, and his eyes travelled with business-like impartiality over both sexes of soldiers represented, and to the expressionless face of the British bobbie. The latter regarded him for the briefest of moments.

"Not the slightest," he said, a world of distance in the inflection, and, stepping round the provost, he paced away without another look.

The sergeant was not to be put off the hunt so easily.

As Estelle and Turvey began to sidle away, he halted them.

"Hey, jus ta minute, you two. I'll see yer passes." He seemed disappointed when they both produced their magic slips, properly stamped and signed. He handed them back coldly.

"I seen that cawnstable take you outa there. Enterin a forbidden militry area, that's whatcha was doin. I've half a mind ta putcha on charge."

"You wouldnt do that to *me*, now, would you, sergeant?" said Estelle with a more fetching smile than Turvey had yet seen on her face. She inched a little closer to the beefy tower and fluttered her lashes. "It's my first leave in London, you see, sergeant, and I didnt know – *he* said it was a shortcut to the Haymarket. We were going to buy theatre tickets. Which way *is* it to the Haymarket, sergeant?" and her cheeks dimpled.

"But – but I didnt say I was – I cant – she – I aint got enough dough to take her –"

"Yur impropaly dressed," the sergeant cut in. His square face, which had been rounding under the sun of Estelle's regard, clamped again as he turned, still majestically bestriding the path, upon Turvey. The latter instinctively felt his fly; no, it wasnt that. He followed the sergeant's stare down to his feet. One loop of the bow on his left boot had come undone and about an inch and a half of black lace lay on his toecap. He squatted hastily, obliterated his crime, and was just straightening up when the sergeant added:

"Boots not polished either. Time ya learned ta look like a soldier. Take a lesson from the corporal here." The provost's face collapsed into meaty folds again and he shot a long-toothed smile at Estelle, who returned it with interest. Turvey gazed at the boots he had so carefully shined before leaving camp. The heels of two Royal Sappers and several allied soles had left their mark on them since. He sighed.

"My what a hard job you have, sergeant!" Estelle's

voice was now a coo. "I think *you're* the smartest-dressed soldier I've ever seen. Do you have to do the whole park every day?"

"I don't walk a beat," he said with superiority. "I got two men on this park and a lotta others scattered round. But," he added with a bashful rumble, "I'm off dooty tamorra. Er – stayin with friends, corporal?"

"My, now, you really *are* a fast worker, arent you, sergeant?" Estelle lowered her lashes. She allowed the red delicious tip of her tongue to appear thoughtfully, then withdrew it. "Suppose you ring me at the CWAC Club tomorrow around eleven. Corporal Taylor is the name, Estelle Taylor."

"Sergeant Bashkin at yer service, corporal." The provost first came elaborately to attention and then positively sagged with pleasure. "Percy ta you. And I hadnt fergotten yer name. Memorized it on your pass. A little habit we have. Quack Club, alaven hunerd hours. Roger!" His face clamped again. "And I ramember yers too, Private Thomas Leadbeater Turvey. I'll letcha off this time. But you see he gets his boots cleaned right away, corporal."

"O, I'm afraid I'll just have to leave him in *your* care, sergeant," said Estelle gaily, glancing at her watch. "I arranged to meet an officer friend who's coming off duty at four. We're going to The Dancing Years tonight. Bye-bye for now, then. I go up this way to CMHQ, dont I, Percy?"

"That's right. Next door ta Canada House. I'd show ya the way but I –"

"O, no, thanks a million, I'll find it. You mustnt neglect your duties, must you? O, and *good*bye, Private Turvey. Thanks for everything. Perhaps we'll run into each other again sometime." Before Turvey could do more than gurgle she had trotted off in the direction of Trafalgar Square. He suddenly understood why he had been parked by one of Nelson's lions for twenty minutes. His thoughts were interrupted by the provost who, having followed Estelle with sheep's-eyes until she faded with a wave from view, rearranged his jaw and renewed a professional interest in Turvey.

"*And* ya gotcha wedge-cap over yur ear." He stared speculatively in the direction of Turvey's concealed right ear, then slid an official-looking pad from his breast pocket. "Think I'll just take a note a yuh unit and the number a that pass anyways. Never know when it'll come in handy." Turvey meekly drew out his pass again.

Then as the sergeant began writing there was a startling interruption. A civilian walking by boggled hard at Turvey, hesitated, regarded the two appraisingly, and wheeled back. Turvey was sure of the face until the stranger spoke. The voice was unfamiliar and thickly English, even more BBC than the bobbie's.

"I say, sawjnt, I hope my friend Tuhvey hasnt been doing anything he shouldnt. I'm shaw," he went on before the sergeant found words, "yaw only doing yaw duty, but I can vouch faw Tuhvey. Shall I take cah of him faw you? I'm Gledstone-Hetherington, Waw Office, you know." He spoke as if the name should be magic. It was a new one to Turvey but – "I'll see you get mentioned faw this, sawjnt uh – what's the nem? Yaw provost-mawshl, CMHQ's a pehsonal friend of maine."

"Bashkin, P., Provost Detachment, CMHQ," said the sergeant automatically, quite off his guard. He came to attention and added heavily, "I wasnt gonna do nothin to him, sir."

"Excellent," said the stranger breezily, winking quickly at Turvey. "Come along, Tops, we'll nip oveh to Pall Mall. If yoh fawst we've just taime foh a couple at the cleb and –"

"Mac!" shouted Turvey, "it *is* you! Wot are *you* doin in civvies –" and stopped, for the stranger's black eyes burned a warning that fairly sizzled him.

The bewildered respect on Sergeant Bashkin's face hardened to suspicion. He looked more closely at the stranger. "Say –" But at that second there was a tremendous whumph and crash such as Turvey had never heard in his life before. A black cumulus spouted from somewhere behind the nearby roofs of Whitehall, and on the heels of the blast came the long rising hysteria of a siren.

"Kee-riced! Sneak-raid!" shouted the stranger. In his excitement he had dropped the BBC and it was indubitably the voice of Turvey's oldest pal, Mac MacGillicuddy of the Kootenay Highlanders. The provost grabbed at his whistle cord but whether to add his warning to the siren or to summon aid for an arrest Mac did not allow Turvey to discover. He grabbed his compatriot and began propelling him at top speed up the path toward Piccadilly shouting officiously: "Air-shelter this way."

Even as Mac spoke there was a curious faint whine in the air that grew instantly to an appalling whistle. The next thing Turvey knew Mac had jumped on him and sent them both flat on the grass. In no time the whistle was a shriek which dissolved in a chaos of sound and light. There were murderous whines in the air and a great cascade of dirt and tree-branches ascended on the other side of the duck-pond. A spatter of soily pebbles pinged and plopped around them, and there was the faint smell of cordite. Turvey felt a strange airy sensation in his mouth.

"Up we get. Make the shelter in this bound," Mac panted, and they tore up the path. Behind they heard the pleep of the provost's whistle and muffled shouts of "Halt!" Over his shoulder Turvey glimpsed the valiant Bashkin sprawled bellowing on the turf. "Dont worry. Got his wind up from the bombs. He wont get up," Mac said hurriedly. "Shake-a-leg."

Suddenly an anti-aircraft gun awoke, so close and savage Turvey was afraid at first the provost had got hold of it. Looking back again as he ran he saw a vicious quivering of the air over the little grove from which he and Estelle had so recently been ferreted by the bobbie. The War Department's sign was now explained, but Turvey had no mind to think of that now. As he pounded after Mac he wondered if the deafening splat-splat of the gun was concealing the whine of the next bomb, and he uttered a little prayer that if a bomb had to fall on anybody it would be on Sergeant Percy Bashkin. They arrived at the shelter before the next one clumphed, farther away now.

Turvey was about to duck around the concrete blast wall into the shelter but Mac swung him sideways, bawling in his ear above the moan of sirens and the bark of the ack-ack, "Got to shake that jeezly provost. Get the lead out of your pants. Jerry's thrown his stick. Only one probably. Tip-an-run. No more bombs."

He pelted across the street on the park's lower edge and into a side-lane, Turvey panting behind. Through a pause in the ack-ack came more faintly the provost's pleep. He must be still whistling from the ground, Turvey guessed, pleased at the picture of the speckless sergeant lying with grass-stains on his pipe cord and anklets.

But his next thought quenched his happiness; he suddenly understood the empty sensation in his mouth, which the excitement had momentarily dulled. His bridge was missing. It must have shot out when Mac batted him to the grass. He tried to make Mac hear: "Gotta go 'ack," he shouted, "los' teef! Teef!" but Mac raced ahead unheeding.

As Turvey followed through a rabbit's warren of streets, the ack-ack whammed intermittently, and the clangor and screech of ambulances and fire-trucks rose in the distance, but no more bombs dropped. Mac kept up a tireless dog-trot, uttering renewed entreaties to Turvey to hurry, until they had jogged into a wider tram-tracked avenue and swerved into the dark lobby of an ancient block of flats.

It was evidently familiar territory to Mac; they lumbered up wooden stairs to the second floor where his companion unlocked a door and led Turvey panting into a surprisingly cosy flat with chintzy curtains. There was no one visible. They collapsed for breath, Mac on a large

chesterfield that flanked a neat fireplace, Turvey on a
cushioned couch by a baywindow.

Mac was the first one to recover. Unfolding himself
from the chesterfield he opened a little cabinet in a corner
and fishing out glasses and a bottle of rum poured two
generous drinks. "Looking at you and going down me."

"Bottoms up," said Turvey, and shortly felt better.
Mac supplied Canadian cigarettes from a humidor, and
settled back. Outside, the prolonged victorious All Clear
sounded.

"Lucky I drifted along. Poor type that provost.
Where've you been the last year? Looking older. Face
sagging." He regarded Turvey critically with the old
dancing light in his dark eyes.

Turvey gazed at him long and reproachfully. "I fought
you were wif 'uh Kootenay Highlanders."

Mac wrinkled his brows. "Lost your ivories again! Explains the a-ged look."

"You knocked em outa me. When you frew me on a
grass." Mac seemed to find Turvey's plight so amusing
he had to pour another round. Turvey took his glass but
he said stubbornly, "Gotta go 'ack and fine em."

Mac snorted. "Not just now, Tops, old fellow. Provost. Awkward character. Should thank me for springing
you."

"He was just goin to let me go, when you come!"

"Never mind, Topsy. Get another set from His Majesty. Buckshee Army dentistry. We'll have a gander for em
too. After Snooper's off duty. He'll be laying for *me*
now, you see." He pointed to his tweeds. Turvey looked
blank. "Wouldnt matter, baby-face, if you hadnt asked
what I was doing in civvies. Flatfloot convinced I'm
limey bigshot. Then T. L. Turvey opens yap. Now he's
sure I'm deserter. Can't be mended now, of course, as
farmer's daughter said after – Vexing though. Wearing
civvies specially to avoid bother from Gestapo. No permission. Pass not signed either. But tell me about yourself, numskull. When did you smuggle over? Where you

hiding? Why didnt you write? Been long in the heart of Emp –''

"I *did* write, to uh Kootenay High'anders, weeks ago!"

"Ah, poor boy. Letter may never reach me. Bad news. Didnt have heart to write it. Regiment came unstuck in Halifax. Broken up. Never found why. Not enough sober officers to take us over, expect. Cant wear badge even unless you're officer. See one of em occasionally. Scattered around. Odds and sods. No-fair-holdin units. Take a dim view of them. Expect you're in one now, eh? Number Twenty? Right. Languished there myself once. Posted now, thank God! Okanagan Rangers. Weird lot. Colonel's moustaches second-longest, Allied Armies, barring Ghurkhas. NCOs all farmers. No discipline. I'm one myself. Intelligence Corporal." He narrowed his eyes like an actor. "A natural for the job. But here, you need another rum."

And in truth Turvey did. All his dreams of kilted glory, shoulder to shoulder with Mac in the one and only regiment, lay shattered on the carpet. It was necessary, in fact, for the two of them to tilt the bottle steeply before Turvey began to feel his old self again and they could begin to catch up on each other's odysseys. Among other things, Turvey learned that the snug nest in which he now sat was inhabited by a young creature with the dazzling name of Daphne, who was paid rather well to be somebody's private secretary.

"Delectable child. Blonde. Unheard-of combination: lovely gams, adequate income, able to read and write. Be home any time now. Have a ball. Celebrate. Pub-crawl. Take in a show, something. Got a steady up here yet?"

Turvey quailed, remembering first Estelle and his vanished pounds, second, his still missing teeth. A wave of self-pity broke over him.

"I got no girl, and no dough, and no teet'."

Turvey thought it unfeeling of Mac to laugh but when Mac insisted Turvey was his friend forever, and guest for the week-end, giving him the last of the rum to prove it, Turvey began to narrate his brief expensive life with Estelle.

In the midst of it Daphne arrived. She was such a dainty thing with such blue English eyes and such a tinkling English voice that Turvey felt all hands and feet, but she quickly put him at ease and made him start his story all over. He had scarcely finished when Daphne and Mac went into conference. It turned out that Daphne was secretary to the manager of a theatre booking agency and had an inside drag for tickets. Next moment she was on the phone in the hall and had talked Peggy, her girl-friend, into coming right over. Then she rang a minor mogul in the theatre world and got him working on the problem of seats. Five minutes later he called back. Would they care for a small box at the Adelphi? A sudden cancellation. Since their escorts were Canadian soldiers, tickets were compliments of the agency. Daphne clinched the deal at once and hurried to change, leaving Turvey, what with the rum and the general glow of friendship, almost happy again. But there was something nagging at the back of his mind. Sipping the final drop from the glass he remembered.

"I hope Peggy aint good-lookin," he said mournfully to Mac.

"Not good-looking! Just a moon of delight, that's all. England's Nut-Brown Maid. Plumpish perhaps, but you like em that way. None of your CWAC teasers either. And eyelashes! Three inches. What's the matter? Never saw you fighting off beauties before. *Thought* you were getting old!"

"What about my teet'?"

"O those! Wont need em, Tops. Peggy likes mature types. A-ged men of distinction, you know. Dont want to bite her, anyway, do you?"

Turvey's smile was weak. Mac stopped in the midst of another mysterious attack of laughter.

"Tell you what, gramps. Might scrounge an old set for

you somewhere.'' He went off snorting into the bathroom and Turvey heard the splash of a faucet. When Mac returned he held up a partial bridge of newly-washed teeth. Turvey could have sworn they were his own.

"Try these for size.''

Turvey took them bewilderedly and after a moment of doubt fitted them with ease into the gap in his mouth.

"They *are* my teeth! Where'd you get em?''

"Spotted em on the grass just as we jumped up. Slipped em in my pocket. Forgotten clean about it. Anything else we can do you for?''

There was nothing else, and what had been an afternoon of some tribulation turned into an evening that reconciled Turvey even to a world containing Sergeant Bashkin. Peggy's teeth, though a trifle noticeable, were her own, and she was as plump and charming as Mac had said. In addition she showed, for a citizen of England, a surprising curiosity about Canada, so that Turvey began to feel himself a man of romance and adventure. "Positive whiteskinned Othello he is,'' Mac had remarked over dinner. "All the way from the Colonies. Now tell em about the grizzly you bopped, or bopped you – never can remember which.'' This was in a pub a few blocks away on the Thames, where they had hurried to eat, since the theatre began early. Here for an outlay less than Turvey's investment in double whiskey sours at the Savoy, the four of them ate surprisingly well, with a faster service than Turvey had thought possible in the Old World.

Then they nipped on a bus which rushed them, more quickly than Estelle's taxi, almost to the door of the theatre just in time for the six-thirty curtain. There had been no more drinks since the rum, but Turvey needed none. The theatre was the most glittering, the tunes the catchiest, the actors the funniest and the leggy ladies the most beautiful in the world. But more beautiful than even the leading lady were the long lashes and the tip-tilted nose of Peggy whose palm he was now fitfully squeezing as they sat chair by chair in the kingly splendour of a second-story box. And Turvey had his teeth.

There was more. When the lights went up after the first act, Turvey, roaming his round eyes over the crowd, and the golden scrolls and icicles on the ceiling, caught sight, in a back row of the topmost gallery, of a uniformed couple leaning forward in the strained attitude of sitters in the gods. Something about the look of the girl prompted him to lift the little pearly opera-glasses Peggy had thoughtfully brought along. He swept them over the man, a pimply Canadian two-pipper with a furrowed forehead. The girl was in the uniform of the CWAC and wore two chevrons on her sleeve. What was the name of this show now? Of course, The Dancing Years! As Turvey stared with growing contentment the corporal fitted sixpenny-rental binoculars to her own eyes.

"This I must see," muttered Turvey. He held his glasses on the CWAC corporal until her own visual guns began to pass over his box. Then he carefully took his from his face and, grinning hugely, waved.

He saw her swivelling binoculars freeze, move on, and jerk back. As they quivered to her lap, Turvey brought his own glasses to bear on the cheated and bewildered countenance of Estelle. But he couldnt look for long; he began to feel sorry for the lieutenant; he even began to feel sorry for Percy. And anyway he had to get back to Peggy's hand.

Turvey Fights on Many Fronts

NOT ALL a soldier's battles are conducted under the fire of mortars and dive-bombers. As the summer of 1943 waxed and waned Turvey developed rapidly into a veteran of the highly varied if seldom lethal campaigns of a Canadian private in England. First, of course, there was a second sortie with his Commanding Officer; Provost-Sergeant Bashkin had whipped a report in to Turvey's CIRU even before Turvey himself got back two hours pushed on pass Sunday night. (He couldnt understand the station-caller's cockney and got off five miles too soon). His social liberty again suffered a wound from the teeth of King's Regulations and Orders (Can.). But Colonel Stimkin seemed to be in a forgiving mood and gave him only three days' confinement to barracks (for appearing improperly dressed in a public place, to wit St. James' Park, London).

Even before he had recovered from his little indisposition, Turvey was forced into a skirmish with a Spo. He trotted rather eagerly over to the Spo's office when his corporal told him to report there on Tuesday. He didnt know what a Spo was – the corporal, when he asked him, had just narrowed his eyes and said, "Suspiciously Pale Officer" – but Turvey hoped he might be a special kind of spy who would assign him to intelligence duties or something – maybe in North Africa even. But all he found was the unit's Personnel Selection Officer who had, for reasons known only to CMHQ, been renamed a Selection of Personnel Officer on arrival in England. SPO or PSO, he showed the same skeptical interest in Turvey's intelligence, proof of which had been lost with all his documents somewhere in Canada. Turvey was ambushed at a barrackroom table and once more machine-gunned with the O-test.

Evidently he stood up better than ever – it was his fifth ordeal of this sort – for the Spo, after the usual fiddling with his pay book and over-casual enquiries about his health, asked him straight off if he'd like to be a driver.

"Please sir, I sure like drivin but I'd rather be posted to the Okanagan Rangers."

"Well now, Private Turvey," the Spo was a long-suffering sort, "there arent any vacancies in their draft just now. Perhaps by the time you finish the driving course –"

"My pal Mac's with the Okies, sir."

"Now I'm sure you would like driving army vehicles –"

"Tanks?" Turvey got interested.

"You're in the Infantry, you know, Private Turvey. Now we've some wonderful trucks –"

"How's chances for a motorbike?" Turvey compromised.

"O.K. I'll try to see if I can get you on an M/C course. But," he sighed gently, "the colonel would be very happy if you'd learn to be just a plain ordinary driver."

A week later, a corporal called Turvey from an after-supper horse-shoe match, just when he was three ringers and three beers up, to warn him for Driving School immediately. Evidently the colonel was going to be happy. There was no mention of a motorcycle course on the order. But by now it *was* an order.

After some minor setbacks, involving damage only to passing mudguards and the nerves of the corporal-instructor, Turvey reconciled himself to the absurdities of steering with a wheel on the right and driving down the left side of highways, even at crossroads. He was duly recorded in his pay book as "Driver I/C England" and returned to his squad at the CIRU.

One of the fitful training speed-ups was in process and there were no passes. For the next two weeks Turvey dissected his Bren again and stabbed dummies. His temper was not improved by a cryptic letter from Mac reporting another bang-up forty-eight at Daphne's flat involving Peggy and a Yank sergeant, and he even meditated writing a letter himself, recording for Peggy some of his own passion and warning her about Americans, but he couldnt think how to put it. Then, when he had almost forgotten he had been to Driving School, he was suddenly shifted to another hut and allowed to spend his days steering a fifteen-hundredweight to the nearby station and back, ferrying food, stores and soldiers with equal élan.

On one of these trips, late in August, Turvey called at the guard's gate by the high brick wall of the Glasshouse, the dreaded Detention Barracks of the British Army, in which more recalcitrant Canadians were also at times immured. Turvey's orders were to sign for and pick up a fellow-countryman at the hour of his discharge and return him to the CIRU. He was surprised to find the released prisoner was his onetime companion in Niagara and Buffalo, Private Horatio Ballard, whom he had last seen in March on his way to a ninety-day sojourn in the Hamilton Detention Barracks. He looked leaner and more sunken-cheeked than ever, and he had the complexion of a celery root.

"Well, I'm fucked! If it aint me old pal Turvey! Got a Canadian cig? W'ere can we git some goddam beer? Jeez I cant wait to git swacked and go square-pushin."

"Sure is a nice surprise." Turvey handed him a packet of Sweet Caps. "But I'm on duty till after supper, and I got orders to take you straight home." Turvey reminded himself to be firm with Ballard.

As they drove back to the unit, the latter brought him up-to-date on his subsequent feats of arms, between luxurious drags on Turvey's cigarettes, which he chainsmoked. "Ah Hamilton was a leadpipe cinch, see," Ballard spat happily out of the truck. "I was oney in thirty days wen they ast me did I wanna go overseas. 'Yer fuckin right,' I says, an two weeks later I was in the bloody CIRU."

"Gosh, you got here ahead of me, then. Watcha been doin since?"

"Scrubbin fuckin flagstones." Ballard narrowed his mouth like George Raft. "Been in that shitty Glasshouse a last two crisely munts."

"Two months! You only been overseas three!"

"Sure, sure. I was goin straight, see, but I couldn git a fuckin forty-eight wen I got here firs. Then, wen I was in Hamilton, see, there was a joe back from overseas gimme an address of a hot lay in London; so I hadda git up there. So I wen on a loose, see, jus fer the weeken', but I got mixin it up with coupla Yank sonsabitches in a pub. I had a skinful but I was doin all right, see, till a fuckin limey provost come in an I socked him right in a kisser – by mistake, kina. An a course the bugger had two hooks. So they wheeled me up fer strikin a sooperior fuckin off'cer. They limeys musta put the screws ona C.O. cause he gimme sixty, sixty days scrubbin shitty flagstones. Never agin. I'm really goin straight this time, Turvey, you watch. Thas the goddamest moosh I was ever in!"

"Worse than Romanburg?"

"Yuh can say that again. These limey cooties are twicet as big. An nothin but burn' beans fer supper, fer sixty fuckin suppers. An java outa the same beans. Excep wen I got their Numer One Diet."

"Was that for Sundays?" Turvey asked innocently, his mind partly on a slit-skirted maiden cyclist he had slowed up to pass.

"Sunday, shit." Ballard lit his second cigarette from the butt of the first. "Thas wen I griped to the brass on

account a the rats bitin me nights. I shoulda knew
better'n start beatin my gums. 'There'll be an Inspecting
Hofficer's paride this afternoon,' the guard says. 'He'll
ask if there's any complynts. And if any son of a 'ore
makes a complynt 'e knows what 'e'll get from me when
'e's back in 'is cell.' So I opened my fuckin trap jus the
same, and the shit of a Commandant he says right away
to the I.O.: 'Aow, we've neveh had a complaint about
rats befoh. All we've got heah, majaw, is human rats.'
And he gimme the old scowl. 'This man's a
troublemakah.' An so the I.O. writes sompn in his little
book, see, and the fuckin parade's over. An wen I double
back ta my hutch, that fuckin guard kicks my knackers
up to me neck, an the Commandant puts me on bread an
water in the spudhole fer six fuckin days. Thas Numer
One Diet, my frand. Yer belly thinks yer throat's cut.''

Turvey cluck-clucked sympathetically.

''An wat's more,'' Ballard went on, ''yuh cant never
talk t'another prisner at work, and yer locked in chrisely
sol't'ry evry night, an evry time yuh move it's at a fuckin
double, wit full pack, an these shit-faced turkies from
Dartmoor swearin their fuckin heads off at yuh. All a
guards is from Dartmoor, see, or old sweats from the
army jugs in India. Take it from me, Tops, I'm headin
straight from now on.''

A few days later Ballard hunted up Turvey in his hut
after supper and persuaded him to put away his tonette
(Turvey was having trouble with the last note in ''Roll
Me Over'') and see if there was a vacant pooltable at the
NAAFI. On the way Ballard drew Turvey out about his
driving job and the prospects of getting one himself.

''Jeez, I'd like ta git me one a these here Don R jobs.
Thas till I made the Paratroops or sompn. Despatch ridin
all overa coun'ry in one a them buckin crash helmits. I
betcha could make seventy on one a them Harley-
Davidsons they got here. Yuh could git to know a lot a

skirts that way, see. Nick – yuh know, the guy I was in Romanburg with – Nick an me latched onta a racin bike oncet. In T'ron'a it was. Started off on that fuckin big highway to Hamilton, see, but wit two a us on it wouldn do bettern jeezly sixty. Was a old heap, I guess, an we hadda ditch it an take to the bush wen the coppers started gainin on us. I'd sure like ta try one a these fuckin army jobs though."

"That's what I was supposed to get," said Turvey, "but I guess a fifteen-hundredweight's bettern a kick in the pants."

Ballard thought a moment. "Hell, *you* know w'ere they keep the M/Cs. Les mosey down ta your grage an have a squint at one ennyways."

"O gosh we gotta be careful; no hellin now."

Ballard smirked and made a smacking noise. "Yuh suckin fer a stripe? Whas eatin yuh? We ain doin nuttin – yet. Sides, this C.O.'s a sof' touch. I'm tellin yuh. They had so many fuckin court-martials at this unit Old Buggernuts knows he'll git the axe hisself if he has many more. C'mon, yer chickenbelly!"

The tempo of events fatally quickened. They happened to find the garage momentarily unguarded by the M.T. Corporal, and a shining khaki-coloured motorcycle with its ignition key in place. Ballard wanted to hear how the bucking motor sounded, and then how it steered, and then how it went on the road. Before Turvey knew quite how it happened he was bouncing on the rear mudguard down the nearby highway behind a crouched catlike figure, at a rate which soon reached the dreamed-of seventy an hour. Ten miles later they were flagged down and placed under close arrest by a forewarned military policeman.

The next day Turvey, in the company of Ballard, again took his cap off for the C.O., and again agreed to take Colonel Stimkin's justice. Turvey, whose offense was deemed the lesser, was heard first, grounded, and given three days' field punishment. It was obvious that the

C.O., who was turning out to be as mild a character as Turvey had seen in the breed, had no taste for the judiciary aspects of his office and in particular wanted to avoid increasing the heavy roster of unit courts-martial. The tone of his voice when he asked Ballard if he too would accept C.O.'s punishment was almost an entreaty.

Ballard looked very cunning, and refused. "Them's serious charges – takin a miltry ve'cle 'thout consent, 'cessive speed, an so on. How much 'ud yuh gimme, colonel?"

"It will have to be twenty-eight days, Ballard. But camp detention only. It's a nice clean brig."

"I know. But I'll take my chance wit a court-martial jus a same. Figger I might swing it."

"You know damn well you wont," said the C.O. "With your record it'll be three months back in the Glasshouse. You dont want that. And I dont want my officers' time taken up with court-martialling you again. Tell you what, I'll let you off with fifteen days."

"Make it seven."

"Fifteen. And say 'sir' to an officer."

"You'll hafta crime the M.T. corp fer leavin the grage unguarded – sir. An the gate-guard fer lettin us outa camp without no check-up, – sir. An the Don/R fer leavin the key in his bike, – sir. An yuh let Turvey down easy, – sir. I'll take a flyer on a court-martial comin unstuck. Sir."

"Seven days," breathed the C.O. wearily, and they were paraded out again, Turvey reflecting that he had much to learn about dealing with Commanding Officers.

He spent the week-end not in London with Peggy as he planned, but meandering through the camp spearing old cigarette cartons and envelopes with a sharpened willow-prong and stuffing them into a great gunny-sack hung around his neck. It was the most agreeable field punishment he had yet encountered, made more pleasant by the sparkling weather and the amiability of his guard, a hut-mate. The latter passed most of the time sleeping under a beech tree, from whose shade Turvey would prod him gently with his willow whenever an NCO appeared on the prowl.

The scene of Turvey's next campaign was the back reaches of the Officers' Mess where he was now detailed as a waiter. He ran quickly into difficulty here as a result of the Admin Major complaining to the Messing Officer about the motheaten bouquets on the tables. The Messing Officer ticked off the steward and the steward tore a strip off Turvey and sent him for fresh posies. Turvey ate his fill of blackberries, watched some rooks and one of the new hush-hush jetplanes soaring, then, time being short, gathered a mixture of rose hips and a lot of shiny flowers which turned out to be deadly nightshade. Although the steward now expressed the opinion that Turvey was a fifth-columnist, he carried on like the good soldier he was until a black Friday in September when he tripped – he could never get used to negotiating a rug-adorned floor while balancing a tray – and shot a mixed charge of hot coffee, prunes and heavy crockery down the length of the C.O.'s table, while Colonel Stimkin was telling his best story to a visiting brigadier. That evening Turvey became a night fireman, and gave up the notion of seeing London again.

He served with some success on this little-publicized front until well into October when he incurred a minor but painful wound from the husky door of a small furnace which malevolently leapt on his right toe from the stove's top where Turvey had unaccountably perched it.

Toe bandaged, it was the one with the old hunting-rifle scar, Turvey was turfed from the QM's office to the Spo to see what he could possibly do now. After a hurried conversation – the Spo seemed to have lost a good deal of his former interest in Turvey – he was sent to the Orderly Room to act as a runner.

For the first few days he found this one of the more

difficult of his military missions but as his old toe-nail worked off and he developed a trick of walking on the outside of his foot, he got quite fond of scuttling between the O.R. and the RAP Hut or the Spo's with little armfuls of documents.

After a while, he grew chummy with Wilcox, one of the O.R. clerks, a fat solemn fellow who had in common with Turvey an unsatisfied hunger to be admitted into the family of an infantry regiment. As he outlined his grievances his liquid eyes would quiver with the spirit of the cheated combatant and his pudgy face would screw itself into the most tremendous scowls. But he was the rare sort of soldier who had never accommodated himself to the army's vocabulary, lacking which a soldier cannot detail his frustrations without further frustration. He had been brought up in rural Ontario by a widowed mother, the solitary boy among a brood of sisters, and he had been taught to swear only by grimace and underlining.

"Do you know what I should be?" he asked Turvey suddenly one day as the latter was basking on a bench near the O.R. stove, while October rains splattered on the greasy asphalt walk outside the window, and ash sticks fluttered and crinkled in the smoky grate. "I should be a platoon sergeant in a real regiment. It's this – this *awful* army. They just wont let me be anything else but a *clerk*." He jerked his head angrily.

"My pal, Mac, is goin to get me into the Okanagan Rangers."

"You believe it when you see it." Wilcox frowned portentously. "Look what happened to me. I asked to go to the Royal Timawgani Rifles when I enlisted. The *very* next day they put me in Documentations at the Depot. It was four months before I could talk my way out of that *dreadful* place to get Basic Training. And when I was only half through Basic the adjutant said there was a shortage of clerks and took me off the field and into his darned old Orderly Room."

"Tch-tch."

"I finally told the Aj, well I just about told him to go jump in the lake, and so then he sent me on to Advanced Training. *But* – they did it to me *all* over again there. So –" he gulped for breath, ducking his double chin, "I just *insisted* on getting marched to the colonel. I did it through the proper channels, of course. He was oh a *very* nice man, really, and he said he would take me right out and send me on a Physical Training course. And so he did. But as soon as I got to the P.T. school and they saw in my documents I was a clerk, bang I was in a –" he wiggled with unwordable resentment – "a *dratted* O.R. again. I just never got that course at *all*, but do you know what I did?" He tilted his chins at Turvey.

"No."

"I threatened to go AWL. Course I wouldnt have, but I guess they thought I just *might*. *So*, they sent me to the Manitoulin Light Infantry and I came overseas with them. But, of course, *they* put me in the O.R. too; I was the only shorthand typist in the regiment. I didnt really have the training for anything else by now, anyway. So this time," he paused for emphasis, "I really did go AWL for . . . a . . . whole . . . . afternoon! They looked *everywhere* in camp for me."

"Where'd you go?"

"I walked right down to a movie matinee in Worthing. So then you *bet* they listened to me, and the C.O. sent me here to get full infantry training. But, wouldnt you know it, right away they grabbed me for the O.R. Told me it would be just for a few days till they got a clerk from H.Q. Humph!" He picked up a rubber stamp. "That was six months ago."

"Why dont you go loose for a *long* time, Wilky? Or, or do somethin really stupid, like mixin up all this bumf, or somethin?"

"Dont be ridic! I *couldnt* do that. I'd just *hate* to see documents mixed up." He looked protectively at the heap of files on his desk. "And I'd lose pay if I went *really* AWL. And I wouldnt be in line for my Good Conduct stripe. The C.O. didnt charge me for that afternoon I went away, you see, so I have a clean MFM6. I dont see how I could ever do it again. But sometimes I get so *vexed* –'' He held his breath, bounced the rubber stamp viciously on the ink-pad, and went back to work.

Turvey found Wilcox hard to figure out. He looked like a natural for the fussy bookkeeping routine of an Orderly Room but he would rather be helling around over the downs with a pack, and sleeping out in the rain. Turvey felt sympathetic and wondered what he could do to help Wilcox get out of the Orderly Room.

First he thought that if Wilcox lost his ambition to be a badgeman, all might be well. He tried to cut him in on a thriving little market in Canadian cigarettes and flogged army blankets that had developed between Turvey's hut and the *Duck and Maiden.* Wilcox would have none of it. Turvey took him to another pub to get him tight. Wilcox drank only stone ginger. Finally he lured him into a casual foray on a neighbouring orchard after supper one evening, when he found that Wilcox, who had been brought up in fruit country, was hungry for apples and didnt consider orchard-raiding a crime. He didnt tell Wilcox that the nimble Constable of Lesser Hensfold had taken a scunner against the unit and would certainly be on the lookout.

But Wilcox seemed to have an unlucky kind of luck which protected his reputation. The constable did trail and surprise them, but damned if Wilcox didnt instantly convert himself from clerk to commando. ''Phooey on you,'' he screeched from his treetop, and conked the policeman with a specially large Cox Orange pippin. Then he scrambled down and without losing another apple from his bulging blouse, somehow vaulted both a hedge and the accordion wire on the top of it and scampered down the lane unidentified.

It was Turvey who was treed, and fined by the local magistrate for trespass. Since there had been a lot of orchard-raiding lately, followed by complaints from the civil authorities to the CIRU, the C.O. decided he couldnt appease them without cancelling Turvey's weekend pass to London and substituting one to the guard house. On Monday the adjutant, feeling Turvey was an unsettling influence on his prize clerk and noting that the period of Turvey's grounding was up, tried to bully the Transport Officer into taking Turvey back as a driver. The T.O. declared he wouldnt have him for a spare windshield-wiper. After sounding out every other officer with equal luck, the adjutant sent Turvey back to the Spo.

It chanced that the Spo had just received an urgent message from his own very urgent colonel in London telling him to locate a driver in his unit (any driver, so long as he had two hands and two feet) and persuade the colonel of the CIRU to release him for posting to Number Two Special Defense Unit. Since the letter was unexplainably but clearly marked SECRET in numerous places, the Spo first swore Turvey to keep it all mum and then told him he would, as a very great favour, try to post him as a driver to a most interesting unit.

"Okanagan Rangers?"

"No, but I'm not allowed to tell you anything more about it, Private Turvey."

"Do I get to drive a really big truck, please, sir?"

"You'll get a – uh, vehicle. But now you mustnt say anything about it to anyone. It's Security."

"Not even to the C.O.?"

"Well, uh – what do you want to see Colonel Stimkin for?"

"O, I dont sir, but you never know."

"You just keep out of trouble till I get you out of here and you wont have to see the C.O. Are you willing to volunteer?"

Turvey wondered if the Spo were planning to drop him behind the German lines. All this secrecy was exciting, anyway. He was willing.

Within a few days he was bouncing along once more in

an army truck, this time heading southwest through bleak November skies. After many winding miles Turvey's secret mission creaked into an isolated set of farm buildings on a high Hampshire down within sight of the Channel. Turvey's martial temperature, which had been rising with each mile, climbed almost to boiling point when he discovered the agricultural appearance of his new home was a camouflage concealing a busy little flamethrowing outfit, complete with dozens of hidden storage tanks, coils of snaky big hose, a number of oddly-rigged Bren carriers, and one or two fantastic grasshopper-like Flammenwurfers lurking under an old tile-roofed cowshed.

His temperature cooled a little the next morning when he was assigned to driving neither a Flammenwurfer nor a carrier but just another army truck like the ones at the CIRU. His main job was hauling supplies to the "farm" from the sleepy country station a mile away. And, more frustrating still, he ran truckloads of the gallant human flamethrowers themselves each morning over a makeshift road across the down to their training operations; and he trundled them home at night. The wasps, or converted carriers, were kept permanently under hay-screens on the official battlefield for Reasons Of Security. The smaller throwers were carried like lifebuoys on the soldiers' backs. They reminded Turvey of his mosquito-control days in the swamps west of Banff.

The first morning that Turvey drove out with one of these human cargoes – every man in crash-helmet with mica eyepieces, asbestos-lined coveralls, and a tire-sized tank on his back – he was amazed when one of the Buck Rogers figures hailed him by name and doffed his helmet. It was Eric, the smaller of the two Icelanders Turvey had last seen at the Basic Training Centre in Ontario.

"You lucky stiff," said Turvey as Eric climbed into the front beside him, "how'd *you* get here?"

"What do you mean, lucky? They told me I was going to be a chemist." Eric went on to explain that the unit

had first been labelled Number One Special Chemical
Company and the Security boys in Ottawa had done too
good a job of keeping it dark that the outfit was to train
for offensive chemical warfare. Certainly the PSO at the
Advanced Training Centre had thought this would be
Eric's natural home since Eric had taken first year
Chemistry at the University of Saskatchewan. "We've
even got Ph.D.s in Bio-Chemistry for officers, and are
they cheesed off! Thought they were going to fight with
test-tubes."

"Are they all chemists?"

"O, no, but the rest are browned off too, because
there's bugger all to do."

"Nothing to do! With flamethrowers?"

"Well, it's fun for a few days," Eric admitted, "but
these lifebuoys weigh a ton. And you soon learn to press
the tit and hose the stuff around. Then what? You sweat
it out in these goon suits, and there's nobody to frizzle.
We burned all the rabbits out of their holes in the first
month. There's more on the other hill but we cant get at
em."

"They run too fast?"

"Nah. We aint allowed to take the throwers off the
farm. Security."

"Dont anybody know we're here?" asked Turvey
breathlessly.

"Just the whole damn countryside. You can smell that
stuff for miles, and it throws up big clouds of soot; when
we had night manoeuvres they started ringing the church-
bells twenty miles away in Portsmouth. Thought it was
an invasion. Sure, everybody knows what we're doing.
But it's still Top Secret."

"So what you do now there aint no more rabbits?"

"We've been burning our initials in the grass. It's good
training, I guess. I can do an E real straight and clear.
But now we got the whole damn hillside black. So we just
shoot a few bursts and sit on our fannies the rest of the

morning. Same after lunch. Fuel's scarce as hen's teeth now, anyway. SM says it nicks the taxpayers a hundred bucks every time we squirt a quickie. And a real typewriting costs a grand. Sometimes I wonder if we'll ever get to fry a single Jerry. I sure as hell missed out on Iceland."

"Still sounds more fun to me than drivin this dinky truck," Turvey sighed. "Say, Eric, what happened to Emil?"

"O Emil's doing O.K. He's an anxiety neurotic now, so they keep him at the District Depot and he can billet at home."

"Gosh, that's one job I never heard of before. Does he get trades' pay?"

"It aint a job, Tops, it's a new kind of illness. You aint really sick but you think you are, and you worry about it till you just about are. Emil's on General Duties. They wont give him the gate because they dont think he thinks he's that sick, you see. But he's kind of sore about it, last letter I had, because he thinks he is."

"Is what?"

"That sick."

"O, sure," said Turvey vaguely, wondering just where he had lost the thread.

Despite Eric's disillusionment, Turvey continued to hope he might graduate from his truck to the sooty field of action so tantalizingly close. The chill November days droned by, however, exciting stories filtered through of Canadian battlings in Italy, and Turvey remained chained to a fifteen-hundredweight.

One foggy afternoon in December the M.T. Sergeant told him to report back to the garage after supper for a night job. Some Ladies' Guild over at High Puddling was throwing a dance-social just for Canadian soldiers and, though it was twenty-nine miles away, Number Two Special Defense Unit had been ordered by the brigadier to provide its quota of thirty. The communication specified privates only and thirty of the species had been detailed accordingly. This was too many for one lorry, and another driver and vehicle were to accompany Turvey.

"You'll have to lead, Turvey," the sergeant added. "Only other driver I can get for tonight is that new fellow, Cripps. He dont know the roads."

The M.T. Corporal standing by ventured to remind his sergeant that two vehicles constituted a convoy and according to the book required an NCO. "I know the way, and I dont mind going along," he added, somewhat too casually.

"You're not gallivantin to any buggery dance tonight. You know damn well we'll need every driver in the place for the Officers' Mess shindig. Major Flannelhead's off up to Surrey already with his gin palace to get that piece of homework of his and there's a flock of dames comin in on the six-fifteen from London you and the other drivers'll have to taxi. Dances. The whole goddamn Canadian Army dont do nothin but dance these days. Every fuckin ve'cle a passion wagon. Turvey and Cripps will take the 'hundredweights."

"Supposin the Aj or M.T.O. sees the trucks goin out without a non-com, though," the corporal persisted.

The sergeant was in a hurry. "Balls, they're all tyin one on in the mess by now. Anyway, Turvey can be actin-lance-jack. I got some extra hooks in my hut. You see me right after supper, Turvey, and I'll pin one on your great-coat."

Turvey's round face dimpled with joy. "Gee, you mean I'm a real NCO now?" It was the first time anybody in the army had thought of promoting him. He didnt realize it was so easy.

"Sure, sure. Just for the trip, of course. And *acting*-lance, – get it? *Without* pay. And by God you remember to take the stripe off as soon as you get back. It's on the q.t. and dont really count."

Even these limitations scarcely lessened Turvey's new pride of office. When he rolled out of the camp gate that night, conscious of Cripps and his truck following dutifully, no general felt more masterly. But the troubles of generalship were soon his too. For fear that the sergeant would change his mind and take him off the expedition, Turvey had not confessed that the road to High Puddling, after the pub at the third mile, was as strange to him as the road to Lhasa. Moreover, the sea-fog was now billowing in, obliterating even the roundtopped flint walls on the roadsides. And to cap it, there was an alert and they had to switch off all lights.

It took them fifteen mintues, nose to tail, to make the pub and, since both truckloads were unanimous that beer was necessary before facing further perils, it was another half-hour before they set off again, primed with somewhat too many directions from the proprietor. Before long they came to an unpredicted road-fork.

There were no signs, and Turvey discovered neither he nor Cripps had remembered to bring maps. Two soldiers in the back who had once been as far as Puddling Green were equally certain of the route. One wanted to take the right fork, the other the left. They tossed for it and went left a mile, coming to a crossroads. After some stumbling about in the misty darkness Turvey found a weatherbeaten sign pointing right to Middle Puddling. But Eric, one of the destined dancers, whom Turvey had arranged to ride in front with him, pointed out cannily that Middle and High Puddling might be miles apart and, anyway, during the invasion scare all road indicators had either been taken down or twisted to point wrong. He thought they should turn left. Then a soldier in Cripps' truck who was sure he knew the way argued them into going straight ahead. The road shortly petered out at what seemed to be a chalk-quarry on the coast. All the Puddlings were miles inland.

Turvey drove back to the crossroads and took the way the Middle Puddling sign pointed. After he had crawled along blind for another mile, he realized that somewhere in the shuffle he had lost the following truck. They drew

up and waited, but fifteen minutes passed and Cripps and
his cargo failed to appear. Not a sound of any car, not a
light, not a dog's bark. Turvey managed to turn his truck
around and feel his way back to the crossroads. No
Cripps. He tried the third road, strayed into a farm lane,
backed out, and droned along on second to a pub which
several soldiers recognized as being leagues off the route.
It was now ten o'clock; the dance had started an hour
ago. Turvey and his fifteen adjourned to the light of the
inn for a council of war.

Since the public room was warm, and contained three
Land Army girls, there was not much difficulty in
deciding to settle down and shoot the breeze until the fog
lifted.

Turvey, whose one stripe shone out in this company,
soon became mately with the least pimply of the girls
and, when he discovered they had to leave almost at once
to walk the two miles to their hostel before eleven, he
gallantly put the services of himself and truck at their disposal. With the ladies, Eric (who had come to discover
Women overseas), another compatriot, and a dozen
bottles of ale, Turvey set off, assuring the remainder of
his flock that he would be back for them promptly at
eleven, when the pub closed. But what with British fog
and the blackout around him, British beer inside, the
pneumatic warmth of Bertha, close beside him in the
front seat, and the confusion of crossroads and twisting
lanes that immediately descended upon him, Turvey
managed to get so thoroughly lost within a few minutes,
that even the Land Girls werent sure where they were and
didnt seem to care. An attempt to return to the stranded
thirteen at the pub ended when Turvey ran out of gas.
There was a blanket in the back for each of the men and
for Acting-Lance-Corporal Turvey, and the sextette
managed, despite the continuing fog and chill, to pass a
fairly cosy night.

But this proved to be Turvey's last battle as a chemical
warfarer. Some of the abandoned thirteen who had

shivered through the dark in an outbuilding of a farm-house behind the pub were too annoyed to remain loyal to Acting-Lance-Corporal Turvey when they were rescued the next day, and the story of the Land Girls came out. Since the Land Army was an auxiliary military unit the adjutant was not able to charge Turvey with unauthorized transportation of civilians in an army vehicle, but he did stick him for thirteen hours AWL (it was afternoon before Turvey and his two mates got back), retaining an army vehicle without permission, conduct to the prejudice of good order and military discipline, wearing rank insignia without rank entitlement (he had forgotten after all to take his stripe off), and consumption of alcoholic beverages on army property, to wit a fifteen-hundredweight. After the usual session with the C.O., a tougher gentleman than Colonel Stimkin, Turvey found himself grounded for another three months, refused the week's leave aleady overdue, and slated to spend Christmas and New Year's in the camp brig. When he emerged from these quarters he was promptly returned to Number Twenty CIRU as a hard case.

Here he was interviewed again by his old acquaintance, the Spo, and in consequence served a brief campaign as a handyman sorting boots in QM Stores. Turvey felt this was a bit of a demotion but he comforted himself with the thought that even General McNaughton was being shoved around by this time. At January's end he was suddenly transferred without explanation to another CIRU, in Aldershot, and interviewed by a new Spo there. The latter, after a long and puzzled sifting of Turvey's overseas file, which had now grown as thick as the one that was lost somewhere in Canada, asked Turvey if he'd ever tried working as a batman.

"We're very shorthanded for batmen just now. Dont forget you get an extra two-bits a day, and living quarters with the officers. Officers' food too. Of course you dont have to take it. All batmen are volunteers. You seem to have tried everything else though. Only other job for you

right now would be General Duties. Scrubbing floors,
cleaning out latrines, you know; things like that.'' Turvey
volunteered to be a batman.

The Corporal Batman to whom he reported that afternoon showed him his palliasse in the batmen's room, a
dark cement corner in the basement of a brick barracks
which the British had built at the end of the Crimean
War. He was given the room numbers of four officers on
the first floor to whom he should report for duty after
supper.

Lining up for his hash, Turvey was pleased to find,
among his fellow-batmen, none other than Roach, hero
of the assault course at Number Umpteen Basic Training
Centre. Roach had at last got overseas when his documents had been lost, including his O-score. After the
usual biographical exchanges Roach persuaded Turvey
that it would be time enough to report to his four bosses
in the morning.

''The pricks'll only make you clean a pile a shoes for
em, an they wont know till tomorrow you been laid on
anyways. There's a coupla pubs in The 'Shot youghta
sample.''

They ambled down into town, past sedate Canadian
NCOs pushing baby carriages beside buxom English
wives. Before closing time they managed to visit six of
Aldershot's more prominent public houses and rolled out
of the last one in comradely contentment. There was a
raid on now, near enough for ack-ack fragments to be
clattering on the tile roofs. On the way up the long hill-
street to their martial eyrie the two, not surprisingly,
developed a considerable amount of bladder pressure.
Roach contrived to relieve himself without incident
behind a piece of ornamental shrubbery in a private
lawn. Turvey tried to imitate his example but, just as he
was set, a chandelier flare lit up the whole town, and
froze his muscles. He was the sort who had never been
able to produce little samples for the M.O. on demand.
After the flare died there was still such a thump-

thumping of batteries, and bursting of ack-ack like high fireworks, and crrumphing of bombs that, when Roach finally guided him into the batmen's cavern, Turvey found himself still with his problem.

"Upstairs, turn ri', las' door on lef'," said Roach sleepily as he rolled boots and all onto his palliasse. There was only the dimmest of bulbs over the stair and none in the corridor. Turvey stumbled down it until he came to a blank wall and turned the doorknob on the left. There was no light in the room except a diffusion from the window, whose blackout curtain had been rolled up. Sober enough to remember that he mustnt switch on the light and violate air-raid precautions he stood trying to feel where the toilet was, when a muffled snore startled him. It seemed to be right in the w.c. Showed how thin these darned partitions were. Must be an officer sleeping up against the wall in the next room. Stretching his hands out Turvey shuffled forward, urged now by desperate need. His left fingers encountered smooth flat wood, almost like a wide chair-arm. Yes, here was the other arm; one of these English johns with a big wooden seat. No time to lift it. Ahhhhh. But just as Turvey began to think it odd that the sound was of liquid descending on cloth rather than on liquid, there was a sudden creaking of bedsprings between him and the window and a voice, husky with sleep and puzzled alarm, shouted:

"What's going on? Who's that? What the bloody –" Then, as Turvey's tired bladder muscles leapt once more into control, the voice changed to a roar of rage and Turvey fled from the bedroom down the corridor, one hand still fumbling vainly with his fly. Halfway to the stairwell he was brought low by a sinewy pair of arms.

The new C.O., to whom Turvey explained next day that he had turned left instead of right at the top of the stairs, was not impressed. He told Turvey he was a King's Bad Bargain and fined him five dollars for drunkenness. Then he relegated him to the brig for two weeks for wandering around billets after lights out and committing a nuisance in a public place, to wit, the sleeping quarters of Major Thornton, M.C., O.C. Training Wing. There was some talk also of his having to buy a new pair of khaki serge trousers for the major in place of the ones that had been so neatly folded in the lap of the big chair by his bed. But Turvey managed to clean them satisfactorily and the C.O. contented himself with promising Turvey he would get him out of the unit so fast, once he came out of brig, he wouldnt have time to look for a W.C. in his camp again.

Turvey had scarcely settled down to pack-drill and floor-scrubbing in the unit's detention barracks, however, when the tide of battle suddenly changed in his favour and, it might be said, in favour of his C.O. It was a somewhat miraculous shift of fortune since it took the form of an official request from the Commanding Officer of the Okanagan Rangers for the posting of Private Turvey to that regiment. What gave it the genuine touch of miracle was an accompanying document, signed by one Private Turvey, William Rockefeller, who stated himself to be a kinsman of Private Turvey, Thomas Leadbeater, anxious to avail himself of the privilege of an older brother to claim young Thomas for service in his unit. Turvey dimly remembered that one of his half-brothers was a William but he had never seen him and was therefore all the more puzzled as well as touched that William should have reached out a fraternal hand at so timely an hour.

Supported by one of His Majesty's travel warrants and relays of directions from station guards, Turvey shortly advanced through Surrey and most of Sussex, dug in temporarily in the quiet station of Wartle-on-Chick, was rescued by a fifteen-hundredweight, penetrated between two roly-poly downs, and halted among a conglomeration of mottled tents scattered through a twilit oak grove within sound of the Channel waves.

The unit was so small that the Orderly Room was only

a large tent and for the first time in his experience there wasnt a Spo within sight. Nor, for that matter, were Mac or the mysterious William. There was no time to look for them. He was rushed through the O.R., issued with a sleeping bag, and assigned to a tarpaulin for quarters. For the first time Turvey fancied he sniffed something like the atmosphere of real war.

The runner who piloted him to his shelter had never heard of any Private Turveys. There was a Sergeant Mac-Gillicuddy though – and at that moment Mac descended on him, adorned with three stripes, and talking faster than ever:

"Ah, there, Tops old man. Welcome to the Battle of Sussex. Told you I'd get you with the Rangers. Splendid body of fighters. Hope you can live up to the traditions. Every one of us a bottle-a-day man. What's new?"

"Wonderful to see you, you old honyak," Turvey said somewhat abstractedly, since events were crowding rather thickly upon him, "but it's my brother got me down here. We'd better go find him."

"Dear old Tops. Havent changed a bit. No gratitude! Brother indeed! You're looking at him. Sergeant MacGillicuddy at your service. Finest brother you ever had. *Buck* Sergeant, please note. Headquarters Platoon. Happened to be getting my chuck or I'd have spotted you when you came in."

"Yeh, sure, Mac. Congrats. S'wonderful. But I better go look up Bill, my half-brother, you know. He claimed me."

"Tops, brace yourself for a loss in the family. Half-brother Bill; no longer with us. Gone west. In fact, he, he – never was. That is, you probably *did* have a fractional brother Bill – or did you now?"

"A course I did. He signed a claim for me from this regiment. I seen it!"

"Little deal between Aj and humble servant, Tops. Tried several ways of worming you out of that mouldy

CIRU but no soap. So we filled out older-brother claim-slips. Adjutant signed for colonel one day when Old Man away. I signed for dear brother Bill. Seemed to remember you saying one of your half-brothers was a Bill. He *could* have been here. Colonel wont mind, *if* he twigs. Wants reinforcements. Scarce as beefsteak. And Aj will cover up, knows I'll do it for him next time he's swacked."

"You been havin casualties?" Turvey asked, quickly recovering from the loss of his kin. This was going to be even more exciting than he thought.

"Casualties? Good Lord, yes, every day. Chap cracked his toe only last week. Tripped in a rabbit-hole coming off guard. Great loss. He was i.c. latrines. *And* a pom."

"What's a pom?"

"Potential Officer Material. Never heard of it? We're lousy with it. Then QMS carted off yesterday to hospital, poor fellow; Section Corporal day before. Piles, both of em. Battle wastage. War is hell, Private Turvey. I'm on my knees myself. Masses of rheumatism. But carry on. Keep the old flag flapping. Reminds me. Get Stores to give you regimental flash for that martial shoulder of yours. Shuck that flaming arsehole you're wearing." He pointed to the maple leaf in the yellow circle on Turvey's upper sleeve, the badge of the unregimented soldier in a reinforcement unit.

"Sure will," said Turvey. Gosh, he thought, a real Ranger! It's at least halfway to being a Highlander.

Neither the March winds, which continued through April, nor the April rains, which began in March and brought out white daisies and little peagreen leaves everywhere, could squelch Turvey's conviction that he had at last reached the potential battlefront. For one thing, he had never negotiated a latrine before that was called a Musical Chair and was just a peeled pole suspended over a pit. And now he wore a beret instead of a wedge-cap, had exercises with smoke bombs and live ammo that went A-BOWW, and threw grenades and worked a Piat and a two-inch mortar – until it was thought wiser for the general welfare that he learn how to dig a new latrine pit. The conviction mounted within him each day as he saw more convoys of tanks and guns crashing down the seaward roads, and heard new rumours of the Second Front, and tried to memorize new and more elaborate pre-invasion instructions to the Okanagan Rangers. Beauforts rushed comet-like and fleets of Lancasters groaned far above them daily. When the whole unit spread out in May along the Channel cliffs, abandoned tents, and rose to a bugle at 0530 from a single frosted blanket and a groundsheet, and ran in dank clothes two miles before breakfast, even Mac abandoned his skepticism and agreed that something was going to happen. Air-raid precautions were doubled and no leaves granted. Barbed wire was strung around the unit area. Turvey had to deposit with the QMS the long woollies Peggy had given him and scrap his souvenir piece from a Heinkel propeller, to reduce his kit to assault size. When even the nearest pub and finally the nearest farmhouse, where he had been getting to know one of the farmer's daughters, were placed out of bounds, Turvey began to taste not only the thrills but the privations of modern warfare.

There were disappointing aspects to their instructions, however, which Mac was quick to point out. "Shouldnt get your balls in an uproar, Topsy, old man," he said one evening in early June just before Turvey was setting off, shiny-eyed, with his Section Corporal, for night guard post on the cliffs. "Be sitting on our fannies when the big push starts. Havent you noticed? We're getting no assault boat training. Strictly land animals. D-Day units all assembling down the coast now, jumping in and out of LCs."

"But gee, we got shell-dressin issue Friday, and water-proofin kits, and, and that new anti-German battledress!"

"Anti-*vermin*, dough-head. Take it from me. Grapevine. I hear things in the O.R. Old Man told the Aj we're for Counter-Invasion, blast it. Strictly Security, of course. Keep it up your frock."

"O, sure," said Turvey, "but what kind of invasion's that?"

"Bugger all, my boy. Means we park here crosslegged in the bluebells. As Yorkshireman said to parrot, 'Thou's been 'ad by a duck.' Course if Jerry takes a notion to beat us to the draw or tries diversion raids on Sussex, we've had it. Get your bellyful of ammo then, old man. But Jerry's not that crazy. Might as well relax. Wonderful weather. Lilacs out. Rhoddies. Larks singing heads off. Lap up while you can. You'll die of diarrhoea yet. Heard the one about Lord Chumly and the new butler –"

But when Turvey padded off behind Corporal Boggs like a stealthy Indian, he was still convinced that any moment now a shoal of landing craft would appear below the cliffs and chug him straight to Berlin. Huge fleets of RAF bombers had been pulsing over all day, as for the past three weeks, their exhaust trails under the high clouds looking like shipwakes in an upsidedown sea. Now as darkness descended, the great droning birds, in smaller, more fitful groups, or singly, sometimes with sputtering motors, were moving back like stars into English skies. Turvey and the corporal, clutching brand-new Stens, nestled themselves on each side of a broom bush halfway down the cliff in a shallow ravine which fanned out below them into a dim cove. The Channel glimmered in starlight and a monotonous succession of dark wavelets nudged themselves into oblivion on the beach.

"Jeez, I wish I were back in Badger Tooth tonight," Boggs mumbled, sighing and settling back under the broom, having already stowed his Sten between two rocks.

Turvey could have wished for a more sympathetic companion on such an occasion. Boggs was very disappointing. He was one of the redoubtable tribe known as P.F.ers or Permanent Forcemen, a member of Canada's pint-sized professional army, and Turvey had expected him to be a regular fire-eater. Instead, Boggs was about the tiredest soldier he had ever struck.

"Golly, I'm glad I'm right here," said Turvey. "Why the Jerries might try to land in this cove anytime. Right tonight, just as we're sittin here!"

There was a superior sniff from Boggs in the darkness. "I bloody well hope not. We'd be up Shit Creek if they did, 'thout a paddle too. Couldn' run fast enough to get outa here fore they potted us. Aint enough cover."

"I bet we could mow em down before they even got out of the boat."

"So what? They'd jus be more of em." Boggs paused, and went on, his voice languidly philosophical: "Watcha wana get n'a shootin match for anyways? Watcha allus dreamin of fightin Jerries for?"

Turvey felt stumped at first by such a question. He thought it over: "That's what we come over here for, werent it? That's what we joined the army for, aint it?"

Boggs yawned. "Mebbe you did." He shifted himself into a more comfortable position. "I joined for a good place to sleep n'eat thout havin ta work m'ass off. That was in 37. Dint figger on no crappy war then."

"But gee whiz, you gotta have a war or they wouldnt have no army for you to join. Like you couldnt get to play baseball if they werent havin games."

"Well, why not jus games then, for an army too?" Boggs argued equably. "Frinstance, take me. I don mind this p'rade-square stuff an the spit'n-polish you fellers r'always beefin 'bout. An gasperators and Sunday-mornin Knee Drill. R'even the RSM's p'rade. Square-bashin's somepn to do, an af'er you get the hang of it there's worse ways a makin a livin, 'less there's too much of it. 'R take summer trainin camps, 'r manoeuvres'n night schemes. Though marchin aint my favourite. It binds me. Sittin, that's what I really like. And you c'n get a lot of sittin in an army. Back in Can'da, that is. But comin all a way over ta *this* jeezly place to sit on a cliff waitin ta get plugged by some fuckin German, while some fuckin zombie in Badger Tooth is probly in bed with my old woman – no sir, I don' see it, I don' see it *a* tall.''

Turvey brooded, trying to find the flaw in Boggs' logic. "Well, you see," he said after a while, "I aint married.''

"Naw,'' Boggs conceded, "but yaint armour-plated either. You c'n stop a bullet as easy as me. All this god-dam shootin and pig-stickin, thas what tears it. An bombs'n mortars, an booby traps yuh gotta delouse. An rockets'n poison gas an – an droppin bugs from planes and cri' knows what all. 'S no percentage in it. I wish ta jeez sometimes I'd jus stayed a bum.''

"Was that what you were doin before you went P.F.?''

"Yeah. Bummin round. Played hockey one year, semi-pro, but mosta time I lived off the ole man till the ole jeezer made me take a job in a grage he was a partner in. Borin fuckin cyl'nder heads all day. Couldn even sid-down t'it. Thas when I hit the freights.'' He plopped a pebble aimlessly over the cliff. "'S fate, I guess.''

"I guess everythin is kinda that,'' said Turvey, begin-ning to fall under Boggs' metaphysical spell. There was a long silence during which Turvey grew conscious again of the lapping waves and the mysterious rustle of wind in the broom flowers.

"If I'd tossed tails stead of heads, I'd still be in Can'da, I bet,'' Boggs said suddenly, as if seeing clearly into the tangled web of his days for the first time. "I took up with a sidekick, see, an one day we got tossed off a freight in some yards near Camp Shiloh an my pal had a brother was a P.F. Corporal there. So we looked him up for a touch, though Wart, that was the guy I was with, he dint like his brother any too much and I hadda talk him int'it. Well, anyway, I kina liked this corporal myself, an he looked pretty well-fed'n give us a big line 'bout the ar-my. I begun ta think I was jus a sucker ridin the rods. Was 37, you know, still purry tough.''

"Your darned tootin! I was ridin em in 38.''

"Oke. Well, you know how that recruitin shit sounded.

Three squares'n a real bed. No worry 'bout lookin for a job or losin one. Learn a trade free an get exter trades' pay. Reg'lar promotion. I started fallin for it. Wart was the smart one, he wouldn bite. But we kina dint like to break up, kina fonda each other. So we decided ta toss for it. Tails, we both go in. Heads, we both hit the freights again. An tails it was, two outa three. So the corp he gets busy for us – they was a recruitin drive on jus then – an got us all set. Then Wart, night fore we was ta be sworn in, he bogged off. Grabbed an empty I guess. Never seen nor heard a him since. But I bet he's sleepin 'na soft bed in Can'da right now. An not alone, neither. Smart guy." Boggs spat softly over the cliff.

"But holy smoke," Turvey had had time to marshal some arguments, "if we all stayed home like that, who'd down the Germans and, and Eyeties and Japs?"

"Well, if we gave em the wire we was stayin home, praps they would too. I bet most a them Jerry soldiers like tup-threein'n goose-steppin round the playground, an Naffy-time breaks, an sleepin home at nights, a buckin sight better'n gettin a mess a Sten slugs in 'ir guts, jus like you an me."

"But we gotta fight fascism and – and, for democracy and, and things."

"Me, I don' wanna fight nobody. Aint no future in it. I love peace, see. The Sitz. That was a best part a the war. Jus sittin. Thas what I love bes'. Oney at home, where's a fuckin sight dryer on the ass, and I c'n get my tail reglar."

"Well," Turvey sighed, "mebbe you're right." He stared at the dim Channel, dimmer now that there was a low mist creeping over the water from France. The waves were getting bigger. Every once in a while a really big one would swell in. "There's lots of girls over here, though."

"Horse shit. They're all dosed, the bitches. The two I slep with anyway. Two trips to the V.D. Ward, thas what I got out a it. Roemance!" Boggs gaped. "Built like brick shithouses they was too."

"Well, you get free safes in the army." He was about

to add "and prolifaxes", but a painful memory intruded.

Boggs yawned. "I cant never be bothered with socks."
He yawned again, wriggled himself into a khaki coil, and
was soon asleep.

Turvey sat for a long time watching the waves curve
out of the mist onto the beach. The occasional large ones
still would give him a start; with the growing murkiness,
each could so easily be the stealthy prow of an enemy
raider, the first scouting craft of a German invasion of
Britain. Somehow he didnt feel as happy about the
possibility as he had thought he would. Far away the
complaining murmur of a big bomber grew to a drone.
Among the steady stars a gliding one, passing over,
homeward bound from some scene of lightning and
death. Turvey shivered. He wondered what it felt like to
stop a bullet where, he had learned a few days ago,
Calvin Busby had got one at Cassino. It occurred to him
that somewhere just a few miles across the foggy strait
some Jerry private might be thinking much the same
thoughts. It mightnt be very long before one or other of
them would be dead. Both of them. Turvey had a sudden
acute desire to be lying warmly in the upstairs bedroom
on the old Skookum Falls farm. The first strawberries
would be ripe about now. But there would be cucumbers
too, and the fuzz on the leaves that got under his finger-
nails.

Was that – that must really be a boat! But no – it was
just another wave.

TEN

Turvey Is Considered for Knighthood

THAT EVENING hundreds of bombers moved high and steady across the sky, like letters on a teletype, and their deep throbbing, as night came down, seemed to fill the world and well out of the earth itself. From midnight on, bombardments flashed on the French coast. And in the warm dawn a whole division of troop-carrying gliders paraded slowly over the camp, two by two, some so low Turvey waved at pilots in the tow-planes. This must be it! And it was. At 0930 the radio in RHQ crackled out Eisenhower's announcement. D-Day.

After supper, Turvey was summoned to the Orderly Tent by Mac. He was holding a roll-sheet at arm's length, as if it were a rattlesnake. His lean face was dark with rage. It was the first time Turvey had seen Mac really angry. "Of all the cockeyed armies, this one takes the fucking cake. Bad enough sitting here. But now – now! – on *D*-Day! – they're sending me all the way to Buckinghamshire to make me into a bloody officer." Mac paused for breath and looked wildly at Turvey; the sight of him seemed to restore the sardonic light in his black eyes. "What puts the plush-lined cork in it, Tops – *you're* coming too."

"Me?" said Turvey. "O no! I'm goin over to Normandy. The corporal give me a pamphlet this mornin all about how I gotta behave myself in occupied France."

For answer Mac passed him the roll-sheet order a

Despatch Rider had just brought in. It announced that Sergeant MacGillicuddy and twelve other Okanagan Rangers (including Turvey, Private Thomas Leadbeater) would proceed immediately to Number Three Canadian Testing Panel for the usual three-day appraisal. "Serves you bloody right for applying," said Mac, grabbing the paper back and hauling him out of the tent with him.

"But gosh I didnt ask to be a nofficer! I aint even a lance-corporal yet!" They were walking back to Turvey's lines, the noise of Normandy guns tantalizing their ears.

"Dope! Remember about three months ago? Unit parade. Everybody ordered to fill out forms, from the RSM down to you. No crime-sheet barred. Well, some screwball's gone and taken it seriously. And it's Top Priority. Got us by the short and curlies. To hell with a little thing like D-Day!"

In the early morning train next day, Mac gave Turvey and the rest of the compartment his reconstruction of the events leading up to the catastrophe. "The scene, fellow-victims, is London; nice airy room in CMHQ. Half a dozen purple brigadiers in confab – AAGs Three and Five, let's make it; at least one general; chest and shoulder hardware everywhere. Civvy steno, with a lush pair of charlies, taking notes. General with five-row fruit salad tells em Ottawa wont send any more new officers. One brig figures exact number of loots to be killed between D-Day and next Christmas. Engineering Bigshot whips out sliderule, shows em they'll have to promote every third corporal overseas to supply deficiencies. Admin Brasscock says unit colonels wont let their good NCOs go. Another Redflannel, full of piss and vinegar, brother-in-law of the general, has memo ready for issue to Commanding Officers all overseas units, threatening em, pain of something or other, to let every NCO and private in army fill out officer application if he wants to. General says that's just the job and they give it to the steno to straighten out the grammar. Then they knock off, Royal Auto Club, to hoist a few.''

"But why did we *all* have to sign it if they only wanted one in three?" asked Randy Crane, who had been following Mac's analysis solemnly.

"Ah, that was our C.O. Took a poor view of it, and quite right. Wanted his sergeants, tried and true, for Do-and-Die Day. Keep Rangers at battle strength. So he played safe, made everybody apply; *but* he signed the recommendation line for only thirteen. But why *this* thirteen, only God and the colonel –"

"Hold your hosses," said Flighty Bagshaw, an RHQ clerk, suddenly. "*I* know which ones the Old Man recommended because I saw em before they went out. And you want to know somepn? He didnt sign for a bloody one of this crew. Not one!"

"Ah, calls for slight revision in Situation Report," Mac went on unperturbed. "Applications go up to CMHQ, see, masses of em, every overseas unit. Pile up in hallways. Fatter brigs cant get past. Complain. Junior officer told to sort out recommended files, stack rest in basement. So makes clerk do it. Long job. Teatime, clerk bored rigid, wool-gathering, shoves rejected Okey Rangers in accepted heap, puts C.O.'s recs in basement. Right? Only hole in theory is – C.O. must have passed *me* over. Improbable, I suppose, except, yes, of course – he wanted to keep best sergeants with regiment! Explains how my dear old Mucking-in Pal Turvey's with us, and I wont have a word against him."

"By God," said Crane slowly, "it could be."

Whatever the reason, by early afternoon the thirteen were detraining at a quiet Buckinghamshire way-stop. They bounced in a big sixty-hundredweight past a field with sleepy cows and a mouse-coloured donkey, under pylon wires neatly arranged with sparrows, and beside cosy gardens dripping with roses and tiger lilies. Then they crowded against a box hedge while a covey of Tiger tanks went whang-clanging by. They turned by a stone keeper's lodge into a grove of oak, and up a long elm-way to a high turreted mansion surrounded by lawns and flower beds.

"Cripes," said Mac, "this cant be for us." It wasnt. Their vehicle veered around the back to the usual tin-town, a collection of corrugated Nissen huts lying like black caterpillars among the greenery. Just beyond were lawn-tennis courts with a sign OUT OF BOUNDS TO OTHER RANKS.

After stowing their kit into the twilight of one of the caterpillars and scoffing a late lunch in another, they were paraded, along with an assortment of candidates who had arrived earlier, on to a clipped lawn bordered with tall spikes of lupins. Here they were harangued by a tiny cropeared lieutenant-colonel wearing a green beret, a battle tunic with a great bank of ribbons, and muddy fatigue trousers shoved into a pair of gleaming leather boots that reached his knees.

Turvey couldnt follow very clearly what the colonel was saying. He spoke with great urgency and an odd accent, sometimes waving his arms like a band conductor, but Turvey could find no beginning or end to his sentences.

"What I wan a from you, my fellows, I wan," he was shouting, "is a *goosto, goosto*, plenty of dat is better dan, you know we no try to fail you boys we wan a know how moch you got, you got a veem you got a drrrive, here is where you show, we don expect you are officer already no but you be smart on a toe and you jump, for it only tree day so you keep your nose a clean an an uniform a too and I don expect you do more dan anybody, you take all a dese test wis a *goosto* an an a drrrive an don be afraid a nobody get hurt unless a maybe he don go in dere wis a poonch on a my catwalk an an my officer when dey interview now you boys a be natural joos a speak up de troot because a we don fail you for, now . . . ."

His teeth shone very white and healthy in the sunlight and when he had finished the sweat gleamed on his swarthy little face from his own gusto. The candidates, as they now found themselves called, were issued with fatigue coveralls, each with a large number chalked on the back, broken up into squads of six, and doubled along cinder paths to various parts of the estate. Mac and Turvey were separated.

The latter's squad was taken in tow by a rosycheeked lieutenant who talked in a cheery vague English voice which reminded Turvey of Victoria. He led them into a hazel copse and put each in turn through a series of large-sized puzzles. "Great mistake to be all over active with these; horsesense, you know, that's all you need. Spot of agility perhaps. I mean to say, it's all under battle conditions."

Turvey, looking at Test One, thought a bit of luck would be handy too. It was a wide gate wrapped round with barbed wire and so constructed that it twirled like a murderous millwheel as soon as weight came on it. He decided the best idea was just to walk around the whole thing, since that was clearly what he would do in a battle, but the lieutenant wouldnt let him. Then he noticed a long pole lying beside the trail. While the lieutenant was entering something in his notebook, Turvey grabbed the stick and ran back up the cinders. The colonel had said he wanted them to be smart and jump to it and have something or other. He came charging down with a warning whee, plunged the slim rod in the "contaminated" sand in front of the gate and perilously, with less than an inch to spare, polevaulted the barbed monstrosity before the alarmed officer could block him.

"I say, I say, old chap," Pinkcheeks called almost apologetically across the gate, "that's not really the way to do it, you know. I mean to say, you've done it, I suppose, but that pole wasnt meant for that, you know. Not supposed to be there, in fact. Might have broken. Fact, you can consider it has." Turvey looked at the pole but he couldnt see a crack in it. "I mean to say, for purposes of the test you know. Too risky – what?" He chuckled hollowly. "Supposing you were under fire, dont you think, old chap? However, you're across. No harm done. Carry on." And he put another mark in his Field Notebook.

After some more hocuspocus involving blindfolds and concealed ramps, Pinkcheeks turned the squad over to a middle-aged captain with an artillery badge on the side of his wedge-cap, and Mutt and Jeff medals from World War One. He took them off at the double through a break in the woods to a spidery trestle of tubular steel that rose twenty feet to a level with the middle branches of the knobbly oaks nearby. Sucking on a cold sway-backed pipe the captain ignored the ominous affair and briefed them on other, invisible dangers ahead.

Turvey was sent along a ditch which very rapidly acquired a roof of turf and withes, under which he had to crawl. Soon it shrank to a point in utter darkness where crawling became belly-wriggling through marshy slime. Then the tunnel bent, and Turvey stuck in the bend.

Only a few yards ahead he could see a gleam of light, the exit; going back was impossible; the next victim was already snorting and slithering up the tunnel. Turvey grunted and sweated, lost more breath, and began to feel a touch of the claustrophobia the designer of the tunnel had been interested in. He framed other words for it but they didnt help, and his squirming only planted him more firmly in the surprisingly cold sub-soil of England. Desperately he arched his back – and felt the roof give slightly; he put everything into another upward hoist – and poked his head up through a canopy of dirt and leaves into the blessed sunlit air. Buy try as he might he couldnt get his shoulders through. He swivelled his neck for a better position and saw a vaguely familiar pair of boots, brown, high, and gleaming. His eyes travelled up, over the soiled dungarees, the five tiers of ribbons, to the little open mouth and astonished eyes of the colonel. The sight added the needed erg to Turvey's martial power; he pressed with his boots, shot his shoulders up, and scrambled panting to his feet. Then, thinking rapidly, while the colonel's mouth was still ajar, he put everything he had into a wide magnificent salute, and spoke first:

"Please sir, we was told to hurry and I couldnt get my stomach round the corner so I come this way. Where do I go next?"

It may have been the salute, the expressed morale, or the novelty of Turvey's solution to the tunnel problem. The astonished glitter in the colonel's eyes softened. "Madre de Dios!" he said, "I wan you com a straight wis me for a my catwalk. Dis I mus see!" Following the rapid little strides of the colonel – he walked very upright but splayfooted like a pigeon – Turvey chugged safely past the Artillery Captain, who stood glaring at him near the tunnel's legitimate outlet. They bypassed several lesser instruments of torture to which the candidates in advance of Turvey were being submitted. Bagshaw perched dismally, not daring to move, midway on a greased log suspended between trees; Crane sat trapped in a set of barbed-wire hurdles; Callicutt was hurtling in a rope cradle down a high wire slung over a muddy swamp. Circling, Turvey and the colonel came to the tall spindly trestle where the course had begun. The Commandant, who had been silent since his first remark, now wheeled on him, teeth bared and sparkling, black eyes snapping with imagined battle:

"Ok-*kay*, you got *eem*portan message you save a de lives if you, *oop* a de ladder now, *ovair* my catwalk an down a catch a catch can. *Urry* now let see you got a *goosto* – but *carajo* don you bus notting no more!"

Fired by the colonel's excitement Turvey felt himself already in a world of shell and smoke, carrying a despatch of life and death, a message he must give personally, immediately, to the Commanding Officer of the Kootenay Highlanders. Up the rope ladder he swarmed to the plank. It was along its twenty swaying feet and down the trestle's steel legs to the ground that the message must go.

But as soon as he made his first step the catwalk took on a mad snaky life of its own, springing and shaking so much he couldnt, for all his will, get the next foot down. Something flicked his cheek and a twig fell on the plank.

"A-BOWWWW, PEEENG! A-BOWWWW! Dats a boollet. You under a fire!" It was the colonel, his booted legs stamping with excitement, his canines flashing. He hurled another handful of twigs.

Turvey took another step and the catwalk curtsied and bounced. His feet glued, his knees swayed with the watery sway of the board and his eyes were drawn and pinned by the dizzy sight of the hard pathway and the scraggly bushes below. When had all this happened before? He was back at the Basic Training Centre; already he felt a shooting pain in his wobbling left ankle from the jump he hadn't yet taken, or had he?

Then across Turvey's rigid vision, while the shouts of the colonel continued to spurt skywards to him, appeared a new face. It belonged to an officer who walked over and was now looking up. Ordinarily it was not a face that inspired bravery in the rank and file; it was puffy and alcoholically veined, and the expression was a mixture of meekness and boredom. But above the face there gleamed something that sent the blood of courage rushing through Turvey's veins; it was the badge on his cap – the golden-feathered head of an Indian chief set in the silver cross of St. Andrew and surmounted by a limp salmon – the badge of the Kootenay Highlanders! With a yell like a stifled warcry Turvey bounded in three great leaps down the catwalk. The third bounce took him almost to the end, and its impact, coinciding by some dynamic chance with a tremendous buckle of the now thoroughly aroused planking, catapulted Turvey forwards and up so that he sailed clear of the whole mundane trestle, clear and out in a neatly turning khaki ball.

He landed mercifully in a leafy limb of the nearest oak from which, after some delay, he was able to unhook himself and descend fairly intact to the ground. Then

Turvey executed for the first time a salute which, though directed by military requirements at the astounded colonel, was intended for and delivered in the presence of a lieutenant of the Kootenay Highland Regiment.

Over a supper of tinned herring, under the curved iron walls of the Nissen, where the candidates at last got together to compare notes, Mac was holding forth. His squad had tackled a set of educational tests, then spent the rest of the afternoon loafing in their hut, getting the lowdown on the Panel from available members of the substaff.

"Look, fellows, we got it cold. It's a nut house, a loony bin. First, this colonel. Hut Orderly says he's all the way from South America. Most of that chest fruit's from revolutions in Nicotina or somewhere. Came up with the rations. Never heard an angry shot in this man's army. Next, place is crawling with psychologists, psychiatrists, every other kind of psychic. They all have a bang at you first two days. Then they hold a powwow, a Panel, pool scores, pick the winnah. Ah well. People have more fun than anybody!"

"I heard," said Bagshaw, "some a them psycho-low-gists are snoopin around dressed as privates and pretendin to be orderlies and the like. That's how they get the real gen on you."

"Gosh, maybe that's who you were talkin to, Mac," said Turvey.

"Nonsense. Heard about that too. Latrinogram. Started by that pint-size doorman. Old soldier type. Seen him? Even smaller than the colonel. Most of him's turned under for feet. But little joker goes around pretending he's officer in disguise. Probably palms odd quid that way."

"Frig him," said Bagshaw, "I'd pay good foldin money to fail, that's if I thought it'd get me over to Normandy."

"It wont," said Mac, "might as well play it their way. Might get over sooner. All a rat-race anyhoo. Six Spos; six Flos (that's Field Liaison Officers, johnnies putting you fellows through the hoops today); one Toe (Tests of Education Officer), two Sikes; and a Major-2-i-c. If all of them cant down you, there's always Little Carioca to boot you out for being short on a goosto."

"What's this agoo-?" Turvey began but Crane spoke at the same moment and louder.

"How the hell did he get to be a colonel?"

"How do any of em?" Bagshaw put in.

"Ah, got the gen on that too. Gets chucked out of Uramania, wherever he was, before the war, counter-rev. Beetles up to Vancouver, becomes Export Bigfart, gets to know right people, joins Permanently Non-Active Militia. Need I go on?"

"Then that little shatterbust aint a psych-a-low-gist too?" asked Bradshaw.

"No bloody fear. Got one speech – you heard it – and three questions. Still, maybe he's the smart one."

"Let's have the questions," said the rest of the table at once.

"Ahh. Corporal wanted ten bob a piece for em. I'm not that crazy to pass. Besides, one of the sarges tipped me off. They dont matter a hoot. All you got to do is walk his wormy catwalk. Course the others can scupper you in the Panel. Bless em all. Friend Turvey here's a cert, from all I hear, for the colonel's fur-lined jerry. Most of em crawl across, or shamble. Nobody ever made that oak tree before, I'll bet a pretty. Tops, you kill me, daily. But I love you. You're in for one of the colonel's special diamond-studded interviews, dollars to doughnuts."

Mac was right. Turvey had scarcely settled down to a game of hearts in his hut when a runner pulled him out to the colonel's office. The converted master-bedroom of Great Buzzard Manor was an impressive chamber with an ancient beamed ceiling. As Turvey padded in and saluted he was confronted not only with the little figure half hidden at the huge desk but with two knights in full armour looming in the room's corners behind. He took a second look and was glad to see the armoured figures were empty. On the panelled wall between them were tacked two crossed flags, the Union Jack and a strange brightly striped affair Turvey had never seen before, Nicomania or somewhere, he guessed.

The colonel had his hat off; his black hair was cropped stiff as a Fuller brush, his black eyes gleamed like shoe-buttons. But his voice, though still full of urgency, was friendly. He invited Turvey to remove his headdress and take a seat. Then he seized a large leather-backed pad and picked up a massive fountain pen.

"Now my boy you don have a no fear a for me, we two a soldier we jus sit for a talking togezzer." He leant back in his big swivel chair. "An I sink you are a good soldier, *verdad*? You have fear, a sure, when you start a my cat-walk – de brave a soldier he know what it is to fear – but you trow eet off, you run, you leap, you got what I like for to see, you got, *positivamente*, you got *entusiasmo*, you got a *goosto*!"

"Yessir," said Turvey grinning vaguely and looking first at the thick carpet and then at the crossed flags to get away from the colonel's little coalfire eyes.

"*Bueno*. An firs I ask you –" the colonel leant forward intently – "why you apply for a commiss-i-on?" He inclined back again, folding his arms over his stunning cascade of ribbons.

"Well, I didnt exactly sir, that is, they were handin out forms and I was told to fill one out like." Turvey started to scratch his stomach – he was having trouble with grass nits.

The colonel seemed to sag a little. He swung sideways in his chair and stared mournfully at one of the knights in armour. "Dis *gringo* army . . . . Ok-kay." He swivelled back. "Secon' I ask a what you do in de ceevil life?"

As Turvey stumbled through the labyrinths of his oc-cupational career the colonel started big scrawls on the

pad with his pen, but he soon gave up, eyes glazing.
Turvey had just got to the winter of 1940 when he interrupted:

"*Bueno*. You have a know life yes. I ask a now tird
question." He half-rose on his elbows over the desk, light
quivering again in his eyes; he leant so close Turvey
thought their noses would touch. "What make a good officer in battle, yes?"

Turvey pondered and grinned feebly. He felt very
much behind the eight-ball. "Well, I guess he oughta be
in there punchin, like you said, sort of in the lead like,
and puttin out –" he had an inspiration – "this here
agoosto." He scratched again, lower down.

The colonel suddenly drew back .as if Turvey had
stabbed him. Had he said the wrong thing after all?

"*Caramba!* You mock a me! You, you *bobalicon* –
take off a dat *green*! You try to be fleep? Maybe I can'
help a speak a de Spanish way, what a for you make insult to your Commandant hey?"

"Gosh I didnt mean nothin, sir! I dont know what
agoosto means. I just heard you sayin it."

The colonel's expression passed from anger to incredulity, to disappointment. "You don know what de
word it mean? You – *imbécil!* I sink I wait for to hear
what a my psychiatreest he have to say about you . . . Okkay, you go now. You have," he sighed, "disappoint a
me verry moch. *Totalmente!*"

Turvey found the rest of the candidates in the NAAFI
waiting on benches for a free film, title as yet unkown.
He sat down beside a big pimply infantry sergeant who
soon mooched a cigarette and began giving Turvey his
woes in a loud mournful voice.

"If it werent for the stripes, I'd tell the whole
cocksuckin issue to go plum to hell. You know when I
come to England?" he asked Turvey with a glower,
"December-fuckin-thirty-nine."

"Golly, you musta seen lots of action by now. Where've you been?"

"Where've I been? Listen. First I was a whole bloody winter in Aldershot. Then they put me on a train for Norway."

"Gee, I never met anybody who fought in Norway before!"

"Well, you aint now. They turned us back at Dunfermline. Next month I got another train ride – to Dover. Whole First Infantry Brigade was goin to France."

"You mean you was fightin there in 1940!"

"Who, me?" He laughed sourly. "First time we never even sailed. Then next month we got all the way to Brest. And I sat in the friggin harbour two days. Then we got the bum's rush back to Aldershot. June 1940, that was. And now it's June 1943, and I'm fightin Hitler from a Buckingham castle. What kinda shitheels runnin this army? Dont tell me they aint got a saw-off with the Krauts. Last year they didnt even send us to Dieppe – took the Second Div boys hadnt been overseas a year. You know what's wrong with those cunts back in Ottawa?"

The lights went out suddenly and the projection machine whirred. "It's these tycoons that's runnin em. The bosses only want one of these phony wars because –"

"Stop the jawin," somebody yelled, "show's on."

It was a National Film Board short on the herring industry in which a young man with an artificially lively voice assured everybody millions of cans of Canadian herring were pouring over to England's defense.

"See," the sergeant whispered, "ca-pit-alist b.s. The guy that owns the herrin industry must be cornholein King's Cabinet. Canned herrin for supper. Smoked herrin yesterday for breakfast. I'd like to tell em to work it. And now herrin for movies. Propaganda, that's all it is."

The next film was a pre-war western with a soundtrack so old the actors all seemed to have quinsy. The projector broke down at the end of a reel, in any case, and couldnt be fixed. The candidates filed out for bull sessions in their huts.

"Well, anyway, you got sent to Sicily and Italy with the First Div, didnt you?" Turvey asked the sergeant as they groped out of the NAAFI.

"O sure," he said, "and we got torpedoed on the way down. Funny how they would know we was comin, eh? And I bloody near drowned. And the boat that picked us up took us back to England. And I got pneumonia and landed in hospital – Aldershot, of course, that twathole. When I come outa there they shot me to a Third Div outfit and I trained for D-Day." The sergeant laughed dismally. "D-Day they send me here! Aah, I tell yah there's pricks high up in this army dont want any of us to mix with the Krauts. They're savin us up."

"What for?"

"For the Russkies, of course. World War Three. You wait and see. Ca-pit-alist swine. And now I get a Blue from my wife my dog is sick. Always somethin."

The next morning Turvey's squad was taken over by a Field Liaison Officer with fat cheeks and a behind as plump as a matron's. He walked them sedately out to a small damp meadow and, after hunting through a big folder of notes, read them a long set of directions for a game called Sandbag. It was designed, he said, to test their ability both to lead and be led, under emergency conditions. The next thing Turvey knew – he had gone into a slight coma trying to memorize the directions – he was blindfolded with a sour-smelling towel and set loose with similarly handicapped comrades to blunder across the pocked terrain trying with outstretched arms to capture Bagshaw, who, blindfolded also, was carrying the sandbag. At least that was how Turvey understood the game. But it turned out that Callicutt had been made Squad Leader and wasnt blindfold; he had been shouting

directions at the others to guide them in seizing the bag-
toter, using the numbers chalked on the backs of their
coveralls to preface his cries. "Number Eight!
halt – grab! . . . no, about turn," Callicutt would shout,
"Number Six, two paces back – grab, GRAB!" and so
on. But most of the squad had forgotten their numbers,
including Turvey, so that the game quickly degenerated
into a confusion of human collisions, rollicking shouts,
howls of pain, and tumbles. Bagshaw, still untagged,
meantime wandered off the meadow and fell into an ornamental lily-pond, sack and all. This was an accident
which the plump Flo would no doubt have prevented if
he had not been at the time fully engaged in picking
himself and his folder of notes out of the mud into which
he had been toppled when Turvey, in the belief that he
had found the candidate carrying the sandbag, tackled
the officer from the rear.

The next half-hour Turvey and his squad cleaned up
at the stock pump by the stables and then paraded into
the ex-nursery of Great Buzzard Manor, a bald room
decorated with peeling white stars and pink fairies. They
were sat down to benches around a barrackroom table
for a Discussion Test.

The officer in charge of this experiment was a squarefaced young man with cold grey eyes and a great air of efficiency. "All right, men. We will spend the next" – he
flipped his wrist watch – "fifty-three minutes discussing
any subject you wish. You may converse with complete
frankness. I am not interested so much in your opinions
as in how well you can verbalize them within a group.
Any suggestions for a topic of discussion?"

Bagshaw, who had had to change from the skin out
and seemed to have decided he didnt want to be an officer anyway, muttered, with heavy irony. "We oughta
discuss Discussion Tests." The squarefaced lieutenant
looked as if he hadnt heard. His eyes travelled over the
candidates and lighted on the one with the smile. Turvey
was still wondering what "verbalize" was, and praying

he wouldnt be called on directly.

"Number 22. Candidate Turvey. What do you suggest?"

There was a long tense pause. What subject would last out a whole fifty-three minutes?

"Women," he said finally.

There was a guffaw from Bagshaw, and a feeble un-identified cheer.

"Subject normal," said Trail.

The lieutenant flinched slightly but spoke with careful calm. "If the *majority* of you wish to carry through a discussion of that subject, you may. But I'm sure we could find a more *fruitful* topic –" there were several quick sniggers – "topics relating to world problems, economics, politics –" he flashed an empty smile.

In the end they accepted a topic which the lieutenant picked for them, The Problem of Civil Rehabilitation. Turvey, once he realized that no one was going to order him to talk, sat in cheerful absentmindedness for the rest of the hour scratching his harvest-bugs.

After the ten-minute break for a smoke, they went back into the nursery for another parlour game with a new officer, a greyhaired Infantry Major with a kind apologetic air. He explained this was a Leadership Test and that each in turn was to imagine he was already a Platoon Commander; he would be given a paper with a typewritten "situation", allowed two minutes to brood on it, and then asked to give an extempore lecturette.

Turvey was unlucky enough to be the first goat. He read his slip. "Two men in your platoon have both become V.D. casualties within the past week. Give a talk to your platoon on the subject." This was fun, after all. He spent his two minutes deciding which men he would pick as casualties, finally choosing Trail and Bagshaw. He began his talk by announcing their names and was going on to an imaginary but detailed account of how each had acquired his injuries when the fatherly major interrupted.

"I think it would be better, lad, if you, umm, used the

situation given you to say something *generally* about the dangers of venereal infection and the soldier's responsibility to, umm, you know –" He waved vaguely.

"O yessir, I was just comin to that. Fellahs, I guess you know it aint no fun havin clap. You oughtnt to get it." The eyes facing him all had a skeptical look. Turvey paused to think of some good reasons. "None of us oughtnt. Cause why? Cause you know it's a hang of a thing to get rid of. A shot in one arm now, and the next arm three hours after, and then your behind three hours after that, and they keep on needlin you like that for four whole days and nights."

"You're bloody lucky it wasnt a packet a siph you caught, you'd been in for ten," said a large sardonic corporal whom Turvey didnt know.

"Chuch-cha," said the major, "he's supposed to be your officer. You, you wouldnt use that kind of language to your officer, now would you boys?"

"That birdbrain an officer!" the corporal muttered, subsiding.

"Anyway," Turvey struggled on, "it's a month before you feel like havin a girl again and –"

"What about the consequences to platoon morale or, umm, the family, umm, wife and children?" said the major, pursing his lips in deprecation.

"O yes, fellahs, the kids! You know what'll happen to em if you get a real dose, like siph?" He paused dramatically. "They wont be no good in the head. They'll grow up to be, to be illiterate!"

The sad face of Candidate Sorensen paled with alarm. He put up a hand slowly. "Ay tank is not right, major. A fellah he yoost need to get fixed up with the doctor." Sorensen's phrasing was impersonal but there was no mistaking the quiver in his voice.

"Well, umm, yes, I suppose," the major broke in hurriedly. "Ummm, always go to the M.O. for anything like that, son. But, umm, better not have to go at all, you know. A real family man, now, he should love his wife and children and not play around, or he should want to have umm, wives, I mean a wife, and now who is next? Corporal Trail, isnt it?''

By mid-afternoon, in the former bedroom of the pantry-maid in the cramped flag-tower of Great Buzzard Manor, Private Turvey was once more rendering up his Occupational Record to a Personnel Selection Clerk. Just before lunch he had taken the O-test again, since the documents containing his previous scores had not yet arrived at Number Three Testing Panel. Lunch itself, and breakfast for that matter, had been a bit of a test, for at both meals the officers of the unit had sprinkled themselves over the tables. The dimple-chinned young Spo who sat with Turvey each time, however, seemed even shyer than the candidates and concentrated rather greedily on his food.

After lunch Turvey had been exposed to a Universal Knowledge Test, a Level of Education Test (Part I: English; Part II: Arithmetic), and a set of puzzles called the Z-test Non-Verbal. Now the Preliminary Interview was over. The Personnel Sergeant had covered all the available spaces in a long sheet, added some extra foolscap notes, picked them up and disappeared up a dark passageway.

After an hour's wait on a folding chair Turvey was led down the same corridor and abandoned at an open door.

"Number 22?" asked an impersonal voice. Turvey entered, saw a captain's three pips behind another barrackroom table, and saluted. It was a Spo.

He was a young man, but no slouch, Turvey decided. He seemed to have all of Turvey's test papers spread over the desk and was embroidering calculations from them on a yellow sheet. He had large deer's eyes, moist but searching, and rounded as if always asking a question.

And never had Turvey, as hardened an interviewee as the Canadian Army possessed, been asked such questions. First the captain wanted to know all about Turvey's health. The mere "how" of breaking an ankle and getting the wrong prophylaxis in Niagara, and bashing a toe in Aldershot, were not enough for Captain Youngjoy. Was he sure – the captain raised his head in a slow dream-like stare at Turvey – that he had *wanted* to take Basic Training? Had he really, frankly now, this interview is absolutely secret, he could take his back hair right down, hadnt he really, deep down within him, *wanted* to break his leg just a little – it was only an ankle chip, wasnt it? – so that perhaps he would be discharged into civil life again? Turvey stopped scratching the rash on his rear and indignantly repudiated the suggestion.

The captain waved his hands gently. "A natural wish, we all get fed up with the army, especially at first. Well, let that go. But tell me. . . ." The captain's voice went on and on, vibrating in a strange way that made his questions seem of the utmost importance – how did it happen that he didnt *see* the night orderly pour the prophylactic from the wrong bottle? . . . Had he been having trouble with his girlfriend about that time? . . . Was he sure now – the liquid eyes held him while the captain's right palm curled suggestively – was he sure that he hadnt wanted to *revenge* himself on his girl by making it impossible for him, just for a little while, to have intercourse with her?

When it came to Turvey's toe, Captain Youngjoy's voice mellowed with exchange of confidences. Now he himself, we're all human, had had a touch of diarrhoea when he found himself in a Holding Unit. And do you know how he had cured it? By facing up to the fact that he didnt like the P.T. Instructor, who had doubled the P.T. period before breakfast. "Now why do you think you got yourself in the hospital while serving in this particular unit, Turvey, and yet stayed out all the rest of the time in England? . . . ."

Turvey, because the captain's eyes were so overpowering, found himself saying "yes" rather sleepily all the time except when assent seemed like a betrayal of the spirit of the Kootenay Highlanders. Even that spirit was burning low in Turvey since Mac had discovered that the Kootenay officer Turvey had seen yesterday was just a junior accountant from CMHQ checking up on messing balances.

Then the captain shifted to Turvey's crime-sheet, and they settled down for the rest of the afternoon.

After supper he reported to the psychiatrist, a shaggy-headed man with an abstracted stare and a Groucho Marx moustache. He was very kindly and after he had looked over Turvey's Educational Test answers and asked him to tell what he saw in a lot of comical big ink-blots, he showed little interest in Turvey's life, sexual or otherwise, and seemed curious only about what Turvey had said to the colonel to make him so annoyed. Turvey explained that he didnt know till Mac told him later that goosto was just the colonel's way of saying pep. The psychiatrist promised he would clear it all up with the colonel before the Panel met the next morning but warned Turvey not to expect to be made an officer right away.

Next morning each candidate, as he was called, marched stiffly into the Great Hall of Great Buzzard Manor, saluted the assembled Panel, announced his name, saluted again, and marched as stiffly out. Turvey provided one or two variations. First he tripped over the surprisingly large feet of the peewee doorman just as he was marching in, smart as a CWAC. He did remember his name and number, and the first salute, but he forgot the second till he was in the door on his way out, and ran back in and gave it. This (Turvey heard later) thoroughly confused the absentminded major-2-i-c, who had been dozing and thought there were two Turveys, and wanted to pass only the second one.

Ceremonies were completed by noon when all the candidates were drawn up on the lawn and harangued by the colonel with much the same speech as two days before, except that this time he also bid them goodbye and warned them apparently (it was hard to get the drift) that some had failed but, to know which, they would have to wait for a posting of the information in their unit orders after it had flowed through the Proper Channels of Communication. Just before dismissal Turvey was startled to hear the colonel say he wanted to see him in his office.

It turned out to be a meeting of reconciliation and destiny. "Now my boy I wan you should know how happy I am you are not a de fleep kine. My psychiatreest he tell me you are a jus dumb. Das a too bad, because he say you are too dumb even to be officer but now you are very brave a soldier. No? You have a goos –, you have veem an an pep, yes, an I take a fancy for you. You like to stay here an work a for me?"

"Gosh, thanks sir, but I'd rather stick with my pal Mac, that's Sergeant MacGillicuddy, and go back to the Okie Rangers. They oughta be goin over to Normandy anytime now."

"Sergean Makeelacuttee? Ah, him I pass. He's a tophole! Two-tree day he get his order an leave you for OCTU. And I don sink your Okie Ranger dey get action for a long a time maybe. Now how about a my nize job? I am going a fire my doorman das a fac' he is no bloody good. How you like a to be my new doorman, hey? An a maybe you bat a for me a little?"

Turvey's opinion of the colonel had gone up a good deal, but – "But heck, then I'd *never* get to the front. No, thanks just the same sir. No hard feelins, though."

The colonel pattered around from behind his desk and reached up a fatherly hand to Turvey's shoulder. "What if I promeese I get you a draft to de fron' before Okie Ranger I bet you ten poun? One, maybe two mont?" His eyes glittered and he launched an utterly fascinating smile with all his teeth. "An now I attach you here till your colonel he give a permission I take you on a strengt, yes?"

And that was how Turvey came to spend the next three months in one of the more charming country estates of Buckinghamshire.

ELEVEN

Turvey Invades the Continent

"WAKEE! WAKEE! Rise and shine."

It was the ungodly hour of five-thirty, the eighth morning since Turvey had arrived in an Aldershot Holding Unit, tagged for immediate despatch to the North-West Theatre. And it went much like the other seven. Half an hour after the corporal with the hysterical voice had winkled them from their straw ticks, Turvey and the fifty-nine other bodies in Draft 606 were standing, shaved and in full marching kit, swollen packs at their feet, yielding up sleepy "Here's" to a bellicose sergeant.

"Stan easy pay tention. You fellows better git it in your skulls boat-train'll leave ANY time. You're confined to your quarters till fur'r notice n REMEMBER – any s.o.b. absen any rollcall'll be mediately listed DESERTER. N REMEMBER, messin hut for this draft is 83B, 83B ONLY, other side prade square; n you fall out you *pro*-ceed ROUND the square not cross it. N that means YOU, Turvey, wipe at smirk off your face, n YOU, Kolt. Four years at war n some a you still swannin cross a MILTRY PRADE GROUND. You don know whether your rear-end's bored or punched. All ry Ten-HUH! Dissssss – MIH!"

Doubling fast, and remembering not to cut corners on the sacred square this time, Turvey and Kolt, a beefy Manitoban he had casually teamed up with in the draft, managed to reach the mess-hut before all the porridge and sky-blue milk were gone.

"No salt in the mush again," Kolt grumbled loudly. He flicked the one slice of fried ham out of his billytin. "Smells like an old hoo-er. Last night was Mystery Fish again. What kinda grub is this fer a athalete like me. I'd like to tie that cook's knackers to a stump and push him over backward."

Turvey shuddered at the thought and tried to be cheerful. "There's some jam for afters this mornin though, Mike."

"So what? They cant kid me there's strawberry seeds in that pozzy. Sawdust, that's what these limeys put in. Same stuff's in the slingers. How they think I'm goin to keep up my strength?"

"Slingers? What's that?"

"Sausages, stoope. Those ersatz barkers we get. Hitler's secret weapon. I wouldnt care so much if this fuckin army gave a fightin Canadian a decent cup of java in the mornin stead of this limey oil." He took a reluctant pull on his mug of sugar-clouded tea.

"Well, anyway, there's toast. Little hard, though."

"Little!" Mike wiped a hairy paw across his lips as if to obliterate the memory of the tea. "Like a old cowpad in August. Come on, let's get back to barracks and scoff the rest of that parcel you got." Later, after Mike had licked the last brown stain from his thumb of the chocolate bars donated by the Kuskanee Ladies Aid, and Turvey had just rounded up two others in the hut for a game of penny high-low on his palliasse, the hysterical corporal, as usual, exploded in the doorway:

"Fall in! On a double! Outside! Hurree. Embarkation Order! Packs on! This is IT, fellahs!"

Turvey doused the butt from the last of his makings, wormed it alongside his field-dressing in the little pocket below his belt, shoved the cards and headless matches into his haversack and swarmed painfully, with inoculated muscles, into a tangled octopus of webbing that led to his respirator, waterbottle, belt, haversack, and great goitrous pack. Then the rolled anti-gas cape. He and the whole cumbrous little army heaved and staggered outside, formed up, and clumped down a familiar mile of pavement through a sudden September heat. Once again Turvey's bed roll, which was supposed to be looped like a great trim doughnut around the outside of his pack, silently unrolled behind and tripped him. He had to fall out, stuff the ends frantically back into the crevices of his pack, and double to catch up.

Then, after they had massed into the Entrainment Point, a little cobbled rectangle behind another set of barracks and nowhere near a train, there was, as usual, an hour's wait in the midst of a bawling flurry of orders and backing trucks and dithering officers. Finally another corporal appeared, intoned their names, and singled out certain victims for the M.O. or the eternal line-up at QM Stores. The rest, including Turvey, still in full christmas tree, were stood "easy" for uncounted minutes and then marched back to their barracks, not quite too late for the fag-end of lunch.

The afternoon was much the same except that Turvey was pulled out of the rollcall at Entrainment Point for another inoculation. It was a change anyway, he thought; instead of his hummocked arms it was his rump. Almost as good as the day he had no inocs at all, only a wisdom tooth pulled.

The next day they were shambling through the same routine in the cobbled rectangle when suddenly a string of empty lorries began backing into the yard, squeezing the warriors against the side-walls. There was a delay, then a rollcall, another delay, another rollcall, and all the A's to H's were ordered into the farthest truck. The I-to-M-including-the-Macs clambered painfully into another vehicle. Just when they got to "T", and Turvey had wedged his blanket roll again, ready to climb on, a Despatch Rider came roaring into the yard, and scurried into the Orderly Room. A few minutes later all the men were ordered out of the trucks and the whole draft marched back to barracks without a clue.

Then at two-thirty on the tenth morning they were roused by no less than four corporals, rushed in record time over the black streets and within an hour were rumbling through Aldershot and out onto the southern trunk road, tires whistling on the wet pavements. They spent most of that day huddled by a railroad siding in the rain waiting to get into a troop train. And it was dark before the train released them at a tiny station, still inland. Here, by some surprising reversal of the pattern, empty lorries were already waiting for them. Now they swayed through dim woods, the rain still beating down, the roads growing muddier and bumpier. Soon one of the trucks bogged down, blocking the way, and the whole contingent was ordered out, sloshing for another hour on foot through slithery lanes. They were met by vague figures with shaded torchlights. Efficient English voices, descending mysteriously from a loudspeaker system in the dim trees, conducted them, dog-tired and stumbling, over the duckboards and into damp marquees.

"Dear jeezis, this all I get?" Mike swore into his mug of cloudy tea. "One spam sanwich and a sinker on the train, a mug a oil this mornin, and now all these limeys give a fightin man is more oil. Good job I had my comp this mornin." He was scarcely placated when the tea was followed by a lump of cheese and a piece of NAAFI cake.

"Bunghole and yellow peril. What they tryin to do, bind me fer the duration? My long-gut's on a sitdown now. This is really the payoff. And I shouldnt be goin to the Front at all! It's all on account of those buckin trick-cyclists at that Testin Panel. Fat bastards of officers, sittin out the war in a palace and sendin me over to fight fer em. 'Fuck you, Jack, I'm all right,' is all they gotta say. Just wait till I write my old colonel at CMHQ about this. They can just about kiss goodbye to their team now."

"What team's that, Mike?"

"You clueless bugger. You'd ferget your own mother. Dont you remember I told you I play fer the Canadian Army Lacrosse Team? They send me out of England and the team's a shimozzle, that's all. Just wait till –'' But an orderly cut off his complaints and guided them to a tarpaulin and sleep.

The next day, fortunately after a breakfast that even Kolt found ample, they marched six miles in a downpour to another camp, and from there were trucked to a shed on a Southhampton dock. After the usual hour wait, while haughty officers with crimson bands on their hats stalked about fluttering papers, they were all given numbered tags and lined up beside a little Channel packet, under the stern eyes of a cordon of M.P.s.

"Jeez, they gonna try takin us across in that punt?" Kolt growled. "After the war I'm gonna track down the O.C. a this draft and knock his suckholin teeth in."

Turvey was disappointed too because he had expected a destroyer or at least a landing craft. He had pictured himself on an invasion beach, rifle held high above waist-deep water. (He hoped it wouldnt be higher). But anything taking him to the Continent was good now. "Golly," he said, "it looks like the old *Nasookin* back on Kootenay Lake, kinda. Got a stern-wheel paddle'n all. They're good boats, no foolin." Kolt contented himself with a wordless grunt. His temper was growing steadily worse, and was not improved by witnessing a group of junior officers being ushered aboard ahead of them into the cabins. With the other O.R.s Kolt and Turvey were each allotted an oblong of deckspace, a corduroy lifebelt, and an ominous paper bag. At least the rain had stopped.

It was night again, cloudblackened and still, when their packet nosed from the Solent into the invisible waters of the Channel. Turvey and his mates lay awkwardly on their lifebelts, heads resting on damp packs. Inoculated rumps rolled and throbbed in time with the ancient pleasure craft. Kolt was too annoyed and Turvey too ex-

cited to follow the lead of the old soldiers who, despite
the hard spray-soaked wood under them, dropped off
almost at once to sleep. Smoking was forbidden, since
blackout rules were being rigidly observed; nobody on
their side of the deck had found a sailor with liquor to
sell; the only alternative to slumber was low-voice talk.
The soldier on Turvey's left, who responded to Wood at
rollcall, but was generally known as Chuck, was also
sleepless, and struck up a conversation. Turvey learned
he was an American, from a small college in Nebraska.

"How come you're in the Canadian Army?"

"Got tired of waitin for Roosevelt. Thought I'd get into
the scrappin sooner." Chuck sniggered ironically. "That
was four years back. And here I am, still suckin the hind
tit. Still, we're on the way now, I ho –"

"I been in Nebraska," Kolt cut in from Turvey's right.
"Been all over the States. Played pro-hockey down there.
Mike Kolt's the name, you probly heard of me." He
paused modestly.

"Cant say I have," the American replied amiably.
"Sure glad to know you though. Who'd you play for?"

"Why? You play hockey?"

"Naw, just follow it a bit. My game's football. American football, that is."

"Pro?" Kolt demanded quickly.

"Naw. Just amachoor. We were State champs,
though. Kind of put old Pugton College on the map.
But –"

"Amatoorin's a sucker's game," Mike cut in, his voice
rising with superiority. "Take me, I went to one of them
small colleges too. Private one. Kind a exclusive; only
about five hundred students. Most of us was really there
to play basketball and lacrosse; we was scholarship
students. But jeez they tried to make us study practicly
every day. You get scholarships at your collage?"

"Yeah. But they always passed us anyway. Didnt have
to crack any books. We were too busy, with night prac-
tices and –"

"Hell, the horse's pitoot we had runnin our place

wouldnt pass us. We was too valuable, see. We won all
the junior provincial titles, lacrosse, baseball, basketball.
So this principal would keep on givin us scholarships but
he wouldnt let us graduate. I was twenny before I got my
junior matric and I didnt have a plugged nickle. I coulda
been out making real dough all that time if I'd wised up
sooner. Course there was scouts around every year wantin
some of us to sign up pro, but just bush league stuff, and
I was waitin fer somethin big. Then this fuckin war came
along."

"Guess you got in right at the start."

"Nyaah! Who you kiddin? That's what the old blather-
skite wanted us to do, all right. Got up and made a big
patriotic speech; told us we was all graduated and he was
sure we'd want to enlist and all that shat. Me, I wired one
of them talent scouts had left me his address and got
myself in the States, but fast."

"That's funny," Chuck laughed. "That's just when I
lit out from Pugton to enlist in Canada."

"What a sucker you were."

"Well, in a way," Chuck laughed goodnaturedly. "I'd
seen action with my own army by now, I guess, if I'd
stayed right in Nebraska till the draft. But I havent any
beef. I'd been readin a book, anyhow, by some guy, all
about drivin ambulances for the Canadians in the First
War, so –"

"Listen, bub, take it from me, amatoorin dont never
pay," Mike broke in again. "Unless it's kina semi-pro,
like when I got down to Cleveland, after wirin that scout.
He got me a paper job with a big firm there so's I could
play on their hockey team. Sweet f.a. to do. Just carried
me on the books. Lots of time fer movies or mebbe a
pool game. But pro's the only stuff."

"Gee, nobody ever asked me to go pro," Turvey
chipped in wistfully. "I started to play softball for
Kuskanee High, though. That's in British Col –"

"Twenty-five hunerd and expenses for the season,"
Kolt carried on as if Turvey hadnt spoken. "That's what

I got in Cleveland soon as I wised up. And all summer off. That aint hay, brother, at least not in them days it werent. If I hadnt come up to Canada barnstormin in the summers I'd a been sittin pretty."

"You mean helpin on the farm?" asked Turvey. Kolt ignored him.

"Trouble was I was afraid the Yanks would grab me for their army if they come in, so I was keepin up membership in the Reserve Battery the coach was in cahoots with back in the home town, and I had to show up there in the summers to do it. I'd get in on summer ball and take a few boxin matches to make it pay. That worked all right till – what in hell's that?" Kolt interrupted himself suddenly. A low siren was wailing ahead in the darkness. "That's a Moanin Minnie! Air-raid?" Nobody knew.

"Wonder where we're goin to land," Chuck mused.

"Dieppe," said Kolt authoritatively. "Aint nowhere else."

"We got Le Havre now too," Chuck said, "and Ostend. Though maybe they aint got the harbours cleared yet. Course there's Antwerp but the Jerries are still in the Schelt."

"Dieppe," said Kolt.

"You're a boxer, too, eh?" Chuck threw in conversationally, after a pause.

"I can use my mitts, chum, believe you me. I was finalist in the Golden Gloves in Shy, '41, middleweight, and I was robbed at that."

"Let's see, '41 . . ." Chuck said quietly. "Charlie Hayes was top middleweight that year, wasnt he? I used to follow the Golden Gloves."

"Yeah, yeah, Hayes was pretty hot but the ref –"

"And it seems to me it was Al Tribuani he defeated in '41."

"I didnt say '41, I said '40."

"You said '41, Mike," Turvey chipped in, "but I guess you meant –"

"You keep your nose outa this. You twerps think I'm slingin you a – jeezis, what the fuck now?"

Far ahead, the blackness was suddenly slashed with orange light. As they sat up on their elbows, a great low boom pressed their ears. "Holy God, they're firin at us!" Mike's voice rose, losing its pugnacity.

"Stow it," came in crisp cockney from the forrard lookout, "aownly a Chennel gun. Dauveh. Moiles orf. One of aours, ennywiy. Dint y'eeah the soiren?"

"Yeah. That big stuff can shoot miles too," Kolt muttered, staring uneasily into the black sky; "limey buttinski!" There was a general stir on the deck, that increased as the gun continued to split the horizon in some slow unknown anger. But soon it fell into silence, and the men let their heads drop, squirming again into positions of sleep. Chuck Wood, however, was still awake.

"You were sayin you were second in the Golden Gloves in '40," he said casually. "Then it was Joe –"

"Yeah, yeah, but I was really tellin you how I got landed in the army. Summer a '41. I had a big contrack that fall, back in Boston, forty, er, forty-five hunerd and found. But when I started across to the States the bastards held me at the border. My call-up had come and they'd got wind of it."

"Golly," said Chuck, "I thought all you Canucks was crazy to get into the fightin, like I was. Here was me hitchhikin to New York to drive an ambulance in '39, and the Canadian Embassy werent havin any. Nor the British either. So I had to hitch up to Montreal and join the Black Watch."

"Gee, that's a real snazzy reg –" said Turvey.

"Whatta you mean I dont wanna fight?" Mike suddenly rose on an elbow. "I can fight any bastard on this ship, see – includin Yanks."

"Okay, okay," said Chuck evenly, "nothin personal." He sat up and scratched his neck reflectively. "Guess it was just that book made me kinda romantic when the war was startin up. Wish I could remember who wrote it."

"I read a book once all about the Rover Boys drivin ambulances in some war," Turvey ventured. "Would that be by the same fellah, Chuck?"

"You sure were a fall-guy," Mike threw over Turvey's head before Chuck could reply. "Longer you stay outa this cornholin army the better. Jeez, when I think – I coulda had a commission, see, if I'd gone Active when they drafted me. They woulda fixed it fer me to play lacrosse over here, like I've been doin. But my old coach talked me into goin to Ottawa to build up an army team for the Beaver Cup. He got me a job up there as a P.T. instructor. Then, by God, the beauty part was I hadda turn Active after all. And it wasnt three months when some pigfucker crossed me up. Some efficiency joe tryin to clean up NDHQ. Bingo, I get two days' notice for overseas draft."

A gull swooped across them, out of the dark into the dark. Kolt flinched.

"You wouldnt get time to see your folks before you left then," said Turvey sympathetically.

"Who you think I am? I worked that one all right; told the coach I'd go loose if he didnt swing me a compassionate; he fixed me up with two weeks and when I got home I faked me a charleyhorse in the knee – used to have one anyway – and got the local sawbones to get me another month's extension. I was tryin to work my ticket out, but it was no go."

"How'd you get to play lacrosse in England, then?" asked Turvey.

"O, I worked it. Had a soft touch in CMHQ too. Trades'n H.Q. pay extra and livin allowance and a coupla hooks. But shat, that's still peanuts and I couldnt get no promotion, so I fixed it with – well, I better not say – a VIP was an old lacrosse player, used to be with the Red Wings – to get me a commission in Artillery. I might just as well be a amatoor the way I was there."

"How come you're still a private then?" asked the American suddenly.

"What's wrong with bein a private?" Kolt shoved his jaw over Turvey in Wood's direction. Chuck said nothing. "Anyways, that phony set-up, Buzzard Castle or somepn, where they got all those little trick-cyclists, some a them aint dry behind the ears yet, they muscled in and crossed me up."

"Gee, I been there all summer," said Turvey, glad to find an entry into the conversation again. "Must have left just before you come. I went down to be a nofficer and I stayed on as a doorman, then I was a batman and –"

"I'd see em in fuckin hell before I'd bat for em," said Mike with scorn. "The quacks! I hate their guts. They wouldnt give me any pips and then they worked it so I got sent on this chrisely draft, and lost the two hooks I had."

"Perhaps there'll be a lacrosse team over here for you to play in," said Turvey cheerfully. The American snorted. Mike sat up and glared at them in the dimness. "Wise-crackers eh? Mebbe there *will* be a team over here. Mebbe I'll be playin lacrosse in Berlin this winter yet. I'll bet I'll be there before any damn cocky Yankee anyhow."

"I didnt say nothin." Chuck's voice was quiet but no longer friendly. "You got somethin against Americans?"

"What's it to you, if I have?" Mike shouted.

Sleepy protests rose around them.

"Quiet, you lugs!"

"Aw, sleep it off."

"Shovel it!"

"Golly, fellahs," Turvey whispered, "we'd better keep quiet. The NCOs mightnt like it."

"NCOs my fuckin foot. Mike Kolt didnt sign away his right to talk!"

"Shut up," Chuck hissed suddenly. "I hear someone comin."

"Who you tellin to shut up you – you goddam Yankee

amatoor!" Mike swung to his knees and drew back his fist.

Turvey saw a dim shape stepping toward them and involuntarily leant toward Mike. "Shhh," he said, "here's a serg –"

Turvey abandoned the rest of his sentence as his left eye caught the beginning of the right uppercut which Mike had aimed at Chuck in the darkness. Turvey was somersaulted clear over the American. His knees whumped against the advancing legs of the newcomer and brought the rest of the figure sprawling on top of him. By the time the sergeant, for it was a sergeant, had righted himself and hauled Turvey up by his lifebelt, the aroused soldiers nearby had managed to dislodge Chuck from his seat on Kolt's midriff.

"You're under arrest," said the sergeant, dropping Turvey back on the deck. "Dont stir from here till I come for you. If we had room for a brig on this ship I'd slap you in it. Who were you fightin with?" There was a careful silence, modified only by the puffing of Kolt. The sergeant must have come from a lighted cabin for he peered blinking around in the darkness. "O.K. You'll all sit right where you are till I come back. And if there's any more noise or roughhousin, I'll put the whole damn deck in the book." He stumbled aft muttering.

"You all right, Tops?" Chuck whispered.

"Yeah, I guess so." Turvey was still in a daze. "But what'll the sarge do to me?"

"Dont worry. I'll see Kolt straightens this out. He wants to apologize to you, dont you, Kolt?"

Mike sat with his nose muffled in a handkerchief. He made no reply.

"Gee," said Turvey, patting his own cheek carefully, "did somebody hit Mike?"

Chuck laughed. "I was goin to tell Mike, when he interrupted me, that he made another mistake about those Golden Glove middle-weight titles in Chicago. I got a funny memory for sports. In 1940 it was Bob Jacobs was runner-up. And in 1939 it was, er, Chuck Wood.''

"You?" said Turvey.

"Yeah. You see, it's just amachoor stuff. And I couldnt remember a Kolt figurin in any of the records."

Chuck lay back, and after a while drifted into gentle snoring.

Mike, after further silent dabbing at his nose, also stretched out and fell, or pretended to fall, into sleep. Turvey, however, sat thoroughly awake, feeling his face still ballooning and expecting any moment to see the sergeant return. As he leant his eye into the cool wind springing up, he wondered if they would ship him back to England on the next boat. He wouldnt be able to face Peggy after her kissing him goodbye and giving him some long woollies again and a lucky rabbit's foot. He clutched Peggy's charm dangling inside his battleblouse (it was tied to his identification disks) and, hoping for the best, continued to sit dutifully until the boat slowed to a stop and dropped anchor.

As daylight glimmered, the wind rose and the ship began for the first time to wallow heavily. Turvey's concern for his eye disappeared in a greater concern for his stomach. It was a sensation others shared; the tossing deck, in the pink dawn, stirred with shifting profane humanity, and the weaker bowelled, including Kolt, were already draped in noisy misery over the chains of the well-deck or gazing intently into their brown paper bags. Turvey had lost his somewhere in the scuffle. He tried as best he could to obey the NCO's instructions not to move, but nature conquered. Failing to elbow himself a place over the chains he lurched to the rail, vaguely aware that they lay at the entrance to a little harbour with scarred stone jetties and, behind, a yellow battered town on a hill. Remembering first to take out his top plate, he greeted Ostend with a retch and staggered back to his lawful place just as the sergeant appeared, followed by an officer.

Perhaps it was the sight of Turvey's eye or the general

fat woebegoneness of his face, or it may have been
Chuck, who now gallantly explained that the blow had
been meant for himself, and called Kolt over from the
rail to sullenly admit having delivered it. In any case, the
officer seemed to consider it more important that they all
fall in for debarkation, and the charge against Turvey
was dropped. He was too concerned with making a parting salute to the Channel from the weaving gangplank to
care, but once on the dock he began to feel he would live
again. Perhaps it was just as well, he thought, we didnt
come in a landing craft.

Turvey rather expected everything to be full of shells
and speed once he had landed in the North-West Theatre.
But the next few hours proved to be very much like
Aldershot. First there was the usual everlasting halt-and-
march through the rather lifeless town, the usual slipping
of his helmet, the treacherous pack-blanket trailing and
tripping him. Then boredom in a draughty railway shed,
everyone standing or furtively squatting on his pack until
an officer remembered to give them a break-off. Turvey
lined up for his turn in the one fragrant w.c. and then
toured the shed's glassless wire-screened windows to stare
at a pile of rusting shell-cases and the back alleys of the
town.

In a short time the screens became clustered on the outside with eager urchins who chattered to each other in-
comprehensibly or demanded in shrill pidgin English:

"Ceegarette, sirs?"

"Shocolate, johnny? Please gimme shocolate?"

One full-lipped cherub, the most sophisticated Turvey
encountered, beamed at Turvey's black eye and went
through a delighted pantomime of punching his own and
collapsing by the shed-wall. Then he scrambled up with a
sweet smile and said, as if reciting a school poem: "Got
any goom, choom? Got monay? You got monay, I got
nize sistair, she slip wit you."

There was much speculation about the kind of train
they were waiting for by the empty platform since most

of the visible track was twisted around bombholes. But it turned out that they had been marched to the wrong place, and they were marched out again, through another mile of town and into a courtyard. Here, eventually, they were bundled into sixty-hundredweights and went rattling off south. Turvey kept on the *qui vive* for a sight of the enemy or at least the front lines but all he could see, from the third standing layer in the truck, was a monotonous succession of lombard tops and telephone poles. Later in the journey he got his good right eye through a hole in the side-canvas and decided that Belgium was a very wet country, a bit like the Kootenay Flats near Kuskanee except that it had more farms, and no mountains behind, and was chock-full of rambling canals with collapsed bridges and sunken barges. Once in a while he saw a flaking tank-wreck in a field, and his martial pulse quickened. But more often what caught his eye were the neat German cemeteries, looking very fresh.

After two hungry hours, the convoy swerved off the cement highway, bumped and clanged over cobblestones through winding uphill streets, and halted, long past lunch, in the middle of a huge courtyard. Here they were disgorged, bewildered and hollow, to stand or squat once more, now on damp paving stones surrounded by a square of brick buildings so grim and dirty as to be obviously a military barracks.

And barracks they were, none less than the Royal Albert of Ghent, temporarily at the disposal of the Base Headquarters of the Canadian Army of the Twenty-First Army Group of the North-West Theatre.

By the ninth day of his imprisonment in one of its smellier basements, from whose walls more water oozed steadily than could be wrung from the greasy taps in the Ablution Room, Turvey was quite sure they were the most uncomfortable of the long panorama of barracks he had come to know. What made things worse was his growing conviction that he was never going to get out of them. For no one seemed to know whither he was bound, or to be much interested, no one at least who came in contact with Turvey. Each morning, after the coldwater shave and the issue of semi-cooked sawdust-sausages looking as putty-pale as the one potato beside them, he would line up for rollcall with several hundred others and hear the names of the fortunates who were to be released to various units in the Theatre. By the sixth day, Kolt (still sulking) and everybody else he could remember having been on his draft had disappeared into the world of adventure. Only Private Turvey, Thomas Leadbeater, remained, noting new faces as fresh drafts were trucked in and dumped in the courtyard. Each day looked like his day of pardon for, instead of being assigned to a training section, he would be warned to remain in his quarters between meals awaiting further orders. It wasnt until the eleventh day that the sergeant, who had felt Turvey's chin on an early morning parade and found stubble under it, took sufficient notice of him to shove him on fatigues. But then it was discovered that he had really been assigned long ago to the Goon Squad for a repeat of Basic Training; his file had been mislaid in the Orderly Room. A new drill had been invented for taking apart a Bren gun, and neither of the systems Turvey had learned in Canada or England was considered adequate for braving the enemy.

Turvey began to feel as if he had landed in Jerry territory by mistake and been captured. Probably the food was better but no Heiney guard could have served it with more suspicious reluctance than the cookees who bounced an ersatz barker and some watery rice into his billytin at supper time. There was the same uncertainty about release, and the same total confinement to quarters. The latter, he had to admit, was partly his own fault. He had sallied downtown with Chuck the second night, on pass to twenty-three hundred hours, and sampled the Ghent beer. (Each of them had been issued with a crisp fifty-franc note that morning.) And they had got lost on the way back, mutely following some Canadians who, it developed, were headed for another barracks the other side of town. Evidently an hour's lateness on pass was considered a serious offence at the Royal Albert; they were both C.B.-ed for a week. To cap it all, Chuck was wafted away as a reinforcement to the field, and Turvey, once his week was up, tried to nose out the estaminet alone, got lost again, and reaped another week's confinement to barracks.

Then one night, when he was sitting alone on his lumpy palliasse drying his newly-blancoed webbing and playing "Bury Me Not on the Lone Prairie" on his tonette, with another day still to go on his second C.B., an angel walked in. At first Turvey thought it was just another battledressed soldier. The only light in his corner of the basement came from a fuzzy bulb not much larger than some he had seen in flashlights, and several yards down the ceiling. But as the stranger strolled in with a rolling swagger that was a little familiar, Turvey caught sight of two pips on the shoulder and jumped to a salute.

"Hi, Tops," said the lieutenant, "happy in the service?"

"Mac! Holy cow! Where'd you spring from?" Turvey had gripped Mac's hand and was swinging it in happy amazement when he beheld, in maroon letters below Mac's shoulder, two magical words. "Mac! Jumpin gee, you're in the – there *is* – a Koo –"

"Now, now." Mac sat down briskly on Turvey's palliasse and brought out cigarettes. "No womanly emotions, please. All very simple. Phoned Buzzard Manor. Aj said you'd gone to join Montgomery. Flown over myself this morning, reinforcement draft. Tracked you down from the O.R. Aj here tells me I'm off up the line tomorrow, so thought I'd better haul you out for a quick one. How's the stagger juice in Ghent? And the female talent? What's the gen? Why arent you up hurling back Huns?"

But Turvey was only half-listening. Something was worrying him. "You'd better not walk around dressed like that, Mac. You'll get into trouble."

"What's wrong with the way I'm dressed?" Mac went through a pantomime check-over. "Fly's buttoned. Tie's tied."

"Dressed like a nofficer! That's personation, and you know it. That's a real serious crime!"

"I *am* an officer, lamebrain! Lieutenant MacGillicuddy. Rosy-cheeked graduate, still clutchin me sheepskin. Officer by Grace of God, gentleman by Act of Parliament. Rather expected your congratulations by now. What you think I've been climbing all over Monkey Hill at the OCTU for? Peanuts?"

"But – but – dont it take seven months at least to do all that trainin?"

"Ahh, not for a MacGillicuddy, my boy. Skipped Educational Pre-OCTU – knew all the answers – had a crib anyway. Jumped One-Two-Pause at limey OCTU first week – initial training crap, you know – had it all taped. Brilliant cadet, but brilliant! Also, must confess, course speeded up. Great shortage of infantry loots. Somebody keeps killing them off. Ack-I's burned their bottoms off getting us through on the double. Then whizz – one-two – we're all posted, and here I am. Cant keep cannon waiting, old man. But come, we're wasting time. Got to show me fleshpots of Old Ghent. Get organized, and stop that sickly grinning."

"I'm *not* grinnin," Turvey wailed, "at least I'm not grinnin inside. I'm C.B. And even if I werent, I couldnt walk out with you, never again I couldnt, and you know I couldnt."

"My dear old half-section, why in hell not?"

"Cause you're a nofficer now, that's why. And they dont walk around with O.R.s. And I'm gonna be here forever. I'm just, I'm just a body, that's all. I wisht I were – I wish I hadnt never gone Active, that's what!" It was the first time Turvey had said anything so desperate in his army career.

"Well, you old sad-sack! As the limey girl said when the baby turned out black, 'It was night and 'e said 'e was a Caneyedian but I didnt know 'e was *that* browned-off.'

Here! Have a genuine Montreal coffin-nail, and sit down, take the sweat off. Unlike you, Tops, unworthy of you, must say. So you cant paint Ghent with me today. Previous engagement. O.K. Pull that pudgy neck in and be the sergeant's whitehaired boy around here for the next couple of weeks, and I'll wangle you up the line with me or my name isnt Gillis MacGillis MacGillicuddy.''

"Holy smoke! Honest, Mac? With the Koot – ?''

"Well, strictly'' – Mac looked almost embarrassed, for him – "no. I'm on loan to the British. Liaison spot of some sort. Dont know what unit yet. Rolling up Belgium, you know. While you Canadians piddle around with the Channel ports. But I didnt want to greet the limeys without a regimental background and all that. Had these Kootenay flashes in my housewife since I snared em in Canada. Tacked em up flying over. However, point is, I'll need a jeep driver. And the Admin Officer here's brother to a pal of mine from OCTU. Maybe fix it from this end, if the limeys'll play ball.''

"Gosh all hemlock, really? I got a pair of Kootenay flashes still, too.''

"Spoken like a true son of the regiment. But sit on em till I can spring you out of this rat-trap.''

"You'll really get me –''

"As sure as you're Thomas Arse-Over Turvey . . . Bung-ho! Be seein yuh.''

And somehow Mac wangled it. Within a fortnight Turvey was banging beyond Brussells in a HUP. The following night he was sitting in his sleeping bag in a draughty corner of a half-ruined hat factory, engaged in the most blissful domestic chore of his army life; by special permission of the Royal Bogshire Regiment he was sewing Kootenay Highland shoulder flashes on his tunic. The next day he reported for duty as batman-driver to the battalion's Liaison Officer, Lieutenant G.M. MacGillicuddy.

TWELVE

Turvey Liberates the Belgians

FOR THE first time Turvey was in a position to engage the enemy. He was with a mechanized unit, the unit was pursuing the Germans across Belgium, and, as driver of the officer detailed to establish liaison with the advanced reconnaissance squadrons, Turvey was the very glittering tip of the Kootenay Highland spearhead of the Royal Bogshires. Unfortunately the Germans proved also to be mechanized and, at this stage of the war, to be almost singlemindedly absorbed in using their own vehicles to get the hell out of Belgium much faster than Turvey's jeep could get into it. In consequence, Mac and his eager batman-driver spent the next few weeks skirting smouldering tanks, rotting horses, fresh shellholes, and very stale canals, while they tore back and forth over a bewildering succession of roads without ever seeing a declared enemy. Often, in fact, what with maps giving out, and petrol scarce, they never caught up with one of the armoured jobs on whom they were trying to keep tab.

There were a few hazards to all this, of course. Snipers were presumed to be lurking in every golden wheatfield and half-shelled village they rattled past. But none ever shot at them. Enemy artillery rumbled and smoked the sky's rim, but not even a stray eighty-eight passed the time of day with them. V-Ones occasionally came buzzing and clonking and snarling out of the horizon, each sounding like a gigantic truck with a loose con-rod, and one roared so close behind that Turvey absentmindedly drew over and waved it by. When he leaned out to see why the lorry wasnt passing and beheld the spitting tail of flame almost overhead he yanked the jeep into a very fluid ditch and the jolt sent his top plate spinning into the murky water. They spent the next hour groping for Turvey's teeth, hauling the jeep free, and wringing out their clothes. In fact the chief threat to their physical wellbeing was undoubtedly Turvey's driving, as Mac never tired of pointing out. And the hazard ranking next in seriousness was the liberated population. The armour generally rushed through villages pursuing the enemy, so that it often happened that the Turvey-MacGillicuddy jeep would be the first allied vehicle with the leisure and inclination to pause and properly free the inhabitants. On one such occasion Mac collected a black eye from a bag of plums, and the same day Turvey suffered a nasty cheek scratch from the stem of an apple hurled too joyfully at the jeep. It was his first wound on operational duties.

There were days, of course, when there was time only for Mac to stick his helmet out the side as Turvey slowed their flower-decked jeep, and accepted an egg or two from some farmer alert to declare his partiality for the Western Powers, and a kiss from his daughter, or to park long enough for an excited shopkeeper to dig a ham or a bottle of wine from concealment and slide it into the liberating chariot. Since Mac sat with Turvey there was room enough behind to collect an appreciable store of thank-offerings.

One day they had been so occupied with trying, unsuccessfully, over a hundred miles of bad road, to locate even a single representative of a forward recce outfit, that they still found themselves a good way from their unit by six o'clock, decidedly hungry, and with nothing but a tangle of allied flags on the hood, and of bottles and Turvey's souvenirs in the back. Turvey lollopped the jeep through a mudhole beside a rather imposing farmhouse of mottled red brick set almost flush with the road.

"Hold everything," said Mac, "time we liberated some chow."

As Turvey brought the jeep to a halt by the farm gate, Mac blew the horn. Almost immediately a massive sack-shaped female emerged from a side-door bearing a mop and pail.

"Hi!" Mac greeted her with the V-sign as she opened the gate. "*Vivent les Belges.* Got anything to eat?"

The farmwife gave them an impassive glance, padded past, and silently set to work mopping off the mud the jeep had splashed on the tiled wall under the window.

"Must be deef. Hey, lady, *madame*, we want *food. Nous desirez* uh – *manjay.*" Mac leant puzzled out of the jeep. The madame swabbed the last speck from her seagreen tiles, picked up mop and pail, and sailed her great oblong face past them back into the house, without word or glance.

"Jeez. Smack out of an Antwerp Old Master, she is. Dont understand French, I guess." He leant over and blew the horn more vigorously. "Dont these hicks want to be liberated?" A large cartdog came to the gate, growled bitterly, and slunk away. Mac grunted. "I'm going to turf out those corny souvenirs of yours and make room for the tommy-cooker next time. Well, let's break out something to drink while we're waiting. What we got in the back looks good, Tops?" Mac bounced the horn again.

"Jeepers, we got just about everythin, only it's all foreign. Maybe cider. You cant read what it says." Turvey reached back and rummaged. "Here's some wallop, I think. Only they dont spell it right. B-i-e-r. That aint the way to spell 'beer', *is* it, Mac?"

"Here, you gormless nitwit, let me look. Course it's beer. *And* you know what you can do with it. I want something really smooth. Didnt we get champagne today? You go smoke these hayseeds out while I make a rekky."

Turvey was about to climb out when a shrivelled old man opened the bright blue side-door of the house and shuffled to the gate.

"Ah, got it!" Mac held up a fat bottle with an ornate label. "Ben-e-dict-ine. Never heard of it. Must be good though, classy bottle like that. Hey you. *Mess-oo!* We want a *drink*. And eats. *Nous sommes fatty-gay*, see. Bring us, uh, tumblers. What the hell they call em, I wonder?"

The farmer stared at them over the low gate. He had a brown face, wrinkled like a collapsed football and about as animated.

Mac walked to the gate and shoved the bottle under his nose. *"Bong? Goot?"* The old man edged back, regarded the label without touching the bottle, and nodded.

"Okey-doke then," said Mac briskly. "Bring us *tumblers. Tassen,* er – as you were – *Glassen.*" He went through an elaborate pantomime, filling an imaginary glass from the bottle and hoisting it. Then he put up three fingers. *"Gros verres,"* he shouted with sudden inspiration. The farmer made a weary moue, and toddled off to the house, coming back in a few minutes with two of the smallest glasses they had ever seen.

"Christ," said Mac, "those aint worth a pinch of coonshat. Strictly from hunger, rather drink out of the crock. Scare up some *gros verres*, you *savez, gros, grands, stark*. These aint big enough for a mouse to pee in. – Must be a baron or something. – And bring three, one for yourself. *Trois. Drei. Een pour vous.*" He shaped three enormous vessels in the air. One of the ancient's hoary eyebrows seemed to go up a few millimeters but otherwise his face remained dormant. He went slowly back and returned silently with two water tumblers.

"That's more like it. Bloody-minded old clam-puss, think it was *his* liquor, trying to palm off those eye-droppers on us. Old codger's bomb-happy. Dont even speak Flemish. Well, here's mud in your eye.''

Turvey and Mac stood beside the jeep and downed their tumblers while the farmer watched, now with a faint show of interest. Mac poured a second in his glass and proffered it to the old man. "Perhaps he's only got two real glasses.'' But the old Flamand backed away as if the glass would burn him, and continued to stare.

"O.K. No offence. Have it myself. Here, Tops, pour yourself a slug. This is bang on. Tastes almost like coke. Any more in back?''

While Turvey hunted and discovered another of the fat little bottles, Mac tried to talk the farmer into bringing them food or, at least, frying them some bacon from a smelly end that had turned up in the search. He exhausted his French, his eight words of Germanized Flemish, and his English, without getting a reaction. But by this time they had both begun to feel too warm and jovial to be really troubled.

"Five miles to Oomberdenderwinkei,'' said Mac. "Scoff something there, then beetle back to the unit. Havent enough petrol for any more swanning around anyway. Here, look sharp with that corkscrew. Sample that second bottle before we push off.''

They looked for the glasses they had set on the gate posts, but while they had both been vainly endeavouring to quicken a response by waving at what looked like the farmer's daughter framed in the parlour window, the old man had unobtrusively taken the *grands verres* back in and himself with them.

"Bugger em. We'll swig this one out of the crock,'' said Mac cheerfully. When they had put the cork in again and Turvey had turned the jeep around and they were passing the mudhole under the farm window, the blue shutters clattered back and the flat face of the girl poked out at them. Even under a Flemish bonnet, it had the same deadpan quality as the old man's. "Hold it,'' said Mac, but there was no need to warn Turvey. He had already shut the engine off. Mac quickly slid out of the jeep and, after a moment's teetering, saluted the damsel debonairly from the edge of the mudhole. *"Bong jour, mamselle,"* he said. *"Enchanté. Weedersine.* How about me coming in?"

"Me too," said Turvey doffing his battle-bowler and waggling his head happily out of the jeep.

"Shush, you're stinko. Dont rush her. People arent just riff-raff. Probably Counts or something. Lashings of em hereabouts. Proud, you know. Shy too. Explains why they wont talk. Need finessing. Leave it to me. You got your back teeth awash." He was about to address the maiden again when the latter's lips, until now as immobile as the rest of her broad face, began to move in a kind of circular squirm. She closed her eyes briefly, then jerked her chin forward with such sudden vigour her bonnet fell back from her head. In that moment there was a flash of strong yellow teeth and a fine jet of brown juice spouted towards them. It was a good ten feet to the jeep but the lady spanned it, catching Turvey neatly on his bared crown. At the same moment, the face disappeared and the shutters clattered to. Turvey, in a belated attempt to duck the lady's tobacco, bumped his head on a roof-strut.

While Mac climbed back into the jeep, swearing carefully and with attention to the principles of variation, Turvey started the engine again and stepped on the gas. When they had gone a few yards they heard the door of the farmhouse open. Peering back Mac saw the old woman emerge with brush and pail and, without a look in their direction, set to work scrubbing the tiled wall under the window again.

"Mac," said Turvey, "that biddy in the window didnt have no hair. Looked kina like her head was shaved. You suppose –"

"You know," said Mac thoughtfully, "I dont believe that family *wanted* to be liberated."

But the strange Belgian coca-cola, once Mac had swabbed the tobacco juice from behind Turvey's ear, soon helped them pass over the puzzles of the Flemish character. Turvey, in addition, so far forgot his immediate problems that he plopped the jeep in an enormous mudhole at the next bridge, so deep that, after some talkative attempts to rev it out, they decided to settle back and finish the benedictine while planning the next move. Half an hour later, a Despatch Rider from their unit found them. Message for Lieutenant MacGillicuddy. Colonel calling an O-Group. All officers, including subalterns. Twenty-thirty hours.

There was just time to make it. With the help of the motorcycle and some rope they got the jeep back into operation and Mac, slightly sobered by the cold mud and the thought of an O-Group, took over the wheel from the now thoroughly carefree Turvey. The latter settled back to massacre "Lord God Almighty how ashamed I was!" on his tonette.

"Thas torn it," Mac muttered as they swayed along in the gathering darkness trying to keep up with the Don/R, "f'all times for Ole Man to start a blitz, and me soused. Firs time he's had two-pippers at'n O-Group. Somethin up for sure. Uc!"

"He wan' me too?" Turvey wiped the tonette on his tunic sleeve. "Whassa No Group anyway?"

"O-Group, dimwit. Strickly for off'cers. Stradishy 'n tactics. Firs, Ole Man 'tends *his* O-group w'other colonels at Brigade, see. Brig-Brigerdier tells em wurr they goin' 'tack, 'r somepn. 'N Ole Man tells us wurr *we* goin 'tack. Chalk-talk, 'n all that. Wouldn' unnerstan."

"Course I unnerstan. 'N then uh privates 'tack. 'S called O-Group cause a Ole Man." He laughed uproariously but Mac was not amused. When they finally drew up by the schoolhouse temporarily occupied by the regiment, Mac reached over and shook the now snoring Turvey into semi-consciousness. "Listen, you drunken numskull. Snap out a it. You gotta stay ver-vertical. Cause you're to look arrer me an' I'm lit. You mark time ou'side O.C.'s t'l I come out, see I getta bed, see I ge' up whenerr we gotta be up. Uc! Go stick finger down'r throat 'n *stay awake*. Thash *order*."

Turvey staggered around the side of the schoolhouse, painfully carried out part of his instructions and groped his way back to the jeep. But after several manly efforts to stay conscious by knocking his knuckles on the sore lump where his head had hit the jeep-strut, he sank into a blissful labyrinth of dream. Then he felt someone shaking him, and Mac bawling in his ear.

"Three hours we're movin up to Hollan'. Ge' your finger out, an shove over!" He crawled in the jeep and was immediately asleep. Turvey's head ached down to his ears.

Three hours later, somewhat restored by coffee, he tried to rouse Mac, but that gentleman seemed sounder asleep than ever. While Turvey was determining what cold water could do, liberally poured down Mac's neck, the Mortar Platoon Officer came swaying out of the darkness.

"Pleasir," said Turvey saluting, "cant wake him up. He's swamped. It's that benzedrine, I guess."

"Benzedrine!" yelled the captain, seizing the now board-stiff body of Mac and plunging a hand down his chest to feel his heart. "Good God! What shall we do!" Turvey thought the captain rather excitable for a limey. He had a nice rich breath, too. "How much did he take? He's in a cold sweat!"

"O, we just killed a coupla crocks between us, sir. Share and share on the first bottle. But I got some longer drags on the second."

"You've swigged two whole bottles of ben – O, I say, not reahlly! You couldnt stand theah and tell me about it." The captain giggled. "Not, not even a Canadian –"

"I hadda bring mine up, sir. Orders of Lieutenant MacGillicuddy."

"I say! What did this stuff look like?"

Turvey rooted in the back and found one of the empties.

"Benedictine, you ass! Benedictine. Well, my lohd,

that's bad enough, a whole bally bottle he's had. Fun *and* games. No wondeh he was so noisy in O-Group. Old Man pointing to the map, saying 'We'll go in theah' and MacGillicuddy bawling from the back 'That's the stuff, let's give em hell.' Old Man looked a bit stahtled, I must say. That map must have been reahlly whirling around for old Mac, eh? What a head he'll have when he wakes! *When*, by Jove! He looks as if he'll be horizontal for the next two days. Heah, you'll just have to look ahfter him." He fished through Mac's pockets. "Heah's his map ref'rences and timing beginning 0300 owahs. Yoah to go ahead and make liaison again. Prop him up in the seat when you drive off and nobody'll twig if he hasnt come to."

And so it was that a half-hour later, Turvey led the Royal Bogshires out on the first leg of their new offensive. It was two in the afternoon before he finally got Mac alive enough to talk to, by which time Turvey was so thoroughly lost it was night again before they found the unit rendezvous. There Mac had a painful session with his C.O., the gist of which he passed on to Turvey the next morning.

"We're in the bloody doghouse, Tops. All account of you. You and that li-koor stuff. In future, dont liberate anything but gin and cognac."

"No sham-pag-nee?"

"Well, if you're sure it is. But no benedictine. Know what we're going to be now? The stinking rearguard!"

True enough, within a few days, the regiment had disappeared ahead of them and Lieut. MacGillicuddy, assisted by Private Turvey and a small detachment of NCOs and men, found themselves officially holding the quiet Belgian border village of Wuustschot-op-den-Bosch, which the rapidly moving armies had bypassed.

At least it started out quiet. But next day the brigadier's push got thoroughly confused with a German flanking movement on the south and a successful holding action in the west. Wuustschot-op-den-Bosch, by rather sketchy wireless orders that filtered through, was officially

sealed off, and Mac was exalted to the role of second-in-
command to a British Artillery Captain who had been
squeezed back into the town with a twenty-five pounder
and a scattering of gunners. These, with other mislaid
soldiers from various units who had straggled into the
village, and the crew of a broken-tracked Churchill,
made up a garrison of about seventy, which the captain
bedded down in the ground floor of the village convent,
below a covey of suspicious nuns. Turvey, as an attendant moon to Mac's rising planet, now added daily a
score of new duties to that of batman-driver. He scuttled
with messages between Military Command (set up in the
Burgomeister's livingroom-parlour) and the convent, and
the Town Hall, and the Town Jail, and the estaminet
where the Wuustschot local of the Belgian Underground
had emerged hilariously to the surface. He found the
company and fare in the last of these very much to his liking. But it was all very confusing, especially as there
seemed to be new Police Officers and new Burgomeisters
to deliver chits to every few hours, and the old ones were
continually being shifted into the cells. Mac tried to explain it to him.

"Bit of a snafu, Tops. Jerry's only six kilometres down
the west road. We've a road block and twenty-five
pounder there, see. But Jerry's somewhere north. South
too. And this burg's chin-deep with collaborationists.
Cant trust a single native. So we've sealed em off.
Nobody leaves town without a pass, and only me or the
Arty Captain signs em. Any bastard crosses us up, into
the hoosegow with him."

"Like the mayor and the Police Chief yesterday?"

"Check! Underground laddies tipped us off on them.
And Burgomeister's sec today. He brown-nosed the Arty
Cap, got promoted to Burgo. Then we caught the twicer
signing passes on his own, and one of our Brens in his
digs. So he's in the clink. Thank God we got a Navy.
Trouble is, damned jail cant hold many more. Full of
civilians tried to take a powder at night with velos;
baskets on the handlebars stuffed with food. Off to hawk

it to Jerry. And now what to do with all these fuggin farmers romping in on dogcarts to peddle their hen-fruit and butter? Maybe they just want to sell em; maybe they want to get military gen and ship it to Jerry. And there's characters sidling in here from Allah knows where, want to sell us the wire about Jerry troop movements. Maybe it's on the up-and-up, maybe they're giving us a bum steer, maybe want to snoop, selling advance gen to both sides. Cant take chances. Anybody gets in this burg, stays in, unless we say so. Tops, my boy, you're practically my adjutant in all these matters now, you know. But dont forget to call me 'sir' when the Artillery johnny's around. Upsets him when you dont. Bit of a blimp, between you and me.''

''Yessir, Mac,'' And Mac sent Turvey trotting off with a rifle on one shoulder and a large painted sign in incomprehensible languages under the other, to paste up on the last house on the High Street. ''That tells the hicks they cant come closer, market days is 0900 Monday and Thursday only, and no goddam haggling and palavering. Just come there, peddle what they got, and bugger off. That'll fox em.''

Turvey got back just in time to escort another civilian to the Police Station. It was the local butcher, who had applied for a pass to deliver outside town. He had made the mistake of asking for one for his wife and daughter too, and an aunt. The Underground reported he hadnt been delivering for two years, and the aunt wasnt an aunt.

On the way to the jail Turvey thought it well to double-check with the Underground, and perhaps pick up a cognac or two. At the estaminet he found four men in assorted handout uniforms, the green bands of the Resistance on their coatsleeves, engaged in an excited babble punctuated with wide leers and rather lecherous laughs. The sub-lieutenant in charge, who spoke English, told Turvey they had just discovered four ladies in a house on the outskirts of the town.

''Nize bebbies, eh, you call dem?'' the Belgian said,

arching his eyebrows ecstatically. "But not too nize."
Then his expression suddenly grew venemous. "Boche
beetches. They are, what you call, a-good-time girls, for
Boche officers wen déy were 'ere. De Boches bring em in
from Allemagne, yes. An wen dey go, dey got no time to
take em wit. Now wot we do wid em? Hah? Shoot em
just? Or slip wit em first, hey? I write a note to your captain to fin' out, yes? Meantime we 'ave de guards aroun'
dis, wot you call in America, lover-nest, hah?"

When Turvey had delivered the sullen butcher to the
jail he reported back to Headquarters, where Mac, in the
captain's absence, was pondering the note which had
meantime arrived from the Underground's sub-lieutenant.

"Stick the little twots in the jail with the rest of em,
that's what," said Mac. "On the double."

"Cant do that, please Mac. P'lice Chief told me to tell
you. Jail's full. Includin corridors, he says. Cant take
even one more."

"Dear God! Have to acquire another klink."

"The Underground loot says they got guards out
around the house."

"Ah, but his note says they got to take em off. Need all
their men for night patrol. So they do. Havent half
enough. Four school-kids sneaking out last night; every
little bastard with two kilos of butter tied on his velo-
frame. Dug it out of em they were off to flog it in
Aalstraat. Right now that's a Jerry town. Notion to
shoot the little muckers."

"Please, Mac sir, if there aint anythin else you want
me to do tonight, I could go guard those women."

Mac regarded him skeptically, but Turvey's face was a
round disc of innocence. Mac blew out his breath wearily.
"Well, O.K. Just for tonight, till I think of something
better. And your orders is to *guard* em see. These arent
ordinary bims. Underground loot says they found a
bleedin arsenal in their place – rifles, ammo, revolvers,
cases of food. Watch em like a mother." He peered at
Turvey. "I'd better send Allen with you. And I'll see the

sub-loot checks up on you both tonight. Better sashay over there now,'' he added, ''so the Underground guards can –'' But Turvey was already off at the double.

It was nearly midnight before Mac could free himself from a welter of pass-signing, telephoning, and the comings and goings of soldiers and civilians in the mayor's parlour. Feeling the need of a breather before turning in, he belted on his revolver and walked out into the moonlit Hoghstraat. Artillery growled and belched on the horizon. He was rambling without much thought of direction when he noticed a street sign. St. Niklasstraat, he thought, that's where they found those four dames. Must be the end house. Wonder if the sub-loot checked up on Turvey.

On one side of the street the wall of old grey dwellings stopped to give place suddenly to farmland. On the other, there was a vacant lot and then a lone two-storey house of modern stucco with a marsh beyond. Seems thoroughly blacked out, he thought. Not a chink showing. Not that it matters with this moon. But where are the guards? He walked up to the front door and found a Quarter-store's chain and padlock stapled lopsidedly between frame and knob. Tacked on the varnished door was a notice; thick-pencilled letters covered a piece of feminine stationery, small and violet-hued:

SEALED OF
NO ADMITTENCE BY
ORDER
T. L. Turvey, Pte. i.c.

After several futile poundings and chain rattlings, Mac paced to the back of the silent house. A similar notice stared at him from the kitchen door. There was no padlock, but the door wouldnt budge. Mac thought he could hear vague movements from beyond the kitchen, but his thumpings and shouts brought no more response than at the front. O God, some kind of shambles, I'll bet. Had enough grief today. "Open up, Tops, or I'll shoot the bloody lock off," he shouted.

Faintly there was the voice of Turvey. "Hold it, Mac. Comin."

But it was Allen, the guard he had sent to companion Turvey, who inserted a key and opened the door. As Mac came in Allen switched on the kitchen light. He was wearing nothing but his dogtags, a pair of grey army socks, and a trapped expression. The rest of the house was in darkness.

"What the merry hell's going on here? Thought you were guarding this house. Where's your clothes? Where's the women?" Allen, who seemed to have been struck speechless, was saved by the arrival of another figure which stumbled blinking in from the hallway, still in the act of binding about its middle a tasselled cord attached to a silken dressing-gown of decidedly unmasculine size and cut.

"Please, sir, Mac, that's what we're doin. We're guardin em. Didnt you see my signs? And we got the house all locked up. Nobody could get in."

"No, you waffling fathead, but they could get out. With you two Naafi Romeos asleep they could slit your silly throats, and climb out a window."

Turvey regarded him with the eyes of the accused innocent. "O gosh, Mac, they wouldnt do that! Not *these* girls."

"You two eternal letching duckheads. You, you're, you're as useless as tits on a washtub. Where's your rifles?"

"Please, sir, Mac, the sub-loots' got em hidden. The girls dont know where. Even we dont know. Somewheres in the house, though," Turvey added triumphantly. "You want him to show you?"

Mac found the occasion beyond words. He stared at Turvey, then at Allen, and shook his head.

"And where, if you would be so good, Private Pathfinder Turvey, where, please, is the sub-lieutenant?"

"Oh he's in the livinroom too. We're all in there. To guard em, you know."

Mac's eyes widened in slow understanding. He shoved past Turvey. "Where's the bloody light?"

Turvey, somewhat reluctantly, came to his assistance and, trailed by the shivering Allen, led Mac through the dim hall. Snapping on a switch at its end, he revealed a spacious but complicated living-room.

Ranged along the walls, under huge gilt-framed pictures, were several chairs and small tables decked with bottles and tumblers. The furniture had evidently been cleared aside to make space in the centre for three cots and a chesterfield. Between the beds, on the lush carpet, stood the lieutenant gendarme in G.I. serge jacket and British battle trousers, stiffly at attention as if in a tableau. He at least, thought Mac, is in some kind of uniform, but something about his stance made Mac's eyes travel downwards. The lieutenant was in bare feet. And, on second look, Mac saw beneath his jacket, instead of shirt, a V of hairy bosom.

"We brought the beds down from upstairs," Turvey added brightly.

"And the ladies on them, I see," added Mac with stunned acceptance. For from one side of each of the beds three pair of feminine eyes regarded him with a curious mixture of fright and triumph. And he was becoming slowly aware that a fourth pair were mutely speaking to him from the blanketed chesterfield, a pair of very handsome sky-blue orbs in which the expression was further complicated by a touch of coquetry. This, he decided, was the girl who was, so far, sleeping alone.

"Excusez moi, s'il vous plaît," said the sub-lieutenant gendarme, still erect on the carpet but now breaking out into the most courteous of smiles. "Eet is verry late, *mon lieutenant*, for to walk back alone, hah? *Dangereux*, no, *les collaborateurs*, zey snipe. We would be *enchantés* if

you would 'ave ze goodness to, 'ow you say, make ze fourt'?''

Mac gave a sigh of defeat. "Carry on, gentlemen. But for Pete's sake remember – I havent been here.''

Turvey could never understand why Mac didnt stay. He expressed his puzzlement the next evening when he caught Mac alone.

"Gotta draw the line somewhere, Tops. Those were Heinie splits.''

Turvey pondered. "Yessir, Mac, but, well, they dont chew tobacco anyway.''

"My God! Touché! But I've enough grief without you coming all over witty on me. Remember we were fraternizing that time, liberating our gallant allies. Anyway, you had me loco with that swampjuice benedictine. All your fault. But these square-tacks are strictly bad news.''

"Yes,'' sighed Turvey, having fired his only shot.

"Besides. Hadnt heard from Daphne then. Should tell you. Seems my last missive did the trick. Got a sugar report. We're to be spliced. Arent you going to congratulate me?''

"Holy cow, that's – that's wonderful.'' Turvey dazedly tried to adjust to the thought of Mac married. If it could happen to Mac – "Did she, she, uh, mention Peggy at all in her letter?''

"Who? O Peggy. Not a word. Why dont you write her?''

"Daphne?''

"Peggy, dope.''

"O! Yeah. Say, maybe I could do that . . . Uh, Mac?''

"Ummm?''

"O, nothin. You stopped that too, more'n like.''

"What *are* you nattering about?''

"O, nothin. Just I got somethin left from last night. Looks kinda like cham-pag-nee. You could, uh, sorta wet your engagement with it, like.''

"Private Turvey, there's two buttons off my trousers. Report to my quarters 1830 hours with issue kit, sewing."

" 'Sir."

"And bring the bottle."

"Yessir."

"And two tumblers."

"Comin up, Mac!"

THIRTEEN

Turvey Becomes a Casualty

"Hmm. You look pretty fit. What's wrong with you?" asked the M.O. in the outpatient wing of the Ghent Military Hospital.

"Please, sir, Flanders crut, sir."

"Hmm. How many times a day?"

"Well, sir, today there was twice before breakfast, and –"

"More than a dozen a day?"

"Oh, yes, sir. Coupla dozen maybe. And Mac, that's my officer pal, he got fed up with stoppin the jeep all the time when we were out lazin and –"

"Gripes in the belly? . . . Hmmm. Spot of vomiting? . . . Hmm. Been to the M.O. at your unit?"

"Yes, sir. He give me lead pills till he run out of em. Then I come here on leave and it's been kinda interferin with things and down at the Canadian Legion Club they thought I better see somebody here."

"Hmm. What do you drink?"

"Gee, thanks, sir. Dont mind if I do. Anythin you got."

"I'm not offering you a drink, numskull. What liquids do you take at meals – and between?"

"O! Just the old shoeleather coffee, you know sir, at meals. I like this here conack all right and cider, and the beer's not bad, or even this here sham-pag-nee. But I dont go for benzidictine, it –"

"What about water?"

"Water?" Turvey thought hard. "No, cant remember drinkin any water lately. You see I been keepin cider in my waterbottle. Clean my teeth in water, though."

"Hmm. That might have done it. Have to give you an examination. Bring you into the hospital for a few days. Soon have you fit."

For Turvey the rest of the morning was clover. He was ordered into a real bed, with sheets and a spring. He lay in a large lysol-smelly ward full of pajamaed soldiers, thumbed old copies of the *Maple Leaf*, and listened to the American Forces programme over the loudspeaker. His gripes almost immediately subsided and he had only two trips to make down the corridor before the orderlies began passing through with the lunch-trays.

But there was no lunch for him. Lonely on his tray was an enormous beaker of castor oil. The orderly, a sullen Flamand dressed in janitor's blue jeans, stood ominously over him.

"Please," said Turvey, "just set it down. I'll – I'll have it later."

The orderly shoved the tray under Turvey's nose with one hand and made a vigorous gesture of downing the tumbler with the other. "No speak Ang-lish. Ooomps." Turvey managed it in four desperate gulps.

The orderly was shortly succeeded by a grim white nurse, who suddenly bore down on him carrying between two muscular arms a small salver. On it instead of meat and potatoes such as he had seen parading past him, lay a set of wickedly gleaming vials and instruments. Within three minutes the nurse had silently recorded his pulse and temperature, stabbed his third finger-tip, squeezed a bubble of blood from it onto a glass slide, skewered his arm with a long stinger, and pumped out a test-tube full of the same precious fluid.

"Got anything to eat with you?" she asked in the middle of executing the last operation. They were her first words.

"Gosh, no, sir – uh, miss . . . sister. You have to bring your own food?"

"Doctor says nothing for you today. Got to have your stomach empty." Then she added, as if conferring a favour, "You can drink this water." She set a small tumbler by his bed and was off.

"Jeez, you must be goin to the operatin room, eh?" It was the patient on the next bed, right. He had been a sleeping huddle in the blankets till the orderly had plopped down a tray for him, minus the meat. Now, lunch over, he was somewhat listlessly fitting curlicues of cardboard into a jigsaw puzzle, with a pair of mustard-coloured hands. Turvey was startled to see that his face was also yellow as a bullpine, even to the wart on the tip of his long drooping nose. "They allus flush em out like a toilet before they operate." There was a brooding dispassionate quality to his voice which began to alarm Turvey.

"Jeepers, you think so? All I got is Flanders crut. They dont operate for that, do they?"

The yellow one was silent while he dovetailed a particoloured scrap into its place in the wooden frame.

"You wont know – till they wheel yah in."

He gave Turvey a speculative peer. The smoke-yellow of his eyeballs, surrounding sad blue pupils, made the look vaguely sinister. "Anyone stick around here long enough they put the knife in 'im for damn near anythin. Wouldnt surprise me if they started cuttin *me* up anytime, even though all I got's jaundice." He looked around the ward carefully and then lowered his voice "It's these kid doctors. They figure this is their big chance to get lots a practice." He twisted a corner of his mouth meaningfully and resumed a study of the jigsaw.

Turvey began to feel goosepimples coming out on his stomach. He lay wondering on what section of his flesh a surgeon might begin excavating to cure his particular complaint. Soon, however, and for the rest of the afternoon, he was too busy shuttling up and down the south corridor to indulge in sustained brooding.

By supper time Turvey had given up his sheets and lay bellydown in fitful quiescence on the top of his bed. He couldnt remember ever feeling so tired or – now that the clatter of trays and the steam of food spread through the ward – so hungry. He raised his chin and watched mournfully the overalled orderlies serve to right and left of him and then shift operations downward as if Turvey's bed were empty. The jaundiced patient, whose name was Whiteside but who was more often referred to as Yellowbelly, rolled his smoky eyeballs meaningfully at Turvey and went back to a peckish probing of his own meatless tray. Turvey, afraid Whiteside was about to retail another of those rumours about unsuccessful experimental surgery in Ghent Military with which he had entertained him during the afternoon, struck up a talk with the husky French-Canadian on the other side of him. This was a thoroughly cheerful soul who was being treated for boils that had appeared in some two-year-old shrapnel scars from Dieppe. But the sight of Trudeau's hearty enjoyment of a full-sized tray made Turvey hungrier than ever and he moved carefully on to his back to stare at the faded peagreen ceiling.

He was practising "Lili Marlene" on his tonette and trying to decide whether the upside down object in his field of vision was a cockroach or just a fly when a large white something interposed. It was the Grim Nurse, complete with tray. It contained a roll of Army Form Blank, a large porcelain beaker of anonymous liquid, and a strangely shaped hot water bottle. Turvey thought the latter a homey touch but his stomach shrank at the sight of the beaker.

"Please, sister, d'I have to drink all that?"

The sister's voice was as hard as a Kootenay crow's, "All right. Down to the toilet and take an enema."

Turvey was puzzled and a little alarmed. "Please, I've been goin to the toilet all afternoon. I'd like somethin to make me stop. That's what they sent me to hospital for."

The sister gazed out the window as if for something to

do while waiting for him to move and she spoke mechanically without looking at him. "Doctor says you're to have an enema now and another in the morning. You know how to take one?"

Turvey regarded the tray. The name was strange but he didnt like to confess ignorance. He could feel the nurse wanted to get away in a hurry. So he said yes, slid into his slippers, and began flip-flapping toward the south corridor. The voice of the nurse arrested him, weary with patience.

"You're forgetting the enema."

"Oh, thanks," said Turvey weakly, "but I'll fill it when I get back and put it at the bottom of the bed. It's my feet'r coldest."

The nurse's stare, at first suspicious, changed to pained recognition of the fact Turvey was not being facetious. She instructed him, slowly, carefully and even with some modest attempts at pantomime, in the use of the beaker and bag. Turvey trundled off with them, wishing very much that he were back with the Bogshires, and nothing worse than Flanders crut to bother him.

Back in bed he drifted off into a sleep of exhaustion, from which he was gently wakened, just before lights out, by another nurse, a rather shy thin creature. She took his temperature, dabbed his face tentatively with a warm sponge, placed a glass on his table, clinked something under his bed and, breathing, "Doctor's orders," in a sad apologetic little voice, fled without further parley, turning out the lights at the door. Turvey lay in a desolate torpor, in which his only pleasant thought was that the little sister had not waited to see if he really drank the castor oil. He remembered the clinking sound under his bed. In a few seconds he made a somewhat more direct disposition of the castor oil than the M.O. had intended. He sank into a troubled world dominated by a whitehooded sexless creature in a respirator who, brandishing a butcher knife in one hand and an enema bag the size of a blanket roll in the other, pursued Turvey down endless corridors.

Hunger awoke him even before the orderlies had rattled in, snapped on the lights and hustled him, with the other up-patients, down the familiar hallway to wash and shave. By the time he was back and had his bed made the Grim Nurse was on hand, complete with thermometer, beaker and bag. At any rate the bag was no bigger than yesterday's.

"Oo goes dere? Friend or henema, heh?" Trudeau's bed quivered with his joviality. The nurse paid no heed.

"Take your enema right away and shower after. Then the orderly will take you to the doctor."

Turvey found the enema superfluous. To save argument he poured the contents of the beaker down the lavatory. On the way back he had to sit down twice on the cold tile of the corridor, but he finally made it to the ward. He had just collapsed on the blessed island of his bed when Marcel, the Flemish orderly, came wandering by, looking at the numbers that hung on metal discs, one from the foot of each bed, and consulting a paper in his hand. He stopped at Turvey's. Then he jerked a soiled thumb over his shoulder. "Komm," he said.

"Where?" Turvey stalled desperately. "I just been."

The orderly stumped around to Turvey's head and shoved the paper under his nose. With growing horror Turvey read it:

ADMIT .... Private Turvey
BED 9
TO..................... Operation Theatre C
FOR .... Stereosphagoscopy

With a grubby forefinger the orderly touched Turvey's name and then poked the finger enquiringly at him. "You?"

"What's it say?" asked Whiteside, who had been watching the scene with fateful tension.

"I gotta go to Operation Theatre C," said Turvey bleakly.

"Whad I tell yah? Boy, they're knife-crazy in here. Knives and scissors and stitches. Bet they got more knives than in Canada Packers' slaughterhouse."

Turvey climbed in stunned silence from his bed and tottered after the impassive orderly. "G'bye, Turvey; was nice knowin you," Whiteside called after him.

"Don you worry, soldier," Trudeau countered, "Dey won fine nutting in you now, heh?"

He trudged wearily behind Marcel, down draughty stairs and along a duplicate corridor in the basement to a door market Operation Theatre C.

Turvey braced himself for a big room full of floodlights and masked doctors, but what they entered was only a narrow dimlit anteroom with two doleful soldiers sitting in wait on the usual barrackroom bench against a wall. Marcel pointed to the bench, thrust the fatal paper into Turvey's hand, and shuffled off without a flicker of interest.

Facing him now was a white partition with a sign – SILENCE – hung on its closed door. The wall was evidently of thin plyboard for through it, despite the placard, filtered along with the smell of antiseptic, a succession of sounds of an uncheering character. Turvey could distinguish the voice of the doctor who had examined him when he had been admitted – when was it, only yesterday morning? He tried to picture what was happening on the other side. The doctor must be talking to another one: "All right. Shove up on his knees . . . steady now . . . head down . . . wont take a jiffy." Turvey thought for a moment they must have a horse in there but then he knew it was a patient; there was the clink of glass, a breathy silence, a sound like a bicycle pump, and a gradual crescendo of grunts that suddenly broke into a deep masculine howl, stirring the hair on Turvey's scalp. This was worse than last night's dream. Now the doctor's voice, routinely soothing: "A little tender there? Just relax. Over in a jiff. Just a couple more inches." Then the breathings and grunts and pumpings began again and rose to another and even more prolonged howl that made the "Silence" sign rattle. Turvey closed his eyes, mentally forming and sadly discarding several plans for escape from the hospital back to the Bogshires. He could think of no way of passing undetected in a suit of hospital pajamas.

His mental state was slightly eased when, not long after the third and most heartrending cry, a surprisingly small patient emerged still on his own feet; but the soldier's eyes were those of a man who had experienced everything. He walked as if astounded that he still could. Without a glance at the waiting three he made swaybacked for the outer door, obviously fearful of being recalled. As he went out he cast one dreadful look behind him as though he thought somebody or something were following him.

The next two, fortunately for Turvey's endurance, must have had different ailments; they were in but a short time and didnt howl. At last a whitejacketed male nurse beckoned him in to a small whitejacketed room, brilliant with light from an overhead globe which was reflected brilliantly back from a neat operatingroom table. It was a table not unlike the one he had once sportively rowed with his crutch down the hospital ward of Number Umpteen Basic Training Centre. Ah, if only it were a broken leg he had now.

"Hmm," said the doctor, glancing at the slip, then at Turvey, then at a clip-board of documents on a corner table, "this must be the other stereophag, Tom. All the instruments sterile?"

"Yessir," said the male nurse briskly. Turvey's unhappy gaze lit on a glittering double row of scissors and venomous little crooked knives immersed in a shallow tray on a side table. He felt his knees give.

"All right, lad, off with the pajamas."

"Please, sir," said Turvey, lingering miserably in one

pajama leg, "it if aint against orders, could you tell me about where you're goin to cut into me."

The doctor snorted. "Good Lord, soldier boy, we're just going to take a look at your lower bowel. Make sure there's no ulcer there. A little blood in your stools, you see. You're not afraid of us, are you? Wont take a minute. All done with mirrors." He smiled broadly but at some secret joke, and Turvey noticed the same smile on the attendant. Somehow he wasnt much comforted, but he could see he was expected to be a soldier about it all. Probably chloroform was too scarce over here to use on privates, even for cutting into a lower bowel. If that other guy could take it and walk out, he guessed maybe a Kootenay –

"*All* right, my lad," said the doctor with a too-elaborate heartiness, "up on the table with you. No. On your elbows and knees. That's it. Head down. Hunch that fanny up as high as you can. That's right. Arms out. Take a grip on the table-end. No. Get the top of your head on the table, not your chin. That's better. Now, dont move, whatever happens."

Out of the side of his eye, Turvey saw the rubber-gloved hands of the doctor lifting a long gleaming glass tube, longer than a rolling pin and almost as thick. It couldnt be that they – he was going to – No. The enema had been big enough. But this!

"All done with mirrors." The voice had that phoney ring which Turvey had noticed in dentists just before they stab the drill into a nerve. "Little mirrors inside this tube do the looking for me. And a little airpump to dilate the bowel. Wonderful invention. No knives. No operations. Only last a jiffy. I just take a look with this tube . . . hmm . . . like . . . *this*!"

"Whoo-ow!" yelled Turvey, with a roar of shock and unbelieving surprise. He brought his behind down with instinctive rejection of the doctor's wonderful invention, which leapt free and was dexterously caught in mid-air by the waiting attendant.

"Good work, Tom! Saved the army three hundred dollars again. They always do it." His voice hardened. "Now, soldier, I told you not to move. We cant have you breaking this stereophagoscope. Take a grip around his knees, Tom." He felt himself folded like an accordion. "I'll pump . . . Hmm . . . Convolution acute here . . . *Whump!*"

Turvey never knew how many hour-like minutes passed before he was released from the triple grip of Tom's two hands and the doctor's anal telescope. It was long enough for him to understand and to duplicate all the grunts and howls he had heard through the partition. And when he made his first unbelieving steps into the freedom of the ante-room and back to the corridor he could understand the look on the other patient's face. It was the stare of a man who has not only experienced the ultimate indignity of life but who still believes himself to be walking with a stereophagoscope permanently imbedded in his inner-most recesses. Even when he staggered to his bed, Turvey involuntarily glanced behind him before venturing to slump on the blessed blankets.

"Let yah off this time, eh?" Whiteside looked up from his interminable reconstruction of a jigsaw Buckingham Palace as Turvey sank back on his pillow. He sounded disappointed.

"Dey cant kill a hinfantryman," said Trudeau triumphantly, (Whiteside was from the Army Service Corps). "What dey do to you, Turvey?"

Turvey struggled to find words for it, failed and contented himself with an understatement. "They goosed me," he said. "With a two-foot telescope." And with returning strength he related his latest ordeal.

"*Tabernacle*, dat worse dan a mortar bumb. Me, I keep my boils, tanks ver much."

"Yeah, but they aint fed yah yet, have they? Seems to me they'd feed yah if they werent going to operate." Whiteside fitted another piece of the palace gates into his foreground.

There was an hour still to lunch, an hour for Turvey to reflect that Whiteside might still be right. The now daily V-Twos had begun to drop, one of them near enough to shake flakes of plaster from the ceiling onto Turvey's bed. He'd never cared less.

He managed to spend the first fifteen minutes watching the scene outside the window. Beyond the narrow lawn, the laurel hedge and the iron railings of the hospital, a withered woman in mourning clothes pushed a drab cart over the cobblestones. A van banged past her, drawn by a great speckled horse. Turvey saw that its tail was docked cruelly short, and winced in sympathy. Beyond the road a row of lindens, bare and scabby, sprayed from a towpath into the gloomy sky. An enormous barge crept into the picture. On its broad prow a man sat placidly smoking while a thin boy ran up and down the gunwales prodding the bank with a fantastically long pole. On the towpath a squat old woman and a scrawny girl stumbled along in sack-harness; by ropes attached to the barge they pulled it along the brown canal water with infinite sad slowness and yet with a curious crablike dexterity. Turvey sighed and rolled over to talk to Trudeau.

"Gee, it sure must have been excitin at Dieppe, Trudeau. How'd you get wounded?"

"O, dat. I don know. I don like much to tell about dat. Me, I'm plenty scared."

"Come on, Trudy," said Bradley, a bald-headed sergeant across the aisle. "You're the only one here was at Dieppe. Give us the real gen, eh?" Several others added their encouragement, glad of distraction.

"Aw, I don really see wat appen. But hokay – we make Turvey forget about 'is henema till de lunch, heh?" He propped up his pillow. "Well, me, I was just de corporal for company 'eadquarters, wit a Bren and tree riflemen. My capitaine, 'e say, 'Trudy, you suppose look hafter me, see I don get los.' But by ca-ripes it me dat get los; so soon we hit dose beaches everyting is smoke an noise like de parade Saint Jean-Baptiste in Mo'real: heverybody bang-bang wit heveryting dey got. Pretty soon we aint got one bullet lef', we can' see de rest of Ead-quar-ters nor de capitaine and by ca-rice, we walk round a hupset carrier in de smoke and pow! – we is captured." Trudeau fished for a cigarette.

"Gee, they take you to Germany?" breathed Turvey.

"Sure, he's still there." Whiteside didnt take his eyes off his Palace, and Trudeau went on as if he hadnt heard.

"I guess dat w'ere we were 'eaded. De Jerries take hour weapons and march de four of us hup tru de *ville*, and push us agains a wall. I tink maybe dey goin shoot us ri' dere an I star' for to say my prayers, but no – you know wat dose bastairds do?"

"Took your pitchers," said Whiteside promptly, "Canada's Secret Weapons."

"Shuddup, Yellowbelly. Let'm tell his story." It was Parsons, next to Bradley. Most of the ward within earshot were now listening, and registered agreement. Trudeau again ignored the interruption.

"Dey make us take hof de boots an trousairs. By gar, now, dat make me one engry fellah. Dere is dis leetle Jerry punk mebbe ten-twelve feet away wit a Spandau sticking at my sto-mach, and I 'ave to take down de trousairs, mine. Dat someting I don like for to do."

"What, never?" asked Whiteside.

This time Trudeau laughed. "Sure, sure, for a nize girl, ouai, but not for no Jerry. No, sir, dat and saluting, dat's two tings I don like for to do." He took a puff on his cigarette and seemed to pursue a side-memory silently.

"So?" said Turvey impatiently.

"O sure. So we stan' dere in hour sox an shir-tail an we keep one heye on de guard and 'e keep two heye on us. Bimeby one of my *gars* 'e was lose some blood, a lot mebbe, from a bullet in de harm, 'e is near faint, I tink, 'e ask for one drink of watair. De Jerry 'e turn de heyes. An I jump eem. I get eem good." Trudeau unconsciously hooked and stiffened his big fingers in front of him on the bed. Whiteside cocked a cloudy eye but said nothing.

"You choke him?" Bradley asked.

"You betcha my life, I strengle im for good mebbe. I got ver' strong fingairs. Dat Jerry 'e make me engry, 'e take my pants." Trudeau puffed. "Sometime I get dream wit beeg snake. Honly way I wake up myself is by strengle im. I ave beeg fear of snakes, me."

"Sure you didnt dream up this Jerry too?" Whiteside poised his hand on the way to completing the royal shrubbery and winked ponderously at the ward.

Trudeau sat up and looked across Turvey at the jaundiced one. "Was a matter, Yellowbellee? You wan mebbe I should dream habout you?" He made a mock threat with his great hands. The laughter was not with Whiteside, who went back to his puzzle.

"Hennyways, we grab 'is gun and ron like hell for de beach. Boy, dat was de wors' run I tink ever I make. De Jerries dey star' shooting wit M.G.s an we got no time for trousairs and boots. Dose cobblestones dey haint made for stocking feet, and I kip tinking some part of me dey is make one beeg tar-get."

Preston guffawed. "By God if it'd been me, I'd a been trippin over em."

"Mebbe I do. I sure fall hover someting in a halley, me. But bimeby I make de trees by de seawall; de ozzer boys dey go differen way an I don see dem no more. Dey all POWs now excep one, e got a packet, poor fellah. Me, I jum down dat wall some'ow – dey was so much stuff, smoke-screen, shells, bumbs too, I couldn tell oo was Einies an oo was our boys."

"It was hell on the beaches," Whiteside muttered.

"Is that when you got hit?" Bradley cut in quickly.

"Me? I'm lucky Trudeau for sure. Noting it me. Right away I crawl tru some barbwire and mebbe I run like hell for a bumb-'ole, den a bus' tank, I don remember much, cause I'm one scare' fellow. Dey was bodies everywere, poor devil. But all de time I kip look-hout for my capitaine I was suppose look haftair. An by car-reesmas I see

im. 'E was tuck hundair one rock afway from de water.
Dey was plenty mortar wang-wanging aroun dere, but me
I'm lucky Trudeau an bimeby I get me across by 'im.
Poor fellah. Bot' is legs is ver bad. But 'e don seem to
know. 'E don remember me needer, cause wen I say,
'*Mon capitaine, c'est moi, Trudeau*, I take you to de
boat,' 'e shout right away 'Boogair de boat. You Franch-
man, yes? We going charge de Boches.' 'Look,' I say,
cause just den de smoke she clear a leetle, 'dere's one
L.C., real close. I carry you on de back.' 'Wot you
mean?' he yell. 'We got to cap-ture Dieppe. I'll ave you
court-martialled! W'ere you trousairs? You're him-
properly dressed!' Well, I tink maybe 'e is not quite right
in de 'ead. An' by gar, dere was too much Jerry crap was
flying all round. So me, I tap 'im a lettle." Trudeau il-
lustrated a delicate punch with his hairy fist, and glanced
slyly in Whiteside's direction. "Dat halway a good hidea
for to settle a hargument. Jus a leetle tap on de chin an
den I slide 'im on my shouldair an beat it like 'ell for dat
boat I see, cause me I was plenty scare. But my capitaine
'e's plenty 'eavy too an I slip on de loose stones an 'ave to
put im down. Right den I say 'Trudeau, maybe dees is
hit.' But by gar, hup come anozzer capitaine, hout from
no-were, a padre capitaine 'e was, an e catch holt de feet
widout say notting and we carry heem to de water. Den 'e
say, 'hokay, now you can manage,' and 'e beat it back
hinto all dat smoke. I never see im no more. 'E was one
fine padre for sure." Trudeau paused. "Well, das habout
all. Like I tole you, I don really see wat appen moch."

"Gosh, but what then?" Turvey had quite forgotten to
worry about whether he was getting lunch. "Wasnt your
captain sore at you for bashin him?"

"Aw, 'e nevair remembair. Firs I wade hout an put im
in de L.C. And goddam, whoosh, she go harse hovair
kittle from a bumb splash right beside 'er. I jus habout
sheet breeks, me. So I 'ave to tow im to anozzer L.C.
And by Jay, me I'm tire, an my backside she is more cold
dan hever. But some fellow dey 'elp us on board. Dey is

in bad shape in dat boat, from some h'air burst, so me I 'ave to look haftair de capitaine myself. So I get me one h'oar an break 'er in two across de boat-side –"

"You dirty bugger, Trudeau, what yah want to do a thing like that for?" Whiteside was still determined to be the kidder. "Aint no way to treat a lady," he added, since Trudeau only looked bewildered.

"H'oar, I say, for to row boat. Wat you tink – You tink I said 'oo-er'? You clean hout de h'ears, mebbe, hey?"

"Aw for chrisesake, drop dead, cant yah, Yellahbelly?" yelled Preston. "Go on, Trudeau, dont mind the silly twerp, he's allus like that."

"Geez, cant you guys take a joke? . . . Nnnuts!" Whiteside dropped his eyes sullenly to Buckingham Palace.

"Hokay, hokay, fellows. Me I'm one beeg man for de joke too. But like I was say, I 'ave to break dis h'oar to make me some splints for de legs of my capitaine. Bimeby, a destroyair, she pick us hup."

"What the captain say when he come to?" Turvey asked.

"Well, w'en we get on de destroyair 'e is still hout. An I don know I tink maybe I was tap 'im a leetle too ard an wat 'e need is one good scotch. So I go downstair in dat boat, for fine a docteur. But heverybody is ver busy an I don like to bozzer dem. I see w'ere is de hoperating room an by Joe is two *bouteilles* cognac in leetle rack on de wall. Nobody noteeze, so I jus take one to my capitaine. 'E come to, den, hall ri' but 'e is ver bad shape an once more 'e start shouting crazy talk. So I go back downstair to dat ospeetal, wat dey call seekbay, yes? an fine me some bandage an one hinjector for put him to slip."

"Morphine? How'd you know how to do that?" Bradley asked in surprise.

"O me, I 'ave dis Hambulance *Saint Jean*, sure. Hennyway, dat's all. My capitaine he is lucky, I tink. Lose honly one leg. Ah, 'e is very fine fellow. I get letter from 'im only las mont. 'E is selling plenty life in-sur-ance by Trois Rivieres now. Wit *une jambe de bois* – 'ow you call, de tin leg?"

"But how about those mortar wounds of yours?" asked another patient farther over.

"O, dose, I jus get leetle pepper in dat landing craf'. Jus small shrapnel dat. Mebbe I get some in de *ville* before, I don noteeze. De Sawbones he dig hout twenty, mebbe twenty-five piece from de back, but dey ver small. Nex week I'm hokay 'cep mebbe I ave two-tree boil. Dat what I ave now. De *docteur* tink some shrapnel still dere. But it don bodder me moch."

"Jeez, I bet yah get the fems to lie back when yah tell em that story." It was Whiteside again.

"Listen, *mon petit ventre-jaune.*" Trudeau swung carefully half out of his bed. "Me, I don need for to tell stories to some floozies. Jus now I got me a wife, she is nize girl. In Scot-land. You wan maybe to make someting of dat, you yellowbelly truckdrivair?" He made a further movement as if he were about to leap over Turvey's bed and vindicate the honour of the infantry to all lesser arms and services. Turvey, thinking of the last time he had lain between two in an argument, got set to roll off his bed out of the way.

"O.K., O.K.," said Whiteside sourly, "dont get your balls in an uproar. You Frenchies cant take a joke."

"Mebbe you don like Franchmen, hey?" Trudeau poised alertly on the side of his bed, one hand gripping his pillow. There was a dancing light in his blue eyes now. "Me, I don like Hirishmen." He held Whiteside's yellow stare in his. "Mebbe," he added almost hopefully, "you're Hirish, hey?"

"For crisesake, Yellowbelly, go get yer liver scraped," yelled Preston.

"Aw, ferget him, Trudy," Bradley growled. "He dont mean nothin. He's just all loused up with janders, aint yah, Whiteside?"

"That's better'n bein yellow clean through like a

Frog," Whiteside retorted, picking up one of the last un-
fitted stones of the Palace. But it was never to be adjusted. Trudeau's pillow came hurtling over Turvey's
head and whammed accurately against the frame edge of
the jigsaw. Buckingham Palace exploded in cardboard
shrapnel. There was a howl of thwarted art from Whiteside, and Turvey rolled under his bed just in time to duck
the jigsaw's wooden frame which Whiteside hurled at
Trudeau in a frenzy of revenge. Then having nothing else
to throw, the two joined battle over Turvey's bed and it
took the combined operations of two up-patients, an
orderly and the Grim Nurse to restore order.

Trudeau was the first to apologize. "Engrey like me
dere is none," he said cheerfully. Turvey couldnt make
out if he were being penitent or boastful. "Engrey is my
favourite. I should 'ave my wife 'ere for to look haftair
me. That would be nize, hey? You like to 'ave your girl
come for to see you now, Turvey?" he asked as they gave
Whiteside token help in retrieving the jigsaw curlicues
from the floor.

Turvey agreed it would be swell. There was only one
person he would like to see better, and that was an orderly
bringing him chow. But he instantly reproached himself
for the thought. It was unworthy of a Royal Bogshire
Kootenay Highlander whose bed was right next to a hero
of Dieppe.

Incredibly, in a few minutes, the Flamand did plunk
before him a full-sized dinner with not a drop of castor
oil on it. Turvey gorged and sank back happy. The whole
ward seemed to have grown suddenly into a den of cozy
comradeship, a resting place for old campaigners before
hurling themselves finally and victoriously at the Jerries.

Sun streamed through the windows, and Turvey saw
that the street view had magically improved too. Over the
cobblestones an army truck bounced sportively, its high-
boxed chassis splashed with a white star. On the nearer
towpath a cycling gendarme coasted by, one hand on hip,
peaked cap tilted jauntily into the sun. Behind him came

two more velos pedalled by girls, their black stockings weaving like serpents. As they passed, the wind suddenly blew their skirts into their faces and their legs quickened in a snaky dance. A limping Polish officer in a blue beret stopped in evident delight and saluted the passing legs gallantly.

On the towpath on the other side of the sparkling olive canal a mincing lady in an imitation leopard coat pushed a streamlined pram. Beyond her an applegreen streetcar jounced to a stop. A plump brown friar clambered aboard, and two bobby soxers with gay kerchiefs. The tram squealed away, disclosing on the far sidewalk a little girl prancing in white rabbit coat, muff, and hat, with a rubbery dog lolloping beside her. Behind the sidewalk the misted stone and cinnamon brick houses of Old Ghent, striped with the shadows of the bare lindens, mounted high-chested to comical staired gables and tiles agleam in the sun. It was, Turvey decided, a good world after all. He had an hour's nap despite the radio and felt even better.

"Psst." Whiteside had got out and was sitting confidentially on Turvey's bed. "Got somethin to tell yuh." Turvey leant his ear up obediently. "Yuh dont wanta get too chummy with all these guys in here." He rolled his yellow eyes sinisterly toward Trudeau and over to Bradley. "Yuh see that type with the head bandage, Preston?" Turvey nodded. "He's a bad actor. From my home town. He's been writin my wife tellin her I was playin around with the Dutch fems."

"Gosh, that aint good, is it?" Turvey blinked sympathetically. "How'd he find out?"

Whiteside gave him a distrustful glance. "He been talkin to you too?"

"No," said Turvey, puzzled at this turn.

"I aint sayin I been cuttin up, see. I jist said he wrote my old woman I had."

Turvey didnt quite know what comment he should make now. "Your wife write and tell you she heard from him?"

"Naw, she wouldnt say who told her, but it musta been him."

"Why would he do that?" Letter-writing was such a chore Turvey couldnt imagine anybody going to all that trouble.

"Cause he thought I wrote *his* wife about the mouse he was shackin up with back in Aldershot," Whiteside hissed craftily.

"Golly, how could he get that idea?" Turvey was beginning to lose the thread.

Whiteside weighed the question suspiciously. "Never mind," he said finally. "I'm jist warnin yuh, see, the kinda drips are in this ward. As for that big Frog," he lowered his voice to an apprehensive whisper though Turvey could hear Trudeau still snoring in his after-dinner nap, "he's just a fuckin windbag. If he was such a brave bastard at Dieppe like he was shootin off, why didnt he collect a gong or somethin?" Turvey couldnt think of any answer to that one. Whiteside, after an impressive yellow stare, added, "There's a lot a other phonies in here too. You're new, so I'm tellin yah the score. Dont trust any of em." He went back to his bed and began rebuilding blitzed Buckingham Palace.

Turvey stared out the window again. The scene on La Coupure seemed to have become less gay since Whiteside's little visit. An old squat woman in a head-shawl trotted down the far towpath, stopped suddenly, looked around, and plucked something from the asphalt with a surprisingly deft motion. Cigarette butt? Or was she a spy? Along the companion towpath on Turvey's side of the canal two Belgian police stalked in high boots, white-helmeted heads rigid, blue capes ruffling importantly. On the roads a monotonous dribble of grey army lorries, jeeps, motorcycles. Under a leprous linden three black-robed priests stood talking, glancing occasionally at the hospital windows. Then, as Turvey watched, the long black snout of a hearse crept at walking pace into his field of vision just beyond the hospital railings, its glassy centre clotted with dim flowers. Behind it plodded a triple line of mourners whose end seemed never to come.

Turvey began to count them and got to forty-eight when a familiar voice interrupted. It was the Grim White Nurse. Turvey stared in sombre fascination, for in her muscular arms was the special tray again, with the same generous tumbler breathing the same oily nausea.

"Drink this now," she said, setting the tray down and looking out the window. "Another funeral!"

"Eighth this week," Whiteside volunteered.

She yawned and turned her attention to Turvey. "Hurry up, I've got other things to do than stand here."

"But, sister, I just had a big lunch."

"That was the orderly's fault. He shouldnt have brought you one."

"Please, sister," he tried again, "I'm all better. Everythin's under control. I think I'd like to go back to my unit now." If only he had been peppered with shrapnel and had something heroic like – like Trudeau's boils.

The nurse looked bored. "You men are all babies. Afraid of a little castor oil. Come on. Doctor's orders."

While Turvey lay getting his breath back he heard the nurse as she swept off with the empty tumbler, "Doctor says you're not to eat anything more today. And you'll have an enema for breakfast." Turvey groaned and rolled on his side. Through the window he saw two panting old women, the last of the procession, limp by in wooden clogs, and then a solitary shining hansom stuffed with the chief mourners.

"Whad I tell yah?" Whiteside scrambled among the bedcovers for a wanted cardboard shape. "They aint through with yah yet."

Nor were they. After another busy night shuttling up and down the south corridor, Turvey was taken firmly along the same trail by the silent Flamand the next morning and made to perform with the hateful bag and beaker under his sullen gaze. Then he was led shambling back and, instead of breakfast, given a quarter-tumbler of water and warned by the Grim Nurse on peril of his life not to put another thing down his stomach.

"In half an hour I have to test your stomach juices," she said cryptically and tramped off.

Turvey didnt need Whiteside's sinister nod as she left to begin picturing the horrors to come. Obviously you couldnt test stomach juices without carving into the stomach somewhere. The nurse said she was going to do it herself, though.

"It's only doctors that operate, aint it?" Turvey asked Trudeau. His voice didnt sound convincing even to himself.

"Sure, sure; mebbe dey jus look in wit de Hex-ray."

Whiteside sniffed. "Hex-ray," he mimicked, but not too loudly. Through the window Turvey could see a small thin girl on a bicycle hauling behind her a smaller even thinner child on a tricycle by means of a rope like a trailing navel cord. Three burly Canadian nurses hustled across the lockbridge before it should open. Another enormous scow was sliding toward the bridge; two frail boys walked rhythmically slantwise, pulling ahead. The ropes slacked; Turvey thought of intestines again. He drew his tonette from under his pillow to distract himself, but the competition of the radio was too much.

Slowly, almost as slowly as the barge, a long dark snout slid into the foreground of Turvey's gaze. A gilt cross on a black tonneau writhing with carvings like an ornamented chocolate cake. Another hearse. Another funeral. Automatically Turvey shifted his gaze back into the ward. Sure enough, as if it had been a signal, the Grim Nurse was halfway across the ward to him. On the tray was a cluster of little bottles and syringes. As she set it down with a clang on his porcelain tabletop, Turvey saw with misery that the server also included an odd-looking pair of scissors and a long rubber tube with a suction bulb at one end. Thank God it looked only a quarter-inch in diameter. But he felt the goosepimples again, running down from about his midriff, spreading around his legs and creeping back up his spine.

"Not another one!" The nurse gaped at the window. A vague odour of carbolic spread from her white presence.

"Ninth this week," said Whiteside promptly. "And we dont see the ones that go to the militry cemetry," he added darkly.

"Just as well." The nurse turned briskly to Turvey. "Now then, we need more light here." She swung his cot so that his head came close to the window. "You can look at the funeral while we do this. Something to occupy your mind." She gave a gurgle that was probably meant to be a chuckle but her face was a professional mask and she was already busy greasing part of the tube with vaseline. She fixed the scissors-like object halfway down – it was apparently only a clamp, Turvey saw with relief – and poked the ungreased end in through the hole in the cork of a beaker. Then she propped him up with pillows and, shoving the tray into his hands, suddenly began squeezing the greased end of the tube up one of Turvey's amazed nostrils. He squirmed and sneezed in automatic protest, almost upsetting the tray.

"Now then, now then," said the nurse angrily. "This wont hurt a bit. Just keep still. Doctor wants some of your stomach juices," and before Turvey could utter more than a few strangled gurgles the cold slithery tube was in his throat and snaking nightmarishly down and down until he felt it actually come to rest somewhere in his most secret and miserable depths.

"See, doesnt hurt at all. Now, you hold the tray on your knee with your right hand. That's it. Now, hang on to the tube with your left. Here, like that." She squeezed Turvey's fingers around the tube just below the spot where it disappeared into his nose.

"Now whatever you do, dont you let go of that tube. I'm going to take the clamp off and pump a little juice out. And if you let go, the tube will go down in your stomach and we'll have to operate to get it out." Turvey, deprived of speech, and afraid even to nod his head, could only blink at her in trapped consent.

"This is it, Turvey!" Whiteside whispered loudly.

"You just keep out of this or you'll get one too," the nurse spoke over her shoulder. The rest of the ward watched in fascinated silence.

At least, as the nurse had said, he could look at the funeral. And with Trudeau watching he mustnt get in a flap. But the procession had been a short one and was already past. The usual scramble of military vehicles and civilian bicycles had replaced it, with the occasional little Belgian auto looking strangely out of place. A trickle of yellow fluid began mounting in the beaker as the nurse pumped. Turvey quivered and rolled his eyes back to the window. Some of the ward's attention had shifted to an argument about MacKenzie King.

A green box overflowing with rusty iron scrap bobbed over the stones, its two pink-hubbed wheels seemingly self-propelled. Underneath, however, Turvey could make out a hulking lion-coloured dog in harness and now, at the cart's rear, an old man shoving, also in harness. As Turvey watched only half-aware, most of his consciousness lying at the tube's end in the pit of his stomach, a trio of brown-robed friars pedalling in stately unison on a bicycle-built-for-three began overhauling the cart. Suddenly from the towpath a large yellow cat started across the road, hesitated, was barely missed by a motorcycle, and dodged under the green box. The cart reared, swerved sideways. Through the windows of the ward came a muffled medley of noises, a dog's howl, a caterwaul, shouts, the shriek of bicycle brakes. And Turvey saw the friars, no longer stately, skid and crash into the green cart's side. In a hazy brown arc, like circus performers, the three clerics took to the air in a harmonious aura of rusty iron bolts and stovelids, vaulting the yelling old man, the slowly overturning cart and the emerging maelstrom of cat and dog. Turvey involuntarily shouted and pointed his left hand at the window, – and felt the long tube slide softly down his throat.

The next thing he knew the tray went crashing from the bed, he had been seized and was being held upside down and ruthlessly shaken by the Great Grim Nurse. "Trudeau," she yelled, "come slap his back." In the midst of what he was sure was his last strangling breath, Turvey felt the sky fall on him. He gasped and out shot the tube.

"Good work, Trudeau." The nurse turned to Turvey: "I told you to hang on. Now you pick up that mess on the floor. We'll have to start all over again."

And so they did. But this time Turvey kept his hand like an eagle's talon around the tube, and his eyes unswervingly fixed on his hand. Every halfhour for the rest of the afternoon the nurse returned to pump out any moisture that Turvey's stomach had managed to recapture. Then, just when he felt he must inevitably dry up and die, she came and pulled the tube out and allowed him a whole glass of water. Turvey would never have believed that mere water could taste so good. He looked at the nurse with new eyes.

"Thanks, sister," he said risking speech for the first time in some hours. "And thanks a million for bangin the tube outa me."

She permitted herself a softening around the mouth, and her eyes actually looked pleased, but she spoke as gruffly as ever. "Thank Trudeau; it was his thump on the back did it. You were too heavy for me to hold and slap all at once. Next time you wont be so lucky." And she sailed out.

Next time, thought Turvey. That means no supper, and the tube again tomorrow. "Thanks, Trudeau," he said weakly. Even if the crick in his back, since Trudeau's paw descended, was permanent, it was worth it.

"Aw, it's notting. I feel sorry for you, by gar. Dat tube like one snake, hey? You're brave fellow, Turvey. Me, I couldn' take it. I run like hell from dat nurse if she bring me dat tube. Like I run from snake. Me, I'm awful coward."

"Jeepers, you werent no coward at Dieppe."

"Ah, dey werent no snakes dere. Dat was jus fighting. Me, I'm great man for fight. But not for snake, or dat tube, not me. I go h'over de 'ill firs. I like de frogs, dough, dey ver good for to heat, you know dat?"

"I hear Quebeckers eat toads too," said Whiteside as if to himself, but loud enough for the ward.

Trudeau stared at him thoughtfully over Turvey's bed. Then he smiled. "No, sir, h'our toads got warts, and yellow bellies. Dey not moch good – for hanyting."

With supper came a turn in Turvey's fortunes. The orderly had a tray for him, and it was no mistake this time. Next day, it was true, the Flamand walked him down for what the nurse called a barium enema, involving a deadly-grey liquid; and for lunch he had a mush the same colour, looking and tasting like wet ashes. Then he was marched to the Operating Room again. But it was only an X-ray. And from then on, for the rest of his stay, there were no ordeals more severe than the yielding up of daily test-tubes of blood and daily milk bottles of urine. At the end of another week, during which Turvey waxed plump with regular food and scarcely more than regular expeditions down the south corridor, and began tootling on his tonette again, the doctor told him he would be discharged from the hospital the next morning. Turvey was bursting with morale in any case because of a letter from Mac. He told the doctor about it.

"Please, sir, my pal Mac wrote me the Kootenay Highlanders are a real unit now, and they're up at the Sharp End, in Holland and everythin. So can you tell me how I get up there with him?"

"You wont be going to the Sharp End for a while, my boy. We didnt find the source of that enteric infection you had. It may come back. Have to slap a P3 on you for a month. That'll let you out of here, though, to the Redistribution Centre. They'll find you a job in Lines of Communication till we're sure you can go back to your outfit. Unless, of course, you'd like to stay a few more days while I take another look at your lower bowel." Turvey assured him quickly he would rather take the P3.

The next morning he waved goodbye to the ward. The Grim White Nurse unbent enough to say he'd better keep away from alcohol or he'd be back, and the doctor told him not to drink any water. Trudeau had departed the day before, healed of his boils and grinning lustily, but Whiteside was still in bed, building up Windsor Castle now. The day after Turvey swallowed the pump, the mail-carrier had left a letter for Trudeau at the yellow one's bed by mistake and Whiteside had discovered it was addressed to Sgt. Jules Trudeau, M.M. He must have decided that even a Frenchman couldnt get a Military Medal at Dieppe without deserving it, for he announced Trudeau's decoration to the ward, and from then on ceased to bait him. Indeed, as Whiteside's colour changed gradually to a delicate cream and his eyes regained their whites, his general opinion of the ward improved. He couldn't resist a parting shot, however, when Turvey shook his hand.

"Watch it, Tops. Dont let em bring yah in this butcher shop again with the crut. Second time they're bound to operate."

FOURTEEN

Turvey Engages a Paratrooper

UNDER THE cold New Year's Moon, a hundred miles away in the fabled forest of the Ardennes, General von Rundstedt was very busy getting bogged down in the last hopeless counter-offensive of the German army. But neither Turvey nor his humble sources of information knew that it was the last or that it was bogged down, and the hundred miles between him and the formidable general were insufficient to ensure him a restful time of it in his new unit. Not that Turvey had become jittery; on the contrary, he was spoiling for a fight, and the inaccessibility of his foe was making him all the more trigger-happy. It was only a few hours, in fact, since the General's Focke-Wulfs had appeared from nowhere like disturbed hornets and shot hell out of the nearby airport at zero level, catching the American ground-crew with New Year hangovers and the American planes in neat rows on the field. And Turvey, himself with a bit of a hangover, hadnt got out of the hut in time even to see the tail of the last Jerry returning unscathed to its homeland.

Now it was night, two in the morning, to be exact, and through the usual ochre ground-fog that seemed to well straight up from the mud of Plaatschat's farmlands, the general's wizened moon brought Turvey only enough light to stumble in. From the camp gate of Number Five Redistribution Unit, where he and another soldier were marooned on guard duty, Turvey could sense rather than see the rising skeletons of lombards along the nearby road, and, behind him, the bulk of the archway leading over the moat into the chateau which quartered the officers. Dim on each gate post sat a battered plaster-of-paris sphinx; the brick ribs of their bodies gleamed red where machine gun bullets had bared them. Over the head of the right-hand sphinx a tin sign dangled. In daylight it read OUT OF BOUNDS TO OTHER RANKS. But in the fog it was only a yellow smudge.

The air was raw and eerily still; Turvey might have been cold even in his greatcoat if he had not been excited with the thought that he was at last actually engaged in combat. For had there not been a General Stand-To, a general multiplication of guards (in pairs too) through the sprawling byways of the camp, and, as a result, a general flap involving everyone from the Commanding Officer to the night fireman? Paratroopers had been dropped scarcely twenty miles away (some said two miles), and the whole camp had blossomed with Stens, Brens, rifles, revolvers and even one or two bayonets.

"They got grey uniforms, aint they?" Turvey asked his fellow-guard, a lank worried-looking batman by the name of Morrison.

"How you goin to tell colours in this fuckin fog?" countered Morrison; there was a catch to his thin voice. "Besides, the Officers' Mess Steward told me he heard the paymaster sayin at dinner these paratroopers are comin down in our outfits, and in Yanks' . . . Droppin whole jeeps of them all dressed up like Canadians," his voice went on in the darkness, rising with almost tearful complaint, "and they're ridin around from here to Brussels blowin up bridges and jesus knows what. They might walk right up to us here lookin like our own officers." Morrison, needled by his imagination, had edged so close to Turvey the latter could see his dilated eyes rolling as if he already suffered the paratrooper's dagger in his bowels. Turvey took a tighter grip on the dank Sten under his armpit and felt a tingle of excitement.

The familiar fecal smell of the moat swirled about them, waxing richer with the night, and reminding Turvey of the tannery he worked in back in Montreal. They began to walk silently up and down together in the lane that led from their gate to the cobbled road, but they halted as one body at the expanding growl of a plane coming low and fast toward them. In a few seconds it had roared over unseen like a huge projectile. Before the noise had faded Morrison was hissing excitedly:

"That was Jerry! 'Ja hear that err-ERR-a, err-ERR-a, I-SEE-yuh? A Jerry motor!"

"Yeah?" said Turvey, breathless with bottled adventure.

"Yer goddam tootin. They got desinkanized motors. Dont hit together or somepn. Just like the ones this mornin. We better go report this." When Turvey didnt move, he added urgently: "Supposin it dropped paratroops! They could be creepin up on us already!"

Turvey visualized enormous square-jowled men wearing German helmets above Canadian battledress; they were festooned with grenades and gleaming knives. He saw himself surprising three, four of them in the foggy lane, marching them, hands high, to the guard house.

"You go if you want." Somehow he felt Morrison wouldnt be any help to him in rounding up Jerries.

Morrison shuffled his feet and peered down the lane aimlessly. "Jeez, I dont feel so good," he muttered, shuddering elaborately, "I need a cup a coffee or somepn."

"Gosh, I'm *hot*," said Turvey. "I'm gonna shed this coat." While Morrison held the Sten, Turvey clambered out of his greatcoat and, reaching, hung it by the nape from the plaster mane of the lefthand sphinx. Now he felt more like coping with the S.S.

"I know where we can get some java, too," Morrison said again, with growing enthusiasm. "Dick said they was keepin it on all night at the NAAFI. Maybe we could get a line on what's goin on too. Aint nobody gonna come and tell us anythin here.''

"You bring me back a mugful," said Turvey. "If the sergeant comes around I'll tell him you've gone to the can. I'll have a couple of paratroopers lined up for you when you get back.''

The last suggestion did not seem to settle Morrison's nerves and Turvey had to walk down to the blind end of the lane with him, past ash trees, their mossy butts queerly luminous in the half-light, and then around to the first row of huts. He watched the lean batman melt with increasing speed in the direction of the NAAFI, his rifle held rigidly in both hands like a pitchfork. As the pad of his boots in the mud faded their pulse quickened. Morrison was taking the home stretch on the run.

And now there was the silence of night and fog, not even a dog's yelp or a stir of wind. For the first time, also, the officer quarters were properly blacked-out; not a gleam of light anywhere. Turvey, walking back, felt again to make sure the safety was off his Sten, and he rehearsed mentally the official movements and stance for firing a direct burst from the hip. Now if he could bag a paratrooper alone, before Morrison got back, it would really be something. He hoped he could capture him without having to shoot. Turvey's belligerent dreams always stopped short of doing actual bodily injury to anyone, even a paratrooper.

He stopped halfway back to the gate as the hum and rumble of a truck grew on his ear, coming along the cobbleroad from Brussels. Might be a petrol supply lorry, but they didnt use this road lately. Might be the HUP with one of their officers liaising with the next unit's guard posts. But it was moving smoother and faster than any HUP. Turvey tensed as he heard it slow down opposite the chateau, then immediately speed up and rush into the closing silence. Had someone dropped off? Or had they just eased for the mudhole where the lane came out?

As Turvey stood, the yellow-brown fog opened up in a

mysterious swirl, and a flicker of moonlight shone up the lane and went out. In that moment of amplified sight Turvey saw by the gate they had been guarding, not a hundred feet away, the outline of something, someone. Though his ears told him nothing, he was sure he had glimpsed an enormously tall yet hunched figure. He seemed to have his back towards Turvey as if frozen in the act of climbing over the gate. Then the yellowness slid compactly back into place and there was only it and a total sinister silence.

Turvey's first thought was to shout a challenge. But he reflected that the paratrooper might not have twigged him; why give his position away? Yet he couldnt stand here, making no sound, forever. Perhaps there was another Jerry with him, a dozen, from the airplane or that truck. Still, there wasnt a creak. But why should there be? Paratroopers could walk right up to you without so much as a grunt and slit your throat from behind. Turvey circled in his tracks; then he stopped, for the squelching of his boots interrupted his listening. The paratrooper might be moving up on him in little rushes every time Turvey made a noise. Well, like Sergeant Swingle always says, you gotta take the nishitive. Stealthily he shoved the Sten out in front of him, made a sudden forward run for a few feet, then halted, holding his breath to hear if he could catch the Other One moving too. Hadnt there been the click of a boot-heel against a stone just as he stopped? Or was it his own? Turvey waited, charged another two yards. But then, and succeeding times, nothing. The fog and the night were so thick now that he was not even sure if he had arrived at the gate where he had seen the apparition. Then, with a leap of his heart, Turvey heard the thumps of running feet, steady, soft – was the softness from distance or from sly murderous caution? Turvey's back prickled and he pivoted, Sten pointed.

Hastily, as he wheeled, he saw the man at his back, climbing down from the gate without a sound. The face

was hidden but he could see the whole length of his overcoat. Turvey took no time to recall how to make a formal
challenge:

"Hey, you, halt! You wanna get shot? Hands, hands
up!"

But the Figure made neither sound nor movement and,
so far as Turvey could make out, seemed poised to leap
straight on him from the gate. Before he knew what had
happened Turvey's gun went off with an uproar that temporarily numbed his wits; he remembered only to keep
pulling the Sten down so that the leaden spate held
straight at the Figure, before the long burst was over and
the magazine empty.

And now, for the first time in his rational if picaresque
life, horror was visited upon Turvey. Even though he had
seen the cloth of the greatcoat flying where the bullets hit,
it now, terribly, slowly, sank in upon him that the Figure
had scarcely stirred, was, in fact, with twenty slugs
through its body, still arched to leap upon him. As shouts
rose in the night and footsteps came running from both
ends of the lane, Turvey made his last heroic attack. Seizing the Sten by its butt he hammered with mounting
savagery the Thing on the fence until the gunstock broke
in his hands and he fled yelling into the shaky arms of
Sergeant Swingle and Private Morrison. As he was
brought to earth, one part of his mind began to register
the fact that he wasnt wearing his greatcoat.

FIFTEEN

Turvey Is Psychoanalyzed

THE NEXT morning Turvey, who had spent the fag-end of the night in Baron van Duffelputten's authentic seventeenth century coachhouse (now serving as a brig), was marched between two armed guards into the Orderly Room and plunked on a bench outside the C.O.'s office. The Old Man's door was shut but plyboard was scarce and the partition, like most in the German-built hutments added to the estate, stopped a yard from the ceiling. Turvey had no trouble following the loud nasal voice of his Commanding Officer and the precise tones of the adjutant.

". . . one that raised the rumpus last night, sir."

"O God, *that* one. Woke me out of my first good sleep in a week. What's he pegged with?"

There was a pause and the rattling of papers. Turvey held his breath.

"Destruction of one greatcoat-for-the-use-of; breakage of one Sten-mark-one-star; unlawful discharge of a weapon; unlawful expenditure eighteen-rounds-ammo-nine-millimetre."

"Now who the bloody hell slapped all that on him?"

The adjutant said something about Sergeant Swingle and an Enquiry.

"Court of Enquiry my backside! We've got a bellyful of them now. And if he turns out to be a barrackroom lawyer and –" The C.O. lowered his voice and Turvey didnt quite get the next sentence; but Colonel Rawkin was not used to soft-pedalling anything, particularly his own tones, and soon Turvey and his guards and indeed the whole Orderly Room (the clerks had kindly stopped typing) were able to follow again. ". . . Love a God, Charlie, cant you stop these sergeants from throwing the book at every dimwit that steps out of line? What's wrong with this, this Tur – Turkey – ?"

"Turvey, sir."

"– Turvey anyway? Trying to work his ticket?"

The adjutant's reply didnt quite carry.

"Thought his greatcoat was a par – Say, maybe he's really shell-happy." The colonel's voice rose with hope. "O God. If we could just get him boarded out!"

The adjutant murmured something.

"Listen, Charlie; if the Swami will play ball and call him Mental, we can bang him off to England on tomorrow's outdraft. And the quartermaster can bloody well write off his Sten."

Turvey's righthand guard elbowed him slyly and the one on his left whispered in admiration, "By jeez, you're gonna work it."

"But, sir, you know the psychiatrist. He wont play. Not unless there's really –"

"Dammit you cant tell me this Tur-, Turnkey isnt crazy as a coot. Hanging his greatcoat on a gate and coming right back and shooting it. Unless, of course, he's swinging the lead. And the Swami will soon put a rocket under that. That's what he's for, Charlie. And he can start right now. I wont see the bugger till the Swami sends me a report. If he says the fellow's swinging it I'll chew his bollocks off and you make sure Spo gives him the worst job on the X-14 list, shovelling coal or something, – but away from here."

"Yessir, . . . right, sir . . . different if it were one of our Permanents . . . court-martial . . . Sergeant Swingle got in a tizzy." The adjutant seemed to be climbing over on the winning side.

"Hell's bells, Charlie, you *know* the brigadier shot us down in flames last time he was here about the number of courts-martial we have. Cant make him understand it's because we're always filled to the gills with these loony transients. You bloody well tell the R.S.M. to see the sergeants dont go around putting the hooks on em or it'll be bowlers for you and me, Charlie."

"Yessir."

"After all, there wasnt anybody inside the coat and, and, well, it *might* have been a paratrooper!"

"Yessir . . . send him to the Sike at once, sir." The adjutant sounded worried. Turvey wasnt feeling too well either, despite the envious winks of his guards. If the Nut Doctor decided he was crazy, they'd send him back to England. If the Nut Doctor decided he wasnt crazy, and trying to wangle it back to England, they'd keep him in Belgium, but behind the lines. It looked bad for getting with Mac again.

"Doggone," he muttered, "just after the Board raised me to P-One and I'm all set for the front."

"Shh, there's the Old Man again," one of the guards whispered.

"Wait, Charlie, I'll get Pugs on the ticker. I'll make him put the squeeze on the Sike." There was the whirr of a field telephone. "Senior Medical Officer." Craarh, crackle . . . "Major Pugston, please . . . Pugs, about that cuckoo fired off the Sten last night . . . Yeah. Listen, I want him out of here. I'm sending him over to the Sike right away. He's a menace. Must be S-Five . . . Sure, sure, I know you have to . . . Well, S-Four anyway . . . But if Hairy dont give him an S something or other, we'll have to hold a Court of Enquiry on the Sten he bust . . . well, there you are. Court-Martial, too, maybe . . . Listen Pugsy, if there's a C. of E. and C.M. about this, you and your Standing Medical Board, every mother's son of you, will serve on it every day for the next two weeks . . . No . . . You'd have to hold your boards at night and sleep when the courts are damned well over . . . O.K. Then you better ring the Sike pronto and tell him he's got to slap an S on the bugger . . . Roger." The receiver banged on the cradle. "O.K., Charlie, Pugs'll make the Sike play ball. Get that Turkey over to him, but fast."

"Yessir." The adjutant shot out the door. "Guards!" Turvey and his watchdogs scrambled to attention. "Conduct the prisoner to Captain Airdale's office and wait outside. When the psychiatrist is through with him, take him back to the guard hut."

Another conversation was floating across another partition when Turvey and his guards sat down on a bench outside the psychiatrist's door. It wasnt as loud as the previous one, but two benchfuls of soldiers were already tuned to it in happy silence.

"That's Pugston, Senior M.O. He's givin Hairy the bee on you," one of Turvey's guards interpreted after a moment. "He sure hotfooted it over, after the Old Man's blast. You'll get an S all right, you lucky split. You'll be in Blighty by the week-end."

"I dont wanna S. I wanna get back to the Koot –"

"Can it; listen! Hairy's talkin now." It was a tired voice and Turvey caught only phrases:

". . . eight ahead of him . . . back to their huts . . . half an hour just to read his file . . ."

"Well, Hairy, . . . worth it if you can justify an S. Of course . . . not attempting to influence your diagnosis, but you know how the Old Man . . . ."

"Yes, sir, . . . play it the way I see it, but . . . examine him as thoroughly as I can . . . write it up big . . . Old Man cant say I didnt try . . . ."

"That's fine, Hairy, W.A.T. I suppose?"

"T.A.T. too, if I have time." He added something else that sounded like "having a bang at a Roar Shack."

Turvey trembled at the unfamiliar prescriptions and one of the guards nudged him. "Boy, you're goin to have to sweat shit for that boat."

"I dont wanna boat, I just wanna get back to the Koot –"

"Sergeant!" A very young captain emerged from the psychiatrist's office.

"Sir!" a voice echoed and a hoarheaded NCO popped from the second cubicle down.

"W.A.T. for Private Turvey. Immediate. And send the others away, cant see them this morning."

Turvey went along, baring his arm for another inoc, but he found that W.A.T. was only a very amusing game called the Word Association Test. The sergeant sat him with a sheet of foolscap at a table in his dinky office. Then he droned off a series of words at ten-second intervals and Turvey had to scribble the very first ideas that tinkled in his head after each word. He tried hard to put down as much as he could because he figured the more he wrote the more proof the Sike would have he wasnt an S-something-or-other and was O.K. for the Kootenay Highlanders.

When it was over there was a wait. Capt. Airdale, the venerable sergeant explained, was still ploughing through Turvey's file. The sergeant filled in the time with sedate chatter about the captain, whom he rated high.

"He's really going to enjoy talking with you, Turvey. Isnt often he takes time to lay on a W.A.T., poor fellow. Generally he interviews twenty in a morning and has to write out a diagnosis and recommendations on all of them by 1500 hours so I can type them in time for the Medical Board."

"Gosh, are there that many nuts around here every day?"

"Well, of course" – the sergeant coughed good-humouredly – "we dont use such a word as 'nut'. Not in psychiatry. We have all sorts of *cases* though, you'd be surprised. Psychopaths, aggressive or inadequate," the sergeant rolled the words fondly, "suspected epileptics, schizoid personalities, manics. And scads of neurotics – compulsives, depressives. But battle fatigues mainly.

Anxiety states, you know."

"What're they all in a state about?"

"O, about getting killed, mostly, though some'r more worried about their wives."

"Because they cant get home to them, you mean?"

"Or because they *have* to go home to em, or," the sergeant considered dispassionately, "because somebody else's home with em. O, you'd be surprised the things fellows worry about. We had one in here last week, depressive type, couldnt sleep because he had it doped out the Second Coming was due at dawn sometime this year, but he hadnt got the exact day taped. Another chap sent in with undiagnosed headaches. Up at his unit they thought he was a malingerer. But Captain Airdale found out he got them every time he saw wire. Had an emasculation obsession, of course."

"A what?"

"Emasculation obsession. He'd got it in his head he was bound to lose his testicles the next time he got into barbed wire. Course it's all very hard on the captain. He's very young, you know." The sergeant smiled paternally. "Had a sheltered home life, then went direct from interning into the army. Hasnt had much of a chance to develop himself as a clinician. Sent straight over here just a month ago. Now he gets enough material in one day to last him a year on Civvy Street, and no time to analyze it. Some of it really shocks him, too. He's kind of a shy type really. Has personality problems himself. All these psychiatrists have. We had one was transferred to a Base Hospital at his own request. Having trouble with sprees. Course they're all supposed to have been analyzed. But it doesnt always take."

When the sergeant finally led him into the captain's office, Turvey entered feeling that at least he wasnt as crackers as some who had been here before him. It wasnt a feeling that gave him much comfort, however, and it disappeared under the strain of explaining to the young captain a number of complicated chapters in his martial career which were hinted at in his file. Then they got on to Turvey's W.A.T. The captain was plainly fascinated by Turvey's big pencilled responses to the stimulus words. As his eyes ran down the column he would pause, scratch his curly head and wrinkle his nose.

"Why did the word *naked* make you think of a can of green peas, Turvey?" His voice was professionally colourless but high and it squeaked a little on "naked".

"Well, sir, in the cookhouse, where I was pearl-divin, sir, they got a lot of cans like that – picture of a pin-up type, without any duds on."

Captain Airdale looked disappointed. But his nose quivered again immediately, like a hound-dog's.

"What did you want to say for *Body*? 'With her head tu –' is all you have."

"Didnt have time to finish, sir. Words was comin at me awful fast. It's just the song. You know." But the captain didnt. "With her head tucked underneath her arm." The captain poised an eyebrow. "The fellows in my Iron Lung sing it sometimes. All about Henry the Eighth and the Bloody Tower."

"Of course, yes," the captain murmured, but he didnt sound at all convinced. He began reading Turvey's responses aloud, in a brooding kind of way. " '*Love.* I love animals.' Hmmm. Farm boy?" His voice held a touch of anxiety.

"Yessir, Skookum Falls, B.C."

"Ahhh . . . '*Women.* I love women too.' " The captain flashed a relieved smile. "Hmmm . . . '*Soldier.* He's not a soldier he's a –' What were you going to write there?"

"Canadian, sir."

"Ca-Canadian!?"

"It's a kinda wise-crack, sir. The limey girls say it."

"Oh." The captain's soft brow contorted. " '*Money.* I'm flat . . . *March.* Wonder where June is . . .' Hmmm. What was your mother's first name, Turvey?"

"Mary, sir."

"Ahhh . . . '*Red*. Blanket drill'?" The captain's forgetmenot eyes came up blinking.

"Oh, sorry, sir. Thought the sergeant said *Bed*." The captain still looked puzzled, and disappointed. "Blanket drill is what the fellahs call grabbin off a nap durin duty hours."

"Oh . . . '*Bang*. Petrol'???"

"Bang-water, sir. That's petrol."

"Yesss . . . '*Kiss*.' You've got S-W-A-K in capitals???"

Turvey blushed. "Sealed with a kiss, sir. 'Swhat we write on the back of a nenvelope, to a girl, like."

The captain cocked his head as if he were memorizing it. Then he went on. " '*Drink*. Red ink.' Have you ever, uh, had the impulse to drink ink?"

"That's just what we call that red wine, sir."

"Oh, sorry. '*Patrol*. Skirt'?"

"O, shucks, that's just skirt-patrol. You know, lookin for beetles." The captain stayed blank. "Well, just sorta moochin around lookin for girls to pick up."

"Ahhh. Ummm . . . '*Blast*. The C.O. gave me . . . *Happy*. As a pig in . . .' Pig in what?"

Turvey tilted his head bashfully. "I didn't like to write it, sir."

The captain stared, saw light, and struggled on. " '*Medal*. Shoved my arm'. Now *how* did you come to associate those ideas?"

"Well, this *is* kinda tangled, sir. You see, a chap I was out drinkin wallop, er, beer with a few nights ago got a skinful and started foolin around and he shoved my elbow just as I was goin to take a pull, and it sloshed on my battleblouse and it's kinda on my mind because I havent got the stains out quite and the sergeant noticed it yesterday."

The captain thought this over. His nose twitched again. "But I still dont see the connection with *medals*!"

"O, canteen medals! That's what we call beer-stains on a blouse, that's all."

"Ahhh." The captain scratched his head. " '*Armour. Crabs.*' That's an unusual one. I rather like that. Streak of poetry in you, eh? Lived sometime on the Pacific, havent you? Thinking of crabs as armoured, eh?"

"Well, it's kind of a sayin, too, you know, sir. Armoured cooties, some of the fellahs call em. And," he added, warming up – he was enjoying this very much, "I've heard em called ballplayers." But again the captain seemed to be left in a daze. This time he didnt try any further but dropped his eyes to the next word, wriggling his brows.

" '*Blood.* Ketchup . . . *Steady.* Peggy.' That – that wouldnt be" – he seemed quite unsure of himself now – "your girl-friend?" His voice squeaked again, and he jiggled his pencil.

When Turvey admitted it was, the psychiatrist's face came alive like a flashlight. He made Turvey tell him all about Peggy. "Now," he said, "just three more words. *Killer.* You thought of, er, *knickers.* Er?"

"Passion-killers, sir." Turvey looked abashed again. "???"

"What the Airforce girls wear. Kinda big and blue. And, and baggy. It's what I hear the fellahs call em."

The captain sighed. "Well, at least the next one's different. '*Sentry. Greatcoat.*' You were thinking of last night?" Turvey nodded, trapped at last. "Tell me all about it." Turvey told him. When he'd finished, the captain leaned over impressively and twitched his slender nose at him. "And now, Turvey, I want you to answer this question very carefully and truthfully. Why, when the sergeant said *father* did you write down the word 'greatcoat' again?"

Turvey was startled. "Did I?" The captain pointed a soft finger at the revealing line in the W.A.T. and twisted the paper for Turvey to see. "Gosh. I guess I was still thinkin of pottin my greatcoat. *Father's* the word right after *sentry.*"

"Ah. I wonder if it was that simple. The mind doesnt

make these errors without reason. Tell me about your father. He was nearly seventy-six when you were born. Did you get on well with him?"

Turvey told the captain what little he remembered of the old boy, how he'd tie one on over in Kuskanee, and come home and play his fiddle to the cows in the barn when the old lady threw him out of the house. The more he talked the more the captain nodded his head and made rapid little sniffs with this nose. "Turvey," he said finally, "honestly now, werent there times before your father died, when you were so angry with him you wished he was, well, that he would die?"

"Holy gosh, I dont think so. Maybe I might have when I'd get into some hellery and he'd give me the end of a trace, but not really for long or like I meant it or anythin. He wasnt such a bad old bird, the way I remember, but course I was only eight when he died."

"Umhmm, think carefully now, in answering this. Did your father wear an overcoat much?"

Turvey thought. "Every winter. Course everybody did. It was cold."

"Was he a big man? Tall?"

"Yeah, as I remember, he was quite a size . . ."

Later Turvey was allowed to look for things in the same comical ink-blots the psychiatrist at Great Buzzard had shown him, and then make up stories to fit some rather vague pictures the captain brought out of a drawer. He found it as interesting a morning as he had spent in the army though he couldnt help worrying whether the captain hadnt found an S somewhere in it all. He told him how much he wanted to get up to the Sharp End with Mac and the Kootenay Highlanders."

"Well Turvey," the captain said finally, sagging back in his chair as if he were really pooped out – he had been writing steadily for the last twenty minutes – "I think we can make everybody fairly happy about this. I'll give you an S all right and the C.O. can wash out the charges. But it'll be the smallest S I can find. An S-Three-*T*. That

means you have a slight nervous condition which will
clear up of itself, probably, once you're out of here. In
thirty days another psychiatrist can examine you and pro-
nounce you fit for the field. *And*, meantime, I'll send you
up near the front, to a Special Pioneer Detachment.''

"Gee, that sounds swell," said Turvey, relieved and
impressed. "Thanks a lot. My mum and dad were pioneers. In the Kuskanee Valley."

"Er, not at all. Best of luck, and take this chit to the
sergeant on your way out with your guards."

"Very interesting," said the sergeant, gravely scanning
Turvey's report. " 'Temporary hysteria . . . Possible la-
tent father-rivalry . . . Mild anxiety condition . . . .'
Havent had one quite like this before. But he says you're
getting over it fast. What you've got my boy is probably
an Oedipus complex, though the captain wouldnt come
right out with it."

"What's that?" asked Turvey anxiously. "It aint anything you get from girls, is it?"

"No, no, my boy. Father complex. Mother too. There's
the dinner gong. No time to explain. Anyway he's marked
you for No. 29 SPD. You'll leave tomorrow."

"Is that at the front?"

"O, couldnt answer that, Turvey. Security, you know,
confidential info . . . Guards up!"

"O yeah, sorry. Anyway, I'll be a specialist till I get all
right again, wont I?" Turvey had to talk over his
shoulder as the guards hustled him off; they were hungry
too.

"A, uh, specialist? O, yes, sure. But dont worry. Prog-
nosis . . . very favourable."

"What's a prog nose?" Turvey asked his guards as
they trotted him out into the sunlight. But neither of
them knew.

SIXTEEN

Turvey Is Employed as a Specialist

Turvey was a little surprised to find he was the only one in his draft who was bound for Number Twenty-Nine Canadian Special Pioneer Detachment. The others were for Number Thirty-Nine, which the more knowing in the truck declared was at Poperloo, only about twenty kilometres from the Redistribution Unit and, now that Van Rundstedt had been shoved back, a long way from any front. He was even more surprised when their vehicle drew up in the little market square of Poperloo and he was ordered out with the rest and marched down a side-street into an Orderly Room.

The O.R. had evidently been the overstuffed parlour of a town bigshot, now expropriated. The walls were still cluttered with modern Flemish landscapes of an impressive size. Clerks and typewriters were noisily at work around an enormous oak diningroom table, before an ornate but empty fireplace with gargantuan knicknacks on the mantelpiece in bronze and mottled stone. The room was barely warmed by a number of electric heaters, the largest of which had been shoved perilously on the mantel to focus its rays down on an inkstained mahogany desk. Here sat the adjutant and his O.R. Sergeant in lonely splendour, checking the nominal roll and the personal documents of Turvey's draft.

When the beefy pouch-eyed sergeant with the big diamond ring called his name, last of the draft, Turvey saluted briskly.

"Please, I'm S-Three and the Nut Doctor says I'm to go up to the front for specialist duties. Number Twenty-Nine Special Pioneers."

The sergeant looked up quizzically and then consulted Turvey's file. "This, my fine feathered friend, is number Thirty-Nine Detachment. Somebody's mailed you to the wrong address." The adjutant, a dapper youth with a sly sallow face, glanced at his sergeant.

"That Re-dis Aj dont know his arse from his elbow – that's the third time he's sent bods here shoulda gone to Twenty-Nine."

"Well, we wont have a wagon going up there for a week. Shall I turf him back to Re-dis?"

The adjutant looked at Turvey for the first time. "Seventy thousand zombies back in Canada with machine guns and we gotta have this! Had any army drivin experience?"

"Oh, yessir. I could drive myself up to the front if you tell me the way." He grinned anxiously.

The adjutant stared. "Smart guy, eh? You do any drivin around here you do it for us, see. Ever been grounded?"

"Only three times, sir."

The sergeant sniggered.

"Only thr – Maybe I better send you the hell outa here before we lose another truck. You like drivin?"

"Yes *sir*!"

"Sarge – we got a driver for that, uh, special job tonight?" He lowered his voice below earshot of the rest of the room. The sergeant's reply was even softer: "We still got Wilson. Everything else is off the road. But by tonight he'll need a helper to spell him or he'll go bye-bye at the wheel. This character's the only driver in the draft."

"Yeah." The adjutant thoughtfully bit his pencil tip. Turvey noticed he too had a really large diamond ring on one finger and a glittering emerald on another. "Hard to dope out a way to give em enough shut-eye." He paused, and looked Turvey over. "How'd you like to do somethin *really* special, right tonight? Confidential job."

"Up at the front, sir?"

"Oh yeah, yeah," he said reassuringly, "one a the fronts all right. Hundred miles from here. Try it tonight. You'll be back in the mornin and then we'll see when we can despatch you to Twenty-Nine." He dropped his voice another notch and looked very mysterious. "And understand this is strictly a hush job, see. It's curtains for you if y'open your trap about it to anyone. *Anyone*, understand? Anybody want to know where you're goin tonight, tell em you got a heavy date. O.K.?"

"O.K., sir, thanks, sir," Turvey whispered happily. "Kind of a secret mission, eh?"

"It sure is," said the adjutant with a puckered sideways look, "top hush"; he went back to his papers.

"Runner!" boomed the beefy sergeant promptly. A loose-limbed private started up from dozing in a morris chair by the door. "Show this young gentleman where our schoolhouse is and our Pally de Dance. You eat in the Pally and sleep in the school," he said to Turvey, "that is, when you sleep. Report back to me right after supper, for your *special* job." Turvey thought he saw a wink pass between the sergeant and his officer. Later, he was sure.

Tug Wilson seemed at first to be a rather uncommunicative type who kept his mind on the driving, and a deadpan expression on his face. But as they slithered and jolted over the snowy roads in the darkness he gradually made it clear to Turvey that their mission consisted of taking the truck a hundred miles south to a coal mine, loading it with sacks of coal, driving it most of the way to Brussells, dumping the load at a factory, and returning the truck to the unit before rollcall at seven-thirty.

"Gee, when do we eat?"

"If we're lucky we'll be back in time to grab a bite first."

It was after eleven before they reached the dark pithead and there was a half-hour's delay until a certain foreman with the odd name of Plute could be found to say it was O.K. for them to begin heaving the sacks on. It was certainly a secret mission, Turvey thought, since Wilson, instead of presenting the usual warrant and signing for the coal, simply counted out franc notes from a wad he drew from his hip, whereupon Plute counted them carefully in turn and then with an "Hokay. Allez vite!," dodged into the darkness.

Wilson, for some reason, seemed sore that they only had a three-quarter load. He muttered vague abuse of the adjutant and then, having turned the wheel over to Turvey as soon as they were headed back, fell sound asleep. Turvey, understandably, lost the way twice and had to wake the annoyed Wilson and be set back in the right direction. Turvey thought it odd that Wilson didnt seem to regard the adventure as anything but an imposition, cheating him of his rightful rest.

"If it werent for the kale, I'd tell those scroungers where to stick their coal," he said once, after a particularly skiddy bit of road. He had taken the wheel again to guide them through Brussells to the factory.

Turvey stopped in the middle of a bar from "Jolly, Jolly Sixpence" he was so surprised, and laid his tonette on his lap.

"Do we get extra for doin this?"

"Say," said Wilson, a new suspicion in his voice, "aint they told you what slice you get? By gee, they aint aimin to cut you in on my crummy twenty francs a sack are they?" Turvey, not knowing what it was all about, said he was sure not, and Wilson relapsed into silence.

As the evening progressed Turvey found their expedition more and more puzzling. They werent anywhere near the front. Yet, approaching the factory on the

Brussells outskirts, Wilson turned the car lights out, crept into the deserted yard as if he expected an ambush, and parked by a vacant shed with the engine idling. Immediately he became a quiet dynamo of activity, hissed to Turvey to get the lead out of his pants and stow the sacks in the shed pronto. His fear of making a noise seemed all the odder since the factory looked completely deserted. Even in the darkness Turvey could see the vague outlines of roofless ruins and twisted girders. It was definitely bombed and kaput, needing more than coal to come to life again. But Wilson seemed intent only on getting rid of his load with the utmost speed and silence. And as soon as the truck was empty, he slid it out as quietly as he had entered. Then, once in a thoroughfare, he gave it the gas and roared down the boulevards at top speed until he was on the highway home. It was already past six and Turvey was beginning to feel thoroughly sleepy but Wilson drove the empty truck at such a rate and the roads were so bumpy with hardened snow he found himself bounced into wakefulness.

"It'll sure be good to hit the hay after rollcall," he sighed.

"O yeah? Better get forty winks now. You'll be on duty all day and we might have to make another trip this evenin."

"Holy cow! Dont we get excused day jobs if we work all night?"

Wilson shot him an amazed look. "Say, I'm beginnin to get it. Boy, are you wet! You just come in this unit, didnt you?"

"Today. By mistake. But I'm to go up to the Sharp End right away for specialist work. Number Twenty-Nine."

Wilson began to laugh dryly. "This is rich! I bet you never see Number Twenty-Nine now. And I bet you dont know what was cookin tonight. Aj just told you to string along with this truck, eh?"

"O, no! He told me it was a secret mission and I wasnt to tell anybody. Guess it's all right to tell you, though, aint it?"

"Yeah, yeah," said Wilson heavily, and sniggered. "You can tell me all right, sweetheart. You can tell me you're in the black market, with a couple years ahead in a Belgy hoosegow if they nab you." He shook his head over the steering wheel and swore softly. "What an operator that Aj is!"

"Black market?" Turvey thought it might be a gag. "You mean cause we get all dirty with this coal?" He had been startled when investigating a pimple in the rear-vision mirror to see an Al Jolson face peering back at him. It put him in mind of scurfing days in the coke plant. And now in the dimlit cab all he could see of Wilson in his sootcovered fatigues was the sombre flash of his eyeballs.

"Look," said Wilson, becoming expansive for the first time, "let's cut the comedy act, eh? You know there's a fuel shortage, dont you? And a coal-strike? Occupation troops supposed to be gettin most of what there is. Civilian rations about enough to cook one good meal a day. Unless they can pay a thousand francs a sack for it under the table, eh? Same racket as when the Jerries were here. Only then the miners didnt strike. I heard it's even the same tycoon runnin the market still, too, some fuckin millionaire in Louvain. Got a brother in the Cabinet, they say, so he's pertected. But you and me, buddy, we're just the little bastards on the spot, the goons that get the stuff from the mine to the black warehouse for twenty measly francs a sack. Only it looks like you're doin it for love, if that's all the sarge told you."

"But gee whittaker," said Turvey, still floundering, "I heard the army was tryin to stop the black market. Dont seem like we get enough coal ourselves."

"Yeah, yeah. I dont know about the army, bud, not all of it. I just know if I dont run coal any night that cunt-face sergeant passes the buck to me, the Aj'll damn well shoot me up the Schelt marshes so fast my ass'll be burnin. And I had all I wanta that.''

"But I thought all the fellahs here at Thirty-Nine was sorta unfit for the front.''

"Yeah, yeah. I'm an L3 myself. Got a slug in the calf last November on Walcheren. But they aint been nothin wrong with me for weeks and all that Brylcreem's got to do is dig out my file and send me down to the Standin Medical Board; two days later I'll be lyin in the gumbo waitin to stop the next one in the kisser. That's my story and I'm stuck with it. So I'm playin along with the dear little Aj. But by the holy ole mare if the smoothie's goin to make me cut you in on my twenty francs I think I'll tell him to go take a flyin fuck at himself, and take a chance on bein an honest-to-god-infantryman again. Twenty jeezly francs! And they soak you fifty for a lousy run in one of them spam-an-egg caffs and I gotta run a whole truckload to stay overnight with a Brussells floozy.''

"You mean the sergeant and the adjutant are in on this black market too?''

"I didnt say a thing, bud. Not a thing. No names no pack-drills. What could they do with francs anyway? Cant send em back to England. And they live on their pay. Yeah! In a pig's asshole. But if they aint got nothin on you, you'd better ask a certain sarge what you're gettin out of this. Looks like they must be short a fallguys if they roped you in. It's on account a that new Spo we got, I bet. I guess they're scared to try cuttin him in. And he's been hellin around checkin documents and pullin the old sweats up for Medical Re-board or shovin em out on attachment jobs. They lost most of us night drivers that way.''

There was already a sullen glow over the flat white land in the east when the highway at last funnelled between lombards frosted like bleached fishbones, and narrowed into the town of Poperloo. They passed ragged old men plodding topcoatless in sabots on their way to the morning Winter-Help queue, and a single labourer in patched

green corduroys clutching a dinner pail. They rattled past
the milkman and his dwarfish horse, creeping townwards
in his high sled, and the paper boy shivering in a cutter
behind his limping dog. Shutters and blackouts were clattering up in shop windows as the truck whirled up the
powdery snow in the Grande Place and swung into one of
the military parking lots.

"Step on it," said Wilson, leaping out of the truck.
"We got fifteen minutes to shave and make rollcall. Too
late for breakfast now. Make sure you get all the black
off and keep your mug shut. Anybody want to know
where you been, you been out on the tiles all night."
Turvey rather wished he had. He couldnt have felt
sleepier or hungrier, certainly.

At rollcall he was picked off with five others and marched
briskly down the narrow mainstreet following a "runner"
to a tile-fronted house with a heavy glass door almost
flush with the sidewalk. The runner pulled a fancy
wrought-iron geegaw, a bell rang flatly inside, and they
pushed into a long cold hall. Their guide gestured to a
line of ancient chairs near the door and departed, after
handing their documents to another runner who had
emerged from a side-room. The new runner yawned, told
them to wait until they were called, and likewise disappeared. They sat, a muddle of shivering sleepy-eyed men,
while their boots silently spread fans of muddy water
over the pink tiles of the hall. The bell rang dully again
and a squat moustached captain stamped in, tailored
overcoat buttoned snug around his neck. He looked the
benchful over quickly with cold green eyes. The most
alert of the five stirred hastily and then all squirmed to
their feet, shambled to attention, and saluted.

The officer returned the salute with an elaborate and
chilling irony.

"As you were." His voice crackled. "Sit down. Let's
try that again. Some of you gallant gentlemen dont seem

to be awake yet." He turned, methodically paced out the door, rang the bell, and shot in again, small eyes glittering. The five rose almost as one man and saluted.

With another poised flip from his cap the officer walked by and up the stairs.

"That's a trifle better. You could do with some practice though." There was no smile in his voice.

"That's Biles, the fuckin Spo," whispered the man who had first stirred from the bench. "You dont want to cross that fucker up. He can send you any damn place he wants to." The group lapsed into gloomy silence until a very young and very haughty lance-corporal poked his head around the doorframe and called one of the benchers in.

When Turvey heard his name he followed the downy-cheeked lance-jack into a room cluttered with desks and tables ranging in quality from wooden boxes crammed with files to a giant mahogany desk. The lance-jack slid himself delicately into a cushioned chair behind the latter object and proceeded to type Turvey's military particulars on a paper so padded with carbons and undersheets Turvey wondered how he had ever got it into the machine. As he answered the lance-corporal's questions Turvey edged his back carefully near a large porcelain stove; but there was no fire in it. The whole house was apparently unheated; the clerks were shrouded in greatcoats, and fumbled their papers through knitted gloves.

When the solemn lance-corporal had come to the end of his septuplicated sheet he sent Turvey back to wait on the bench again. He managed to sleep upright most of the hour that followed, and was wakened only by the dim crying of his name up the stairway. An arm was beckoning. He stumbled over a thick stair-rug black and soggy from many army boots and past a cubbyhole on the halfway landing. Two cardboard signs dangled from its open door. The top one was marked TOILET; the under OUT OF ORDER. Turvey glimpsed a floor half-carpeted with yellow ice.

The hall above the second flight was deserted and

Turvey paused, wondering where he was to go. Two bedrooms led off on each side. The door of one was ajar and, coming abreast of it, Turvey saw the torso of the dread Spo behind a table covered startlingly with a leopard skin.

"Well. What are you waiting for? In here. In here." Turvey gave his special Salute-for-Generals as he entered and the little jade eyes of the Spo looked approval.

"That's better. Sit down." Turvey sat on a hard little folding-chair facing the Spo. The latter, leaning back in a black leather morris, let his sardonic gaze roam over Turvey.

"Dont you know you're in the wrong unit?" he asked coldly.

Although Turvey tried hard to explain, the captain continued to stare at him as if he blamed Turvey for it all. Turvey's voice gradually petered out and, to avoid the captain's petrifying stare, he started looking for face-patterns in the mesmeric leopard-spots on the table-cover. The patterns were complicated by violet blobs which Turvey first accepted as part of the original animal, but then realized must be ink-blots. There was a little jam-jar of violet fluid at one end of the table. Turvey felt a twinge in his vitals, suddenly remembering Clarence and his first prophylactic. He shifted his gaze to a mountainous wardrobe with glass panels that stood against the wall behind the captain.

"What's the matter? Cant you look an officer in the face when you talk to him?" There was a smile at the corner of the captain's thin mouth, but not of the kind to bring comfort.

"O, yessir."

"What are you grinning about?"

"Me? I'm not grinnin, sir. At least, I am, I guess, but I dont know it." He paused helplessly.

"You arent and you are and you dont know it." The captain repeated the phrases with saturnine relish. Then his eyes focused on the side of Turvey's head. "Dont you ever wash your ears?"

Turvey automatically put his hand up to his ear. His fingers came away sooty.

"Yeah," said the captain. "Go take a look."

Turvey stood up and examined himself in a heavy gilt wallmirror to which the captain had pointed. He must have missed one ear in his hurried morning wash. And there was more coal dust, a long streak, on his neck. "I see you've been listening at a black market door." Turvey turned with alarm, but the captain's little smirk suggested only that he was enjoying his own pun. Turvey did his best to wipe the betraying smooches off with his khaki handkerchief, and sat down again.

"The sooner we vet you for Twenty-Nine the better. They'll teach you to wash up there. Meantime," the captain paused and opened the door of the walnut cupboard behind him, fishing out some blank forms and, as an afterthought, a box of Laura Secord chocolates, "meantime, we'll have to complete a record on you here and put you to work. It will be two days before the next vehicle goes up to Twenty-Nine." While Turvey watched hungrily, he lifted the top lid of the chocolate box and, after some musing, selected a large brown cream and popped it in his mouth. He began to write, copying information longhand to a new form from the papers the lance-corporal had evidently sent up while Turvey had been waiting in the hallway. The captain's pen went dry; he shook it bad-temperedly, adding two more violet spots to the leopard's, then proceeded to renew his supply from the jam-jar.

A raucous auto-horn sounded outside and there was a dim puzzling clatter that grew quickly into a huffing and roaring in the street below. Suddenly, between the dirty lace curtains and the brown blackout hangings that framed the one window, a great puff of acrid wood-smoke rolled into the room, blanketing the panes and darkening everything. The auto-horn sounded again, deafeningly, as if under Turvey's very feet. He leaped back alarmed. But the captain looked up with cynical boredom. "Come on, now. You're only S-Three. You've got to jump higher than that to work your passage. Havent you heard our train before?"

"Train?"

"Yes, my brave soldier lad. That's the Toonerville from Antwerp. Twice a day. Narrow-gauge, next the sidewalk down there. As you see, they at least have some wood to burn."

The captain settled down to write again, but stopped to wring his fingers and cast a venomous look at the green porcelain stove next his desk. Reaching up savagely, he squeezed a signal cord hanging from the ceiling. Faintly below a buzzer sounded, there was an immediate "Coming, sir!" and feet dashed up the stairs. Then a breathless runner skidded at the door, saluted jerkily, and stood to attention.

The captain regarded him evilly. "Why the hell dont you keep this stove stoked? It's gone out."

"Sir," the private gulped, "the coal's all gone."

"Well get some more."

"Sir," the private picked his words apprehensively, "Sergeant Perkins says QMS told him we c-couldnt get no more this week."

The captain squinted. "I thought you told me you'd been a duty fireman before," he said quietly, and immediately built his voice to a shout. "Dont stand there! Get off your knees! Scrounge something somewhere! Coal, briquettes, horsedung, furniture, anything, as long as it'll burn! How do you expect me to work without a fire?" The private saluted and fled in the same motion. The captain picked up his field telephone and spent the next few minutes getting through to the quartermaster. He munched two more chocolates while he waited, paying no attention to Turvey.

"Captain Briggs?" There was a sepulchral crackle at the other end. "Biles here. I need some coal right away . . . No, we're fresh out. Must be below zero right here where I'm trying to work . . . Not even a half-sack? . . . Not even –" There was a long crackling from the other end.

"Well, if I whip up a driver could you get some today? . . . Yeah . . . Hold it a minute." He turned to Turvey. "Done any army driving?"

Turvey sighed. "Yessir."

The captain turned back to his telephone. "Send you one over in five minutes. How's that for service? . . . Sure, sure, he's experienced. . . . Sure, you can have him for the next three days . . . Okey-doke . . . Yeah, four sacks up here soon as he comes back. Roger." He hung up and began busily writing on a field message pad. Turvey stared forlornly around the walls. Several brighter squares on the florid wallpaper recorded the size of vanished pictures. The only surviving ornament was a large calendar. The illustration was of a gaunt old miner silhouetted in front of a pit head. "Kalender van den Mijnwerker", it was headed, and there was a border of red type listing the appropriate miners' saints throughout the year. Turvey wasnt able to read which one he should pray to today. It was too late anyway. The captain was holding out a pair of violet-scrawled messages.

"Take this one to the Orderly Room. Then the other to the Transport Office. They'll give you a vehicle. You'll be trucking coal from Army Stores in Brussells." Turvey, a paper in each hand, stepped back the required pace and saluted sadly. "Who taught you to salute? Put both messages in your left hand and try again." The captain watched with mysterious pin-points of enjoyment in his eyes as Turvey obeyed. In the hallway he heard the captain's acid voice again: "Make sure you wash when you get back."

But by the time Turvey had rattled back from Brussells with a now lawful load of coal – he recognized his truck as the same one he had driven during the night – it was a choice between being too late for supper, and washing. He hadnt been able to wangle much lunch at the Brussells Army Stores, so he chose food. After some argument with a cookee he managed to get his billytin filled and its contents down him before he had to hustle over to the

Orderly Room again on prior warning from the fat
Orderly Room Sergeant.

That night was very much like the previous one except
that Turvey found himself quite able to sleep through
every road-bump whenever Wilson was at the wheel.

The sacks they had stowed under the deserted shed at
the back of the Brussels factory had disappeared when
they slid in with their second load, sometime about three
in the morning, but there was no one around. Wilson was
jittery, however, because there was an air-raid somewhere near the horizon toward Antwerp and the fitful
radii of searchlights occasionally swung overhead, making their operation far too visible. And though they got
away on the home highway without incident, the air
above them groaned with unseen planes, the far thud of
bombs and the pop of ack-ack.

"You find out what cut they're givin you on this?"
Wilson asked next time Turvey took over the wheel.

"I dont like to ask," said Turvey. "I dont want to
make any trouble or perhaps they wont let me go up to
Twenty-Nine at all."

"Mebbe you're right," said Wilson reflectively. "Once
they got somethin on you you're a dead pigeon around
here. But all you're doin is buyin the Aj another diamond
ring. Boy, is that drape-shape coinin it! I heard some of
them buy up Dutch guilders with all these francs, up in
the Brussels Bourse. Get em seventy-five percent off.
Then they drive into Holland, cash em in the Officer
Clubs for francs at standard rate. Wotta racket. Salt it
away in sparklers and spend the rest on dames and
throwin do's for the local nobs."

"Yeah?"

"Yeah. But dont let on I said it. And somebody, I'm
not sayin, mind, some wise guy with shoulder brass, is
doin a paint job on these watchacallums, Captured
Enemy Vehicles, and sellin em to the Flam dealers in
Ghent. I'll bet there's real foldin money in that. But dont
start yappin or we'll both be in a slittie waitin for the one

with our name on it." He lapsed into silence, yawned, and was almost at once asleep.

Unfortunately the drone of the planes made Turvey sleepy too. At a right-angle turn still two miles from their unit he nodded and before he knew it they were completely in the ditch, the back axle buried in mud and slush. It was only five-thirty, too early to hope for another vehicle to come along and haul them out before breakfast time or even rollcall. The only buildings in sight were a row of cracked, deserted greenhouses.

"A great life if you dont weaken," said Wilson, climbing gloomily back into the cab after they had made several vain attempts to rev out. "We'd better toss to see who hoofs it to the unit." They matched. Turvey, as he more or less expected, lost; it was not his lucky month, and he'd forgotten to touch Peggy's rabbit foot before he flipped.

"For chrisesake pull your finger out and get goin before I freeze em off," said Wilson. "And if they start makin it tough for you tell em you're delicate, you need a sleep once a week. If that dont work, get yourself marched. Ask to see the O.C. That'll throw a scare in the Aj. Twenty fiddly francs. Jesus H. Christ!" Turvey nodded dubiously and set off with the truck's flashlight down the still-darkened road.

Fortunately the adjutant, when he heard that the truck would have to be rescued from two miles up the highway, seemed to decide that Turvey had outlived his usefulness at Number Thirty-Nine. After breakfast he was allowed to go to his three-biscuit mattress in the school basement. He washed and flopped, but he was no sooner asleep than he was waked and bundled into a HUP, kit, documents and all, and despatched with a driver and an S-Three sergeant along Maple Leaf Up, bound at last for Number Twenty-Nine.

SEVENTEEN

Turvey Reaches the Sharp End

H EADED for the front! For the Sharp End! Well, for
Nijmegen anyway, which everyone said was within
shell range, almost at the very tip of the Canadian salient,
in danger of being nipped off any time. Yet somehow, as
on other occasions when he had drawn near to his martial
goal, Turvey wasnt nearly as happy as he thought he
would be. It wasnt that he was scared; he always found it
difficult to imagine dangers he hadnt experienced.
Perhaps it was the chill January day and the bleak sights
along the highway. He had nothing else to do but doze,
when the roadbed permitted, or stare at the receding
pavement from the HUP's backseat. The sergeant was
sitting in front; he and the driver, ignoring Turvey, were
deep in reminiscences; they had discovered they were
from the same home town.

Over the barren saltmarshes sped the truck, under the
floating Disney elephants of a balloon barrage and into
the winding hubbub of Antwerp. Past multitudes of
giraffish old houses they clattered, past enormous
churches, past barbaric ruins, some old and weedy,
others (like the Rex Cinema, where a whole Saturday
matinee of soldiers still lay hidden) bright with newly-
shattered brick. Then north into a flat straight highway
again. Now over a groaning pontoon bridge subbing for
a blasted canal lock; along the ice-choked ditch was a
sprinkling of mounds, and one by the roadside held a

faded stake on which a hoar-bright billytin clunked mournfully in the Flanders wind. These, and a crazily-twisted tank marked with a Maltese Cross – the little harvest of some almost forgotten fight a few months earlier for the possession of the canal. Then the Maple Leaf Up ran straight for miles between a boulevard of ground-level stumps, all that was left of lombard avenues cut for road-blocks or fuel or mine-props. Through the raw mists swirling across from the colourless fields Turvey could see ragged old men and shawled women silently carving chips from some of the stumps with long butcher knives, and stowing the frosty fragments carefully into straw baskets and pails. The road swung and narrowed into cobblestone. They bumped through a dead village, fiercely killed in some artillery or aerial duel, a shapeless collection of rubble through which chimneys reared like broken old teeth. The occasional despatch rider roared by them, slithering madly on the glazed stones, always about to careen into one of the ditches but always just escaping. A monotonous succession of grey blobs whined out of the horizon, grew into trucks and station wagons or shrank into jeeps, and passed. Civilian traffic was barred from the Maple Leaf but cyclists, risking military wrath, would come bumping wearily toward them, sometimes women in billowing skirts riding on un-tyred rims, tossing and bouncing like grotesque sailboats over the cobbles.

A detour now through the side-lanes of a village. The main street, either by bad luck or some diabolical aiming, was hit a few minutes ago by a V-Two. That was the white flash, the feathery arc in the sky they had seen from the highway, and the following roar like a distant express train. Sombre men with incongruously bright orange sleeve-bands are re-routing traffic, for they have passed into Holland and these are the Dutch Underground. And these are two Dutch bodies lying half-revealed by the acrid wind that has blown askew the sacking thrown over them. But they are now someone else's concern, and

Turvey's HUP jounces on as if it would run forever. The road turns asphalt again and their speed increases. But soon icy patches multiply, they rush past two trucks abandoned in the ditch, and stop to help pull out a third which just skidded its way in. Now on, more slowly, for there is a repair sign, and the verges are still mined. Some kind of bomb has torn up a hundred foot of paving, and there are three heaps of slaggy asphalt, sweepings from some other bombing, dumped here to repair the road. Each heap is clustered with children, some with naked blue legs, thin as willows. With frayed gloves or bare hands, they are fingering the heaps for nuggets of tar or burnable flakes of asphalt, and stowing their loot in shopping bags. No, Turvey somehow could not fall into gaiety on the road to Nijmegen as the mist thickened to rain and then to sleet. But he took out his tonette and played "Clementine" to himself in the draughty back of the HUP until the sergeant and the driver bawled at him to stop.

They entered Nijmegen in darkness, moved under dim ghostly trees limned in white, and climbed wearily down from the high truck in the backyard of what seemed in the vague light to be a large oblong apartment house, but which Turvey learned later had been a high school. It was long past suppertime and he got set for the usual Orderly Room hold-up, after which he saw himself confined to barracks as a firstnighter in a new unit, too late for food and barred from estaminets, and flopping hungry to sleep on a floor. Or even setting out on another black market journey.

But everything at the Sharp End turned out to be strangely different and simpler than Turvey was used to in the army. The three of them were whisked into a mess-kitchen and given great bowlfuls of hot soup from a gleaming pot on a giant Flemish stove that soon spread warmth through their cramped limbs. Then a runner helped Turvey with his kit up to the second storey of the big schoolhouse to a real mattress in a bunk fitted against the blackboard wall of what had been a classroom. It was a cold stoveless place, breezy with draughts that seemed to come not only from behind the paper blackout blinds but down from the top-floor stairs. The runner, however, had an extra blanket for him. With the help of this and the pair from his pack, his greatcoat, battledress, sweater, and the new long woollies from Peggy, he was asleep in the shake of a lamb's tail and stayed that way until the Orderly Corporal poked him awake at 0630 the next morning.

By 0900 he had breakfasted, checked in at the Orderly Room, and was sitting on a three-legged stool across a table from a Personnel Sergeant in a bare office on the ground floor. The little sergeant with the round brown eyes was absorbed in Turvey's dossier. He seemed to find it interesting and would raise his vaselined head frequently to send him a shining speculative glance. He didnt look an unfriendly type but Turvey braced himself for the shooting, calm yet tense like the veteran he was, hardened from many a battle in S.P. offices.

"Have a Dutch horsetail?" said the sergeant suddenly, proffering a packet of odd brown cigarettes. They both lit up and the sergeant returned in fascinated stillness to Turvey's documents. When he had finished he inhaled, placed his cigarette on the table edge, and crossed his arms with a curious wide sweep. Then he leant back in his rickety cane-chair, blew out a coil of chestnut smoke, and smiled genially:

"So you're an S-Three now. Well, you're in good company. We've got three hundred of them right here in this building. Fine lot of boys. You'll like them. Some of them get the wind up when Jerry starts popping shells over, but in between it's a good show. A lot of nice jobs around here too . . . Hear the eighty-eights last night?"

"Shells? Jiggers no, I was poundin my ear all night."

"So?" The sergeant looked pleased. His voice was suprisingly deep and vibrant for such a little man. "You're not jittery about being up at the Sharp End then?"

"Heck, this is where I been tryin to get since gosh knows when. I'm for a specialist job," Turvey rushed in, fearful it might be his only chance to get the record straight. "Pioneerin. The Nut Doctor at the Re-dis said I was to come here cause I got a father complex and that's why I shot up my greatcoat by mistake."

The sergeant seemed a little mystified. "I thought it was a paratrooper," Turvey added placatingly.

The sergeant looked even more puzzled, picked up his cigarette and went back to the dossier, but the full psychiatric report from the Redistribution Unit must have been left behind. Turvey had to reconstruct his latest personality as well as he could from what he thought he remembered. It wasnt a very clear account. Meantime the sergeant was examining Turvey's Pay Book.

"Why, you're only S-Three-*T*," he said. "You're just a *temporary*!" He seemed to feel the discovery merited another horsetail each. And once again the sergeant laid his cigarette on the table's corner and folded his arms with a slow gesture almost as if he were tossing a cloak aside. This time he leant forward peering compellingly at Turvey through the heady brown smoke streaming from the parked cigarette.

"You feel O.K.?"

"Sure! I'm sittin on top!"

"Do you want to get into the infantry again?"

"You bet, yes, please. Koot –"

"Sure you haven't any jitters?"

"Not that I know about."

The sergeant relaxed with a pleased little crinkling of his eyelids, but he spoke cautiously.

"Of course I'm only the sergeant here, old man. Maybe Bob – that's Captain Janes, the Spo – wont agree with me. And even if he did, we'd have to get the Area Sike to see you."

"Maybe he has," said Turvey. "I oughta seen most of them by now. Course they're generally quite nice to know. I dont mind meetin him a second time. Which one have you got here?"

"Major Malkechinski."

Turvey shook his head. "No, havent met any inskies."

"O you'll go for him. He's a real Sky-artist. And very fond of S-Threes. And *specially* S-Three-*T*s . . . But look," the sergeant consulted his wrist watch, and turned his eager stare on Turvey again, "the Cap wont be along for another ten minutes. How about a little preliminary test or two while we're marking time?"

Turvey must have looked a trifle unenthusiastic, for the sergeant went on hastily: "Just for the hell of it. I havent a thing to do this morning till Bob comes. You'll like these."

"I think I've had all the tests," said Turvey flatly. But there was something alluring about the sergeant's soothing voice and dreamy stare.

The sergeant flipped back again through the fat folder. "By crikey, I really think you have. All the *official* ones, that is. Hmmm." He cocked his glossy head sideways at the ceiling. Then he leaned persuasively at Turvey.

"Look, old man, I have a wonderful idea. You can do me a favour and I can do you one. Fact, I'll put you on the road to S-One again, so you can get to an infantry regiment."

"Kootenay Highlanders," said Turvey automatically.

"Of course," the sergeant went on hurriedly, but softly. "Now, I want you to let me try out some little tests which we dont use officially. Matter of fact, they're all my own. And really on the beam. O, nothing unpleasant," he added quickly, sighting suspicion in Turvey's face. "On the contrary, very amusing. *And* instructive. Humdingers, in fact, the oldest psychological tests in the world." His dark eyes were heavy with mysteries. "You see, Turvey –" his voice was quite confidential now – "in civil life I'm a Magician and a lot of things like that. Astrologer, Palmist, Seer, Graphologist. And Psychologist, of course. Perhaps you've even seen me professionally?

Rama, the Seer of Destiny?" The sergeant's supple lips framed capitals for each important word.

Turvey was ashamed to say he hadnt.

"Ah, of course, you're from the west," the sergeant said forgivingly. "I've never appeared beyond Hamilton. Had engagements in all the principal eastern cities, of course – Toronto Casino; Ogilson's Department store, Hamilton; grand foyer of the Papineau, Ottawa; Cabaret Click-Clock, Montreal. Wore a turban of course, and brown make-up. The women like that."

"Jeepers, you have a crystal ball, too?"

The sergeant made a moue. "Only in the smaller centres. It's an outdated technique now in the profession. Mine is more the Scientific approach. I interpret Handwriting. Read Palms too, of course, plot Destiny from birth-stars and all that. Now your handwriting," he flipped through Turvey's file until he came to the Officer Selection Form Turvey had been required to fill out personally, "is very, very, interesting, packed with Character. I would say to begin with that you are Versatile. Look at the variety of those capitals. A little restless by nature perhaps . . . well, Adventurous. You'll take on anything. I should guess you've had a great number of occupations both in the army and in civil life. Right?"

"You're sure right there," said Turvey, beginning to be impressed.

"Now these i-dots, and the long t-strokes. I could tell you a great deal from these." He leant his cheek on the sheet and squinted along it. Then he picked up a small ruler and solemnly measured one of Turvey's dashing t-strokes and seemed to be making a rapid mental calculation. "You're a cheerful sort, easy to get along with. Affectionate. But often Misunderstood. Yes?"

"*I'll* say," said Turvey with feeling, and growing admiration. "Especially in the army."

"Especially in the army," the sergeant repeated, but as

if he had said it first. "You do not always make yourself
clear to your superior officers."

"You can say that again!" Turvey wagged his head
with astonished delight. "I never had anybody read me
like you can."

The sergeant waved a deprecating hand. "Let's take a
glimpse into your Future. Just put your left hand on the
table . . . Ahhh, a fascinating Life-line. Still not married,
I would say. Not churched, at any rate. I can see," with
deft fingers he paused to tauten Turvey's calloused palm,
"I can see many more Women in your life. Umm, yes.
Fascinating. But there is One, perhaps you have already
met her" – he looked quickly in Turvey's face. Turvey
felt himself beginning to blush. "Yes, I'm fairly sure
you've already met her. In . . . ummm. England?"

"Yes, that's Peggy," said Turvey, feeling by now there
was no use concealing anything.

Suddenly a curious noise grew in the room, something
between a whine and a long lamenting cry and a whoosh.
It was immediately followed by a tremendous trampling
overhead, from the floor where Turvey had slept, and a
cascade of confused sound coming down the stairs,
shouts of excitement and fear, the thunder of army
boots. The odd swishing keen, which had been momentarily drowned, now penetrated shrilly from overhead
and passed, and was replaced by the crack of an explosion. The sergeant had scarcely stirred in his chair and
was still holding Turvey's palm.

"Just an eighty-eight," he said offhandedly. "Jerry
trying to hit the bridge, or maybe Army H.Q. Off the
mark, anyway." There were still shouts and scufflings in
the corridor, descending now what must be the basement
stairs.

"What's all the shoutin about?" asked Turvey, a little
bewildered.

"O, that's just our S-Threes. Some of them been on
night jobs and were up sleeping. They try to make the

basement every time even though we keep telling them
the shells always pass over. Of course one did connect
with the top storey. Fell short. But that was a month ago.
Took the roof off. Notice the draught upstairs last
night?"

Turvey nodded vigorously, and the sergeant went on.
"That keeps reminding them." The trampling of ammo
boots could be heard ascending slowly. "Then they
stampede and we stop them on the bottom stairs. Armed
guards. We have to do it, the basement's full of cloak-
and-dagger boys. Range-finders, you know, hush-hush
equipment; they cant let anybody in. It's good for the
S-Threes, though, they say. Supposed to get their nerve
back that way. But george, your nerves are O.K. Now
let's see your other mitt a minute. Peggy, you said her
name was? It's a lovely name. And a lovely girl. I see that
you will be Together Again, you and the beauteous
Peggy. But before that, you will have many Adventures,
some happy, some, umm, not so happy. I wish we had
time to cast your Horoscope. I'm getting rusty at
Horoscopes. But perhaps we can do a little more with this
Secondary Life-line. Now before you're fifty you'll –"
But without warning he shoved Turvey's hand back. His
voice, which had been growing so low, so gentle, so
throbbing with soft wisdom that Turvey was in a spell,
suddenly became casual and brisk. "Yes, you'll have to
wait for Captain Janes. Perhaps he'll let you see the
psychiatrist again." There had been steps outside the
door and now it was opening. The sergeant slid out of his
chair. It was a captain. Turvey popped up and stood at
attention.

"Relax, chaps," said the captain easily. "You're
lookin guilty, sarge. Been up to somethin, I'll bet." He
stuffed his beret in his thigh pocket. He was a young
man, with brown tousled hair and a perky chin. He drew
up a jerrican from the corner, waving aside the sergeant's
offer of the cane-back. "What's the good news this
mornin, Herb?"

"Nothing much so far, Bob, except Private Turvey here. A new S-Three came in last night."

"Pleased to meet you, Turvey. My name's Bob Janes." He shot out his hand. "What's your first name?"

"Thomas, sir, but I generally get Tops – short for Topsy."

"Swell. And unless it makes you feel better to say 'sir' suppose you call me just Bob or Cap while we're here. I get so damn tired of all this sirring crap."

"Like to look at Tops' file, Cap? I've just been through it with him."

"All that bumf? You're kiddin me. Herbert here's a great kidder, Tops. He knows I'm allergic to army documents. Put me in the picture, Tops. How'd you come to get sent here?"

Turvey told him as best he could. The captain seemed very easy to explain things to, though it took a long time; he plainly enjoyed the narrative and went clumping around the room clucking sympathetically. When Turvey had finished, the sergeant added quickly,

"But it's only a *Temporary* S-Three, Bob."

"Top-hole. Maybe this'll be one for the book. Feel anythin wrong with you, Tops? You got a cough, I notice."

"Just a cold. It's nothin. I feel jake-a-loo."

"What kind of a job would you like to have then?"

"O, any of this here specialist pioneerin they told me you got up here. I dont care."

"Well, we could put you on coal deliveries to the Corps units," the captain said grinning. "I'm just kiddin," he added, seeing the alarm in Turvey's face. "But on the level, that's the kind of thing our S-Threes are doin. All this horse-feathers about specialized employment – just a fancy title the L. of C. swine dreamt up down at One Echelon. What we get is a lot of boys with the wind up. The psychiatrists call it Battle Fatigue and they say these ones arent windy enough to get their ticket and they'll snap out of it if they're kept up here loadin trucks with shells, coal, supplies, any damn thing, or just doin the chores around the Corps units – battin, swabbin, night firin, dishin up food in officers' messes, bubble dancin and spud bashin in the cook-houses, carryin slops in field hospitals, *you* know, all the little joe-jobs. One of them's peddlin a bike to make power for a hand-laundry we got. It's a slice of pie really. Then they're supposed to get all steamed up to start throwin things at Jerry again and come and plead with the O.C. here to send em back to the front. That's the theory, anyway. Now how about you, Tops. What'll you have?"

Turvey was unused to the privilege of making decisions on such matters and he had to think.

"Well, Bob, sir, I guess you know best. But I aint nervous. It's just this father complex I got somewhere, I suppose, but I dont feel it. I'd like to get to my regiment and be with my pal Mac again, if I could. The Koo –"

"Herb, it aint possible." The captain slapped his knee ecstatically. "This is really one for the book. Arnhem Annie wouldnt get a look from this boy. Quick. Make out one of those Referral forms – you know, I never can remember the number. I'm goin down to the O.C.'s office and see if I can get the Sike on the blower. He should be over at the Field Dressin Station this mornin. This is bang up our street." The captain glaumed his beret on his head and made a beeline out the door. Turvey noticed he limped a little.

"Nice guy, Bob," said the sergeant fondly. "He hasnt the psychological background some of us have, of course, but he gets things done. He's a combat type, really, but he bunged a knee up in a carrier crash. . . . Now, if we can make up the right song-an-dance for this SP-206, I think maybe the Sike will raise your category." He made a little sandwich of seven forms and six carbons, squeezed them into an old portable on the table and began clattering off Turvey's answers to the requisite questions. He paused after the birth-date.

"Born thirteen May. Yes. You're a Taurus man, Tops,

you know. That means you're really a strong character, Persistent in obtaining whatever Objective you have in hand."

"Like gettin to the –?"

"Exactly. But you have to watch you dont over-do it. Taurus chaps often dont stop to think whether their Goal is worth the Effort and Endurance they expend."

"Well, gosh, there aint any better regiment than –"

"Of course, I didnt mean that. But, according to the Star Signals this week, people in your Sign should beware of Journeys and watch their Health. That cough you have, for instance –"

"Shucks, that's just a cold I got in the black market."

"Ah, but Taurus folks are susceptible to Throat Complaints. And let's see, what Vibration has 1945 for you?" Herb made a rapid calculation on a pad. "Thirteen is four, your Universal Year, and May thirteen is nine, that's thirteen again – your Lucky Number – and that's four again, your Personal Year. That makes 1945 a, umm, let's see, yes, a Three Year for you. Good! This year will bring you much Happiness, Tops, Self-expression, Freedom –"

"You mean the war's gonna be over?" Herb's brown eyes had taken on such a far-off sureness, and his sentences rolled off so professionally, Turvey was ready for any revelation.

"Ahh, to answer that requires more Astrological Study than I have opportunity to make in my position." Herb gestured mournfully at the room and folded his arms again. "But for yourself, I can say that you will share the benefits of Jupiter and Mars – Success in your affairs, Romance, Love."

"Peggy?"

"Peggy. I'm sure of it, Tops. But first there will be Set-backs. Other people will Show a Desire to Manage your Affairs."

"That wont be nothin new," Turvey sighed, "not in the army anyhow."

"True, Tops, and you must continue for a while to

Adjust your self to such annoyances. Also, you will be
compelled to take Long Journeys, and suffer Loss and
Separation from Loved Ones. But I'm sure your sunshiny
spirit will win through the clouds. Provided of course you
are not too Reckless." Herb paused and, fishing a comb
from his pocket, ran it through his glossy hair. "Hope
you dont mind my giving you advice like this?"

"Gosh, no," said Turvey. "It's very good of you."

"Matter of fact," Herb put the comb back and relaxed,
"what with the Palm-reading and the Graphological
Analysis and the Horoscope and the Numerology, that
would cost you fifteen dollars on Civvy Street. That's for
a man, of course. Always charged them less to encourage
them. Most of my clients were women. Nicked them
twenty or twenty-five for all that. Had to, you know, to
make expenses. Management took twenty percent, booking agent ten. Then there were hotels and travelling expenses. And extra laundry for turbans and stiff shirts;
and capital investment you know – crystal ball, two dress
suits, and my Library. There's a lot of studying to it,
you'd be surprised. Astrological Charts, for example. I
used to know them backwards. Getting rusty now." He
shook his head. "Four years in the army. People dont
stop to think the sacrifices a Professional Man makes going to war."

"No more they dont," said Turvey, feeling unusually
at ease and chatty. "I knew a fellah at the Chemical Warfare outfit where I was. He was a nembalmer on Civvy
Street. You'd think a war would be kine of a good show
for a nembalmer wouldnt you? But he hadnt seen a stiff
in three years, he told me. They'd sent him to this outfit
because they thought he ought to be up on chemicals,
like. But its all flamethrowers there. So they put him in
R.A.P. helpin the sarge with first-aid. He was bandagin
up plenty of burns that way but the fellahs were pretty
cagey and nobody ever got really fried."

"You havent been an embalmer too, have vou?"

"No, but I've –"

"Dont mention it to the Sike if you have. He's down on embalmers. And osteopaths. And chiropractors. If you've had a turn at any of those, just skip it. And dont let him hear you whistling."

"No?"

"He's got a phobia about whistles. Told Bob he was scared by a train once. Otherwise he's O.K. though. You'll go for him. These psychiatrists are all a little one-sided, of course. It's their training. They arent even allowed to use Graphology, you know that? The brass-hats in the Medical Corps are against it . . . And dont make any cracks against other Sikes you've seen. Professional Loyalty you know. We all have it. Just tell him how you came to write off that greatcoat. And if you get a chance tell him you Love this girl Peggy and hope to have a settled Home-life and raise a flock of kids. He's all for the Family. Tell him *you* had a Happy Home too. Then he'll be sure you arent crackers. He's a heller for Home Values and all that. Well, we'd better get this bumf ready." And he resumed his clattering on the little machine.

He had just finished when the captain returned. "Hi," he said. "Sike wont believe it, you know, that an S-Three comes up one day and wants to be an S-One the next. Says you're to see him this af'. I'll run you over myself in the jeep. We'll R.V. here at 1.30. Herb, you wanta come too?"

"Well, there's those weekly reports to Spo One. We're two weeks behind now, Bob. And your swindle sheet for that last trip to Antwerp's got to be cooked."

"Forget it. Sun's out. You need fresh air and games. Better come along with me now, Tops, and we'll clear you in the Orderly Room."

Turvey padded happily after him. Everybody was so

friendly and speedy and casual, it was almost like being with Mac and the Bogshires. Must be something about being near a real shootin war, he thought.

Even the Sike, when Turvey sat down for a chat with him, was in his own way just as pleasant. Captain Bob and Sergeant Herb took Turvey in their jeep through slushy woods south of the town to a tiny but surprisingly modern building plumped in the middle of christmassy firs. Turvey was thrilled to learn that for the last hundred yards he had been in Germany.

"The Jerries got everythin teed up here for a maternity ward," Captain Bob explained. "I hear they have a string of em just on their side of the border. Whenever they knocked up a local biddy they sent her to one of these so the little bastard would be born in the Reich. Patriotic codgers, the squareheads. Efficient, though. Couldnt ask for a nicer field-dressin station. Big windows. Tile floors. Course they took all their equipment out."

The Sike was a tall stooped major with a slightly abstracted air but very kind blue eyes and a long lean face like Gary Cooper's. He was very gentle and friendly and showed Turvey around, asking him little questions about his health as they strolled. Turvey thought it better to say nothing about his throat, which now had a curiously precise spot that was sorer than he had ever had with a cold before. The major wasnt in charge here, he just had a field office in the building, but you never knew what would happen if you told a Sike you felt anything wrong with you. The ward was fairly full of soldiers lying on clean-sheeted mattresses on the floor. The major explained they were light casualties from minor wounds or sickness who would presumably return to duty in a few days. The serious ones, after emergency treatment, were flown either to Ghent, where Turvey had been, or to England. Then the major took Turvey into his little office at the

ward's end and sat down beside him on the one bunk.
First he scanned the SP form the sergeant had made out,
and poked warily through the other papers underneath it
in Turvey's file. Then he whanged Turvey's knees with a
little rubber mallet and went through the usual routine
doctors always seemed to follow when they interviewed
Turvey. Later, he called Captain Bob and the sergeant in
and they had an impromptu conference. The captain
made a special point about Turvey being the first S-Three
to recover under the new experiment. "Malky," he said,
"he's the 311th S-Three to clear through our office in the
seven weeks since L. of C. started turfin em up here. And
the rest are still panickin down stairs every time they hear
a poop – except the thirty-five you downgraded and sent
home. He's unique." And Herb added his testimony to
the fact that Turvey's hands and corporeal frame
generally had remained perfectly calm when the most recent shell had come over.

"Yes," said the major thoughtfully. "A very interesting case. Recovered within twenty-four hours of arrival.
Ummm. It's not a question of querying the previous
diagnosis, you understand. He's simply, ah, shall we say,
made an unusually speedy adjustment. The trouble is,"
he scratched the underside of his jaw and wrinkled his
brow, "there's nothing we can do till his thirty days are
up. You see it's laid down for us at One Echelon;
S-Threes all come here for a minimum of thirty days.
Then we check on them. Cant you find him something
martial enough to do for the next month?"

"Well, I could attach him to the Mobile Laundry Unit.
They need a driver. But Spo One is after me because One
Esh is on *his* tail to grab every guy that's declared fit and
transfer him to Infantry. There's a godawful shortage.
And here's this lad all set to pack a muckstick, too."

"Kootenay High –" began Turvey.

"But look!" the sergeant interrupted, "We forgot –
Turvey's only S-Three *Temporary*."

"No!" exclaimed the major, turning quickly to the

file. "By Gad, you're right, Herb. That means I can up-grade him any time without a Board. I'll tap out a form this afternoon. O.K., son, sure it's the infantry you want?"

"Kootenay Highlanders, please, sir."

"The Kooties? They're near here, arent they?" the major asked.

"Yeah, in the swamp somewhere, coupla miles beyond the bridge," said Bob.

"Of course, he couldnt go straight there." The major scratched his chin again. "All we can do is make him S-One and send him back to the Blunt End earmarked for infantry. Then they'll send him back to the Sharp End, to whatever regiment has priority; isnt that right, Bob?"

"O Lord yes, so it is, even for S-Three-Temporaries. Everythin arse-about-face. And they'll probably lose him at the Royal Albert Bollocks, the sods, and find him again when the war's over. You know that dump."

"I was lost there once before," said Turvey anxiously, "I'd rather not go back. And I know my outfit can use me right now. I had a letter when I was in hospital, from my pal Mac. He's Lazin Officer again with the Koot-enays and he's fixin it for me to drive his jeep like I did before. Couldnt I just walk up there now and get started."

"Maybe you could in some armies," said the major sadly, "but not in this one. We'll have to put you on the X-12 list and wait for a truck back to the Re-dis. That's where you massacred your greatcoat. And there they'll put you on the X-14 list. That'll take a few days. Then you'll go back farther to CBRG in Ghent and wait till there's an infantry draft coming up to Corps. That's up here. And Corps will send you to Div and Div to the regi-ment that's been hollering the most in the last few days. Course that might be the Kootenay Highlanders. But it's only about one chance in fifty."

"I told you there would be Unexpected Setbacks,"

said Herb as he and Turvey walked out to the jeep behind the captain and the major. "But the sun goes into Aries on Thursday and that's a better Sign for you. It's a more Auspicious Time for Taurus people to travel. You can expect quite a change in your Status any time now. Who knows, you might be back here in a week, bound for your Kootenay Highlanders."

Turvey nodded. It was obvious Herb was just trying to be comforting. The thought of travelling a hundred and fifty miles back to Plaatschat, going through all the Redistribution routine once more, and then being dumped in King Albert's dungeons until they remembered to send him up here again was not a happy one. And the soreness in his throat was spreading. He sat glumly in the rear seat of the jeep until Captain Bob spoke suddenly: "Say, Herb, old Spud Murphy is Aj with the Kooties now, I think. *You* know Spud. Used to sell for Canamerican Biscuits? Was champion backstroke at the 'Y'? Remember the guy that dropped in here last month with the big colonel, lookin for a bottle?"

"O, him," said Herb, "sure, he's a real live-wire."

"Well, what say we take the jeep up tomorrow and try to find em? The O.C.'s a pal of Spud's too. He'll let us go."

"Have to get permission from Corps to drive into Div area," said Herb cautiously. "And Div Intelligence will have to be willing to give us the gen on how to locate them."

"Hell, Stinky Finkle's the I.O. at Corps now. We used to play basketball together. He'll get us up to Div. And if Div's sticky about it we can ask any Dutchman. They always know where any of our units are. We'll take Turvey along tomorrow and he can say hello to his Heeland pals anyway. Never know; if they're strapped enough for replacements they may wangle a way to keep him."

Turvey, who hadnt missed a word, felt much better. That evening, though his throat burned like the inside of

a hot stovepipe when he went to bed, he drifted happily
to sleep thinking how surprised Mac would be. He didnt
notice the drafts this night. In fact before morning he was
sweating so much he threw off the greatcoat and one of
the blankets, and when he got up he felt a little dizzy, and
his throat was sorer than ever. But these matters were obviously of no consequence on such a day.

By noon Captain Bob had wangled permission to visit
Div area and by mid-afternoon they presented their pass
at the Nijmegen end of the bridge and chugged across its
scarred length and down into the frozen riverland that
stretched, relieved only by willow tufts, black scars from
flamethrowers, ruined farms and the occasional burnt-
out glider, from Nijmegen almost to fatal, German-held
Arnhem. Armed by Stinky Finkle with the password and
a map, they ignored Div H.Q. and by dusk, following the
directions of a courteous Dutch boy, parked their jeep
where the side-road ended in a constellation of shellholes,
and made their way through a thin scurf of snow to a
willow-thick embankment, battalion lines of the Kootenay Highlanders. Just after they were challenged by two
soldiers in ghostly white parkas Turvey stumbled and fell
into an ice-crusted fox-hole. Herb pulled him out.

"Say, you've got a fever! You're all flushed."

"Jus excited," Turvey mumbled, "kind a het up."

"Nerts, I've been watching you. You look like death
warmed over. You're coming down with something. It's
that damned Pisces. You're going to see the Kootenay
M.O., that's who you're going to see first. You can hunt
up your pal Mac later." Against Turvey's protests, Herb
made one of the guards accompanying them take Turvey
directly to the brush-screened R.A.P. dugout in the dyke,
while Captain Bob was directed along its bank to the
smoke-pot marking battalion headquarters.

The M.O. was a sad hollow-eyed youth who looked
very much as if he needed a good sleep. He brought
Turvey out into the fading light and looked down his
throat.

"Say Ahhhh . . . Bit inflamed all right . . . And you've got a temperature. May have a touch of Vincent's throat." The M.O. didnt sound very sure. "Reinforcement?"

Herb explained the technical difficulties in the way of taking Turvey on without sending him back to Base and bringing him up again.

"Just as well," the M.O. said dully. "I'd have to send him out anyway. We've got too many crocks around here now." The tone was weary rather than ungracious. "I'll give you something to gargle with, meanwhile." They stooped and re-entered the damp timbered dugout.

"Been having a lot of casualties?" Herb asked.

"Couple of weeks ago, we did. Farther up. Threw everything but their medals at us. So much grief they moved us here where it's quieter, till those L. of C. swine get round to coughing up some reinforcements. Yeah. We had plenty. Mortars mainly. You heard about Colonel Howlett? One of them got our H.Q. you know. Gave the colonel a trip. Lung. He'll be lucky if he sees Canada again."

From far away came the brrrping and prrracking of machine guns. Turvey felt again the unpredictable anticlimax of war itself that always assailed him when, after months of impatient hope, he approached the reality. This must be Ted Howlett from the Hill Farm near Kuskanee – he was big and barrel-chested, with a jaunty black moustache. Turvey thought of him coughing blood in some hospital bed. Then with sudden terror he thought again of the M.O.'s words. One of them got our H.Q. –

"Is Mac O.K., sir? Lieutenant MacGillicuddy, I mean, sir. The Lazin Officer?"

The M.O. looked at him with brooding, faraway eyes. "You knew – know him?"

"He's my pal, sir, from even before the war. And I was his batman-driver last November. I – he wants me back with him. I had a lett –"

"Sorry, old man. His – he's gone for a Burton." The M.O. put a hand on his shoulder. "Perhaps he was luckier, though. Took the top of his head off. It was the same shell that got –"

But Turvey was already stumbling out of the dugout door, to stand in the darkening air, darkness rising in his heart.

EIGHTEEN

Turvey Is Laid Low

THE NEXT few days were always dim for Turvey. There was a ride in blackness back to Nijmegen, squeezed between Bob and Herb. Then he lay where there was a smell of iodine; somebody swabbed his throat, sprayed it, and gave him a pill. Perhaps the next day, still clothed, he was jouncing indifferent in the front seat of an ambulance. Then somebody pushed him up a steep ladder into a low-ceilinged room half-full of men strapped in stretchers, some quiet, some not so quiet. The room hurtled forward and lifted and in a little while he was looking down on a fuzzed crazyquilt. Someone said it was England. Then the front of another ambulance.

As the car swerved through an ivied gate into a sprawl of low buildings Turvey's head began to clear. His throat and mouth were not painful now, just numb. But a wind struck chills in him and he was glad to follow the driver through a door marked RECEPTION into a basement divided in two by a low partition (like the Bank of Commerce in Kuskanee, he thought). The driver dumped a heap of documents on the counter:

"Where the hell's your stretcher men? I got four in the back."

"Keep your bloody shirt on. They'll be out." The surly little lance-corporal began checking the files against a roll-sheet. "You got one walking case, eh?" He jerked his head at Turvey. "This it?"

"Yeah. Seems kinda crocked; been shiverin all the way from the airport. Dont seem like he can talk even. Better git'm a bunk fast."

The counter-clerk shoved out his lower lip aggressively. "You tellin us whudda do?"

"O.K., O.K., no skin offa my arse."

"Siddown on a bench, wait'll your name's called," said the clerk with a scowl at Turvey. He had puffy eyes which gave him a fixed battling look.

There was the usual string of barrackroom benches against the outer wall, and the usual row of weary-looking soldiers holding them down. Turvey found an empty corner on a rather rickety specimen and slumped, pulling his greatcoat tight around him. There were cracks around the door, and an open window somewhere, through which draughts stabbed and shook him.

"Gonad!" barked the little lance-corporal suddenly, a long time later, frowning at a paper in his hand. "Gonad! Gunnit! What the hell kind a name's this?" He looked impatiently over the benches. "Gorgeous Camel Go-goo-not," he shouted angrily. "Come on. Get the lead outa your pants!"

The two other clerks stopped typing long enough to look up and snigger. The only other man left on Turvey's bench, a big signalman with a head bandage, started up quickly from the other end. There was a crash; Turvey, deprived of his counterweight, was rolling on the floor. One clerk guffawed. The soldier went back, righted the bench with a muscular swoop and helped Turvey back on it. Then he turned to the counter with slow dignity.

"Are you calling me? D-65789432 Signalman Gounod, Georges Camille." His English was perfect though he gave the name its French pronunciation.

"G-o-u-n-o-d" the lance-corporal spelled with scornful care. He shoved a paper at the *Canadien*. "Down the hall. Third door ri –"

There was a second crash. Turvey had fallen off the bench again, and lay still. Another snicker ran through the three clerks.

The *Canadien* took a deep grip over the breast pockets of the surprised little lance-jack and hoisted him neatly over the counter beside him. "Now," he said grimly, holding him at requisite distance with his left and drawing back a fisted right, "do you get him into a bed first or do I sock you first?"

"O.K., O.K.," said the paling clerk, wriggling weakly. "We didnt know he was that sick. You better not hit –"

"And next," said the *Canadien*, while the other two clerks darted through the barrier gate and began lifting Turvey into the little room he had been looking longingly at, "say 'Zshorrh Goo-no, ZZZshorrrzhh Goo-no!" He still held the lance-jack at arm's length.

"Zhjor-guh Goo-no," the clerk gulped. "– I'm your superior officer. I'll put yuh on –"

"Not bad. Third door right, you said?" He released his grip and stalked off.

Later that day Turvey awoke squawking; he had been running from a coal-black bear, tripped belly down and been whopped by the bear's paw square on his behind. The beast held him down and whopped him again, even after he was awake. Then he saw it was a sinewy nurse leaning on his neck while a giant doctor stabbed him in his nether cheeks with serum.

The next day he and his bed and belongings were moved to a cubicle at the nurse's end of the ward, and a sign hung over his outer doorknob: OUT OF BOUNDS. DIPHTHERIA

After a week or so, thanks to the serums, penicillin sprays, and a warm soft bed, Turvey began to feel better, though the sensations in his rear were much as when he had been kicked accurately and twice by Comet, his father's lead mare, in Skookum Falls.

For a while he was glad of his solitude. He was still

thinking about Mac. And he felt a change somewhere in himself that he sensed was permanent. He knew it when the mild little Albertan M.O. told him one day he was making an excellent recovery and barring complication, he might be fit to return to a theatre of war in another three months. Turvey discovered he didnt really care, even though the ward radio, whose raucous voice leapt daily over the space between the ceiling and the dusty top of his cubicle walls, was excitedly chronicling the Canadian sweep through the Rhineland. World War Two seemed to be getting on very well without him.

One day, however, he made a sudden upswing. The beady-eyed day nurse, a scolding type whom Turvey had not exactly taken to, opened his door and tossed a much-addressed letter on his bed, the first to catch up with him since hospital days in Ghent. Since its posting in London, it had gone the rounds of Turvey's multitudinous units, and visited several he had never heard of. Musing at the doggedness of the Canadian Postal Corps, Turvey tore the envelope and was pleased to find that Peggy wished him a merry Christmas, or at least had, three months ago, and hoped he always remembered to change his socks when they got wet, and there was a parcel following. Turvey was so cheered he applied to the nurse again for permission to write. As he expected, she refused on the grounds that he was still infectious.

"What you want to tell her where you are for anyway? She cant visit you. You're still quarantined."

He appealed, not very hopefully, to the M.O. when the nurse was out. The doctor surprisingly agreed to have an orderly phone Peggy's office – Number Ninety-Two was only twenty miles from Hyde Park Corner – to tell her where Turvey was, and even offered to "think about" when he could see her.

The next Saturday afternoon Turvey heard a soft call beyond his half-open window, and, lifting his head, saw a plump vision standing on the grassbank, peering down into his room.

"Hello, you poor dear? I'm so glad I've found you. Are you feeling better? Isnt your doctor a sport? He says I may stay for an hour, so long as I dont come any closer. He's even sending a chair out to me."

Turvey was leaning over the sill assuring Peggy she looked like a million dollars when the nurse bounced in. "Who's that out there?" she said fretfully and hurried to the window. "Go away," she shrieked, "this is an isolation case. No visitors allowed." She shoved Turvey back in bed.

"But I've only just come," wailed Peggy; "and with all the connections it's taken me an hour and a half. Maynt I please speak to him out here, miss? The doctor said it would be quite all right."

"Aw, give us a break, sister," Turvey pleaded.

"You go away or I'll call a guard!" The nurse put her muscular arms akimbo, as Peggy stood hesitating. "You cant tell *me* what the doctor says. *I'm* his nurse here."

Just then a whitecoated orderly stumbled up with a gleaming little chair, and after upsetting it twice managed to get it firm on the turf at the bank-top. "Thank you so much," said Peggy with a defiant glance at the window, and promptly sat down.

"Clarence, you take that chair and that – that civilian away. It isnt visitors' hour for another twenty minutes," shouted the nurse, shifting her attack.

"Doctor's orders, sister," the orderly mumbled, "it aid god dothig to do with be." Where had Turvey heard that snuffle before? The nurse had called him Cla –

"Clarence! Clarry!" Turvey leapt clean out of bed, made an end-run around the sister, and was hanging out the window, which had got stuck and resisted the sister's efforts to close it. "You old honyak!"

"Tops! Topsy Turvey! I didit doe it was you id there!" Clarence rushed down the bank, slipped and, as Peggy squeaked with alarm, went into a complicated tumble, ending on his feet, and grinning, up against the window opening. He had spilled his wedge-cap in the remarkable somersault and his yellow cockscomb hair ruffled in the breeze. There was no doubt about it; it was Clarence, night orderly and ex-clown-diver from Number Umpteen Basic Training Centre, back in almost forgotten Ontario.

"And they call this a Military Hospital!" the nurse snorted. She wheeled and departed, banging the door. "*I'll* see what the doctor's orders are," her voice came vindictively over the partition.

"Jeez, I better take a powder," said Clarry hurriedly. "See you later, Tops. I'b id eduff hot water dow." He grabbed up his wedge-cap, ducked his cockscomb at Peggy, scrambled up the bank and tore away.

Peggy and Turvey had scarcely started to talk again when the sister reappeared, flanked by the barrelchested Ward Sergeant. Turvey nipped back under the blankets, a little late.

"Doctor's gone off duty and cant be found," she said triumphantly. "Besides, I heard him tell you not to get out of bed. If the Isolation Ward werent full we'd have you where nobody could see you. I'm closing the window." She motioned to the stocky sergeant, who obediently wrenched the sash down, and they both departed. Turvey, grown obstinate, hopped to the window again and tried to lift it, but it was too stiff for him. He shouted at Peggy, but she shook her head, unable to hear, and dabbed her handkerchief at her eyes. Turvey had the brief consolation of seeing her put on a brave British smile and blow him a kiss. Then she was gone.

The doctor dropped in that evening. He tried to look stern, but he wasnt that sort of a doctor. "You know the sister is an officer, Turvey. When I'm not here you must take your orders from her."

"Yessir."

"And there are good reasons for keeping you off your feet. You're not to worry at all but you'll have to stay quietly in bed for another month at least. In Italy they let the dip patients up early, and some of them started walking down the ward and dropped dead. Heart."

"Holy cats!"

"However, you're not to worry, and now I'll give you something to tear up." He went to the door and unhooked the QUARANTINE sign. "Here, we've got more of these." Turvey clamped his teeth, tore the cardboard precisely in two, and then under direction, into four and, with a savage smile, into eight.

"Swell! I see you still have a good grip. If you notice it relaxing, dont worry, but be sure to let me know. Your girl-friends can see you anytime now during visitors' hours. And I'll remember to tell the sister."

The next day Clarry popped his head in, looked carefully behind him, squeezed the door to with great caution and wormed a pint bottle of beer out of his blouse, followed by two tumblers.

"Dab, I forgot a bottle-opeder. Doe tibe to go back for wud. Have to do it this way." He broke the bottle neck smartly over the radiator, getting almost half the liquid into the glasses before the rest had foamed over the bedtable and Turvey's top blanket. Then he stuffed the bottle and its jagged top back in his bosom, sopped the table dry with Turvey's towel, and sat down. They had just killed the beer and shoved the rest of the evidence back in Clarry's blouse when the sister swished in.

"You break something?"

"Dext cubicle dowd."

The sister sniffed. "Funny smell in here." She looked around the room shrewdly but, discovering nothing, scuttled off to investigate the next patient. The two resumed the business of catching up on each other's stories.

"Here, have sub chocolate." Clarry reached into a trouser pocket. "Good for what ails you." He brought out a limp grease-spotted bar. "By wife sed it. Tastes a bit fuddy. She sed soap id the sabe parcel. But it's Cadadiad."

"Your wife?" Turvey was surprised. "I thought she lit out on you."

"O nod *thad* wud. They caught *her* for bigaby. She'd bid barried three other tibes. So bide didit cowd. Doe, I god really barried. To a Doofie girl."

"A goofy girl?"

"A Doofie, you dope, a Doofootladder. Lives id Sade Jods. I wad stayshed there for two buds." Clarry's adenoids were worse than ever. What's he mean? Married to a two-foot-ladder! Turvey pondered.

"O, a Newfie!"

"Sure, that's wad I said."

"Gosh, congrats, old man. Got a picture of her?"

A shadow crossed Clarrie's face. "Yeah, I god wud all right." He shoved his hand into his inner breast pocket. It clinked; Clarry ouched and sucked his finger. "Forgod about that bottle," he grinned. More warily this time, he extracted his Pay Book and produced a very crinkled snapshot. It was the side view of a curiously portly lady standing on a wharf.

"How long ago was that taken?" asked Turvey speculatively.

"About four buds."

"Then you must be a proud father now," said Turvey with unusual brightness.

"So thad's the way it looks to you too," Clarence sighed gustily. "You see, Tops, I was dearly a year over here before I got that sed be."

"You mean she always looks like this? Perhaps she's got a growth or somethin."

"Yeah, a growth," Clarence laughed hollowly. "She was flat eduff whed I left her. It's still a bystery to be. You see, *she* didit sed be that stap. It cabe id a edvelope without doe letter. I dode doe who sed it."

"She looks about seven months gone to me." Turvey shook his head in sympathy.

"Eight, the adjuted said, whed I showed it to hib. He says she bust a had the baby log ago. But they couldid fide a thig wrog whed they idvestigated. So she still gets by Depedid Allowids. But she hasit writtit be sidze. Just sed six chocolate bars. With two bars of soap."

"O, well, perhaps she just takes a poor picture. Maybe when you get back everythin'll be all right."

"Yeah? I aid told you all. See, whed I thought she was docked up by sub other bastard I wed off the deep ed over here." He paused bashfully. It was evident Clarry hadnt stopped enjoying his own misfortunes.

"How ja mean, Clarry?"

"I miscodducted byself. With a Digglish girl. Dadcy's her dabe. O, she's really a very dice girl though. She was assistig a kebbist, they call eb. Kide a like a drug store. Id Habberspith. But thed of course she got fired." He stopped and heaved again. "Wish I'd brought adother bottle."

"How come she got fired?"

"Cause her boss didit like seeig her aroud id the fabily way. Said it was bad for trade. Ad dow the Legal Aid wode gib be eddy."

"Any what?"

"Eddy Legal Aid, you stoop," said Clarence, transferring some of his annoyance to Turvey. "They say they cad fide eddy evidets by wife is udfaithful. So I gotta asside her pay, ad the rest goes off by pay too, to Dadcy's pareds. Cause she's livig with theb till she has the baby ad cad go back to work. Ad eeved whed she goes back to work, I'll have to support the baby. I'b what they call the Poo Faw, the P.F."

"You mean you're in the Permanent Force now?" asked Turvey, floundering. "What's that got to do with it?"

"Doe, doe, I'be the Pootative Father."

"Whose father?"

"I docked her up, you dope!"

"O! I get it. Too bad! O, well, cheer up. You're gonna be a poppa after all!" Turvey tried to be genial about the whole thing.

"I guess so." Clarry gave a piteous twist to his narrow shoulders. "But it's geddid so I dode believe eddy thig a girl tells me addybore. Well, I gotta get alog, Tops. I'b suppose to be od duty. Ward X." He lifted an eyebrow eloquently. "V.D., you doe, I'b kide of a specialist id

V.D. dow. You cad feel lucky you aid id that ward, Tops. Makes you thig about wibbid.''

He turned to go. "Well, take it easy, Tops, You dode wad to get doe wooded overcoat."

"Don't forget your missis." Turvey held out the snap from the tabletop. Clarry was stuffing it abstractedly into his bosom when the sister suddenly opened the door.

"You here still? Arent you on duty today?"

"O sure, sister, I'b od by way." Clarence, fumbling guiltily in his battleblouse, suddenly yelped, and snatched out a bleeding hand. Both glasses and the headless bottle crashed to the floor, followed by the fluttering photograph. One of the tumblers shattered.

"Drinking! I thought so! I'll put you both on charge for this! Drinking in the hospital is strictly forbidden. Well, dont stand gawking. Pick up the mess. Staff and patients drinking together! *What* a hospital. *Dont* think I wont report this!"

She did, but the doctor persuaded her to drop the charge against Turvey, and what Clarence got Turvey never knew. A few days later the whole ward was suddenly warned for transfer to another hospital.

As usual, there was no explanation. The husky Ward Sergeant, a gullible fellow at the best of times, rushed around in a sweat getting the up-patients to pack their kits as fast as possible because Hitler had a V-Three ten times as big as the V-Two and loaded with poison gas and bacteria; he had secretly told Churchill he would wipe out London tomorrow unless the Allies surrendered. Turvey's nurse said briskly the move was Doctor's Orders, but in such a way as to suggest she really knew the reason and that it wasnt good for privates to know. The favourite latrino, whose origin was obscure but which spread like a fever through the patients, was that an armistice had been signed and they were all being sent home.

By 1900 hours Turvey, obeying orders, was sitting up in socks and battledress waiting glumly for the stretcher

boys. He felt strong as a lumberjack and aching to be up.
And he was wondering how he could head Peggy off
from another unsuccessful trip. All the up-patients had
already been herded out of the ward, the doctor was not
to be seen, there was no one who would sneak a phone-
call for him to her office. All writing equipment had been
stowed in packs and whisked away. He lay composing a
letter in his mind. In case he was really off to Canada,
what should he say? Just goodbye? Goodbye! Slowly,
Turvey began to realize Peggy was the first girl he didnt
want to say goodbye to. Ever. Holy mackinaw, he
thought, I must be in *love*!

Turvey was so astounded at this idea he scarcely noticed
the stretcher-bearers carry him off. But he came to life
with a bang a few moments later when, firmly clamped
under a topblanket and on the point of being shoved
headfirst into the maw of an ambulance in the courtyard,
he saw Peggy turn disconsolately from an armed guard
barring the gate a few hundred feet away, and start back
to the bus-stop.

"Peggy," he yelled. "Hey, stop fellahs! That's my
girl!"

"Heave, ho!" said the orderly at his feet-end cheerily.
"You can write her from Halifax. We're in a hurry." But
even as they were sliding him into the bottom rack
Turvey gave a mighty squirm, tipping the stretcher and
himself on the tailboard. He bounded to the ground and
raced down the hospital driveway yelling, "Peggy,
Peggy! Wait up for me. I –"

Peggy turned and came running back. "Tops!" she
shrieked in alarm. "What's happening? You'll hurt
yourself!"

The gravel bit through Turvey's socks and his legs were
already wobbling from unaccustomed use. "Peggy," he
panted. "Will you mar –?" He was bowled to the
ground, pinioned and borne by two struggling blasphem-
ing stretcher-bearers back to the ambulance. One wrapped

his long arms so effectively around Turvey's head and
shoulders that Turvey could not even catch sight of
Peggy again. When the car, after much delay, finally shot
out on the highway, one ambulance orderly, warned that
the right lower patient was looney, sat firmly on Turvey's
strapped-in legs.

At least, thought Turvey, he hadnt dropped dead, and
his pins werent any shakier than might be expected after a
month on his back. In fact he seemed to have nothing
worse than a cold in the nose. That, and a pronounced
desire to resign from the army.

Darkness had fallen when Turvey was trundled into a
ward looking much like the one he had left and equally
chaotic with hurrying nurses, orderlies, stretcher-men,
NCOs and doctors. There were so many patients the cots
were all shoved together and the bed-tables moved out to
the centre aisle. But Turvey was pleased to find himself
unstrapped and admitted to an open ward. He borrowed
a postcard and stamp from the Yukoner in the next bed
and wrote Peggy he was now at Number Ninety-One. He
felt too bashful to say anything else on a card.

The next morning, a haunted-looking doctor made a
kind of jet-plane journey through the ward, trailing a
preoccupied corporal who checked patient's names and
bed-numbers against a clip-board of nominal rolls. Two
nurses tried unsuccessfully to keep ahead of the doctor
with temperature readings of the ninety-odd patients.

"What's the matter with *you*?" the M.O. barked,
slowing at the foot of Turvey's bed.

"Me? I feel jake, sir. I'd like to get up." His nose
wasnt any more stuffed than last night and he really did
feel good, except for Peggy.

"Name and number?" The corporal scrabbled through
his disordered clip of papers.

"B-08654722, Turvey, Private Thomas Leadbeater."

The ward-buff scrabbled some more. "Body arrived
from Ninety-Two last night, sir; no documents."

"Blast Ninety-Two. That's the third in this ward

already. Well, soldier, what's been wrong with you?"
Turvey supplied his most recent hospital history.

"Let's see you walk." Turvey obliged, happy to find it
even easier than yesterday.

"Hmmm. No tingling in the toes? . . . fingers? . . .
Throat all better? . . . No fluttering in the heart? . . .
Sister Scowcross!"

"Coming, sir!"

"This patient's temperature normal?"

"Havent had time to take it yet, sir." She plunked a
thermometer in his mouth.

"Shove him on the Convalescent Hospital list, corporal. Number Ninety. Recommend duty after a week if
progress normal."

"Temperature normal, doctor."

"Wonderful! Get him out today. Dont wait for documents. We need the bed."

Three hours later Turvey, booted again, actually
climbed unaided into a lorry and, with a dozen others,
was given an hour's tour of unknown England and
deposited in a posh country estate with wide lawns full of
soldiers in Hospital Blues. Too full, as it turned out.
Turvey had no sooner posted another card to Peggy
cancelling yesterday's and giving his new address when he
was precipitated into another conference with an even
more driven doctor than the last one. Next morning
Turvey was presented with six days' hospital leave and a
pass to London.

Turvey managed a bunk in a Service Club not more
than two miles from Peggy's rooming-house and though
she had no day hours free from her office they spent the
evenings together, talking, going to flicks or the odd pub.
But the breezy patter and the crackling black eyes of Mac
haunted him wherever he went. If he had been able to
forget, the tight face of Daphne, whom they both gently
forced to accompany them on their nightly jaunts, would
have stabbed him again into awareness.

They found it difficult to join in the furore of the newspapers and street-talk, now that the Russians and the Western Allies were within uneasy sight of each other on the Elbe. The war had gone on too long. For Peggy, whose only brother was coming home from Italy without his eyes, for most women of England, Victory in Europe would be simply the conclusion of a chapter halfway in a confused story whose ending could never now be satisfying.

But the weather went on being wonderful, the ducks in St. James' had their gaudy feathers, it was lilac-time in Kew, and Turvey, who couldnt break himself of the habit of waking at o6oo hrs, had time to burn. Following the directions of the girls, he spent solitary daytimes mooching through the parks, Madame Tussaud's and the Zoo. One day he actually wandered into the National Gallery rotunda, and the same night Peggy dragged him to a concert.

But, for some reason, he couldnt get around to saying his piece to her. Had she twigged the proposal he had begun to shout just before being manhandled into the ambulance? Why did she keep on treating him like a favourite cousin one kisses only when saying goodnight to, before disappearing quickly through a heavy boarding-house door? And he, Turvey, who'd never had trouble making love before – what had got into him? Perhaps it was Peggy's long lashes and the tilt of her nose, which he seemed to notice much more now than her buck teeth. Perhaps it was because of all this – this London. Didnt make sense a girl like Peggy would want to leave England and everything for a guy like him.

Suddenly it was the second of May and Turvey had to squeeze unhappily aboard the Aldershot train, the great question still unextricated from his bosom.

There was an hour to kill at The Shot before he could connect with the Toonerville to his Convalescent Hospital, and Turvey ambled over to the nearest pub. The cold in his nose had clung on. Perhaps a glass of bitter would help. He was puzzled when he took his first pull that the beer, instead of going down his throat as it always had, turned round and came back through his nose, giving him the sneezes. It was all he could do to get the glassful down, and he wanted no more.

The next morning, in the hospital, the same thing happened with the tea and Turvey told the nurse about it.

"Doctor's too busy to see you today. We're more crowded than ever. Everybody's wanting something." She took a little wooden spoon and squinted up his nose. "Looks all right. Throat sore: No? I'll get you a little ephedrine. If it's not better tomorrow we'll have the doctor look."

But the next day nobody saw a doctor unless he was very ill. The BBC announced the German surrender and everyone who could get out of bed tumbled hooting onto the lawns, some waving bottles long hidden under mattresses for the occasion. Sisters kissed patients, and doctors kissed sisters, and an orderly dropped a thunderflash behind the colonel. There were far too many patients for the staff to control so that those who were nimble enough and sufficiently clothed went yelling out the gates, kidnapping the guards on the way and carrying them along into the first buses they could board, bound for London and celebration.

Turvey, however, was recognized by a still conscientious Ward Sergeant just as he was streaking out the front door.

"Hey, hold it, you're Turvey, arent you?" Turvey tried to think of somebody else he might be, but couldnt.

"Been lookin all over hell's half-acre for you. You're on draft. Infantry reinforcement. Truck's waiting. For Sixteen CIRU. Where's your kit?"

"But I just got back from leave and my schnozzle is outa whack and I gotta see the doc tomorrow. And, the war's over!"

"Nerts. Your M.O. signed this nominal roll and your name's on it. B-08654722, Turvey, Private Thomas Leadbeater. That's you aint it? Truck's ready. Come on.

Pack it up. I got my orders. No more floggin the dog. They still got Nips to shoot.''

Fifteen minutes later Turvey was on his way to Aldershot and the same Holding Unit where he had languished before invading the Western Theatre last year. This time they must be sending him to the South Seas. It seemed a long way to go without seeing Peggy first. And a long way to go to start plugging Japs. Or anybody.

Turvey found the Holding Unit in the same old groove of last autumn. The War might be over in Europe but not the Peace. They were planning more European reinforcements than ever, more soldiers and tanks to keep tab on the Krauts and spell off the old sweats. At least that was the best logic available in the usual over-crowded, armpit-smelly Nissen Hut that night. And the next two days were an almost exact repetition of the nightmare Turvey had gone through to get to the Continent before. The chief difference for him was that there was now something definitely wrong with his swallower. And also with his tongue. He found certain sounds so difficult that the Rollcall Sergeant stopped, walked over and carefully sniffed his breath after Turvey had shouted "Pwezhent" the first morning.

"Someping wong wif my foat," said Turvey. He was fallen out for sick parade. But both M.O.s in the RAP cellar were so busy with inoculations and last-minute draft-checking that one of them had barely time to pop a look into Turvey's mouth and shoot some ephedrine up his nose.

"Bit of catarrh. Come back tomorrow at ten if it isnt better. Next man."

Turvey returned to blanket and kit parades, and got needled against tetanus, typhoid and paratyphoid. He had had inoculations for nearly everything when he went over the first time, everything but diphtheria, but it seemed it had all worn off.

The next day he could scarcely swallow anything even by cocking his head back and pouring. He got down early to the RAP hut. When a few feet from the open door he heard a vaguely familiar voice rasping a sing-song of orders.

"All-ri'. Nexman. Open up. Squeezit. Nex man. Cmon, yad one wen you were drafted, dinyah? . . ."

No doubt of it. At the head of a disconsolate fumbling line of ex-zombies stood purple-faced Sergeant Sawyer. He acknowledged Turvey with scarcely a miss in his vocal step:

"Nexman. Chokit. Fer crysake! Turvey, ainit? O.K. nexman, huslem up there corprl. Sight fer sore eyes! No, not you, buttnrup. See yuh in a jiff, Tops." And it was probably not more than three minutes before Sergeant Sawyer had polished off his inspection, without undue discoveries, and was over pumping Turvey's hand with one of his, slapping Turvey's back with the other, and squirting brown snuff out the door.

"Yole pisscutter, wotcha doin here? Yuh look skinny. Gittin too much, I'll bet a pretty," and he made a feint at Turvey's vitals.

"I gaw guitar. Can' shwallow proply."

"You got a bloody bun on if yask me. Wotcha been drinkin, yole souse?"

It took some argument to persuade the sergeant he was cold sober. Sawyer stuck a spatula in Turvey's mouth.

"Say Aaah."

"Oouwah."

The sergeant pulled the spatula out and looked at him with surprise. "Your sof' palate's gone phutt. You been sick lately?"

"Hadda difweria."

"Dip!" The sergeant took another look. "O boy, yuh sure did have it. And now yuh got paralysis, I'll bet a stack a bibles. Never a dull momen'. Hey, cap'n." He shouted at a tall gloomy M.O. who was just poking his head out from an inner office. It was a different doctor from yesterday. "Give a look at this. It's real fancy. He's had dip."

"Palatal paralysis," said the captain squinting disinterestedly down Turvey's gullet. "Probably post-diphtherial. Have him admitted at once. Bed-patient. Any V.D.s off that last draft, sergeant?"

An hour later Turvey was flat on his back in Number 89 Canadian Military Hospital, writing another postcard to Peggy.

He had never found speech his long suit but such powers as he had he was not anxious to lose, and he told the very motherly sister about it when she took his temperature that night. The next morning she had in tow a large athletic-looking officer with a purple crown on his shoulder.

"How are you?" he said without preamble in a deep booming voice and stuck out a big meaty hand at Turvey. Turvey was surprised at such immediate comradeliness from a major but he took the hand politely.

"Squeeze it," he roared. "Hard!"

Turvey had a moment's confusion, thinking of Sergeant Sawyer, but he gripped with all his might.

"Good," said the major, not even blinking, "nothing wrong with those arm-muscles, anyway – yet. Say Ahhh . . ." Then he made Turvey strip naked and sit in various embarrassing postures while he whacked him smartly with a rubber mallet on the knees and arms and even across the soles of his feet, making him giggle from tickling. Next Turvey had to prove he could touch the tip of his nose with his outstretched finger, on the first try, and tap his right knee with his left heel and so forth.

"Fine," boomed the major, "nothing peripheral – yet. Now, my lad, if you lie here quietly for at least two weeks your palate will swing as merrily as ever when you push a beer down. *But* you'll have to stay absolutely in bed till it does. See he gets a bedpan, sister." Off he went, and Turvey settled down mournfully to yet another fortnight in a military hospital.

However, by some fafu that no one ever untangled, he

was wheeled out the next day to a different ward at the far end of the long hospital. Here there was a new lot of orderlies and nurses who left him pretty much to himself. Turvey wondered whether the major had lost track of him, or was just too busy to come. Several other M.O.s made daily tours of the ward but they seemed to have their own patients and though one or two would look curiously at him and took to nodding and smiling pleasantly as they passed, they always hurried on to someone else. Not that Turvey really minded. His speech was getting less drunken daily and he was plumping out and feeling almost unbearably well. And Peggy, to whom he sent his new ward number, was coming to visit him that week-end. He was a little surprised, however, re-membering what the major said, when the sister assigned to his side of the corridor made him get up, the third morning, and make his bed.

"What's wrong with you?" she said heartily. She was a very hearty girl, fat and bowlegged, who came from somewhere in the Peace River.

"Pallal parlsis."

"O," she said cheerily, "Just your palate? Then you must be an up-patient. We're terribly short-staffed here. When you finish with the bed you can help the orderlies sweep up."

That night Turvey fancied his toes were oddly numb but he thought it might just be from getting his slippers wet washing the hospital doorstep. The next day he no-ticed he was favouring his left leg a little but decided to say nothing about it because Peggy was coming that evening. Lord knows what would happen if he asked to see an M.O. again.

What did happen was that the hearty sister, just before going off duty in the late afternoon, casually remarked to Turvey (toying with the prunes on his supper tray): "Sergeant just brought the forty-eights. We got fifteen for up-patients. Want one? Do you good to get out for the week-end. Fresh air."

Turvey automatically accepted one of the precious

slips. Then he realized Peggy must already be nearing Aldershot and he would have to wait till she came. Too bad he hadnt known earlier, but at least they could go back together and have a whole week-end in London. Perhaps he could get up enough nerve to put the question this time.

As soon as it was possible for Peggy to be arriving, he limped off into the fading sunshine on the curved macadam leading to the gates. He was a hundred feet from them when a serge-suited figure came walking trimly through. The hat was new but the eager plump face and the slightly squirrelly teeth were Peggy's.

"Hi!" he yelled and broke into a hoppity run.

"Hey!" came a great booming voice behind him.

"Tops," shouted Peggy, quickening toward him.

"Turvey, what are you doing out of bed?" came the deep voice, now at his back.

"I got a forty-eight!" said Turvey, hugging her. "We're headin right back to London."

"How marvellous!" said Peggy and gave him the warmest kiss of his life.

"You're heading straight back to bed," said the booming voice registering at last in Turvey's consciousness. Reluctantly he looked around. It was the major. Peggy disentangled herself.

"But gosh darn it anyway my palate's all gone and the sister let me up and give me a pass," said Turvey, not bothering to say "sir".

"O, do please let him come, just this once." Peggy managed a smile like a small searchlight.

"Why are you limping?" said the doctor, dodging its beam.

"Just a crick in the ankle, I guess."

"A crick, eh? Sit down. There, on the curb. Cross your left leg over your right." With the edge of his great hand he jabbed Turvey twice under the knee-cap and got a mild jerk. "Now cross them the other way." The major tried three times and nothing happened.

"Just as I thought. You'll get off those props immediately, and stay off for a good long while."

Peggy suddenly began to sniff. "O, Tops, they'll lose you again and I'll never find you."

"Please, sir, if I go back to sick bunk right now, can she stick around till visitors' hour is up?"

The major seemed to look at Peggy for the first time. "My dear young woman," he said with a sudden bearspaw of a salute, "if there's anything left of visitors' hour after I get this laddy under the blankets in the right ward, I'll be glad if you'll spend it guarding him. Meantime, have the goodness to take a seat in the main hall until I set off a few firecrackers under the administration of a hospital that can mislay all my patients as soon as I go on a few days' leave. And you walk in front of me, Private Turvey, so I can keep you in sight."

By the time he had been tucked into bed in his original ward, the wall clock showed eight minutes left of visitors' hour; five of these vanished before Peggy was restored to him. Turvey saw with gloom that the major was still in tow.

"All right, my lad," he rumbled. "I wanted to make sure you were bedded down. You're going to lie doggo for a month at least. In a few days you probably wont be able to navigate properly anyway. And you may lose some control of your arms. But if you stay in bed that will all be temporary. If you get up, you may damage the muscles permanently. I'll be in to see you tomorrow." He regarded Turvey balefully. "I should really tie you down. At any rate you have a guard for" – he looked at the clock – "the next two minutes." He blew out his cheeks in a vaguely amiable gesture and departed.

"You poor dear," said Peggy contritely, "dont worry. The major told me you'd be right as rain again soon if you just rest carefully. I think he's rather nice, your doctor."

"Yes," said Turvey without enthusiasm.

"And I'll come to see you every chance I have."

"Will you? . . . It aint the dip I'm worryin about exactly. It's . . ." He sighed and looked around. Two feet away on his right another patient lay staring at the ceiling. His ear was visibly quivering. Behind Peggy's chair, on the other side, an airman was sitting up and, lacking visitors, idly gazing around the ward. Turvey tried whispering.

"Well, it's - O crickets, I wish I was a major or a doctor or, or somethin."

"You funny child, I'm sure you *could* be. But I like you the way you are."

"Do you? No foolin?" If only her eyelashes werent so long. They threw him out of gear. "Uh, Peggy, do you think - how about you and me -"

"Rrrrrrrng," went the electric bell at the ward's end.

"All visitors out," shouted the Orderly Pig with inhuman promptness, clumping noisily down the aisle. There was a general scraping of chairs and a confusion of goodbyes in mixed Canadian and English accents. Turvey slumped back.

"Bye, dear. I'll come again next Saturday and we can have a real talk."

"But right now what I want to say is, will you -"

"All right, vis'tors out. You've had it!" The orderly, a lance-jack was standing fussily beside them. Peggy gave Turvey a soft smile and was off. Did she nod her head just as she turned? He couldnt be sure. He sighed, remembering that he'd forgotten to keep back his tonette when he surrendered his clothes this time.

He might have felt really brassed off that week if he hadnt soon got to know something about his fellow-prisoners. The one who had been staring at the ceiling the night before was, Turvey learned, trying to recover from beri-beri and frozen feet. He had been a Kriegy, a real prisoner, in northern Germany for the past four years, and the last three months before rescue he had spent in solitary, after an unsuccessful break-out. He hadnt yet got back to talking easily. But the airforce sergeant on the other side, whose eyes had been roaming the ward last night, made up for it. He was a cheerful waffler and the nurses' favourite. It was only in passing that he told Turvey he was waiting for the doctors to agree whether an operation to dig a bullet from his spine would kill him or allow him to walk again. He was a husky fellow or he wouldnt be on the mend from the pneumonia he had also acquired when he was shot down two months earlier in the North Sea. Turvey felt guilty about being in bed at all.

Then, that afternoon, an up-patient, visiting from another ward, stopped suddenly as he passed Turvey's bed.

"Well, goodness me! Topsy Turvey! What are you doing here?"

It was Wilcox, the Perpetual Clerk, with whom Turvey had once stolen apples at the Sussex Holding Unit. His right arm was in a sling and concealed under the loose front of his unbuttoned tunic. Wilcox settled at the foot of Turvey's bed, and they brought their biographies up-to-date. Turvey noticed he now had the Good Conduct stripe on his dangling sleeve, for three years of "undetected crime".

"Whatcha do to your arm, Wilky?"

"Oh that! Just one of those things." He looked almost coy. "An SS Man tossed a grenade at me and I tossed it right back at him. But not soon enough." He didnt move his hand from behind the dangling tunic front. He was as serious and ladylike as ever but Turvey felt something different. The pudginess was gone from his face and there was a wistful, wiser look in his eyes.

"Gosh, you musta got out of the Orderly Room, anyway."

"Funny thing, Tops, but you know I never did, really. You see CMHQ made that C.O. we had release all his

A-category clerks for Italy. But wouldnt you know it, we were sent as *clerks*. Well so, after a month in an O.R. at Base, I could see they needed drivers real badly and I went and qualified in my spare time for MT and MC, and managed to get transferred to the Transport Wing. Then, bang, right away, they cut the establishment down and I was sent straight back to a typewriter. O golly I was mad. Then they started that drive for Potential Infantry Officers, you remember? – and I applied for OCTU. The adjutant, of course, just as you'd expect, he said he needed me too much in the Orderly Room. So then I really blew a fuse and when the C.O. wouldnt sign my OCTU application, I got paraded to the brigadier."

"The brigadier! You sure must have been cheesed off."

"You just bet I was. But the brigadier, he was a very nice man. He said I really was a Potential and he sent me back to England to Number Six Testing Panel."

"I was at one of those, too. But it was all a mistake."

Wilcox giggled. "I didnt make it either. That is, I passed all the tests, but the dratted Panel said of course my army experience was limited to clerking and so there wasnt any evidence I could lead infantry in action. After I'd spent three years trying to *get* into action! Well anyway, then they sent me to Ghent, chairborne of course. But there was a wonderful I. C. Draft there, he was from my part of Ontario, and he was *very* good to me. He wangled me right up the field, Corps H.Q. But, of course," Wilcox made a great pout at the memory, "the only way he could lay it on was to send me as a clerk."

"So how'd you get tangled with SS men?"

"O them! They made a raid on our H.Q. one day; had us really cut off for a few minutes." Wilcox smiled almost triumphantly. "Well, at least they wont put me at a darned old typewriter again."

Turvey raised his eyebrows and Wilcox almost slyly produced his hand from behind his blouse. It was in a wire cage. Within the cage a metal spring led from a leather bracelet around the contorted wrist to a sinewy talon that had been a thumb. There was the stump of a little finger, but for the others not even stumps.

The ward talked hospital ships and cursed the delay. Most of the patients wouldnt be used by the Canadian Army again unless the Japs reached Edmonton. The doctors, of course, said nothing, but one orderly overheard two sisters who had overheard two Pills saying it would take three years to get the Canadian wounded back, because the Yanks had corralled all the hospital ships and planes to ferry their own first. The news of American sailings over the Forces Radio strengthened the story.

Next morning, Thursday, the jungle wireless worked overtime after an Orderly Officer materialized in the doorway and announced tonelessly that no further passes would be granted, all leaves were cancelled, and patients' kits were to be kept in readiness for immediate movement. "Any questions?"

"We goin back to Zombieland?"

"Jeez, don' tell me, lemme guess – we gotta boat?"

"Does that mean we're going home, sir?"

"I have no information on the subject of return to Canada. But if you have anyone you want to say goodbye to, I suggest they visit you tomorrow. After twenty-thirty hours Friday, all visiting hours to this ward are cancelled." He turned and went stately out.

Turvey spent the next hour in frustrated misery trying to find someone to phone Peggy for him (she wasnt planning to come till Saturday) but the one telephone permitted up-patients had a line-up that would last the night, and the staff were rushing around in a first-class dither. He was dismally trying to compose a farewell letter with a right hand that wouldnt grip the pencil properly, when the major loomed over him.

"I've just been phoning your girl-friend," he said affably.

Turvey gave him the most suspicious stare he had ever directed at anyone higher than a sergeant.

"Thought she'd like to know tomorrow night was the last time she could see you for a while. She'll be down."

"Golly, thanks, sir, that's very good of – uh, how'd you know her numb – ?"

There was a glassy crash a few beds down, a muffled commotion and an eerie wail. It broke in a scream. The major wheeled with surprising neatness for one of his size, bounded down the corridor, and grappled with the threshing arms and legs of the screamer. It was poor old Spokey Wheeler in another fit.

Despite the fact that it had happened twice before, even to Wheeler's knocking over the water-jug on his bedtable at the start, Turvey's heart began fluttering again in the peculiar manner it had recently acquired whenever something startled him. He lay back, feeling faint. Orderlies and a sister now threw a screen around Wheeler's bed and after a time there was quiet. The major emerged and returned to Turvey as calmly as if he had just been for a stroll.

"As I was saying, it looks as if it will be a while before you'll see your girl again."

"A while," said Turvey wanly, "it looks like curtains."

"Well, why dont you get grounded, and bring her out to Canada?"

"Creepers, she wouldnt have me."

"Have you asked her?"

"No, but shucks, I aint nobody . . . And I'm kine of a cripple now too."

"Well, you *are* a clueless wonder! *I* know you're going to get quite better. And *you* know all you have to do is ask her."

"You really mean it?" Turvey raised his head with astonishment, but felt queer again and lay back.

"Hmm, looking pale. Not all that scared of wedlock are you? Let me feel . . . Heart fluttering a little?"

The next afternoon, Turvey was hefted into a wheel-chair and carted down to the X-ray room. From the out-side corridor along the way he could see great thunderous clouds mounting. He hoped Peggy wouldnt get wet waiting for a bus. He hoped he wouldnt drop dead before she came.

A sleek corporal in hospital whites took off Turvey's socks, greased a precise spot on each ankle, then on each wrist, and wheeled him beside a metal table; fittings and wires led from it to a machine so complicated it reminded Turvey of the mixing floor in the candy factory where he once worked.

The corporal had a little tar-dot of a moustache, and a trick of wriggling it evilly. He was chatty, in a gloating kind of way. "On your back on the table. I'm going to make a cardiograph."

"Yes," sighed Turvey, too used to army mysteries to bother enquiring what that was.

"Now, I'll just strap your arms and legs down for a moment, so you wont move when I turn on the current."

"Current! Hey, wot you gonna do? Aint this the way they 'lectrocute people?"

The corporal moved his moustache secretively. "Is a bit like that, only in reverse. This machine is going to make a little drawing of your heart-beats. So just lie quiet and think of something else. Dont think about your heart. There's no real danger."

Dimly through the hospital walls came a crack and the rumble of thunder.

"Jove, we'd better hurry, though," said the corporal briskly. "Thunderstorm coming up. Sometimes affects our instruments." Turvey wriggled. "Now just be calm. Dont think about your heart." Turvey tried to think of something else to think about, but the beating of his anx-ious pump was like a tom-tom in his ears. "We had a case," the corporal went on, with a kind of wicked brightness in his voice, "of actual electric shock, very nearly an electrocution in fact, from one of these things, when a lightning bolt happened to hit nearby." As if he had called it, a cannonade rocked the heavens. Turvey heaved miserably in his thongs but they gave not at all, and his torturer continued to twirl unseen dials.

But at last he was untied. And he leaped from the ominous bed into his wheelchair before the corporal's little moustache could so much as twitch. Back in his own cot, he could now feel that his heart, whether from fright or simple cussedness, was ticking away without a single flutter again, but he was sure it must have been registering squiggles like earthquake shocks when he was strapped to the infernal machine. He tried to think of what he would say to Peggy. He wished he could phone her right now . . . Say, how did the major know her number?

The ex-POW on his right, the silent chap, had started vomiting the previous day and had been taken away in the night. His bed had already been filled with another patient with an elaborate set of bandages around his neck and on the shoulder next to Turvey. Between their whiteness, a shapeless purple ear stuck out startlingly. He was a lively sort, talked whenever Turvey would listen, and in between borrowed his cigarettes. He told Turvey, after supper that day, that this was his thirteenth straight month in hospital and he sometimes got streaks of restlessness.

"I aint bellyachin though, dont git me wrong. I got the best surgeon, I bet, in the Canadian Army. I sure hope they're sendin him home in the same boat. Y'oughta see what he and the other docs have been doin over at Basin'stoke where I was. Whole wards full a guys with burns, headwounds, amps, you know, the works. Why look at me, I didn have practically no face on this side when they brought me in. No hair or eyebrows, and no ear. Fried off before I could git outa the tank. Musta looked like somethin would make a cow miscarry. Not that I wasn lucky, y'understand. I was the only one got out at all. Course I know I still got a map like a monkey's behind but by God every month they frig around with it some more and it gits a little better. I got mossly a new scalp and a new nose-tip and this eyebrow. And lookit this ear. It aint much but it's all mine now, and they'll do more prunin on it yet. They showed me pitchers a guys with ersatz ears you could hardly tell they werent born with um. Right now I got some new graffs on my neck. They rolled some skin up from my chest till it got rooted in and then cut her loose. I'll have the bandages off that'n a few days."

"Holy gee, how many more operations will you have to have?"

"O, mebbe a dozen or so – but small ones now, you know. They figger it'll be another year before I'm all ironed out. But what the hell, why should I beef? The army stands the gaff, and pays me better dough'n I ever made before the war. And they got all sorts a Rehab plans I guess they kin fit me inta."

"You sure got what it takes," said Turvey admiringly.

"O Chrise," said Evans almost angrily, "this ain' nothin. I'm hung with horseshoes. You oughta see the real sticky jobs at Basin'stoke, the ones they'll mebbe keep there another year before they even dare ship um home to their folks. Some of um, I dunno –" he broke off. "It's good to be alive, see, don kid yourself. But there's a guy with a hole clean through his dome – bullet wen' in his eye and come out the back of his skull. By all the books he oughta be up in Annie's Room. Well, he's paralyzed, and blind, and somethin's wrong with his brain, you know, cant talk worth a hoot or remember from nothin. But he's kind of an exhibit – what they kin do with plasma and pen'cillin and surgery and all that . . . And there's a poor bugger been in there for months with bandages praticly all over what's left a him. Juss a hole for him to breathe where his nose was, and a round thick mouth they stick a toob in and pour soup down. They say he's gunna live all right. But what I wonder is, is that really livin? And does he really wanta?''

His monologue was interrupted by a call for order from a stentorian NCO at the ward door. A small official party had arrived, consisting of the Ward Sergeant, an orderly (who began passing little booklets quickly from bed to bed and waking up the sleepers), a lieutenant fidgeting with a sheaf of papers, and a spectacular padre in a tank beret. He was well over six feet and stood very erect. Over the little black surplice and reversed collar he wore officer's serge, with buttons gleaming like diamonds, and the insignia of a major of the Armoured Corps. The lieutenant standing beside him began a jittery little speech.

"Men," he said, and coughed, "this is the first of a series of Repatriation Lectures you will be getting between now and arrival in Canada." He was interrupted by somewhat ironical cheers. "Now, the padre here, Major Slingsby-Smith, he has had only a few –" The padre bent down and whispered. The lieutenant ducked his head apologetically, smiled nervously, and went on. "The major says he just wants to be called the Armoured Padre." He waited for the appreciative applause but there was now only silence. "The maj – the Armoured Padre, he wants to tell, to speak to you, uh, we persuaded him to come down here, he's a busy man," cough, "and speak to you specially on the –" he coughed again and looked questioningly up at the immobile padre, who remained staring out at the ward – "uh, on the spirit, the general meaning and," cough, "purpose of these Repatriation Lectures." The padre leaned his long neck down again and moved his lips. "Sorry," said the lieutenant, "Rehabilitation Lectures. The title has been changed. Uh, last month we called them Repatriation Lectures. It's uh, it's the same thing. And now, boys," cough, "the Armoured Padre!" He stepped back, bumped into the bored Ward Sergeant, and recovering began clapping his hands energetically.

There were feeble responses from one or two patients and then silence again, except for scattered rustlings from beds where men had begun a mechanical thumbing of the orderly's pamphlet. A waxing snore from the far end sent the orderly scurrying down to douse it. Turvey, glancing at the beginning of his folder, found it was a remarkable parallel to what the padre was saying and put it down, deciding to let the padre do the work.

"Fellow soldiers," he began in a loud platform voice, "we have all at one time or another in the long years of struggle against the terrible forces of evil and oppression, we have all, I am sure, given some thought to the problem of our return to civil life."

"Cripes, wut's his problem, don' he wanna be a Holy Joe wen he gits back to Civvy Street?" Evans whispered.

"And most of all, you boys," the padre went on, adding lush concern to his tones, "you who have borne the brunt of the sacrifice and with God's help purchased the victory – at the expense of your own bodies. Some of you have to forge new plans for the days – soon to come, I hope (" 'ere, 'ere" came a phony cockney voice) when you return to your loved ones. Some of you" – he flung them a smile – "are planning no doubt to marry –"

" 'Raaay," a falsetto shout.

"Not *that*!"

"What, again?"

The padre quickly extinguished his smile.

"Trust a Sky Pilot to plug his line," Evans muttered.

"Nearly all of you are faced with decisions about returning to your old occupations, seeking new ones, securing further education, in short, preparing yourselves for the very important role of soldiers of peace, workers – I would say, leaders! – in the great world of tomorrow that waits us back in our wonderful homeland. It is to help, in what little way I can, to prepare you men for these all-important tasks of rehabilitation that I am here to talk to you today. Now if you will look at the little brochure which. . . ."

Turvey was growing sleepy. Some one had sneaked a

keg of beer, complete with air pump, into the ward the previous night and there had been a party. He couldnt think of a smarter way to start getting rehab – whatever it was – than marrying Peggy. Wonder if the padre would hitch them tonight supposing she. . . . Shucks she couldnt possibly be. . . . But the major seemed to think all he had to do was . . . Say how *did* the major get her phone number . . . ?

Suddenly it was nineteen-thirty hours, the ward was full of soprano English voices, and Peggy was sitting squeezing his hand. There she was, serge suit and curves and brown hair and tippy nose and that shine in her eyes and my gosh those eyelashes. Even her teeth, Turvey realized at last, werent really buck; they were just sort of strong and healthy and he loved them too. He would have to work fast this time.

"O, Tops, are your poor toes still numb?"

"O, them, they're doin good, Peggy, I can wriggle them all again. But," he sighed, "now I got a bum ticker."

"A what, Tops? It sounds interesting and Canadian but I dont –"

"My heart was flutterin and they strapped me in a l'ec-trocution bed."

Peggy looked stricken, but she assured him it couldnt be much. "Your major said you were going to be right as rain in a month or two."

The major. She'd been talking to him again. Had he been gum-shoeing up to London? He tried to find two-timing behind the tenderness in her eyes, but their sparkle melted him immediately to adoration. And gloom.

"Well, a guy with heart trouble, you know," he began and stopped. "Well, it just means I cant ask you to, to – to do somethin for me I was goin to ask you to do."

"Why Tops, anything in the world! What difference could it possibly make?"

"But you dont know what I was –"

"Dont be too sure," she said quietly.

"You mean –?" A large moon began rising some-where inside Turvey. The light it shed was beautiful and golden.

"I'm awfully sorry." It was suddenly the gentle blonde night nurse. "I hate to interrupt you, but we've just got to take temperatures now. There's so much to do tonight." She looked genuinely apologetic. "It's orders, I'm afraid."

As soon as she was gone, Turvey got a grip on Peggy's hands. But his fluency, never much of a flow, had been interrupted and Peggy seemed to change the subject.

"I brought you a couple of little things." She opened her bag, fished through a prodigal assortment of articles, and brought out a tiny parcel and a larger one. She put the first back, after a moment's hesitation, and asked him to open the other. It was a gleaming blue and white sweater, soft and fuzzy as a kitten.

"Gosh, Peggy, you shouldnta done that! All those coupons! I should be gettin *you* things."

"Silly, I knitted it myself. And how could you get me anything lying in here?"

"Right now" – seeing the way to a touchdown at last, he lowered his voice, "there's only one thing I wanta buy you, and that's an ingage –"

"Hey, Turvey, could I bum another cig?" It was Evans. Turvey groaned, let go of Peggy's hands, and hurriedly obliged his bedmate.

"What were you wanting to buy me, Tops?"

"No, it aint fair to you. Besides, there's the – Peggy, do you like the major a whole lot?"

"Tops, what an odd question! Of course he's very nice. But *do* we have to start talking about the major now? Let's talk about us."

"Peggy, supposin I got hittin on all six again, ticker and, and everythin, would you –"

"You gotta bedpan here?" A panting orderly had appeared from nowhere. "We're fresh out of em. I'll fetch it back in a jiff."

Turvey's glare should have roasted him but the orderly was already rattling under his bed.

"O, darling," breathed Peggy piteously, when the whitecoat had clinked off, "if only we could have a few minutes alone."

"Peggy," he said frantically trying a drop-kick, "will you m –"

"Well, well, keeping your patient happy?" Turvey dropped Peggy's hands disgustedly and looked up, wordless, at the large genial face of the major.

"O, Major Erickson, I'm so glad you came. I wanted to thank you again for being so thoughtful as to phone me and everything. I wouldnt have got here at all if you hadnt."

Turvey listened, scowling.

"Not at all, ma'am."

"Do you know what the major did, dear? He thought of getting my telephone number before I left last time." Very thoughtful indeed, said Turvey to himself bitterly – "And as soon as he heard this was the last visitors' night he phoned me for you."

Turvey felt a little better.

"Glad to be of service," said the major. "But I mustnt spoil it playing gooseberry. I just wanted Turvey here to know, before you said *au revoir* to him, that I've had a gander at that cardiograph. The fluctuations are extremely small. Take it easy and in a week or two I think your ticker will be as sound as ever. Nothing to worry about . . . Well, hope I'll meet you two again, in Canada. So long for now." Before Peggy could rise or either of them could say anything he had presented her with his particular lady's salute and was off.

Turvey stared after him with belated admiration and then turned to Peggy. But before he spoke he grabbed the packet of cigarettes on his bedtable and shoved them hurriedly at Evans, together with an agonized gesture for silence. Then he looked carefully around the ward. There was no one approaching, and the patient behind Peggy was closely engaged with a female visitor of his own.

"Peggy," he said, slowly and carefully, his voice rising in spite of himself, "will you, please, – please, will you marry me?"

"Oh Tops, Topsy Turvey," she said with a great sigh, "of course I will. I thought you'd never get it out." The next moment she was sitting on the bed and Turvey was finding a surprising return of strength in his arms, and a new fluttering which no cardiograph could possibly chart.

"Eee*yow*ee!" shouted Evans suddenly, "on markers steady! 'Gratulations, Tops. Hey, fellows, Turvey made the grade!" From the cheers during the next few moments it was evident that several others had been following Turvey's courtship with almost as much concern as he had.

"How does he do it?"

"Better get it in writing, girlie."

"Aint you got a ring for her, Tops?"

"Get up them stairs!"

"Aw, fellahs, gimme a break, cantcha?" Turvey shouted, "I gotta lotta things to say!"

"Yah. Pipe down. Give the guy a chance."

"O.K. Tops, carry on. We aint listenin."

"Much," someone snickered. But soon the news precipitated another couple across the aisle into a similar announcement and the attention turned to them.

"If only we could get hitched before I leave," said Turvey. "Then you could get on a special list for a boat to Canada. If we're just ingaged it might take donkey's years to –"

"Isnt there a padre here, dear, we –"

"You mean you would –? Jiminy! There was one here this afternoon, but he's gone. They're all too busy givin rehabilitation lectures, anyway. Besides I'd have to get permission in writin from the C.O. of the hospital and wait till it's posted in orders. And that takes a dog's age."

"Well dear, perhaps the ship will be delayed long enough." Peggy didnt look as if she believed it.

"I'll try anyways." Turvey didnt believe it either. "Gol darn it, I havent got a ring or anything for you, even to be ingaged with."

"O," said Peggy calmly, "I'd almost forgotten. Your other present. I had to wait to see if – It's really something from you to me." She dived into her bag again and brought out the little square box. When Turvey opened it he saw a slim silver ring centred with a diamond.

"It was my mother's," she said a little sadly, "she willed it to me. It was her engagement ring too. It's a good fit." She crooked her third left finger. Turvey slid it on.

"Then you really knew I was goin to –"

Peggy stood up and waved her left hand. "See chaps, he *did* have a ring."

The mounting whistles and offers to kiss the intended bride suddenly changed to wails at the sound of the hallway bell and the orderly's mechanical shouting:

"All vis'tors out! All vis'tors out!" Today he added a new sentence. "This ward is now closed to civilians until further notice."

The ward's departure was indeed delayed, but only from day to day and finally from hour to hour, and the hospital's colonel made short shrift of an application for marriage from a bed-patient on the brink of repatriation.

Each day had its false flurries, its packing and unpacking. Mostly, however, they waited, bored, sealed off from the lost English world. The boredom was not lessened by the daily Rehabilitation Talks which were inched along, the magnificent padre having disappeared, first by the nattering lieutenant and then, more efficiently but even more dully, by a Personnel Sergeant who intimated that he had once been a High School Principal.

After the second day the sergeant ran out of material, made a dreary "recap" of his tattered pamphlet, and then in despair began a question-and-discussion period. Most of the men wanted the answers to three questions only:

"When's this goddam boat gonna go?"

"How many jeezly days will it take?"

"How long after that before we get out of this fuckin army?"

Turvey asked: "Supposin you wanted to marry an English girl, how soon could she get over to Canada or how soon could the fellah get back?"

Since the sergeant had answers for none of these, it wasnt long before his hold over ward discipline was completely shot, the program was cancelled, and the patients went back to their old magazines, card-games and thoughts. Turvey wrote another letter to Peggy and practised "My Bonny Lies Over the Ocean" on his tonette.

Then, at 0300 one morning, the ward lights flooded on and there was a great shouting of orders and wheeling-in of stretcher tables. By the dawn Turvey had survived another ambulance ride and was being slid into a kind of open cupboard at floor level on an English hospital train. A few inches above his head the capacious bottom of some unseen patient bulged his bedsprings threateningly. On his own level across the narrow corridor lay a sergeant whom Turvey had not seen before. The wards had evidently got shuffled in the process of leaving. Whether for morale or for appearances, all but the sickest had been dressed in their walking-out tunics, shirts and ties, and Turvey was startled to see that the sergeant's bright little band of ribbons was headed by one he had heard much about but never beheld – a maroon rectangle centred with a tiny bronze cross. The V.C.! He took a second and awed glance at the cheerful pink-cheeked youngster. He seemed to have no scars and looked very fit.

"Hi," said the sergeant, feeling Turvey's gaze on him. "Looks like they really mean it this time. Have a cig?"

As the sergeant leaned across the aisle with a cigarette poking from a Red Cross packet, Turvey noticed that just the upper part of his blankets moved. The V.C., he realized, was very healthy only down to where his legs had been.

"Naow then, you boys o raight?" A motherly faded creature in a dingy apron came shuffling past. Turvey thought she looked more like something he had seen in ward copies of *Punch* than a hospital aide, even on a limey train. "Wut's wrong wif you?" she asked with a kind of routine curiousness, bending over Turvey. For some reason the hospital administration had remained several laps behind on his ailments and, just before scooping him onto the stretcher that morning had pinned a little label on his chest: "Palatal Paralysis".

"Pa-lye-shul pral-sees!" she read admiringly. "Cor, you ev got somepn theah naow, evnt you?"

Turvey grinned and she turned her attention to the sergeant. "And wot's wrong wif you duckie?" The sergeant must have removed his tag because there was nothing on his tunic front but his ribbons. "*You* look 'ealthy enough."

The sergeant looked at her quizzically. "Athlete's foot."

"Oaow. An wut's awoll these ribbons abaht? Wut's the little stah on thet one foh?"

The sergeant looked embarrassed but came out with it. "Victoria Cross, maam."

"Garn! You Ca-ny-jins, 'oways pullin' sembody's laig. Thet's somefn big, thet is, the Victowea Crohss. It dahnt look loike thet."

"Your durned tootin it does!" Turvey was unable to restrain himself. "That's it! Honest injun!"

She looked at one and then the other. "Garn," she said again, "oo ye kiddin?" She started up the aisle, looking a little puzzled. "Must be a Ca-ny-jin one, then. Tynt like ahs."

As Turvey was borne through a Southampton dock

and up a gangplank, gulls banking over his defenceless head, he caught a glimpse of giant wharf-cranes and, behind them, bright downs rolling, rolling north to Lesser Hensfold and unexplored High Puddling and Aldershot and Great Buzzard Manor and Trafalgar Square and Peggy. Then the bouncing stretcher carried him into sunless recesses and aseptic smells.

NINETEEN

Turvey Is Rehabilitated

THE HOSPITAL ship – also staffed by British personnel – Turvey found a very pleasant affair compared with the transport that had brought him over two years before. Once they cleared the Channel the weather was calm, the poker parties got organized, and the orderlies were agreeable to smuggling beer regularly in return for Canadian cigarettes or a blanket flogged from a pack. Turvey was even able to attend the ship's concerts and movies because the Scottish doctor who took him in charge had unorthodox theories about the treatment of post-diphtherial paralysis; he decided Turvey should begin walking to exercise his legs, and declared him an up-patient. Turvey was willing, though his feet felt they had already been on a twenty-mile route march; but he had now recovered full use of his hands and his swallowing apparatus, and his heart seemed troubled by nothing that couldnt be cured better by a padre than an M.O.

At last the tossing dories off Newfoundland, the sweet land-smell of Cape Breton, and the crouched hills behind Halifax. Then a dock full of bands and flags and Canadians, brightly dressed girls with pretty expressionless faces and long stockinged legs.

Now the long predictible unexplainable wait by the dock, the gangplank unlowered, while sweating dignitaries howled welcoming orations through a loudspeaker rigged on a little platform. When the orators tired, two curvaceous girls in tights appeared and waved kisses that instantly provoked a prolonged bestial roar from the up-patients clustered like monkeys on the dock-side of the ship. The girls skipped to the platform like ethereal lambs, linked their arms gracefully and crooned into the microphone in a flat imitation of the Boswell sisters.

A large handcart was slowly wheeled through the dock-crowd by two solemn men in brown overalls and visored caps cut to the same pattern. The front of the cart bore a bright placard: WELCOME HOME BOYS. UNEEDA WHOLESALE FRUITS. The attendants dropped the iron push handle with a clang and hauled the tarpaulin off the cart, revealing a great heap of loose bananas. The sight brought renewed bellowing from the ship's rail and a general rushing and pushing to get as near the almost forgotten fruit as possible. Without a smile or a word, two workmen began hurling the yellow treasures blindly at the ship's rails, working methodically down to the stern and up again. Bystanders on the docks grabbed for the cart too, throwing with more enthusiasm, if less accuracy, and small boys darted in between the hurlers, munching the bananas that dropped back.

At last Turvey, suddenly a bed-patient again, was trundled through staring Haligonians across the dock and stowed in another hospital train. Put into berths in a genuine giant-sized Canadian train, only two dozen of them to a car, and with ice-water! And Wilcox in the same coach with him. Then, almost at once, fetching girls waltzing through with free chocolate bars and cigarettes, real orange juice and coca-cola in paper cups.

"Hey, where we put the cups, anybody know?" asked the one-armed Signal Corporal down the aisle, and the one-eyed sapper over his head said, "Hell, this is Canada. I guess yuh just throw em away."

Canada, still only half-real, familiar, and yet, because

so unchanged, curiously foreign and a little frightening. The endless flow again of evergreens, log-flecked lakes, violently rushing rivers and little wooden stations knotted with people in strange variegated clothes, civilians looking bored, even a little resentful, or filled with a childish noisiness. Then it was night and Turvey's car was its own remote world, a swaying dimlit cylinder of snores and sleepless tossings, of persistent hopes and fears and, twice in the long night, of dreams which broke into choked yells from the twenty-year-old Flight Sergeant tumbling once more through the flak over Berlin. Morning brought the Laurentians and the train rushing with full right-of-way through valleys and villages, stopping only to release some of its damaged cargo to a tense group on a platform, and crawling at dusk across the grey St. Lawrence into the dingy excitement of Montreal. And here the hungry boy on the liquid diet across the aisle from Turvey gets dressed and croaks goodbyes all around and walks firmly out. He does not smile, of course, for the ingenious network of wire and metal clasps that he is using in place of teeth and a lower jaw is not quite ingenious enough to provide him with the mechanism of a grin.

Nor does the bombardier at the far end smile when he is lifted into a stretcher and carried out to the town of his mother and his wife. And this is rather unsporting of him, for he could laugh, and at least he might say goodbye to all his mates. The doctors have said he could be walking about and enjoying life if he would only snap out of himself, and they are hoping a few weeks of psychiatric care in a hospital near home will make him right, or almost right. For the only things missing about the bombardier are his testicles.

Night again, and the train moving slower, spacing its time to avoid arriving in Toronto too early the next morning. So there is less sleep than ever, though only one nightmare from the Flight Sergeant. Brockville, and the strapping CSM from the Tank-Transporter Unit is given a little slip of paper telling him he can go straight home for a month's leave and that his wife and children are waiting at the platform. And he smiles and cocks his wedge-cap over the little plate in his skull and walks out with two punctured ear-drums from the silent car into the silent world.

Shortly after they had left Halifax Turvey and Wilcox had been playing rummy on Turvey's bed when they were approached by the train M.O. "Our beneficent government, Private Wilcox, has presented you with thirty days and nights of unbroken leave upon your arrival in Toronto. On its termination you will report to the Christie Street Hospital for further treatment. Here is your pass."

"Dont I get one too?" asked Turvey. Wilcox had already invited him to spend the thirty days with his family in Toronto.

"Most certainly, my boy. After you have completed your hospitalization and been lawfully declared an up-patient. And that reminds me. The same beneficent government stands ready to transport you either to your point of enlistment, which according to my records is the holy city of Toronto, or to the depot nearest to your next-of-kin. And that, I gather, is the unholy city of Vancouver. It is necessary that you make your decision now. In other words, do you want to go to Christie Street Hospital, Toronto, or to Shaughnessy Hospital, Vancouver?"

"Well, jeepers, my next-a-skin's only my brother Leo and he's in Skookum Falls. That's a day and a half by train from Vancouver. I dont see no percentage in goin to Shaughnessy."

"Remember that our munificent legislators are also prepared to pay your way from Vancouver to the main or metropolitan depot in Skookum Falls, *after* your hospital release – but *not* from Toronto to Skookum Falls."

Turvey tried to work it out. It didnt much matter.

Wherever they sent him Peggy wouldnt be there. Nor Mac. But at least Toronto was a lot closer to Hyde Park.

"O, sir, couldnt you please let him have his leave now, in Toronto?" Wilcox broke in eagerly. "My mom's expecting him and everything."

"I dont want any more hospitals," Turvey added. "I'm all better. I can walk as good as anybody. And I was an up-patient on the limey boat."

"Cant help that," said the M.O. serenely. "You're still a bed-patient by Canadian standards and I decline the grave responsibility for altering your status. Christie Street it is, then?"

Turvey had continued the argument throughout the journey by leaping up every time the M.O. strolled through and giving a practical demonstration of his walking ability. The doctor had retaliated by probing him diligently for aches and pains in heart, feet, hands, stomach, and anywhere else he could think of. But the M.O. could find nothing and was obviously torn between professional caution and his natural if somewhat corny geniality. Now, on the final morning, a holiday spirit (aided by a case of rye which had mysteriously got aboard near Oshawa) took hold of the train, including the M.O. When Turvey, on the doctor's first appearance, performed a one-legged hop down the centre line in the aisle carpet, and back again on the other foot, the M.O. gave in. Turvey got his leave pass and relaxed. Now he could walk from the train with the other up-patients, past the hated ambulances, into the waiting room where relatives would be massed, into temporary freedom. He felt ready to lick his weight in wildcats.

The long train with the ruby cross-marks, taking its own time, rolled gently along the shore of the familiar flat lake, gliding past rusty backends of wharves. The grey cliffs of Toronto office buildings, strangely smaller than memory, slid past the right windows, and suddenly the train eased to a stop near the old Horse Palace of Turvey's first army days.

Turvey helped a nervous Wilcox button the battle-blouse over his wire cage, gave his own hair a final slick with his fingers, and the two of them followed the other up-patients out the car door. The platform was cluttered with big-shouldered officials and a row of standing signs pointing the way around the corner of a wide shed to the room where civilians waited. The thump and snarl of a band throbbed from its walls, punctuated by babble from a loudspeaker and faint cheers. An armbanded official stood at the portals to secure and announce the name of each soldier as he entered. But a few yards this side of him a Medical Sergeant was planted, with a roll-book, and around him three girls in natty Red Cross uniforms. Wilcox gave his name, it was checked, and he was waved on. Then came Turvey.

"B-08654722 – Turvey – Private-Thomas-Leadbeater reportin, sergeant."

"Turvey? Turvey?" the sergeant scanned a sheet. "aint expectin no Turvey." He flipped to another. "O, yeah, here we are. Ambulance case. Driver Three."

Immediately one of the Red Cross girls linked his arm in a motherly motion. "This way, Private Turvey." She began nudging him toward a row of ambulances, which Turvey hadnt noticed, parked by the shed's wall.

"Please, miss, there's a snafu somewheres. I'm an up-patient. I'm with Wilky there." He managed to stop, but the armbanded official was already shoving a protesting Wilcox through the door of liberty, and the sergeant was flipping his roll-sheets for yet another two.

"This *darned* old army!" Wilcox struggled to get back but Armband blocked him. "O shoot! I'll phone you at Chris –" He was pushed out of sight.

"That's all right," said the girl soothingly. "You're down for Chorley and your family will be waiting for you there."

"I aint got any family. Waitin for me, that is," said

Turvey desperately. "I just got Wilcox. And they let him through to the shed. And I dont know his address. And he thinks I'm goin to Christie Street." But the girl, a solidly built creature, had now got a surprising grip on Turvey's arm and was propelling him rapidly toward her ambulance. "You're not supposed to be walking, you know, or you would be on the other list." She had the manner of a very kind attendant in a lunatic asylum.

"But the doc on the train said it was O.K. for me to –"

With a supple twist of her free arm she opened the driver's door of the ambulance; then she bunted Turvey in past the wheel, and leaped nimbly beside him. She drove in watchful silence to Chorley Park Hospital and turned him over with canny firmness to an equally protective orderly who insisted on leading him up four flights of marble stairs to a line-up in a hallway. After a half-hour's standing and slow shuffling Turvey reached the head of the queue and saw a distracted sister sitting at a desk covered with little floor-charts and nominal rolls.

"How many *more* are there?" she cried petulantly, looking beyond Turvey at the dozens who had gradually filled in behind him. "There isnt another bed! And Christie Street's full." She wig-wagged a passing captain and they went into a huddle of whispering. Then there was a long wait while they both hurried off, returning with a major. He looked wearily over the line-up.

"If any of you fellows *want* to bed down here, we can fix you up something temporary on the floor, I guess. But the rest of you can have forty-eight hour passes. How many want passes?" Every hand went up. The major looked relieved. "All right, we'll try to have extra beds by the time you get back."

Turvey had to break a dollars' worth of hospital pay into nickels and phone eighteen Wilcoxes before he got Wilky. He spent two days blissfully with the Wilcox family, and the next three back in the slow purgatory of a crowded ward waiting for a doctor to look at him. Then a very precise and remote M.O. told him his documents were not yet available and would he care to have another two days' leave until they secured them.

Whatever they found it was enough, apparently, to strap Turvey to another elaborate Buck Rogers machine for a totting-up of his heart-beats, and to tap him in unlikely parts of his anatomy with the familiar rubber hammer.

"I think we will discharge you to D.V.A.," said the precise doctor after three days of this sort of thing.

"Many thanks, sir," said Turvey, not quite sure what D.V.A. was, but liking the sound of "discharge".

"That means you will go to the Christie Street Hospital; they will decide whether you need further treatment."

"Ah," said Turvey, cheated again.

"And now, have you been hospitalized for anything else in the army prior to the diphtheria?" He began to rummage in Turvey's files and halted at a page.

"Hmm, yes, dysentery, unknown origin . . . Have you had any more difficulty with that?"

"O no, sir."

"We had better have a check. You will report at 1400 hours for a stereosphagoscopy."

Turvey blenched, and a great rebellion began to stir within him.

"You mean that big telescope they goose you with?"

The doctor tried to be hearty. "Well, now, that's one way to describe it. But an overseas veteran like you" – the doctor's chest carried the Spam medal without star – "surely isnt afraid of a little thing like that."

"I aint havin it," said Turvey suddenly rigid. His words sounded incredible in his own ear, but he was content with them. He waited, expecting the M.O. to take out his officer's whistle and blow for an M.P., or at least shoot him down in official flames. But the officer only shrugged his shoulders, and made a mechanical little speech.

"That is your privilege. I shall have to mark you down, of course, as refusing treatment, in which case you will be automatically ineligible for pension in respect to any disabilities that might arise as a result of the dysentery. Will you reconsider?"

"No!" said Turvey explosively.

It was a week later. Turvey, at last free of hospitals, had spent it in a maze of line-ups, interviews, form-signings and other not unusual occupations, in various caverns of the old familiar District Depot. And here was the great morning. He had signed the last sheet, his pocketbook bulged with his back pay and his discharge money, he had received his service button, given up the last shred of his kit and had been pronounced a civilian. Now, thought Turvey, I'm gonna climb out of this uniform and get me a set of real Yonge Street duds.

"And now," said the clerk mechanically, "take this paper to the Horse Palace. Out this door, left three buildings, over one, in the side entrance. D.V.A. Take it to the Personnel Selection Desk. Next man!"

Turvey eventually tracked it down. It was full of clerks in civilian clothes. One of them, a youth with cheeks so downy they reminded Turvey of the fedoras he used to fuzz, took his paper delicately, went back and delved into an enormous cabinet file. After a long time he returned. "Ever had an O-test?" he asked briskly.

For the first time in the army Turvey really lost his temper. "O-test! *O-test?* I – I started takin that blasted O-test before" – he looked at the blank gossamer countenance – "before you lost the cradle marks off a your silly behind!"

The clerk's face merely registered well-mannered disdain. "There is no record of it here." He made out another slip. "First room on your right."

Turvey, already a little repentant, and not quite know-ing himself, joined a score of other soldiers in a bare hall set with barrackroom tables. After a half-hour's wait he took his eleventh O-test from a high-voiced civilian with the proud exact air of a Staff-Sergeant, and was told to report back after lunch for an interview.

It wasnt later than three when he was permitted to sit down before another disguised NCO in a room dotted with similar pairs of interviewers and interviewees.

"Now, let's see," said Turvey's mentor, a bulky bald chap, ineffectually fumbling with the largest file Turvey had yet seen. The grey cover was marked TURVEY, THOMAS LEADBEATER. "Let's see." He sucked his rooty pipe. "Wut was your chief occupation in the army?" . . .

An hour later, Turvey was waved into the doorway of a little office. At a neat desk by a sooty window sat a gaunt gentleman in very new civilian clothes. He wore grand-fatherly glasses, army issue; what seemed a permanent frown forked up from under their bridge. Turvey re-mained in the doorway while the gentleman continued to write at great speed on a long document. Then he laid down his pen, paying no attention to Turvey, sniffed as if something smelled bad and, taking a rag out of the bot-tom drawer of his desk, used it as a muffler for his bony hand while he opened the window an inch. Turvey's memory began to click.

Ex-Captain W. W. C. Smith smothered a burp as he returned to his desk. Though it was past four, the June mugginess seemed to be thickening, and there was still another veteran to interview. A moonfaced fellow, already smirking in the doorway. At least he knew enough to wait until he was asked to come in; the war had made some of them so, so bad-mannered, especially those ones who'd been overseas. Well, he'd better get it over with. Now that he had to eat in restaurants it was absolutely necessary to be out by five or there was nothing left but fried horrors.

"Come and sit down." He took up the typed report the clerk had handed in with Turvey and read it slowly. "Batman" spelled with two t's and "intelligence" with one l again. How did the District Counsellor expect him to produce literate reports with the kind of incompetents he gave him for clerks? He fingered his forehead softly; he was going to get a headache. He laid the paper down with a sigh.

"Mr. Turvey –" the fellow for some reason gave a start – "what are you planning to do in civil life?" He hoped it wasnt a Small Holding; they took so long to explain.

"Well, sir, I thought maybe I'd take a course to be a ninjineer." What's he grinning about? "But first I'd like to be a sailor." O Lord, another one doesnt know his own mind. "Or maybe a fireman or a stewart or somethin. You know, on a boat."

Mr. Smith plucked with irritation at his trousers where they clung to his sweating knee. This man was going to need a lot of counselling. He took off his glasses and wiped them methodically. Why did the fellow stare at him as if he'd seen him before? "Ah, that's quite an assortment. Havent you made up your mind which you would really like?" Mr. Smith listened with a certain pride to the tone of his voice; it sounded absolutely patient and that was something, what with this heat wave and the eternal noises of dischargees galumphing around the Horse Palace. And the smells of this place. To expect a brainworker, a professional man, to –

"Well, just now, sir, anythin on a boat. On the Atlan'ic, that is."

Should he have another cigarette? It was almost half an hour since the last one, wasnt it? He drew out his Cools. It wouldnt help his head but it might stop those stomach flutterings for a while.

"Why the Atlantic only?" This man seemed a bit stupid. What was the O-score?

"Well, you see, sir, Peggy, that's my financee, she's –"

"Fiancée, you mean?" Really, you couldnt let the chap go around saying that.

"Yessir, we're ingaged. But she's still in England, see, and a sergeant today was tellin me they wouldnt let her over for a heck of a time. So first I'd like a job on a ship so's I can go back to where *she* is."

"O dear me, we couldnt do that you know." Goodness, this interview was going to take forever. He glanced involuntarily at the little carton on the window sill. He'd take an aspirin right now if it wasnt that the fellow was sitting there looking at him with that silly grin on his big face. "We want to put you on the road to a permanent profession or, ah, job, you know. As to, ah, Peggy, your – fiancée" – he pronounced the word carefully and gave Turvey a parental smile – "there's nothing we can do for you about that just now, nothing at all, you know. But about this engineering you put down." He checked another burp. This new doctor's prescription wasnt helping his ulcer at all . . . Let's see. Grade Nine, he has. "You realize that you would have to complete your high schooling – there are special classes for returned men, of course – and then go on to university for at least four or five years." That should bring him down to earth. "That's say for civil or electrical engineering or –" By jove, could the chap mean – "What kind of engineering did you have in mind?"

"What kind?" He sounded surprised. "O, I guess any kind of a nold injin would do to learn on, a yard-injin maybe, or a freight. Maybe just a donkey injin to start with. But I'd like to get one of those Trans-Canada flyers to drive someday. Or if injin-drivin's out, how about a tractor-trailer rig? Like one of them thirty-eight-wheel goosenecks? Some kinda really big truck."

My God! What *is* his O-score? I forgot to look. No!
It's a mistake. *Two hundred and two!* Why, why, he,
he'd have to be a genius or – Mr. Smith grabbed
Turvey's report and hurried out toward the steno-
grapher's pool. But the score was correct. Two hundred
and two out of two hundred and eighteen. He came back
and made a systematic thumbing of Turvey's file. Yes,
he'd evidently had the test before, 1942, but there was no
record of the score. The really important documents were
missing, even though what was left would have taken all
night to read. But how could he be that smart and be so,
so, well, so dumb – and a private all the time? Failed Officer Selection! Stayed on as a doorman!

Then ex-Captain Smith began to see a very great light.
He had read of such cases; men with tremendous IQs,
really brilliant, but unable to show even an ordinary
amount of brains, except through accredited psychological scorings such as the O-test, because of profound emo-
tional illnesses, deep-seated inferiority feelings or the
like, going back to, well almost to the womb. Why he
might even have a real psychosis – in an early stage, of
course. It would be wonderful if he spotted something
like this here. And quite possible. All those smug medicos
and alleged psychiatrists piling up reports on this fellow
for three years, and not one of them with the intuition to
penetrate into the real trouble. My Lord, if he could
establish a case like that, he'd shoot ahead in D.V.A.! He
could thumb his nose at the University's measly twenty-
four hundred a year. They'd have to offer him an
associate professorship to get him again. His wife would
be green that she'd left him. Ask to be taken ba – He
realized he was biting his nails again and looked hurriedly
at Turvey. The man's face didnt really betray a thing.

"You certainly have the intellectual equipment to learn
just about anything you want, Mr. Turvey," he said,
with the respect in his voice which was due such an
O-score.

The man seemed about to say something and then

changed his mind, merely simpered in a puzzling kind of way.

"Now supposing you tell me about some of your jobs in the army, the ah, more specialized ones, and then I can help you decide whether it would be a good thing for you to pursue railway engineering. Perhaps you could tell me, also, why you havent, er, ah, let us say, *advanced* in the army in the way I would have expected from one of your, ah, intellectual endowments." But the fellow was definitely having a game with him. His smirk was wider and sillier than ever. Ex-Captain Smith sensed his back beginning to ache, and suddenly felt persecuted. "You dont seem to be taking this very seriously, Mr. Turvey! Do you think it fair not to be serious with me?"

"O, gosh, sir, I'm, I'm real serious." But the simper didnt so much vanish as twist. "It's my grin, sir; I dont mean it . . ." As the man began to explain, ex-Captain Smith thought vaguely that he had heard of a case like this before, but he couldnt be sure. It didnt matter. When Turvey went on to detail with a kind of halting steadiness the long confused saga of his army occupations, ex-Captain Smith saw the pattern taking shape and all his intuitions confirmed. Quietly he opened the left drawer and drew out a blank Psychiatric Referral form. But the chap was really sharp; he must have noticed the heading; his monologue faltered and trailed off into silence. Mr. Smith decided to go straight to the point. "Tell me," he said with what he was sure was just the right mixture of casualness and concern, "how has your health been in general?"

"My health?" Turvey licked his lips, wondering if he would be lucky enough to get the nice fat Nut Doctor he had had after his first Personnel Selection interview. Then he had a thought. "Fine," he said politely, "how's yours?"

The gentleman gulped. "Uh, thank you, but that's not

quite what I meant. I was just wondering if you had anything you would like to talk over with a doctor –
nerves, for instance?''

Turvey felt the cage door about to drop behind him.
As often before at such moments, he thought of Mac.
Mac had always sprung him sooner or later from the army's traps. Now there was no Mac. But suddenly Mac's
sly ghost was whispering in his ear. ''Numskull. Get off
your knees. You're not in His Majesty's Bloody Army
any more. Tell him he knows what he can do with that
file. Here, no, better. Those choppers of yours. Loose
again. Give the little Swami something to write home
about. Just . . .'' Turvey listened and nodded delightedly
while the gentleman's eyes, behind his glasses, popped
with alarmed confirmation. Turvey stood up, putting on
his wedge-cap for the last time. Then he slid his palm
across his mouth, drew forth his little porcelain accessory
and plunked it neatly on the blotter.

The astonished Mr. Wilbur Smith had already begun
sliding from his seat.

''Bite em, teef!'' yelled Turvey.

Ex-Captain Smith leaped back as if already bitten, his
elbow knocking the aspirin box out of the window.

''What on earth! Here! Put those teeth back
in – help!''

But help was not needed. Ex-B-08654722 clapped the
plate neatly back in his face. ''Excuse me,'' he said, ''I
gotta date down at the docks.'' He put a thumb in each
ear and waggled his fingers happily at Mr. Smith. Then
with a war whoop that would have carried across Kootenay Flats, Mr. Turvey scurried like a plump demented
squirrel out of the Horse Palace and into Civvy Street.

Afterword

BY AL PURDY

When I was twenty-one and twenty-two-years-old, I'd reluctantly wake up early every morning and hear — "DAH-DAH – DAH — DAH — DAH . . ." It was the Royal Canadian Air Force band at Trenton Air Base playing "Colonel Bogey" on the parade square. It was the same tune to which many thousands of servicemen marched over dirt roads and highways during the Second World War. And many survivors of that war can probably hear it in their minds still.

I loved that sound, the quick staccato "DAH-DAH." It seeped into your blood and guts like overproof whiskey. "DAH-DAH," and winter was over, spring arrived. I loved the music, but hated the military.

R52768, that was me, Aircraftsman 2nd. class, A. Purdy, from January 10, 1940 until July 1945; nearly six years. During those years I changed from a boy to more-or-less a man. Many things happened to me, a lot of them funny. But I didn't appreciate their humour until much later.

And what has all this to do with Private Thomas Leadbeater Turvey, Earle Birney's literary creation? Well, quite a lot, actually. You see, I am Turvey.

I know, I know – my name is different; and Birney didn't model his accident-prone hero on me. But my age would be about the same if T. L. Turvey had survived into 1989. My character and temperament, however, are very different from Turvey's. Nevertheless, I insist that I am Turvey.

In writing his novel, Earle Birney included a few of his own adventures: Birney was a personnel officer during the war, like those he described administering torture tests to his novel's hero. He read recruits' dossiers; looked into their heads; and knew what happened to them before and during, although not after, their military service.

Birney was there; he knew what he was talking about.

When I first read *Turvey* years ago, I thought yeah, it's kinda funny, things that happened to Turvey. And I thought: when all those similar things happened to me, they weren't a damn bit funny. In fact, I thought they were downright solemn, almost tragic. This wasn't some cardboard recreation of a comic hero, this was me, this was real life, this was earnest.

But reading *Turvey* now, Aircraftsman 2nd. class A. Purdy wears that old uniform again, the fancy blue one with brass buttons instead of Turvey's shit-brown battle dress. And Colonel Bogey is loud in my ears; my toes wriggle with it.

Somebody out of time yells, "Prisoner and escort, 'Foh-wahd mah!' " I march, laif-rye-laif-rye into the O.C.'s office, a hatless prisoner. And scared.

"Prisoner and escort, Ha-h-h!" (That means halt.)

It was not a damn bit funny. The Officer Commanding said, "Will you accept my punishment?" (For whatever it was.)

(That non-flying flight looey's tone was dolorous as an undertaker burying his best friend without charge. I had visions of being locked away from the light for years.)

"Yessir," I said.

"You are hereby reduced in rank to corporal," the O.C. said. (I had been acting sergeant.)

Lo and behold it was so.

Somewhat later, another O.C. said the same thing, and I was reduced in rank farther down; then successively into the depths, to L.A.C., A.C.1, A.C.2, and lower still.

After I had expiated my sins, somewhat depressed in spirit after these swift descents, I was permitted outside the military base. On the streets of Trenton, encountering a drunken civilian, I saluted him.

Turvey was faced with a very similar Officer Commanding when his rank was acting corporal. And at one time he almost became an officer. I too was almost an officer. I took the air crew medical, thinking, "Gee whiz, I'm gonna be an officer" – amid visions of the sexy girls my wings insignia would doubtless attract. The prosodic strains of "The Flying Instructor's Lament,"

> What did you do in the war, daddy,
>   How did you help us to win?
> Circuits and bumps and turns, laddie,
>   And how to get out of a spin . . .

rang in my head along with Colonel Bogey. Alas, Turvey's, I mean Purdy's, blood pressure shot sky-high at the thought of leaving the surly bonds of earth. The excitement aroused by my prospective adventures had been too much for me. Later, I took the air crew medical again, with the same result. Afterwards, my blood pressure went back to normal.

On guard duty late at night, Turvey shoots a German paratrooper with his Sten gun. But it turns out that the German Turvey shot was his own greatcoat he'd hung on a fence and forgotten about. The greatcoat was, of course, ruined by the bullet holes.

I had a similar experience. And it's true, not Earle Birney's fiction. I swear it's true. Here's the scene. I'm on guard duty at #2 Equipment Depot in Vancouver; the Burrard Viaduct looming overhead, wartime traffic scanty late at night. Below the Burrard bridge another much smaller one, for streetcars crossing False Creek. I march back and forth on the R.C.A.F. dock, now less than a civilian, and bored out of my skin.

In oily water below the dock, a gaggle of ducks were

quacking about how nice it was to be a duck and not to be shot at. On sudden impulse, I lifted my Sten gun and it went "rat-a-tat-tat" as Sten guns do. Water splattered. Bridge traffic continued. The ducks just sat there, didn't fly away, trying to decide if there was any danger. Of course they were in no danger. The marksmanship of R52768, A.C.2 Purdy was lamentable, as instructors had oft pointed out.

Reading *Turvey* again, I am mesmerized by the account of how Turvey went A.W. Loose in Buffalo – where, through diligent application of the requisite equipment, he kept two female employees of the Earthquake Aircraft Company busily happy on the swing shift. Punishment, two days confined to barracks. Very mild punishment, I think. Since I did not have a kindly author in charge of me, my own awards were never less than a week's C.B.

Turvey searches for his friend Mac, a member of the Kootenay Highlanders and eventually finds him. Turvey urinates on an army major's head, having taken a wrong turn in the barracks at midnight. Turvey imbibes a little too freely at an English pub, then finds himself trapped in the middle of a minefield late at night. Turvey is quarantined for diptheria. The guy is accident-prone, but survives all mishaps, always swims and never sinks. Me, I sank.

There was the time I was posted from #9 Construction and Maintainence Unit, Vancouver, to Woodcock in northern British Columbia. I had been married not long before, and being extremely uxorious in the early days of nuptials, yearned for my absent wife.

At Woodcock, we were building an airfield in expectation of imminent Japanese invasion. My sergeant there was one Jackson, an ex-typewriter mechanic. (That's his real name.) He was a miserable s.o.b. I made friends with another guy, Leo LaBlanc (that's his real name too), and pulled every string I could think of to get back to Vancouver with my wife.

I wrote letters to a flight sergeant in the #9 c.m.u. orderly room, requesting return posting to Vancouver on compassionate grounds. I wrote my wife, asking her to apply for a travel warrant, a free r.c.a.f. ticket, enabling her to take a train from Vancouver to Woodcock in order to soothe my subcutaneous wifeless membranes.

In the meantime, Leo LaBlanc and I rode the freights to Hazelton on the Skeena River, to drink beer in that frontier town. And the great mountains loomed overhead, surrounding us like picture postcards propped vertically in circular splendour. Eagles surveyed their kingdom; only man was vile; and I do mean Sergeant Jackson.

Requests to my flight sergeant friend for return posting to Vancouver, my injunctions to spouse to get a travel warrant and fly to my arms in Woodcock – both bore fruit simultaneously. She and I passed each other going in opposite directions, about halfway between Woodcock and Vancouver. And she liked it at Woodcock, got a job as a waitress in the airmen's mess, and refused to return despite my womanless detumescent condition.

I have, I hope, made my point. *I am Turvey.* Not exactly the cheerful and rather naive character in Birney's book, but nevertheless a completely authentic version of Turvey's reverse image. Yet I wasn't always sweet-natured and cheerful. Oh, no! Over those nearly six years of military servitude I became a dour and depressed loser, the guy on the sidewalk with his chin scraping the gutter. I saluted civilians. I was less than the least. As I remember that time, only Colonel Bogey remains sweet and nostalgic.

When I say I'm Turvey, it's as another dimension of that grinning creation of Earle Birney's. For how could you write a novel about Turvey or Schweik as depressive characters? Even James Jones and Norman Mailer didn't do that in their supposedly realistic war novels. Nevertheless, Turvey is real; except for the small cavil that he didn't change a bit through all his adventures, the timeless episodes of war.

Those six years of Armageddon are now seen from a distance; events are fixed and unchanging. They involve all of us, soldiers, sailors, and airmen, who went through the war. And our laughter at Turvey is reminiscent laughter at ourselves. Those ex-servicemen – except for Sergeant Jackson – they are all Turveys too.

George Woodcock has observed that *Turvey* is a "poet's novel." I guess he meant one of those strange books that hover on the far edge of reality, a dream in words. Along with *Turvey*, he mentioned Herbert Read's *The Green Child* and Alain Fournier's *Le Grand Meaulnes*. I don't agree. Despite the laughter, there is nothing of childhood and dreams in *Turvey*, as there was in those other two books. One does not fail to see men dying in World War II and all the wars since then. In Afghanistan and Nicaragua and Vietnam. Reality supercedes the image.

But Colonel Bogey sounds in my ears. What an irony for me to have all my blood stir with music as I read the book. No birds build their nests in springtime. The world renews itself annually. And "DAH-DAH" goes that music, as it will again and again, as Birney and Turvey knew it would.

BY EARLE BIRNEY

DRAMA
The Damnation of Vancouver (1977)
*Words on Waves: Selected Radio Plays of
Earle Birney* (1985)

FICTION
Turvey (1949)
Down the Long Table (1955)
*Big Bird in the Bush: Selected Stories and
Sketches* (1978)

LITERARY CRITICISM
The Creative Writer (1966)
*The Cow Jumped over the Moon:
The Writing and Reading of Poetry* (1972)
*Spreading Time: Remarks on Canadian Writing and
Writers Book I: 1904-1949* (1980)
Essays on Chaucerian Irony (1985)

POETRY
David and Other Poems (1942)
Now is Time (1945)
The Strait of Anian: Selected Poems (1948)
Trial of a City and Other Verse (1952)
*Ice Cod Bell or Stone: A Collection of
New Poems* (1962)